Don't Forget Your Umbrella

Forecast sunshine, prepare for rain

Carlene Ness

Infinity Publishing

Although every effort has been made to ensure that the information in this book is correct, the publisher and author assume no responsibility for error or omissions or for damages resulting from the use of the information. The suggestions in this book, especially those pertaining to nutrition and fitness, are not intended as a substitute for consulting with your physician or other healthcare professional to discuss your personal risks before making any major lifestyle changes.

Library of Congress Cataloging-in-Publication Data.

Ness, Carlene

Don't Forget Your Umbrella: Forecast Sunshine, Prepare for Rain / Carlene Ness

ISBN 0-7414-1693-X

1. Self-help women. 2. Aging. 3. Inspirational I. Title

Cover design, page composition, typography, photography, by Donna French

Printed in the United States of American on Recycled Paper

E-mail the author at Carlene@YourUmbrella.net or visit her Web site at www.YourUmbrella.net.

Order books at www.buybooksontheweb.com or by calling toll-free (877) BUY BOOK. 1-877-289-2665

Dedication

For my heroes
My grandmothers, my mother, my children

Acknowledgments

Behind every individual's accomplishments stands an army of assistants. Likewise, any success I've enjoyed, especially this book, reflects the advice and encouragement of family, friends, and colleagues.

Media consultants Ken Fairchild and Lisa LeMaster and Arlington businessman/author Jim Miller were among the first to suggest I use my experiences to encourage others. Family and friends jumped on the bandwagon and have hung on for more than a decade.

Without Rex McRae and my friends and colleagues at Arlington Memorial Hospital, who gave me the opportunity to forge a career, there wouldn't be a happy ending for *Umbrella.* Thanks to all the mentors, especially Ted, Ken, and Jim. I paid for their products and services; they gave me their valued advice and expertise. My special thanks to the public relations staff. I learned something from each and every one — Annelle, Barbara, Janet, Tenya, Ellen, Sue Ellen, Lori, Shannon, Suzy, Alma, Anissa, Teresa, Christy, and Susan.

The Dallas Fort Worth Writing Workshop provided criticism and expertise that helped improve my writing. Writing groups at the Valle del Oro RV Resort, our winter home in Arizona, offered their stories and read numerous drafts. John Dykus' editing of the book proposal bought enough response from agents to keep me motivated, and Tar Beaty's professional expertise bolstered my resolve to finish the job. Dr. Sandra B. Edmonds reviewed Chapter 3 for any medical missteps. Thanks to all!

I'm blessed with the most wonderful friends anyone could have. I've mentioned many of them and left out many more. Some I've lost touch with, some I haven't spoken with in years, some remain close. I call them all *friends*. They each gave me a boost or a shove to push me one step closer to a bright future. I hope I'll hear from many of them so I can say "thanks" once more. I'm grateful to those who allowed me to tell their stories and hope those who aren't in the book know they are also appreciated.

Unless they've given professional advice, I've used only their first names. In a few cases I've changed a name to protect someone's privacy. Although the lives of many have changed, their stories reflect their age and circumstances at the time I interviewed them. I hope the families of those who have died find pleasure in seeing the contribution their loved one made to this endeavor.

To the best of my ability, I've written an honest book, though it may not be altogether true. "Memory is not a literal recording . . . It's an evolving sculpture," explains Harvard psychologist Daniel Schacter. Neuroscience researchers say childhood memories recalled forty years later may have little resemblance to reality, so I apologize in advance to those whose memories of events differ from mine. I've presented the facts as I recall them. For my grandmother's stories I used creative nonfiction based on information passed down through the family.

When scolded by the March Hare to say what she meant, Alice replied, "I do, at least I mean what I say — that's the same thing, you know." I've found it easier to say what I mean than to find who to credit for what *they* have said.

For example, I found references crediting four prominent people with the observation that luck is "preparation meeting opportunity." Buddy Holly wrote his hit song *That'll Be the Day* from a John Wayne line in the '59 movie *The Searchers*. And before Nike's "Just do it!" slogan, came German philosopher Goethe's "Begin it now." The list is endless.

I'm extremely grateful to those who gave me permission to use their material and for the memorable quotes from the famous and not so famous that punctuate the philosophy of aging greatly. To the best of my knowledge, I've credited the proper sources. (Web addresses and toll-free numbers were correct at publication.)

Two very special women helped carry my dream to reality. Editor Jae Malone carefully edited for grammatical correctness and made sure my words matched my meaning. Creative, computer-wise Donna French turned my vision into delightful designs for the cover, text, and marketing materials.

Finally, I wish to thank my family for their support and encouragement, beginning with the man I share my life and office with. My patient (yeah, right) engineer, who finds everything electronic 'intuitive,' kept me alive by retrieving things I accidentally clicked away, troubleshooting software glitches, and splurging on enough computer memory to hold a dozen books (wishful thinking on his part). Thanks to my mother and my children and their spouses — David, Susan, Lori, Robert, Kathy — and the grandchildren for allowing me to tell their stories.

Unwind your mind set

Model the role

Beat the biological clock

Reflect, don't regret

Exercise your options

Listen and learn

Love, laugh, and

Accept the accolades

Introduction

Don't Forget Your Umbrella: Forecast Sunshine, Prepare for Rain is based on my ashes-to-accolades story and the experiences of dozens of other women whose lives affirm our inherent ability to turn tragedy into triumph.

Umbrella is for ordinary women, like me, who became big frogs in little ponds, balancing family and career, perhaps making a splash as PTA leaders, den mothers, or block captains for the Cancer Society. It's for women who didn't take Broadway by storm or become as famous as Amos or Oprah.

We furnished our first homes in "early attic" and proudly displayed hi-fi components on board-and-brick shelves. With ingenuity and a can of paint, our generation turned houses into homes. For us, insider trading meant swapping patterns and recipes.

We're the granddaughters of suffragettes and the daughters of Rosie the Riveter. We're the sandwich generation — the first generation who can expect to take care of our parents for longer than we took care of our children; the last generation with both hands on the cradle. Some of us are wealthy; others are rich in life experiences. We are savvy and sassy, shy and uncertain, PhDs and GEDs, partnered and alone, living in small houses, penthouses, and houses on wheels. *Umbrella* is my story and yours.

My version of our story begins in the year the Golden Gate Bridge opened, the Hindenburg crashed, Walt Disney produced *Snow White and the Seven Dwarfs*, and Amelia Earhart attempted to circle the globe. For almost seven decades, my life has followed a path of mostly delightful, sometimes devastating, events.

November is hunting season, so none of the relatives were in town for my birth. My dad notified aunts, uncles, and grandparents by mail. A 2-cent postcard addressed to a deer lease in Comfort, Texas, broke the news:

> *Just woke up this morning tipping the scales at 6 lbs. 1½ ozs. Went to a dance last night and had a fine time.*
>
> *Love, Carlene Katherine Doolan*

The opposite side of the card pictured Houston's Buffalo River turning basin, calling it "a wonder of the maritime world." I spent the next eighteen years in the shadow of that basin.

Yes, I'm a native of the state known for big ranches, big hair, and big egos. Texans are also known as the friendliest folks on the planet. Since I live in a condo, haven't had big hair since the '60s, and have done nothing to warrant a big ego, I count myself among the latter.

I'm not a psychologist, social worker, or spiritual adviser. Neither am I a scholar or a sophisticate. I'm more inquisitive than dogmatic. Mythology is Greek to me; Aesop is more my style. My royal philosopher is an ex-University of Texas football coach, and I'm more likely to quote Shula than Shakespeare; Twain than Tennyson.

Newsman Dan Rather says an intellectual is someone who can listen to the William Tell Overture and not think of the Lone Ranger. I'm not sure what that makes me. I can't listen to it without singing titty-rump, titty-rump, titty-rump-rump-rump.

I'm a weed — a duct-tape-will-fix-it, God-helps-those-who-help-themselves sort who grows where I'm planted. Life has taught me that the smartest people are those who know what they don't know, who succeed by reading, listening, and recognizing role models worth emulating.

Long before today's corporate world gave rise to networking, women listened to the advice of friends and neighbors. They would gather around a quilting frame in the parlor, sit on the porch with an apron full of shelled peas, or share coffee and conversation around a chrome dinette table. This is the kind of woman-to-woman wisdom *Umbrella* offers, relying equally on the educated experts and the experienced experts — women who have been there, done that, and worn out the T-shirt.

It's meant to be read with a highlighter in hand and to end up looking like a favorite recipe card — spotted with coffee and grease. It's a book to make you rethink your image of old age, to make you forget aging gracefully, and to encourage you to go for "great."

Graceful is elegant; great is excellent. A ballerina is graceful. Loretta Young sashaying onto the set in high-heeled shoes at the beginning of her Emmy-winning TV show — that's graceful. A mature women in sensible shoes and support hose plodding along on her daily walk — that's great! A woman armed with a library card, a Medicare card, a charge card, and enough moisturizer to slather a battleship — that's great, too!

Great advice comes from ancient wisdom, from the axioms our mothers lived by, from business principles, modern psychology, and enough clichés to needlepoint a pillow for every friend you've ever had.

Athletes and coaches provide inspiration with strategies analogous to those women use to surmount life's challenges. It doesn't matter what name you put on your jersey — elder, senior, seasoned citizen, or just plain over-the-hill — winners in life and sport rely on both defensive and offensive strategies. The aging game is not about adding years to your life; it's about adding life to your years.

The chapters of our lives are neither fair nor equal, and *Umbrella's* eight chapters — titled as an acrostic — mirror that variance with long chapters on physical and mental health and shorter ones on reflection and patting ourselves on the back. Each holds a reminder that rainbows follow rain, and each offers practical advice on conquering life's challenges with hope and humor.

Fasten your seat belts; it's going to be a bumpy night.
— Bette Davis, *All About Eve*

Unwind Your Mind Set

The greater part of our happiness or misery depends on our dispositions, and not our circumstances.

—MARTHA WASHINGTON, FIRST LADY

"Buckle up, put it in low gear, and keep it under 2,000 RPMs." A slap on the rear door urges me toward the test track.

"Hi, I'm John."

"Hi John, I'm Carlene, and the only other time I drove off-road it has been by accident."

"Don't worry, you'll do fine. The women are doing better than the men," the young man in the passenger seat assures me.

At my urging, we recently traded our sedan in on a Jeep Cherokee, so here I am on a hot summer day at Jeep 101, Chrysler's introduction to off-roading.

Negotiating giant moguls, roller-coaster hills, rock piles, and potholes with names like whoop-dee-do is more fun than I expected. The instructor needn't have worried about me keeping the speed down. Tilted at a 45-degree angle, I ease around a hillside at three miles an hour. Next, the course leads straight up the aptly named Sky View Hill. I mean *straight* up, as in all you see is sky.

"Now, when you start down the other side, don't put your foot on the gas," John warns. Is this man crazy? Of course I'm not going to accelerate going downhill, but I'm certainly going to find out how well the brakes work.

"And," he continues, "don't use the brakes either." Now I know he's crazy. With elbows locked, teeth clenched, and eyes squinted almost shut, I prepare for a suicide slide down the hill. That's when I fell in love with my Jeep — it eased down the steep slope as sure-footedly as its Indian namesake.

Once I hiked the Rocky Mountains photographing flower-covered alpine meadows and breathtaking sunsets from our 10,000-foot base camp. Now the legs are willing, but the lungs are not, so I've reluctantly deleted mountain climbing from my retirement plans. When exercise and medication lowered my blood pressure and cholesterol, but didn't improve my high-altitude breathing, I knew it was time to shift gears.

Driving to nature's doorstep in style — with heat, air-conditioning, and a cargo area for water, snacks, and camera equipment — beats lugging a loaded backpack up a mountain any day. Swapping mountain climbing for jeeping and foothill hiking comes easily compared to many of the other adjustments aging requires.

Look for the silver lining

That's the *Umbrella* message — expect the best, but prepare for the worst. Be a practical Pollyanna. Enjoy the sunshine with an umbrella tucked under your arm.

Life doesn't tick along as planned. An occasional tock sounds the alarm, awakening us to a new set of circumstances — our well-timed future unwound. On Sept. 11, 2001, terrorists forced us to change our national mindset. We thought it couldn't happen here and it did. We prepared for hijackers; suicide bombers surprised us.

Life surprised me in much the same way. I'd prepared to be a wife and mother, my days overflowing with church and school activities, little league, and political campaigns. I had no desire to join my friends who were going back to college and getting jobs. I had the job I wanted. Like the itsy-bitsy spider, I was doing fine.

I had it all — a loving husband, three children, a house in the suburbs, and a standing appointment at the beauty shop. Five years later, the rains came and washed me out. It was 1977, the year the world mourned Elvis. For my family, grief struck closer to home. My husband's suicide left me with no money, no credit, and no job. I inherited $200,000 in debts. The rent was due, the utility payments overdue, and we still needed to eat.

I had started preparing for the worst a year prior, never dreaming what the worst might be. Fred was becoming more desperate by the day. Money came in spurts. Sometimes he'd bring home $5,000 and we'd get caught up on the bills; at other times, we had barely enough for a few days' groceries. I knew he had missed my car payment when he parked his car behind mine with the bumpers touching (apparently it worked since the car was never repossessed).

My Dad had always paid cash for used cars and liked to brag that he never owed anybody anything. "If you can't pay cash, you can't afford it" was his motto. By the time Fred and I were having our problems, Dad was long dead, but that same pride prevented me from telling anyone about our situation or asking for help. Instead, I'd plead with utility companies for another day's grace, glad the person on the other end of the phone couldn't see my red face.

My vision of living life as a homemaker and volunteer faded. At thirty-nine, I enrolled in college. A pink polyester pants suit and an avocado green station wagon colored me exactly what I didn't want to be — matronly. I'd worked elections, school carnivals, and dog shows, but nothing prepared me for college registration. It took six hours to register for nine credit hours (now a process that takes a few minutes online).

I pushed the up button and the elevator doors opened to a new world — freshman English at the University of Texas at Arlington. Thankfully, forty years of living spins more than cobwebs.

I made an effort to prepare for the financial disaster ahead by taking two summer courses. School, studying, and chauffeuring the kids filled my days. Nights were harder. Nightmares of standing naked on the curb, stripped of all dignity, mingled with dreams of a big investor saving the day. That's what Fred had always promised. Any day the big contract would be signed, the big check would arrive. It didn't happen.

One night I didn't sleep at all. When daylight came, Fred's side of the bed was empty, the sheets were cold, the pillow smooth. *Should I skip class?* I wondered. No, after scraping together the tuition, I felt compelled to continue. Even one semester of college might help me land a better job.

I did my best to shield the kids from our precarious situation. Although later I would learn that they knew something was wrong, the day began normally enough. Kathy slept in, Lori went off to summer school, and David, home from his freshman year of college, left for his summer job. I went to class hoping their dad would be home when I returned at noon.

Fred's best friend found me in Dr. Stone's media class, concentrating on a student presentation. I don't recall going to his car or what he said. We'd driven several blocks before I fully realized that Fred wasn't missing, he was dead. Twenty-two years of shared dreams had just ended in the nightmare of suicide.

The man who was supposed to grow old with me had driven his 1968 yellow Continental south from Fort Worth to Johnson County. On a back road in Cleburne, he'd hooked a vacuum cleaner hose to the car's tail pipe, lay down in the tall weeds, and breathed his last breath. The pipe was so hot it had burned his hands.

Two sheets from a yellow-lined tablet told the story — one a brief apology — was left on the car seat; another was neatly folded and placed in the glove compartment.

The next few days were a sketchy kaleidoscope of catastrophe. David knelt beside the green velour chair with his head on my knee. "He won't see me graduate from college; he won't know who I marry," he sobbed.

Kathy and I sat on the end of our bed, *my* bed now. It was too much for a twelve-year-old to handle. She simply said, "Okay," and went back out to play. That brief denial of grief delayed her recovery for years.

Returning from summer school, Lori saw all the cars at the house and ran in crying. At fifteen she was always first to the phone, but recently she'd begunto let it ring rather than lie and say her dad wasn't home. Her first thought was that someone he owed money to had hurt him.

And owe money, he did. The yellow sheet from the glove compartment listed twelve major creditors. Sums from $900 to $60,000 were owed to banks, big spenders, and small investors. The total was $197,600 — $64,000 in default — and as I later discovered, this didn't include unpaid taxes.

As word spread, neighbors, friends, and relatives arrived with condolences, food, and flowers. It's odd the little things you remember at such times. I remember deviled eggs brought by either the professor from my media class or Billy Bob, the junior high principal. I remember how painful it was to watch my mother and stepfather pay the utility bills. I remember my friend Janet explaining that they were late for the funeral because, while pressing a dress to wear, she'd dropped the iron on her daughter's foot and they'd had to make a quick stop at the doctor's office. I remember wondering if the burn would leave a scar.

Families are forever

Fred's family was (and still is) my family, too. He had two sisters and three brothers, all of them older. Their mother, Mary, had married young. Her husband left when Fred was a baby. She worked in a sewing factory all day, and each evening washed one suit of clothes and ironed another for each child. They had only two changes of clothes each, but Mary's children went to school with scrubbed faces, starched overalls, and a mother's pride. The Salvation Army brought Christmas.

After bearing six children in a dozen years and spending decades of long hours on her feet, Mary's middle-aged body with old-age miles rebelled. She moved in with her youngest daughter when Fred was fourteen. He drifted from one sibling's house to another's, a teenager uncomfortable among newlyweds and young families. By the time he finished high school, he was living in a Houston boarding house.

Survivors often blame themselves for a suicide. I didn't. I was too overwhelmed with the task ahead; and no one ever so much as hinted that anything I might have done could have changed the outcome.

The funeral (paid for by Fred's brother Bob) was on Friday. By Monday, I was working in Bob's office filling in for his vacationing secretary, refreshing my typing skills, and collecting a paycheck for the first time in fifteen years.

For his entire life, Fred had worked hard, determined to make it big. He'd excelled at every job he had, but the fastest track was too slow. He struck out on his own, an overenthusiastic entrepreneur. The latest failure was strike three.

It was my turn at bat, and I hadn't even been in the game. I needed a grand slam, but would settle for a walk. Cheered on by family and friends, I put the bat to my shoulder and started swinging.

For several months our lives mirrored the "when it rains, it pours" adage. The Hogans had been our neighbors for years. Their older daughters babysat for us; their youngest was Lori's best friend. Our sons, both named David, shared the camaraderie and competitive spirit of boys who'd grown up together. Then, on the brink of manhood, while on his route for the Dallas Morning News, their David was murdered for the change in a newspaper rack.

Our families had shared happy times and, until this year, what we'd thought were hard times. During their friend's graveside service, my children's eyes wandered a few yards to where the grass struggled to cover the summer's cracked earth. The absence of a headstone that I couldn't afford didn't keep them from recognizing their father's grave.

A few weeks later, their cousin Sammy Jack was a nineteen year old off to see the world on odd-job earnings when his motorcycle careened into the curb of a rain-slick Denver street, sending him under an oncoming car. His world ended in Colorado.

Three funerals in four months. The children proved more resilient than I expected. I pushed my own grief aside and struggled with an unending to-do list.

Working, going to night classes, and fending off creditors while trying to maintain a June Cleaver atmosphere proved impossible. I had to let go of the home-baked cookies, shed the apron, and pick up a briefcase.

I learned first hand the truth in Eleanor Roosevelt's observation, "Women are like tea bags. You don't know how strong one is until it's in hot water." And, like tea, apparently the longer you steep, the stronger you get.

Hard times strengthened the children, as well. Missing apron strings forced personal responsibility. If they forgot to take lunch money or homework to school, they suffered the consequences — early lessons that encouraged hard work and independence. (To my delight and their credit, they've become joyful adults and loving parents.)

Attitude is everything

When we set our mind on a certain route, we only see the roadblocks and miss the detours to exciting new places. Motivational author Dale Carnegie says, "I am deeply convinced that our peace of mind and the joy we get out of living depends not on where we are or what we have or who we are, but solely upon our mental attitude."

A story about two families moving to a new city illustrates the point. One family pulled off the interstate and into a service station on the edge of town.

"New in town?" the attendant asked.

"Yes, we sure hate to move, but I have a great job opportunity here. The people where we lived were wonderful — friendly and helpful. I sure hope the folks here are like that."

"Oh, you're a real lucky fellow. You'll find the folks here are just as nice as where you came from."

In a few minutes another car towing a U-Haul trailer pulled into the station.

"Looks like you're moving. Planning to settle here?" the attendant asked.

"Well, maybe. We're glad to get away from the last place. I had a lousy job, and the neighbors were as bad as the people at work. There wasn't a decent one on the block. What about the folks here?"

"Oh, I'm afraid you'll find them about the same as those in your last neighborhood," replied the gas-pumping philosopher. This is an old story, but the message is timeless.

Abraham Lincoln made the same point when he said, "Most folks are about as happy as they make up their minds to be." Attitude is everything. "Get your head on straight" doesn't suggest a trip to the chiropractor and "You're as young as you feel" doesn't imply the absence of aches and pains. They refer to mindset.

Looking forward keeps us going in the right direction. Divers and gymnasts perform perfect flips guided by their head movement. Physically *and* mentally, the body follows the head. Wile E. Coyote never falls until he looks down.

A line from Gilbert and Sullivan's *H.M.S. Pinafore* easily applies to the aging paradox, "Things are seldom what they seem; skim milk masquerades as cream." Forewarned, do we reprise our mothers' spilt milk adage, bottle up our feelings, and pretend skim tastes like cream? Or do we adopt our children's put-a-cherry-on-top psychology and churn like crazy? I prefer to combine these generational philosophies and acknowledge that skim is healthier than cream, even as I do what I can to disguise the taste.

In *Leadership When the Heat's On*, Danny Cox advises business leaders to discard their preconceived ideas and be willing to "blow the lid off," and try new and innovative activities. He suggests beginning with a personal mission statement.

Anthony Edwards' eight-year run on *ER* ended with a tearjerker of an episode when his character, Dr. Mark Green, died of a brain tumor. Knowing death was imminent, Dr. Green made a list of things he wished he had done and crammed as many as he could into his final days.

All our days are numbered; we just don't know the number. Why wait for the terminal diagnosis? How about a mission statement that blows the lid off preconceived ideas about aging? Prudent accommodation to health doesn't mean twenty years in a recliner. Shock the kids and grandkids. Add some adventure items to your wish list. It's your turn to circle catalog pictures.

Pat, a spunky lady in LaMesa, California, bailed out at 13,000 feet the day after her seventy-fourth birthday. The gift certificate for a tandem-skydive was a present from her grandson and his wife. Her Christmas card featured a picture of her "free as a bird" experience.

Bird experiences involving binoculars are my preference. We've spotted lots of birds in our travels, but one afternoon while unhooking our travel trailer, I saw some not usually found in an RV park.

Having freshly showered at the park facilities and fed her birds and dogs, our neighbor with the parrots invited me to visit. Jean, a retired college professor, said it had all begun with a Christmas gift of a canary in a rattan cage. At seventy, she and her five parrots and two dogs were traveling around the country in a white Ford Aerostar conversion van, nicknamed for the friendly ghost. An electric cord, which runs through a hole drilled in Casper's side, operates an electric fan and small refrigerator. Her bed, a two-foot platform where the back seat would normally be, leaves room for storage beneath. The dogs and caged birds share the back.

On this particular day, her three-legged dog romped around the picnic table as we exchanged travel stories and she happily explained the difference between macaws, cockatoos, and Amazons. I caught a glimpse of sadness as she explained how if her arthritis didn't improve, this would be her last trip.

As we pulled out the next morning I waved and mouthed "good luck," hoping that ex-Girl Scout would make it to Idaho to complete the badge requirement she's set for herself. "I've taken a picture of every state capitol except the one in Boise," she told me.

Jumping out of airplanes or traveling across the country with a menagerie doesn't appeal to you? Me neither. Nor do I find the thought of getting all the photos into albums and the recipes in order much of a motivator. The thing is, we need to start the morning with more to do than check the obituaries.

Every year for the past forty, the life expectancy at birth has increased by a year. Antibiotics, vaccines and other pharmaceuticals, surgical procedures, lifestyle changes, genetic engineering, and transplanted body parts all contribute to Census Bureau projections of 131,000 centenarians by the end of the decade.

Currently, 85 to 90 percent of all U.S. centenarians are women, so set your sights on the future. Make plans for next week, next month, next year, and for the next decade. As the English poet Robert Browning elegantly points out, ". . . a man's [woman's] reach should exceed his [her] grasp, or what's a heaven for?" Indeed. If you have nothing to look forward to, you're not living, you're merely existing.

How about booking a trip on the highest railway in the world? On tracks stretching nearly 700 miles, most of them above 13,000 feet, pressurized rail cars carry passengers from the Tibetan capital to China's interior. The railway across the Himalayas, which has a top altitude exceeding Peru's 15,700-foot Central Railway, is expected to be complete in 2005.

For something closer to home, visit one of the celebrations commemorating the Lewis & Clark Bicentennial. From 2003 to 2006, communities along the expedition's route from St. Louis to Astoria, Oregon, are planning events.

In 2007, you can go to Jamestown, Virginia, and celebrate the 400th anniversary of the first permanent settlement in America. Then you can continue the history and heritage lesson in nearby Williamsburg.

Maybe you prefer natural wonders like the Grand Canyon and Victoria Falls, or the great cities of the world, the Great Wall of China, the pyramids, or an African safari. If you prefer staying close to home, plan to visit all the museums in your city, all the state parks in your area, or stay put and read all the books written by a favorite author. Whatever you choose, set a goal and anticipate a great adventure.

If travel isn't your thing, pass along symbols of your heritage to the next generation. Irene and Bonnie, friends for more than seventy years, are leaving the next generation samples of their handwork. Wedding ring, window, round the world, and buckeye beauty are just a few of the quilt patterns Irene has made for her children, grandchildren, and great-grandchildren — twenty-five in all. "I make each one a quilt for their first big bed, then another for their wedding or college graduation. The boy's favorites are blue-jean quilts. They're backed with a red print and tied with red thread," she says. In case you're wondering, her quilts are the old fashioned kind — all hand stitched.

She lets neither age nor illness get in her way. "I have two to go," she says, explaining that the two youngest are still in cribs. She tells me, in addition to those made for family members, she's sold eight white-on-white quilts "for a little extra money." Then she describes her latest purchase: "I wore out one weed eater and had to get another."

At eighty-five, Irene lives alone, mows her one-acre yard, keeps a small tomato garden, gives lessons at the Relief Society twice a month, and is president of her Sunday school class. All this is after four heart attacks, a bout with cancer, osteoporosis, and high blood pressure. Mindset counts!

With arthritic hands, two fingers numbed by a stroke, and others tender from daily sticks to check blood-sugar levels, Bonnie worked under a lighted magnifying glass until she had finished five counted-cross-stitch samplers, one for each grandchild's family, appropriately signed — wrought by Nana. "I really did twice that many if you count all the ripping out I had to do," she says.

I suspect some of her ripping out came from watching baseball on TV and paying more attention to strikes than stitches. Her next goal is to make graduation and wedding stitcheries for events several years away. "I want to get all but the names and dates filled in before my eyes give out," she says referring to her glaucoma and macular degeneration.

Expect to rip your list apart every few years. In the '60s, a little red convertible like the one Elizabeth Taylor drove in *Butterfield 8* topped my wish list (the closest I got was a new toaster). Forty years later it doesn't even *make* the list — it's too low, too windy, and only has room for two passengers.

In the '70s, it was Dolores' writing desk I admired. My vision of a perfect desk — curved legs and polished dark wood reflecting an elegant pen set standing beside a leather-lined blotter — vanished with my first computer. Now my sturdy white Formica desk with a keyboard tray, mouse pad, and CD rack is perfect.

Lest you think I'm totally materialistic, I have had other goals, such as getting Lori to finish high school and reading my way through the "great books." The former was realized; the latter was forgotten, though ironically, those books now decorate Lori's family room. No doubt in many cases I missed the mark; but I did finish a twenty-mile walk for the March of Dimes, meet some professional goals (their importance long since faded), and save enough for early retirement.

The point is there was always something on the drawing board. In our younger years, we all had goals. We saved for our first home; rejoiced when the baby was potty trained; planned how we'd spend our days when the youngest started school. We didn't have to go looking for things to do and didn't need lists of goals. We simply looked ahead, struggled, strived, plodded, and celebrated things large and small. Fresh-cut grass, a perfect lemon pie with a flaky crust, or a prize-winning rose carried the aroma of pride — a goal accomplished.

"Life is a journey not a destination," the old proverb cautions. It reminds me of a quote I used when I was a political novice taking the reins of the local Republican Women's Club: "When you're green, you're growing; when you're ripe, you begin to rot."

When we start thinking that the best of life is over, we rot on the vine. That's what happens when we adopt the at-my-age-I-don't-even-buy-green-bananas philosophy. Thinking we may not have enough time for long-term goals, we sit. Well, I say buy some green bananas; plan a future. What's the worst that can happen? If a few items on your wish list prove to be overly ambitious or impractical, you'll still have had the pleasure of contemplating their possibilities.

Sixty-five was my deadline for finishing or forgetting this book. Now I'm toying with the idea of hiking down the Grand Canyon before I'm seventy. It will take training and special equipment, and I may have to do it wearing Depends, but it's possible if I prepare.

Change — the only constant

Expectations change, the language changes, we change. That's good. Futurist Alvin Toffler says, "The illiterate of the 21st century will not be those who cannot read and write, but those who cannot learn, unlearn, and relearn.

Don't expect a perfect list on the first try. Better yet, use five-by-seven-inch index cards. That way you can adjust your priorities and move "done" items to the back of the box. This is what I do — although I wish I had kept lists from the past to see how I've changed.

When my children were growing up, I learned to take 'never' and 'impossible' out of my vocabulary. I've also learned to move preconceived ideas to the back of my mind. It's a long way from River Oaks to south Houston, where I grew up. I didn't learn the debutante rules, but my family had a few rules of their own. Ankle bracelets and red fingernail polish were out; you were never to wear white shoes after Labor Day; and you were always to wear underwear without holes (in case you were in an accident and sent to the hospital). Nice girls *never* rode motorcycles.

Although I'll probably never wear an ankle bracelet, I wear white athletic shoes year round, and I've changed my mind about motorcycles. I love hearing Paula, Ila, Sally, Carol, Millie, and Ann tell about their cycling adventures. They're not the type you see roaring down the streets of Sturgis exposing their breasts. They're just practical women who found motorcycling an up-close and inexpensive way to see the country.

For Ann, marrying an East Texas schoolteacher, and experiencing an old fashioned shivaree staged by his students, was quite an adventure. Now eighty, she hasn't given up adventure, but she and Van have traded their motorcycles for a motor home. "When we were younger, we strapped the motorcycles on the back of the camper and headed for Colorado every summer. We camped in National Forests and explored back roads. We're too old for that now, but I sure enjoyed it," she says.

Now, shivarees are passé, and busy people with more money than time ship their expensive Harleys to interesting locations for a few days of outdoor adventure. What's right at one age or time may be all wrong at another.

Author and syndicated columnist Tom Peters devoted one of his columns to some of businesses' dumb preconceptions. Peters says one of the dumbest statements ever uttered is "Do it right the first time." "We don't do anything new or interesting right the first time," he says. He suggests that today's business environment demands fluidity, not hard-wired organizational charts and strategic plans.

We certainly want to do new and interesting things, and most days our bodies tell us nothing is hard wired. The strategy: Use a pencil to plan your future — and keep an eraser handy!

Don't forget, even the big guys don't get it right the first time. The Newspaper Association of American named Kmart "Retailer of the Year" one day before the company filed for bankruptcy.

American manufacturers save millions of dollars a year with "just in time" inventory, a management strategy that saves capital and eliminates warehousing by scheduling raw materials and parts to arrive immediately before needed in the manufacturing process. However, General Motors discovered a glitch in the plan when a supplier's strike shut down facilities across the country. With no surplus, GM's small inventories were soon consumed.

Gary Giles, a GM plant manager, says they continue to modify their plan by considering backup sources and transportation alternatives. As we age, we must continually modify our plans and look at alternatives.

Perfect becomes passé. The best intentions fall short. Those daring young women of the Roaring Twenties who shimmied around in nighttime attire they called the "cat's pajamas" would blush at today's version in the window of Victoria's Secret.

Successful organizations and individuals continually modify. Farmers across the U.S. and Canada have opened new markets in India by swapping traditional crops for chickpeas. Ranchers have discovered the advantages of raising elk: They are relatively disease-free and, in addition to their low-fat meat, the velvet from the antlers of one mature bull fetches as much as $5000 on the Asia market.

After 115 years, Avon has moved their products into stores. Likewise, Tupperware (which goes from freezer to microwave!) is available in mall kiosks. The Welcome Wagon, as obsolete as its horse drawn namesake, is reduced to brochures delivered by mail carriers.

Today, with 65 percent of women working outside the home and concerns about strangers, door-to-door calls are impractical.

It's also impractical to assume you'll go sailing into the sunset Noah's Ark style — two by two. Widows are the fastest growing segment of our population. The average age of widowhood in the U.S. is fifty-six, and the midlife divorce rate has tripled in the past decade. The latest census reports that 45 percent of women over sixty-five are widows. Include the divorced and never married women, and the number of women paddling their own canoe rises to 56 percent.

Despite these statistics, unless a catastrophic event plunges us into icy reality, we meander through our middle years treading water — worrying more about wrinkles than widowhood, shying away from financial matters, and taking better care of our houseplants than ourselves.

On average, women live six years longer than men, and a second marriage in midlife doesn't assure a lifelong mate. My mother, grandmothers, and mothers-in-law have all outlived *two* husbands. The problem is we tend to ignore this unpleasant evidence — a mindset that leaves us ill prepared to cope with the challenges of spending years alone.

In leading the San Francisco 49ers to three Super Bowl victories, Coach Bill Walsh had his teams practice the most unlikely scenarios involving the last things he expected the other team to do. Then, no matter what happened, his players were prepared.

In his book on building a championship team, Don Shula says the "A" in *Everyone's a Coach* stands for "audible-ready," a football term meaning a team is prepared to respond quickly to a change in signals. "Audibles are not last-minute orders the quarterback has dreamed up out of nowhere. They're strategies the players know about and have practiced," says Shula. His teams practiced their game plan and the fallback scenarios, which played a part in making him the winningest coach in National Football League history.

Women also need to prepare a fallback position in case the unexpected happens. Susan B. Anthony said, "Marriage, to women as to men, must be a luxury, not a necessity; one incident of life, not all of it." It's time to unwind our mindset and realize we may not always have the luxury of a man in our life. This is a perfect attitude to begin a conversation with your spouse about death and dying.

Do you know the passwords to financial records stored in the computer? Do you know where to find the key to the safe-deposit box? Do you have a list of bank accounts, CDs, T-bills, stocks, bonds, and other holdings? If you're the keeper of the keys, does your husband know about these things?

I'm reminded of the time I stepped out the backdoor to water my plants the week after we changed door locks. You guessed it. There I stood in my nightgown, wishing I hadn't put off giving my neighbor the new key. My embarrassment knocking on doors half dressed and the inconvenience of waiting on a locksmith pales compared to dealing with financial matters after the death of a spouse.

It's possible that your husband won't have the luxury of *your* company forever. Younger women won't believe this, but some of us still live in "woman's-work" worlds. So, make sure he knows how to operate the household appliances and knows which cleaning products to use (the high-gloss finish on our bedroom suite should never be cleaned with furniture polish, only ammonia-free glass cleaner). During the learning process, you have the luxury of some household help.

After retirement, couples may spend all their time with each other. That's wonderful until one dies. As best-selling author Jacquelyn Mitchard related in a *Ladies' Home Journal* article, "I didn't plan to be a widow, and suddenly I discovered that I had no idea where my husband's life left off and mine began."

For both your sakes, begin now to have a life of your own. Join a women's club; plan an out-of-town shopping trip with friends; take a painting class or a cooking course. Develop friends and interests that don't depend on having a partner. Encourage him to do the same. You'll have a lot more to talk about around the dinner table than you will if you spend every day joined at the hip. It's good for your marriage today and good preparation for unknown tomorrows.

Research by the National Centenarian Awareness Project concludes that the most common characteristic of people living to 100 is their ability to "renegotiate life" and adjust to change.

Throughout history, women have demonstrated their resilience and creativity in renegotiating life. Civil War nurse Clara Barton found herself with plenty of food for the soldiers but only five tin cups and three plates. As she dished up food, each jar became a glass, each tin a plate. At the battle of Antietam, with hundreds of wounded to feed, she had used the last loaf of bread and the last cracker when she reluctantly agreed to open cases of wine. When she found the bottles were packed, not in sawdust as usual, but in cornmeal, she filled six large kettles with hot cornmeal mush.

Barton refused the woman's role of her day, defied politicians who tried to thwart her efforts, and founded the American Red Cross. She continued working for the organization until she died at age ninety-one. Surely, with role models like Barton, we can refuse the rocking chair and defy the stereotypes of aging.

Author Ellen G. Langer relates a story about doctors dismissing her grandmother's complaints as senility. When an autopsy showed a brain tumor, Langer sadly recalled, "We did not question the doctors; mindset about experts interfered."

The only expert on how you spend the last quarter of your life is you, not your doctor, your children, or your spouse. Listen to them all, study your options, and make your own decisions. The only thing set in stone is the slab that will mark your grave. Everything else is negotiable. So rewind your thinking about aging, and set your mind on a personal mission.

Star Jones, former prosecuting attorney and co-host of *The View*, says it best: "I'm the author of the only dictionary that defines me."

It's time to define you and what you want to do with the rest of your life. We commonly refer to nothing being certain except death and taxes, a comment Ben Franklin made in reference to the new constitution. Fully aware that nothing is guaranteed, he said the document had an "appearance that promises permanency."

Just as we don't wait until April 15 to begin preparing our tax return, we shouldn't put off preparing for the other certainty. As Mother Teresa said, "The important thing is to be ready for anything, at all times."

In the blink of an eye Salvador Dali's painting *Hallucinogenic Toreador* changes from the goddess of love and beauty to a bullfighter. Another blink and Venus de Milo's image returns wrapped in the toreador's cape.

Sometimes a long illness warns us of an impending change. At other times, change comes in the blink of an eye — or ruptured aneurysm — as it did for Carolyn, a longtime Arizona resident. She says the only discussion she and her husband had about death was after a business associate's funeral. "Ron threatened to come back and haunt me if his funeral was a somber and depressing ritual. Of course, we laughed — he was only fifty.

"Two years later I was forced to remember that conversation. He was energetic and full of energy one day and gone the next. Now it was up to me to plan a celebration of his life."

Family and friends streamed through the door of their Scottsdale home. Casseroles, cakes, and pies covered the tables and countertops. Hugs, tears — and equal parts laughter — prompted by favorite stories about Ron filled the house. They did it his way.

"In the spring, we gathered at Rocky Point and scattered his ashes across the water," Carolyn recalls. "I launched a time capsule of his favorite things to carry him into eternity — family pictures, a cigarette and match, Simon and Garfunkel sheet music, a miniature bottle of gin, and a piece of English toffee. When someone asked if I'd kept some of his ashes, I said, 'No, I didn't save any; I was afraid I'd take an arm or a leg and he'll need them to swim.' Looking back, I'm a little embarrassed at such a flippant remark, but actually it was a perfect farewell. Exit laughing, my love."

Ron left something else behind that will bring laughter and joy for years to come — a liver and two kidneys. Maybe that's why Carolyn could find humor in a remark about body parts. Like Ron, she saw them as something he no longer needed, yet priceless to someone else. She's consoled that a father of eight received one of Ron's kidneys.

Others are consoled by a funeral reflecting religious beliefs and familiar traditions. When my daughter-in-law Susan's father died, our grandsons read scripture at the service. Other family members and friends spoke of what he had meant to them, and beautiful music and traditional Catholic ritual brought comfort to mourners of many denominations.

The rituals of death are changing, which — when you consider fathers in delivery rooms, skydiving couples exchanging vows in midair and botox parties as popular as bunco parties — is not surprising.

Longevity and mobility contribute to the decline of church funerals and burial in the family plot. If you die at age sixty, a wide circle of mourners seek the solace of a funeral or memorial service; but for each additional decade you live, the circle shrinks. Many people whose parents live into their nineties find a simple service at the grave or the care facility their parent called home a suitable remembrance.

Funeral directors suggest pre-planned (a blessing for loved ones) and prepaid (a blessing for the funeral home) arrangements. With fewer families spending a lifetime in the same town, you're fortunate if you have a family cemetery plot. Scattered around the country, our offspring take root where opportunity plants them. In later years, we may move to a warmer climate, to be near our children, or to escape the responsibilities of a home and yard. As ties to the former church and community dwindle, many consider burial in their new surroundings comforting and convenient for their family.

It isn't necessary to have a full-blown diagram of arrangements; however, a discussion of your wishes may avert family disagreements down the road. Make a simple list of your druthers. If you want to be buried with your parents on the family farm, let someone know. If you don't care, say so. If you'd rather hear familiar music than a choirs' cantata, list your favorite hymns. If you envision jazz playing while your ashes are scattered across your favorite landscape, tell someone where. And if you want your final resting place to be six feet under lush grass and shade trees, scout out some places.

It's not morbid to discuss funeral plans, nor will it tempt fate. As business guru Peter Drucker tells his clients, "Objectives are not fate; they are direction." Your objective in talking about death is to give directions that ease your family's responsibilities. Without specific directions, you might end up like Ted Williams — a permanent Popsicle.

Some folks are opting to have the carbon from their cremains made into jewelry. For about $2000 LifeGems creates a lovely diamond. I heard a man discussing how comforting it was to have a beautiful remembrance of his daughter. If this appeals to you, numerous diamonds (one for each family member?) can be made from your ashes. It doesn't appeal to a friend of mine. "No thanks," she says, "I might end up on the third finger of a new wife's left hand.

Mary doesn't see anything morbid about her homemade "rocket ship," as she calls the casket waiting in the workshop. She had her headstone and gravesite picked out when she went shopping for a casket and decided even $500 for a pine box was too much. "I'm going to leave this world as I came into it — not owing anybody anything," she said.

What began as a cost-saving idea became a loving project for her husband, a sixty-five-year-old veteran, who stays busy in his woodshop when he's not riding around Phoenix on his Harley. He hopes she won't need her poplar wood casket for a long time.

"Shopping" for funeral services may seem distasteful, yet we spend weeks shopping and price comparing for other things we value. Buying a new dress at the last minute is no big deal; we have years of clothes-shopping experience to draw upon. When shopping for a new car, we already have an idea of the features, price range, upholstery and color that we want; even so, most people take more than one day to buy a car. Yet when a loved one dies, we are expected to make many decisions in an hour or two. Surely it's more easily done without the emotional turmoil and time pressure that immediately follows a death.

When you're asked, "Who will the body be released to?" is not the time to begin looking at options. You're presented with a vast array of choices — how, when, where and how much — cremation or burial, funeral service or memorial service, wake or no wake?

My friend Jean let her family know what she wanted years in advance. She filled out the forms and made all the arrangements so when she died it was all handled just as she wished. A memorial service paid tribute to the TLC she'd brought to patients during her long nursing career and to her final gift to medicine — she donated her body to the medical school for research.

The approximately 25 percent of Americans who choose cremation also need to evaluate costs, services, and reliability with a clear head. Amid recent scandals, checking out crematory references and stability in advance saves the family unnecessary angst. For $600 – $800 mortuaries rent caskets. The most expensive option is to embalm the body and buy a casket for a traditional wake and funeral and then have the body taken to the crematory.

According to the National Funeral Directors Association, going out in style carries an annual price tag of more than $8 million dollars, with the average for a traditional funeral running around $6,000, not including cemetery charges.

A survey of funeral homes in the Midwest found a difference of 300 percent between the cost of the most and least expensive funeral with just basic services. Bill Baker, a funeral director in Arlington, Texas, says the average cost in this area is just under $5,000.

Jessica Mitford's *The American Way of Death* and a later investigation by Congress led to the reform of the funeral industry. Now funeral home operators are required to provide cost lists, respond to telephone inquiries, and inform purchasers that neither embalming nor a casket are required by law.

Survey the scenarios

Sandra Day O'Conner, the first woman Supreme Court justice says, "I think anything you do in life requires preparation." How do you prepare for old age? Take the advice of those football coaches — prepare for the unexpected with a fallback position for every scenario.

Spend an hour brainstorming the many routes your life might take during the next twenty or thirty years. You'll see that each scenario creates its own set of problems requiring different solutions.

Professor Blaine McCormick, of the Hankamer School of Business at Baylor University and author of *At Work with Thomas Edison*, gives his students an unusual brainstorming exercise. It's designed to show that our best solutions aren't always the first ones that come to us, that we go through a lot of bad ideas to get to the really good ones. After students generate at least forty solutions to a problem, they select the best to present to the class. Dr. McCormick says the results are pretty predictable — students find their best ideas between numbers 18 and 42.

Remember the scene in *Dead Poet Society* where Robin Williams tells his students, "I stand on my desk to remind myself we must continually look at things from different points of view?" That's invaluable advice.

What follows is a word quiz that demonstrates how our point of view (our mindset), affects the conclusions we draw. Think of two or more answers for each clue and check the width of your view.

1. Pupil's place
2. Army Brass
3. Tumblers
4. Frank
5. Lean
6. SOS
7. Hides
8. Big revolver
9. Nursery occupant
10. Rainbow
11. Jerk
12. Spring
13. Bee product
14. Rank
15. Shed
16. Objective
17. Cap
18. Ram
19. Top story
20. Scratch

Sample answers: 1. desk, iris. 2. officer, bugle. 3. glasses, acrobats. 4. honest, hot dog. 5. slant, slim. 6. May Day, Brillo rival. 7. conceals, pelts. 8. weapon, planet. 9. pot, tot 10. trout, aura. 11. soda, knee. 12. coil, leap, season. 13. honey, quilt, spelling word. 14. fetid, military. 15. lean-to, molt. 16. goal, unbiased. 17. bottle cover, head cover. 18. Aries, butt. 19. headline, attic. 20. claw, flaw.

As you can see, each can be perceived more than one way. Where you put the accent often changes the meaning of a word. A flexible mindset — a willingness to change emphasis as circumstances change — is the key to aging greatly.

Changing our mind is more than a woman's prerogative — it's a necessary part of successful aging. Don't expect to find every answer, or the best answer, on the first try. Remember that failure paves the road to success, so unwind your mindset, model the role of someone you admire, reset your biological clock, reflect on the wonders of the present rather than regrets of the past, exercise your options, love, laugh, learn, and accept the accolades. You'll be prepared for rain or rainbows.

Model the Role

Every person I meet is in some way my superior; that's what I learn from him or her.

— Ralph Waldo Emerson

She was born in 1916, the year Norman Rockwell illustrated his first cover for The Saturday Evening Post. My mother, Bonnie, could easily have been the model for the mischievous child Rockwell often depicted in his cozy family scenes. She is a wonderful role model and a hard act to follow.

An only child, she followed her dad and the hired men around the farm, curious about everything they did. From the parade of Mexican and Black families who carried a tow sack of belongings into the one-room shack beyond the barn, she got a multi-cultural education. Some stayed just until the cotton crop came in; others hung around for a year or so. The men milked, planted, and weeded. The women would build a fire under the black pot, scrub the clothes on a washboard, and the next day heat a flat iron to press gingham shirts and dresses.

Much to my grandmother's chagrin, my mother preferred squatting next to the Mexican women as they cooked their tortillas on a tractor disk balanced over a wood fire to watching her mother can peaches. She also preferred hanging around in the barn to helping in the kitchen—and from the time she was eight, she carried a .22 rifle. The hired men quickly learned not to mess with this skinny kid. Once one of them challenged her to shoot a pigeon off the barn roof. She squeezed the trigger and breathed a sigh of relief when the bird landed at the man's feet.

This same man got another gander at her Annie Oakley skills one evening when she spotted him hiding behind the wild wisteria peeking in the upstairs window at her mother undressing. She aimed just above the bushes, and lucky for him she was a good shot. The next day my grandfather had the man cut and haul off the wisteria. Then he fired him.

When I was growing up, my mother kept her shotgun handy for hunting trips and scaring pesky varmints out of the yard. Once she spent all day perched on a campstool with a .410 laid across her lap protecting our lot. Workmen laying forms for a warehouse that would sit inches from the property line had trampled her tomatoes and knocked off for the day when she threatened to shoot the next man that set foot on her property. The next morning when the owner showed up to negotiate, he got a surprise. Friends and neighbors had stayed up all night helping my parents erect a six-foot tall fence that ran the length of the property line, forcing him to keep his construction at a reasonable distance.

Mother called him "the man from the northeast" and would say he was a slow learner. He often parked his Cadillac with the tail fins extending well into our driveway. After several instances where she had to wait for him to finish a phone call or some other business before she could get her car out, she borrowed my uncle's truck. The next time the driveway was blocked, she backed the truck out far enough to be seen from next door, walked across the lot, announced she was leaving in two minutes, and this would be the last time she would ask anyone to move their vehicle. "I've never seen anybody move so fast," she says.

Then as now, she's fond of telling you "how the cow eats cabbage." Politically correct is not in her vocabulary. I consider it a victory to have convinced her that *damn* and *Yankee* are two words, although I think she still considers mine a "mixed marriage" because my husband is from up north. To her way of thinking, there's something wrong with anybody who prefers mushrooms to okra. "You know what they're grown in don't you?" she whispers.

The chances of her saying "significant other" instead of "that old boy she's shacked up with" are nil. She can sympathize with people who are crippled, fat, deaf, or blind, but don't talk to her about "challenged."

Her entire life has been a challenge. From a mother who didn't want to see her "precious baby" grow up to the mother-in-law from hell, she's fought for every inch of ground she's gained.

She never liked school and says, "It's a good thing we only had eleven grades back then or I'd have never finished." (No doubt, Epson Downs contributed to her poor academic record, since anytime the horses were running on Wednesday—ladies day—she skipped school.) Yet, she's been a student all her life, always interested in everything around her, a make-do role model combining creativity and common sense. And thanks to her pack-rat ways, generations to come can pass along bits of history.

A small cream pitcher from the 1920s recalls the family scavenging through the Rice Hotel's garbage for napkins, flatware, and china before her uncle slopped the hogs from what he found on his daily garbage collection route.

As a teen during the Depression, she earned spending money raffling off her drawings and paintings. People who couldn't afford to buy one, gladly bought a chance for a quarter, earning her more money than the original asking price.

Mother's recollections and the smocked and embroidered dresses she and her mother wore to the 1928 Democratic National Convention in Houston — the first national convention held in a Southern state since the Civil War — offer a look at Texas politics. Twelve-year-old Bonnie didn't notice the temperance groups protesting Al Smith's anti-prohibition stand, the Baptists holding twenty-four-hour prayer vigils opposing his Catholicism, or the black alternate-delegates separated by a wire barrier. What she recalls seventy-five years later are the music, the old gray mule they paraded through the aisles, and the fistfights that broke out among delegates. "It was like going to a circus," she says.

History books complete her story. Although the Texas delegation voted for a favorite-son candidate and supported a "bone dry" plank in the platform, Al Smith, who didn't attend the convention, prevailed. Despite the platform, the New York Governor's telegraphed acceptance stunned delegates with an anti-prohibition message.

Democratic "drys," anti-Catholics, and anti-Yankees joined Republicans to make Herbert Hoover the first Republican presidential candidate to carry Texas. His election and the Great Depression that followed began my mother's distrust of anyone north of the Mason-Dixon Line and began a fifty-year domination of Texas politics by the Democratic Party.

Pottery from prewar Japan elicits more stories of her family's political activism and defense of the underdog. Her father, who served on the school board, rallied the community to keep local Japanese-American truck farmers from being interned during World War II. Only those sending money home to their families in Japan joined the 100,000 incarcerated.

That sense of fairness stayed with my mother. Years later, our black mailman said she was the only one on his route who offered him water without being asked and brought it in a regular glass instead of an old fruit jar the family didn't use.

She never got too excited about the spider-web-looking stuff and photos she took of strange objects in the sky, but a group of UFO enthusiasts and some folks at the University of Texas were excited enough to carefully examine her snapshots and tape record her recollections. Now all that is tucked in a dilapidated stationary box tied with a length of old panty hose.

Edgar Albert Guest could have had my mother in mind when he coined the phrase, "It takes a heap o' livin' to make a house a home." She's lived in a tiny frame house she and my dad built, a tract house in the city, a log cabin in the woods, a concrete block house on the river, a double-wide trailer in the hill country, and a retirement apartment — all in Texas and all filled with her unique personal touches.

Like the motto of the new Cowgirl Museum in Fort Worth, my mother has "always saddled [her] own horse." And that includes furnishing her retirement apartment.

Her closet holds more craft supplies than clothes. Collections, mostly found rather than bought, take more space than the bed. On the wall near the door hangs a Texas Centennial souvenir plate she bought in 1936 when she performed on the teeter-board with the Gainsville Community Circus, celebrating the state's centennial at the opening of the State Fair in Dallas. (Later that week she and my father were married.)

Beside the plate hangs an original cross-stitch depicting the state flag, an oil well, bluebonnets, and other Texas symbols. Her art work

— on rocks, tiles, canvas and anything else that stayed still long enough for her to find a brush — stands, sits, and leans everywhere. A donkey-cart collection, blooming violets, stringy cactus, rocks, sea shells, driftwood, an authentic railroad spike with a toy metal train glued on top, insulators, arrowheads, and a mastodon tooth complete the decor. It suits her fine, and I've been told in no uncertain terms not to touch anything. "I like it just like it is," she says.

When I get frustrated with the clutter, I remind myself that, at eighty-six, her curiosity keeps her mind sharp, her determination keeps her threading the sewing machine (she won't consider paying anyone to alter clothes), and her independence keeps her giving herself two insulin shots a day.

My mother was a forty-one-year-old widow when she took the first job that paid enough to support her and my teenage younger sister. She supervised a housekeeping crew at a hospital. She knew about cleaning and hard work, but she wasn't prepared for the deferential treatment the high-dollar doctors expected.

"We tangled horns more than once when he blamed my housekeepers for things that weren't their fault. He was wonderful to his patients, but didn't have the time of day for anyone else," she says. No doubt, internationally famous heart surgeon Dr. Michael DeBakey had little time for chewing the fat with the cleaning staff.

Mother, on the other hand, has always had time for people. With plenty of food and lively conversation, our house was a favorite with neighbors and my teenage friends. She tolerated anything but lying, "puttin' on airs," and being "uppity." That hasn't changed.

She's affable and accommodating to the retirement home staff, her neighbors, and tablemates, but doesn't back down when challenged. She "wouldn't be buffaloed" by a particularly "pushy" woman who continually cut ahead in the lunch line. Fortunately, neither was hurt when Mother stuck her cane in front of the woman's walker and gave her the "cow-cabbage" speech. I'm hoping I've inherited half her spunk.

It runs in the family

I actually have several generations of spunky women to draw from. One rainy day (figuratively and literally), after weeks of concentrated composure, rivulets on the windowpane primed a gush of tears. After a good cry, I recalled the stories of a terrible rainy day for my paternal grandmother, Erie Doolan Marsalis.

Erie looked out the window again. The scene was the same — rain, mud, and no sign of the doctor. She had sent word for him to come; but with so many sick, she knew it might be night before he made it. She wished her sister Katy would come.

Erie dug in her apron pocket for Katy's letter, slumped in her sewing rocker, and reread the brief note.

November 17, 1918
New York Harbor

Dear Sis,
I expected to be mustered out and on my way to Houston by now, but my departure has been delayed. The first day out of Southampton the sick bay was full, and by the time we docked, the ship was a floating influenza epidemic. We've been quarantined, so it seems the Navy will have me a little longer. Several of the nurses have it, so the few of us left are near exhaustion. I fervently hope that all of you are well. Give my love to all.

Your loving sister,
Katy

Erie tucked the letter back in her pocket and returned to the bedroom. She wrung a wet cloth and replaced the warm one on Jim's fiery forehead. His eyelids briefly fluttered to acknowledge the gesture as he lifted his head just enough to take a sip of the tea she offered. She picked up a second cup and turned to the daybed a few feet away.

"Mama, please have a few sips," she pleaded. "The sassafras is fresh and warm." After no response, Erie dipped a rag in a bucket of water fresh from the well and squeezed it between her mother's cracked lips.

For three days, feverish delirium, retching coughs, and a blowing rain shook the small frame house. Erie slumped into a chair between the beds, thankful the children were with neighbors.

The morning's hot, mustard footbaths didn't seem to help, and there were no lemons for toddies. Until the doctor brought sulfa, she knew of nothing else to do.

"If I just had a phone to call someone. . ." She looked at the crochet basket as a possible distraction, but her leaden hands rejected the thought. The coughing, so familiar now, went unnoticed as the rise and fall of her chest rocked her to sleep.

Erie awoke to a world of darkness and banging at the door. She stumbled through the parlor and fumbled with the latch.

"Oh, thank God you're here. Let me light the lamp. I must have dozed off."

"Sorry, I couldn't get here earlier. I think half the county's sick. Let me have a look at 'em." The kerosene lamp wavered as Erie led the doctor into a silent bedroom. She knew.

"I'm sorry Mz. Doolan." He pulled the quilts first over her husband, then her mother.

Like me, MamMaw was a widow with three children, no education, and no money. My father, Earl, was nine, his younger brother, Weldon, five, and their older sister, Violet, eleven. Their mother clutched them to her and never let go.

Erie's love strangled them. A second marriage to a gentle, loving man didn't extract her from the unhealthy relationships with her children. She made her daughter and daughters-in-law miserable. My father, the middle child, paid the highest toll. He died of leukemia at forty-seven, still tangled in her apron strings.

MamMaw Eva, my maternal grandmother, devoted herself to her only child. She moved into a separate bedroom as soon as my mother was born. She treated her like a doll to be dressed and loved, and never wanted her to grow up. When Bonnie came to her concerned because she was bleeding, Eva turned pale, slumped into the nearest chair, and rocked back and forth crying, "Oh, my baby, my baby, is gone forever." Thinking she was dying, Bonnie ran to the barn to get her father. "It's the only time I heard my dad curse," she says. "He grabbed my arm, drug me into the house, and told my mother to stop that blubbering and do some explaining to this child." (Understandably, I got the information on menstruation years before I needed it.)

Not surprisingly, as soon as my mother announced her marriage, her father left and married his lady barber. He set Eva up in a little house across town. She, too, was on her own at middle age. This five-foot dynamo cleared the land, planted a garden, raised chickens, and kept a milk cow. She eked out a living doing hard labor for neighbors. She painted barns, chopped wood, cleaned the gun club, even salvaged the nasty handkerchiefs discarded on the clubhouse grounds.

To locate Eva as far as possible from his south Houston home, her ex-husband bought her land that later became one of the fifteen wealthiest communities in Texas. She sold it in the '50s, long before it reached its full value, but she got more money than she ever dreamed of having. A few years before her second husband died, she bought land along the Blanco River in Wimberley, a idyllic spot in the Texas hill country.

Although she had adequate reserves to last the rest of her life, Eva never lost her waste-not-want-not ways. She kept a small garden into her late '70s. Torches made from kerosene-soaked corn cobs lit her way to the river for predawn fishing. She fashioned minnow traps from fruit jars and dug worms to bait her cane pole.

She made her dishcloths from the twine twisted around the daily newspaper. Neighbors saved even the smallest scraps, saying, "Eva will find something to make from it." And she did. She knew nothing of fun, only work, but this was her pleasure — giving something to others. Half of Hays County must have had one of Eva's potholders or an apron she made from scraps.

As it turns out, that lady barber, my step-grandmother, became my favorite relative and was an excellent role model. Her nickname, Pep, suited her perfectly — she was full of energy and enthusiasm. She had more pluck than poise; was more practical than polite; and was always more concerned with substance than with style.

She was the second wife of two men and took their families as her own. She became a role model for generosity. She gave her time, advice, and surprising gifts. She took my mother on a trip to Hawaii. When she couldn't dissuade me from marrying so young, she gave a one-sentence lecture on the importance of sex in marriage. Although shocking at the time, it was good advice. In today's world where children get cars and computers for gifts, it won't seem impressive, but in my modest circumstances, a $100 bill in a graduation card was overwhelming.

She was a barber before the days of unisex salons; she ran a dairy, worked in a factory, and invested in stocks before my family even knew that individuals could do that. She nursed two husbands through years of poor health and chose to stay in her own home until her death.

She grew day lilies, nurturing expensive hybrids that she passed along to family members. When I last visited her, she was distressed that her arthritis kept her from properly caring for the lilies. She died a few months later at the height of their blooming season. Every June, the orange, gold, deep purple, and creamy yellow blossoms remind me of the lessons in living I learned from her.

My biological grandmothers were strong women, great role models for hard work and determination — yet one's manipulating and the other's smothering ways were not a legacy I wanted to leave my children.

I had to make a life for myself, not try to live theirs. My heart raced as curfews approached, skipped a beat at the sound of a siren, and almost stopped at late night phone calls. But as they left with friends, I gripped the doorknob, forced a smile and said, "Have a good time."

For years, I'd been comfortable modeling my mother's role of stay-at-home-mom. Fresh baked cookies after school and family meals together were the norm. Being a good wife and mom were my only goals. Then circumstances forced me into a new role.

For our generation, the glass slipper preceded the glass ceiling. We waited for a charming prince to sweep us away to the castle or at least to a tract house in the suburbs. It was a perfect fit, unless prince charming ran off with the ugly stepsister.

Aside from wife and mother, there were few roles to model: secretary, salesclerk, teacher, waitress, nurse, and of course, the oldest profession, which was by far the most lucrative. But Cinderella was a good girl. She wanted love, marriage, and a baby carriage.

We only became a pumpkin for nine months at a time and lived happily ever after. The suburbs, station wagons, community service, and standing appointments at the beauty shop defined our world. Cart the children, clean the house, cook the meals, and entertain *his* boss.

When the corporation beckoned, the moving van rolled us across the country. With each move, our spouses climbed the corporate ladder and we slipped a rung. It was back to fund-raising chairman — again. The first year in a new town, we found a new church, new doctors and dentists, a pediatrician for the preschoolers, a dermatologist for the zit-teens.

We'd grown up dressing dolls, playing house and school. Boys were swashbuckling soldiers, amateur architects, and hard-driving bargainers. Budding businessmen parlayed paper-route proceeds into bulging baseball card collections. They negotiated and traded like NASDAQ nabobs. They built, bought, and fought. We nurtured.

The midlife crisis hit when our daughters dreamed of becoming doctors, lawyers, and accountants. Balding prince charming, battling his own midlife crisis, welcomed the help with tuition, and stay-at-home Cinderellas by the thousands climbed aboard the carriage of commerce. With clay of courage we modeled new roles.

Changing fairy tales

Now it was my turn to sweep Cinderella's ashes aside and model the Goldilocks role. If first attempts were too cold, too small, or too hard, I'd keep trying until I got it just right.

"The old gray-hairs ain't what they used to be," I told myself. They've trotted out new hair colors and are galloping into their golden years. They're racing through the halls of ivy, charging the corridors of Congress, and stampeding the corporate culture. They pick the mommy track, the fast track, or back track. The kitchen isn't too hot; it just takes longer to find the recipe. Goldilocks across the country sampled the sweet porridge of success. I craved a place at their table.

Today, psychologists call it visualization. In the summer of 1950, it was just plain daydreaming. I leaned against the Chinaberry tree and visualized myself strutting onto the field. My baton flashed in the stadium lights, and a gold satin skirt swished around my legs. (It was definitely a dream because in it I had nice legs, not the toothpick realities.)

The fall that I started Junior High my music teacher told me something my family had been too kind to mention. "I'll give you an 'A' if you promise never to open your mouth in my class. Just take the roll, pass out the music books, and run errands. It's not your fault you're tone-deaf, but if I were you, I'd find some high school activity that doesn't require rhythm."

I'd been twirling a baton for years. My dream was to be a high school majorette, so I just held on to my dream and modeled that role in my head. Four years later, I raised my baton, blew the whistle, and led the Golden Gauchos under the goal post. Since I got to start the cadence, they followed my lead.

The Chinaberry tree was long gone when I searched the job maze for a career path. My skills weren't listed on the typical job application. Interviewers were as discouraging as my music teacher had been. They didn't ask if I could run a political campaign or school carnival; didn't care if I could decorate a cake with a ballerina or baseball diamond. They looked at the fifteen years of unemployment and the four-0 in the age column, not the four-0 for my one year of college.

So I gave my own answers with a resume of volunteer experience. I dusted off scrapbooks, copied PTA award certificates and letters of appreciation from grateful candidates. George Bush's thanks after his failed senatorial candidacy went to thousands of people, but it had my name on it. (Little did I know I was using a future president for a reference!)

I dreamed of a career, not just a job. And just as visualized, a creative resume and charitable recommendations from friends persuaded an employer I could do the work. Appropriately, a brilliant orange sunrise welcomed the last day of October 1977. It was no trick; it was the beginning of my career in hospital public relations. I was on my way. Well, almost.

I altered, borrowed, and bought a work wardrobe of five outfits. To be sure I never wore the same thing twice in one week, I had a Monday dress, a Tuesday dress, and so on — a good plan except in a hospital where volunteers work one day a week. Profuse compliments on my *new* dress from a "Tuesday pink lady" substituting on Friday delivered the embarrassing message. On days like this, I remembered the Chinaberry tree, visualized a better future, and struggled to make the vision a reality.

The eye of the storm

With the children in counseling and night school increasing my skills for a job I loved, I thought the hurricane that spun my life out of control had passed. Turns out, it was only the calm at the eye.

Church on Christmas Eve and black-eyed peas on New Year's Day satisfied the spiritual and superstitious rituals; but ten days into 1979, my life froze. I lost consciousness halfway through my backward count from ten. As the nurse pulled back the sterile drape, the surgeon's eyes revealed an unseen smile behind his mask. A strip of surgical tape across my right breast carried a message to my bridge-playing physician. "Make a grand slam. Get it all!" That small lump was a giant pothole in my road to recovery.

I'd discovered the lump in my breast the same week my boss gave her resignation. I had assisted in the office for only a year, didn't have a college degree or the writing experience the director's position required. Qualifications aside, I gambled on my gut feeling and assured management I could do the job if given a chance.

Cancer gave me that chance. In my case, a hospital bed was the right place at the right time. The hospital administrator with the disposition of a lion and heart of a lamb couldn't turn me down. Years later I teased him saying, "I got the job because you didn't think I would live long enough to screw it up."

There was nothing to tease about at the time, however. "Just remember, you asked for this job, and if you can't do it, you can't go back to being the assistant. You won't have any job," he growled. Then he quietly added, "I've hired an assistant to cover things until you recuperate."

The recuperation wasn't easy. With no sick leave accumulated — and refusing to accept a loan to make up for unpaid time — I was back at my desk nine days after the surgery. Determined to grin and bear it, I held my arm close to my side and moved it as little as possible, which resulted in a frozen shoulder. It took weeks of physical therapy to regain the range of motion. As soon as I was eligible, I became a Reach to Recovery volunteer for the American Cancer Society. For the next ten years, I taught mastectomy patients exercises so they would not lose the movement in their arm.

Losing a breast wasn't my concern, but the cancer was a huge one. It had only been a year since my children had lost their father. I *had* to survive. At the time, a radical mastectomy was the standard surgery, only followed by chemo and radiation in cases with extensive lymph node involvement. In my circumstances, I couldn't have managed either, so I'm glad it was a decision I didn't have to make.

I assured everyone that I'd been given a clean bill of health; then I hid the dates of my three-month checkups and periodic bone scans. Fortunately, the children didn't notice the regularity of mysterious stomach upsets that kept me throwing up the day before each test. Still, I'm sure it was nothing compared to the effects of chemo that today's patients endure.

At the time, doctors didn't recommend reconstruction until at least a year after the initial surgery, which didn't boost confidence in survival. In my case, it was a mute point. It took four years to accumulate enough time off to begin a two-step reconstruction process.

A year after that, I became one of the happy statistics with a five-year survival rate. The sad irony is that the men who saved me physically and financially — my surgeon and the hospital president — both died of cancer in their prime. In life and in death, they modeled a role worth emulating. Rex, fighting his own battle with cancer, spoke at Dale's funeral. A beautiful eulogy to his golfing buddy ended with, "Save me a tee time." (I imagine they're quite a twosome.)

It took more than a twosome to sustain me through the learning process in public relations. Although I never left the 'l' out of the public in my title, there are plenty of opportunities for disaster when you "relate to the public." The temporary distress of a cockroach running across the head table at a banquet, a VIPs name misspelled in a publication, or a ream of stationery with the wrong zip code wanes when an occasional coup makes up for the faux pas. One of the best was giving away inexpensive plastic phone-book covers with our hospital information printed on them to cover the competition's expensive ad on the back of the book.

Only 10 percent of the job involved the media, but fielding questions about emergency room victims — policemen shot, children burned, teens killed in car wrecks — are the things you remember. I saw firsthand the suffering behind the headlines.

The degree of media attention was determined by how sensational the accident or how celebrated the victims. I once found myself sneaking a material witness through the garage to a waiting FBI car; and occasionally used the freight elevator to whisk celebrities to waiting limos. I cradled Baby Noel, an infant abandoned at Christmastime.

Reporters from the National Inquirer and the Globe would sit in my office asking questions they knew I couldn't and wouldn't answer, while their colleagues roamed the halls prepared to pass out $100 bills to anyone willing to talk. (No one did.)

Hospital PR was an exciting and challenging career. I dealt with situations involving medical, legal, police, fire, constitutional, ethical, political, and media issues; and I gathered enough sit-com fodder for a long-running TV series. My experiences are tame compared to those of many, and certainly compared to that of the young west Texas PR director, who was brand new to her job when a little girl fell down a well. Long after retirement, I still sympathize with the spokespersons whose job it is to step in front of the microphone and deliver bad news.

Fabulous family and friends

From casual acquaintances to dear friends, from immediate family to son-in-law, daughter-in-law, step-daughters, brothers-in-law, sisters-in-law, and ex-in-laws — I've been blessed.

Garth Brooks sings about friends in low places. When tragedy struck at our house, I found I had friends everywhere — white collar, blue collar, old friends, new neighbors, politicians, professional athletes, even an IRS agent.

One phone call from Congressman Jim Collins cut through the red tape at the Social Security office and shortened the six-month wait I had been told to expect.

Dick and Dolores had been our friends since they'd moved into the neighborhood. Dick showed up unannounced one Saturday morning to pick up my dilapidated station wagon. "A woman alone needs reliable transportation," he said. The service station where we traded offered their services. The car came back with a purring engine, a wash job, a full tank of gas, and no bill.

The country club management and golf pro canceled the dues and urged me to let the children continue to swim and play golf at Rolling Hills. Members of the Irving church we'd attended ten years earlier collected $500 on Sunday morning. The simple thank-you note I sent couldn't possible convey to the folks at Plymouth Park Methodist the difference their offering made.

The 1966 clock-tower shooting spree at the University of Texas at Austin made a profound impression on a young student. Phillip did the only thing he knew to do — he donated blood. A decade later, as a struggling builder/developer, he was still doing what he could to help others. The offer Phillip and his partner Barton made to me was as life giving as the blood donations he's made a lifelong practice.

We were leasing one of their houses, and they told me I could stay in the house, rent free, until it sold. They only asked that I keep the grass watered — and even offered to pay the water bill. I gratefully accepted their offer and paid the water bill myself. Both men have dozens of trophies, plaques, and certifications of appreciation for years of community service, but none were given with more gratitude than my lush green lawn.

As soon as I could afford a security deposit on an apartment, another neighbor, whose father owned a moving company, volunteered to move me. Physically, it was an easy move — lots of helping hands and only a mile away. But it's a long way from a big house on one end of the golf course to a small apartment on the other end.

Every day's mail brought notes of condolence, often with checks, some from people I hardly knew and some, like the one from my friends Polly and Mike, surprisingly large.

Ralph and Nell brought a stack of inspirational books, which I kept next to my bed so I could read a little every evening. This was the beginning of a lifetime appreciation of self-help books.

Al was dealing with his own grief at loosing his best friend, but he and his wife, Patty, were my anchors. I could write a whole chapter on the large and small favors and encouragement they offered. Most importantly, they told me about the job opening that began my career. Al wrote a glowing recommendation and a vase of roses, with a "Good Luck" card, welcomed me on my first day at work.

Friends and family found creative ways to help me so I wouldn't feel like a charity case. It's amazing how many people bought a ten-pound bag of potatoes without realizing they couldn't eat but half the potatoes before they rotted. And women who had cooked for the same size family for years suddenly had more food than they could eat — "Why don't you join us for dinner? Sam hates leftovers," Lou offered.

But the prize goes to Bob and Al. One day in October they stopped by after a round of golf and asked if they could weigh. I wasn't surprised since they often had a weight-loss bet going — usually dinner paid for by the loser (where they probably gained back half of what they'd lost). This time the stakes were higher. They were determined to lose weight before Christmas, so they asked me to record their weight and hold the money — $100 from each. As you've guessed, in December, they made a big deal about the incredible odds they would lose the same amount. They insisted I keep the money for the children's Christmas. (Writing this book often brings tears and this is one of those times. Thanks guys!)

When we first came to Arlington, several of the Texas Rangers lived in the same apartment complex. I shared the laundry-room folding table with Fergie Jenkins, watched the children in the pool with Tom and Kathy Grieve, and became friends with Janet and Jim Sundberg. When we moved into a house, Fred was working in California so Janet stayed with me while Jim went to spring training.

After Fred's death, thanks to Janet's generosity, I attended ball games as often as I liked and sat behind home plate with the Ranger wives. Daughter Kathy earned her spending money babysitting for the Grieves. Now those little fellows she babysat for are major league ball players.

While making his daily hospital visits with parishioners, my minister often came by my office. He was a good listener and one of the few people with whom I could share my woes. His frequent stops fueled a few rumors I'd like to put to rest. A hug and an occasional kiss on the top of the head were as intimate as our relationship got. On my first clandestine weekend out of town with Vince, it was Bob who had the phone number to reach me in case of an emergency. A year later, my friend and confidant performed our wedding ceremony.

I represented the hospital in civic and charitable organizations and found the business people at the Chamber of Commerce quite willing to accept a rookie. At one of the meetings, I sat next to a CPA. After the meeting I made an appointment with him to discuss thousands of dollars in business taxes owed to the IRS. The children's Social Security and my small salary paid for the essentials, but I could never pay off the business debts and didn't feel any moral obligation to do so. Jim went with me to the local IRS office and eloquently pleaded my case. I don't recall the details, but his basic argument was that you couldn't get blood out of a turnip. "You can spend lots of money in the effort and the result will be the same — except you will have ruined four people's lives," he argued. When the IRS horror stories came out in 1997, I realized how fortunate I'd been to find a friend like Jim and an understanding IRS agent. I never got a bill from either.

I've had wonderful role models, beginning with a family that valued honesty and hard work. As a teen, whenever I thought I might be the brightest candle in the candle shop, some friend gladly trimmed my wick.

Once I related a derisive thought about our biology teacher as if I had said it out loud. Knowing I wouldn't talk back to a teacher, Lanelle snuffed my exaggeration in mid-sentence. This is the kind of friend one needs when growing up. I learned a lot from her mother, too. Although at the time I didn't even know the word, she was the acquaintance who was closest to being avant-garde. She was a delightful round lady with a laugh that tinkled like wind chimes through her unstructured household. I didn't know there were people who didn't sit down to dinner at precisely at 5 p.m., eat, and do the dishes before the gravy dried on the plates. At Lanelle's house we could stand over the sink and eat ice cream from the carton and leave the dishes until the next day. From her I learned to appreciate people's differences.

Another ego trimming came from a dinner guest. Apparently I was in quite a tizzy when the guests arrived and, throughout the evening, was quite vocal about all the things that went wrong in the dinner preparation. When he'd heard enough, he looked across the table at me and said, "If it was so much trouble, why did you invite us." Talk about being cut down to size! I'm sorry I don't recall whom to credit for my improved entertaining skills; but since that day some thirty years ago, I've planned menus I can make ahead and made sure I have time to relax and enjoy my guests. If it isn't easy, I do my best to make it appear easy.

Role models make me better at everything I do. From Heloise-type household hints to serious life-altering events, I learn from other's experiences. We often model consciously. Dianna hopes the patience and kindness she showed her aging mother set an example for her own children. When we become impatient with our parents, we should consider what we are modeling. Someday we'll be in their shoes and hope our children will walk the extra mile to make us comfortable.

Several women of my acquaintance are among the thousands whose husbands have slipped into the abyss of Alzheimer's. Once their spouses designed components for our missions to the moon, headed successful businesses, coached college ball, and managed the finances of large corporations. Like a past president and popular actor, they are among the nearly 4 million Americans losing their memory, language skills, and judgment to this degenerative disease.

"The doctor says it's time to look at a place for him; but as long as I can keep him at home, I want to," one says as we chat in the grocery store with her husband standing near by. She shaves, bathes, dresses him, and prepares his favorite foods. Another visits her husband every day in a care facility, playing simple games and throwing a ball to him, hoping this postpones the inevitable. Yet another sends her spouse to adult daycare to relieve herself of the constant care and concern that he will wander away from home if left alone. They all carry on simple, one-sided conversations like they once did with their babies — more for their own sanity than with any hope of comprehension.

Alzheimer's devastates the mind of its victims and breaks the heart of loved ones. Caregiver services need to keep pace with the strides in diagnosis and treatment to meet the demands of the families of an expected 14 million victims by mid-century.

For Alzheimer's patients, death is a release. Those who die suddenly escape this life without the burden of anticipation. Heroic are those who watch disease slowly unwind their health into a straight line on a heart monitor. If this is my fate, I hope I can be as brave as those I've been privileged to know who left this world giving as much comfort as they received.

To keep from being overrun with cards and letters, I read greetings and thank-yous several times and tossed them away. Only a few are too precious to part with. One of those was from Dolores.

Her retirement plans exploded on April 9, 1995. As chief operating officer of the Oklahoma County Chapter of the American Red Cross, she disregarded her own health to coordinate services for the victims of what, at the time, was the nation's deadliest act of terrorism.

For two weeks she worked around the clock, snatching a few hours sleep on the office couch and postponing her retirement for three months. By the time she and Bob parked their travel trailer in Mesa, her lungs were slowly failing. Two years later, the doctors confirmed the diagnosis — she wouldn't live long enough to collect Medicare. For the last year of her life, she lived with such grace that anyone who didn't know her assumed she was as happy-go-lucky as her laugh.

She never hid from the reality of her fate. Doing her best to prepare her husband and daughters, she was the Morrie Schwartz of our desert resort — asking for little and thrilled by every kindness. Neighbors who brought food always received a personal thank-you note. A ride into the desert to see the poppies and cactus blooming exhausted and delighted her. Near the end, she welcomed short visits and enjoyed listening when talking was too much effort.

Many people have shown me how to live. My note from Dolores, with a bright yellow bird perched on the corner, reminds me of the friend who showed me how to die.

At ninety, Betty was ready to die. She told doctors not to bother with invasive tests because she wasn't having any of the procedures they might indicate. "I've already lived longer than I expected, and I'm confident that I'm going to a better place," she said. When told that the doctors had done all they could, she voiced only one regret. "I knew I shouldn't have let the dentist talk me into a root canal. I told him I wouldn't be needing that tooth for long!"

If you're ready for a better place, a Do Not Resuscitate (DNR) order assures that your wishes not to prolong life will be carried out. Unless you've signed a DNR and made some prior arrangement with emergency personnel, a call to 911 brings emergency workers prepared to do what they are trained for and obligated to do, so check out the rules in your town or care facility.

Watching a loved one's mind and body deteriorate is one of the toughest roles we'll ever play. In case mental decline sneaks up on me, while I'm of sound mind, I'm writing this open letter to my family:

> *You have loved me while I knew. You have cared for me when you could. When the time comes that my care is a burden too heavy to carry, put me in competent hands without regret. As I monitored those who cared for you when you were young, monitor my care when I am old to see that I'm not mistreated. Nod and listen to the same stories without scolding and patiently answer the same questions, knowing I wouldn't ask if I remembered.*
>
> *If I've forgotten your visits as soon as you leave, don't feel obligated to come so often. Don't make young children come along if they don't want to. Bring me a picture of them instead.*

Honor me by taking care of yourself and living your life to the fullest.

Don't spoil every holiday with sadness. Shower me with attention on my birthday and pick a day a week before or after family holidays to visit. Bring me a fragrant flower, a whimsical gift in a beautiful package, something childlike, brightly colored and moving to catch the eye of my dimmed vision, or something soft to cuddle. Hold my hand, gently rub lotion into my translucent skin, kiss my wrinkled forehead, and leave with my love.

Vince, if you find a woman who brings joy to your life, when I don't even know who you are, don't postpone your happiness. Ignore the critics and grab the golden ring (while you can still reach it!).

To my children and grandchildren: Take a cruise, a ski trip, visit far away grandchildren. When that special day comes, celebrate with your family and recall the good days. Talk about the recipes, the Christmas ornaments I've passed along, the funny gifts we've shared. I'll probably never know the day has come and gone, but if by chance in some spider-webbed corner of my brain the date registers, I'll remember those same good times. I promise.

We shouldn't sacrifice our own lives caring for loved ones. My aunt ignored a mole on her cheek while caring for her husband after his heart attack. He recovered; she died of melanoma. A drastic example, but caregivers often neglect their health and become as ill as the patient.

With parents living so long, children in their seventies are often physically unable to handle the demands of care-giving. If they are able, how long should they put their own lives on hold? Joyce, approaching eighty, has a 103-year-old father and a ninety-five-year-old stepmother. Fortunately, they are well situated in care facilities near her home in the Twin Cities, so she's able to leave for the winter and participate in the activities that keep her young.

Drs. Joseph A. Ilardo and Carole R. Rothman, co-directors of the Center for Adult Children of the Elderly and the Center for Caregiver Studies in Scarsdale, New York, have written several books on eldercare and resolving the dilemmas of aging parents. "*Are your Parents Driving you Crazy?*" addresses such problems as an aging parent taking a new spouse or becoming unable to safely drive; approaching your siblings for help; and handling a parent's finances when he or she is no longer able. Local care facilities and agencies on aging offer seminars and workshops to assist caregivers, so take advantage of all the resources available.

Approach this process with a golden-rule attitude, keeping in mind that your children are watching. Accept the care-giving role you want them to follow.

While we're on the subject of acceptance, there comes a time to accept, for yourself or a family member, that death is imminent and request hospice care. Hospice is an end-of-life care option for those with less than six months to live. It provides dying patients and their loved ones with comfort, compassion, and dignity. Hospice services are usually covered by Medicare and Medicaid. Go to www.hospiceinfo.org or call 1-800-658-8898 for The National Hospice Foundation guide. This comprehensive brochure includes a list of questions to use in evaluating different hospice providers in your community.

Smother the dust and soot

Famous Canadian physician, Sir William Osler, suggested that we "Learn to accept in silence the minor aggravations, cultivate the gift of taciturnity and consume your own smoke . . . so that those about you may not be annoyed with the dust and soot of your complaints."

One of the great annoyances to young people is the constant complaining of old people. People who continually complain about their aches and pains and glorify the past aren't good company.

When you meet Aubie, a ninety-three-year-old widow, you know why her family likes to visit. She always has a joke and finds humor in most of the maladies of aging. "I don't have Alzheimer's," she says, "just half-timers. I remember about half of what I'm told." She has as many aches and pains as anyone else her age. She's survived the death of her only daughter, a broken hip, and the loss of all the residents who moved into the retirement home with her sixteen years ago, yet she seldom complains.

Many residents at her retirement home have moved to assisted living, nursing homes, or new facilities. After years of crisscrossing the country following the wrestling circuit with her husband, Aubie is happy to stay in one place. She entertains her tablemates with stories from those days on the road, talking about history, geography, and the humorous adventurers of a nomadic life. "Once I tangled with a woman trying to poke Cowboy (one of many names her husband wrestled under) through the ropes with an umbrella. I took care of her," she laughs.

I asked her son, if she'd always had such a good attitude. "When people comment on the way my wife and I dote on my mother, we tell them that you reap what you sow. She's a wonderful mother. I owe everything I am to her. Neither she nor my father finished high school; they were self-educated, but they knew the value of education," he says.

Aubie had big dreams for her son. Knowing young Billy wasn't getting a proper education, she made the sacrifices necessary to send him to a top-rated military school. After that came an appointment to the Naval Academy, a degree in nuclear engineering, and command of a nuclear submarine. She was a role model for her son to value education; now she's a role model for aging greatly.

My husband Vince is the perfect role model for Dr. Osler's advice. What most of us would consider more than a minor aggravation, he seems not to notice. He has chosen to wear long-sleeved shirts rather than call attention to his missing hand. Having made that choice, I've never once heard him complain about the heat. For that matter, he never complains about any of the inconveniences and never says, "I wish I could . . ." Maybe that's because there's so little he can't do. No one who knows him would call him handicapped. He fastens necklaces I can't manage and buttons the back of dresses like any other husband.

He does home and car repairs, plays cards, shoots pool, and invariably is the one who shifts packages around and gets to his house key while I'm still fumbling for mine. When he went to get a Texas drivers license, the testing officer wanted to put a restriction on his license. No way. Vince left, rented a stick-shift car, and returned to easily pass the test.

He tests himself by what he can do, not by what others can do; and he graciously accepts help with the few things he can't do — an excellent way to look at the limitations of aging. Rather than give up on a task, look for innovative ways to accomplish the job. Use a walker, a reacher, or a hearing aid to postpone the need for help, then learn to graciously accept the help your age and abilities require.

Singing, dancing legend Doris Day's quip puts aging in perspective: "The really frightening thing about middle age is that you know you'll grow out of it." Indeed we will, so look for the role models who are aging greatly and follow their lead.

Beat the Biological Clock

If only, when one heard
That Old Age was coming
One could bolt the door,
Answer "not at home"
And refuse to meet [her]!

— Anonymous Japanese Poem

The words are all wrong. Change of life. Menopause. Oh, no problem. Pause at the crossroads of life, look both ways, and skip across the intersection. Wrong! It's a head on collision, red lights flashing wake-up call. It's hot flashes, mood swings, and a host of other mid-life maladies.

My first clue came one Thanksgiving when the bathroom scale went on the fritz, registering five pounds heavier than it ever had. After Christmas the needle took another leap, but my tight fitting skirts told me it wasn't the scale. Middle age was settling in around my middle. (This is when Barbara, who has fought a lifetime battle with the bulge, plays her imaginary violin and swears she gained that much in her first 24 hours.)

Not so subtle clues — arms too short to read the phone book, more hair on my face and less on my head, marching decidedly into another room then not remembering what I was after — sounded the alarm. I wanted to scream and stomp my foot like a three-year-old, but a leaking bladder prevented such a childish response. Instead, I expressed my frustration with this bit of humorous verse.

Double Nickel Defense

The image I see
Doesn't reflect the real me
The eyes look alive
But the rest looks fifty-five
The hair is thin and gray and limp
I wonder where the beehive went
Send in the double nickel defense
Reclaim my youth with a red-colored rinse
The hair on my upper lip has got to go
But professionals who do it ask a heap of dough
So I used a depilatory to save some cash
Now the mustache is an ugly red rash
Send in the double nickel defense again
This aging game I'm determined to win
My bladder leaks whenever I sneeze
Or lift anything above my knees
I want to pamper myself
Just not from the diaper shelf
Send in the double nickel defense once more
And a sense of humor for the winning score

In a 1940 telegram to a newspaper editor, military leader Douglas MacArthur said, "The history of failure in war can almost be summed up in two words: Too late." Fortunately, in the aging battle it's never too late; but unlike old soldiers, the problems don't fade away — the challenges return every day.

Athletes tell us the best offense is a good defense. As our biological clock ticks past halftime, it's advice worth heeding. It's too late to adopt the "Live fast, die young, and have a good-looking corpse," motto from the 1949 movie *Knock on Any Door*. As birthdays keep knocking, our best hope is to live young and die fast.

For years I wanted to look older. The Fuller Brush man looked past me and asked for the lady of the house. Nurses whispered outside my hospital room that the new mom was actually twenty, not the fourteen they had guessed. Now I take more care with what I wish for.

Like Lady Aster, who said she refused to admit being over fifty-two, even if it made her sons illegitimate, Sandy's children are gaining ground on her. She enjoys the facetious ruse, but when she does let the cat out of the bag, I hope she'll add ten years to the number. It's a great ego booster to look ten years younger than your stated age. Try it. At seventy, say you're eighty and enjoy the compliments.

Young children say they're five and a half, teenagers say they're almost eighteen, but after forty, birthdays aren't so special. Then Medicare eligibility makes sixty-five special; folks throw a big party for surviving to eighty; and somewhere along the line, we begin acknowledging the "and a half" again. Actually, most of us aren't as worried about our age as we are about the effects of aging — how we look and feel. Even the most self-assured among us lament the ravages of time. Maya Angelou, in *Even the Stars Look Lonesome*, describes her breasts at sixty: "It's better not to mention them at all except to say that they seemed to be in a race to see which could be first to reach my knees."

I fret a little each morning at the reflection of my pigeon figure — small head, large tail, bird legs with equal size ankles and knees; but after dabbing on some makeup and dressing to conceal the worst parts, I forget about my age and shape for the rest of the day. Actually, it hasn't changed much over the years, other than the added twenty pounds migrating south.

The good news is I've lived long enough for gravity to pull my breasts, eyelids, and jowls toward my knees. Longevity's bad news is arthritis, diminished hearing and vision, cataracts, declining mental and physical ability, and higher risks for a multitude of diseases.

Beating the biological clock is about quality, not quantity. No one wants to live in a renegade body, a defector of our will. Our greatest fears are uncontrollable bowels, useless limbs, and a mind that refuses to recall our children. Our fears are well founded with bleak statistics for women over sixty-five as proof:

- One in four has some form of heart disease.
- Eighty percent have arthritis symptoms
- One in ten has Alzheimer's disease
- More than half have high blood pressure
- Women are twice as likely as men to experience major depression

- Increased risk of cataracts, glaucoma, and macular degeneration
- Increased risk of breast cancer
- Overactive bladder

Old age ain't for sissies

Art Linkletter had it right — aging is tough. No amount of effort keeps us from aging, but with hard work we can avoid many of the maladies of old age. As Vince Lombardi told his players, "The dictionary is the only place that success comes before work."

It's easy to get hung up on conflicting health claims. Today's cure becomes tomorrow's killer. Hormone replacement therapy, which we thought protected our heart and bones while reducing the hot flashes and other menopausal symptoms, turns out to do more harm than good. Common over-the-counter drugs to ease pain can cause drug-induced liver failure. Several herbal remedies are linked to urinary tract cancer.

I'll drink to that!

Research on the French connection twists and turns more than the car chase in the movie of the same name. The French, eating a diet similar to what Americans eat, have a much lower rate of heart disease. Ah, the red wine they said. A good assumption, since the French drink nine times more wine than the average American. So in the '90s we toasted our health with red wine.

When Vince and I visited the Napa Valley in the mid-90s, the squeeze was on for more red wine. Growers had begun an expensive seven-year process to meet the vintners demand for red grapes. Vineyards switched from white grapes to red for merlot. The assumption was that Americans prefer merlot to the more robust cabernet sauvignons. Well, guess what? Seven years after our wine country visit, research showed red grape juice has a small effect and cabernet sauvignon has the greatest benefit.

The assumptions continued with the thought that healthy, wealthier, better-educated people tend to drink wine. Then a Duke University study designed to eliminate income and education bias indicated that wine drinkers naturally prefer healthy lifestyles. In the same way one might assume that mobile homes attract tornadoes, researchers assumed wine contributed to the good health of their subjects.

A French study confirmed that a couple glasses of wine a day raises your good cholesterol and credited omega-3 fatty acids with increased protection against heart disease. Next came the news that the flavonoids in grape juice may be as healthy, without the effects or the price of alcohol; and the malt or barley in beer may be even healthier for you than wine.

The latest? A twelve-year study concludes that taking one or two daily drinks several times a week lowers the risk of heart attack. Wine, beer, scotch, gin — it doesn't matter. Moderation matters. Excessive alcohol consumption decreases the benefits and invites numerous other health problems.

Is tea better for you than coffee? If so, does it matter if it's green or black? Maybe, since green tea has more flavonoids than processed black tea. However, it has to be something you like. While a small amount of alcohol raises HDL, it takes several cups of tea to lower the bad cholesterol (LDL). An important caveat — the benefits of either are greatest when combined with a heart-healthy diet.

The coffee issue percolates from touting caffeine's benefits to issuing dire warnings. One study speculated that heavy coffee drinkers cut their risk of diabetes. Other studies claim coffee drinkers significantly lower their risk for gallstones and Parkinson's disease, while still others find a link between caffeine and osteoporosis. If the caffeine debate sets your teeth on edge, console yourself knowing the trigonellines, added for flavor and aroma, may prevent cavities.

Since caffeine's not one of the FDA-mandated food-labeling ingredients, you don't know if your coffee or chocolate candy bar has 100 or 500 milligrams of caffeine—switching to decaf may put you at risk for rheumatoid arthritis. Good luck with making an informed decision.

Magnets are in; copper bracelets are out

It's no wonder we're confused. We keep trying to remedy the ills of aging and disease, grasping at the proven, unproven, and sometimes pathetic. Oxygen bars charge health-conscious clients a dollar a minute for a breath of fresh air. Some say shark cartilage fights cancer and eases symptoms of arthritis. Others claim to give your body a "tune up" by hitting your feet with tuning forks to create a resonance between you and the planets. Whom can you believe?

It's not easy to separate fact from fiction. Even the "old wives" are sometimes right. A glass of cranberry juice a day may prevent urinary tract infections. Biometeorology confirms what anyone with arthritis has known for years — that aching bones can predict the weather.

Much to my chagrin, my mother rubbed Vick's salve on my chest at the first sign of congestion. "How silly," I thought. No way could something on your skin effect an internal organ. But, Mother was right. Now transdermal patches deliver heart medications. Several trials are underway using a nasal-spray delivery system — the flu vaccine appears to be as effective in nasal-spray form as with the standard injection.

Did you hear that hairless mice exposed to the sun and massaged with caffeine got 70 percent fewer malignances than mice that were not rubbed with caffeine? What an opportunity for Starbucks — make java cream that stains your skin coffee-colored without roasting at the beach and protects against skin cancer at the same time. What a deal!

Beth Swisher, manager of Green Mama's Nursery and Garden Center, is a great believer in the effects of through-the-skin transfer. She discourages using commercial fertilizers, saying they make lawns unsafe to walk or play on. To prove her point, she asks people to put a peeled garlic clove next to their foot. "It's amazing," she says. "In about ten minutes, most of them can taste the garlic." I haven't tried the garlic, but a tiny silver patch behind my ear means I can leave the barf bag in the seat pocket when I fly. The FDA is close to approving a body lotion that cools hot flashes. Amazing!

Now scientists say there may be some truth to the homespun wisdom that says, "feed a cold and starve a fever." On the other hand, there's no proof that castor oil, my mother's treatment of choice, has any benefit at all. Had I thought about it, I probably could have predicted today's use — lubricating race cars. It kept me running — before (I had to be caught and held down) *and* after the dose!

Like castor oil, there are a few things I don't have to debate. A spoonful of honey to make the medicine go down is fine; a bee sting to ease arthritis pain, forget it. And I'd die before resorting to coffee enemas.

We can't change our heredity, gender, age, or race, all of which may increase our risks for certain diseases. We can, however, make day-to-day lifestyle choices that have as great an impact as those factors we can't change. Reinhold Niebuhr's Serenity Prayer says it well:

> *God, give us grace to accept with serenity the things that cannot be changed, courage to change the things that should be changed, and the wisdom to distinguish one from the other.*

Various treatments dribble between favor and fatal, but a healthy lifestyle is a slam-dunk. As my grandma liked to say, "The best way to pray for cornbread is to plant corn." So plant a few kernels of common sense, dig deep for initiative, and reap improved health.

Winning ways to good health

Wise lifestyle choices put a sparkle in your eye, a spring in your step, and a smile on you face. There are no toxic side effects and no expensive equipment to buy. What's needed is merely the commitment to give it a try. Here's how:

- Wet your whistle
- Wash your hands
- Watch your mouth
- Walk — the more the better
- Weight train
- Watch the numbers and letters too
- Wake up to the wonders of sleep
- Write it down
- Worship

Wet your whistle

Seventy percent of the earth's surface is water; our bodies are more than half water. Water fills our oceans and lakes for commerce and pleasure; it falls from the clouds to grow food and flowers; it boils to power engines and steam vegetables; it freezes to cool our drinks. Its force supplies us with electricity.

The Internet offers 752,000 articles relating to water and our body. On a top-ten list of ingredients for good health, water is second to oxygen.

Like the air we breathe, we take this magic elixir for granted. If you think magic is overstating the case, look at what water does for your body. In addition to its basic functions of flushing waste and regulating temperature, if we drink an adequate amount, water will:

- Moisten skin
- Improve digestion
- Cushion joints
- Increase saliva to inhibit gum disease
- Promote weight loss
- Help prevent kidney stones
- Reduce the risk of bladder, kidney, and colon cancers
- Decrease constipation and urinary tract infections

If that doesn't convince you, look at the effects of dehydration. We're not talking about a person lost in the desert, but all of us who go about our daily lives drinking less than half the water our body needs to function properly. From simple bad breath to serious illness, dehydration contributes to:

- Muscle cramps
- Dizziness
- Headaches
- Increased susceptibility to respiratory infections
- Dry skin
- Disorientation

As seniors we need to be especially vigilant. Like many other functions, the mechanism that lets us know we're thirsty slows down as we age. By the time we feel thirsty, we have already started to dehydrate.

Every day we lose fluid through digestion, perspiration, and breathing. Heat, low humidity, high altitude, and exercise increase fluid loss. In those conditions, and when we have a fever or diarrhea, additional water is required to avoid serious dehydration.

Dr. Sandra B. Edmond, an emergency medicine physician, notices a rise in dehydrated patients, particularly kids and elderly, during flu season. Take this as a reminder of the importance of replacing fluids when fighting bouts of vomiting and diarrhea.

Now that you know the risks and benefits of drinking water, how much do you think is enough? Some question the standard eight glasses a day, but it's safe to say few of us are getting too much water.

It's true; we get a few cups of fluid a day from the solid foods we eat and from fruit juices and milk. However, for each alcoholic or caffeinated beverage consumed, it requires an additional one-half cup of water to establish proper fluid balance.

It's easy to deceive ourselves about how much water we drink. Filling a sixty-four ounce pitcher and seeing how much is gone by the end of the day works for some. Others buy bottled water and drink four or five half-liter bottles a day. It's a funny line, but you *don't* get enough with the multiple pills you take — unless you drink a full glass of water with each pill and before every meal!

Interestingly, cool water is absorbed quicker than tepid water, so chill or add ice to your water. For variety, add a splash of lemon or lime juice.

If you wake up with wrinkles (more than the usual ones) across your body from folds in the sheets or nightclothes, or if your urine is dark and smelly, you're dehydrated. A few foods, such as asparagus, and some medications cause urine to smell, but otherwise it should be a very pale yellow and almost odorless. Also, waking in the night with leg cramps is possibly due to a lack of fluids.

I've experienced all the above, and I've experienced the benefits when I diligently consume enough water. Surprisingly, drinking plenty of water, as long as you stop an hour before bedtime, doesn't increase nocturnal trips to the bathroom.

Limiting fluids in an attempt to curb incontinence risks serious illness. Instead, consult a physician to see if you're a candidate for corrective medication or surgery. What you were told a few years ago may not be true today. If all else fails, drink plenty of water and use the best products on the market for your comfort and confidence.

Almost all weight loss programs include a recommendation for adequate fluids. Water kick-starts your metabolism, burning calories and fat. And water makes you feel full, so you're not as tempted to drink calorie-laden colas and lattés.

And lastly — a concern to everyone over forty — is confusion and memory loss. Our brain is 75 percent water. Like a droopy blossom, a dehydrated brain perks up with a drink.

Water is never an under-the-bridge or over-the-dam issue. It's a lifetime commitment. Begin each day by filling your favorite container with water. Refill it frequently, and take it everywhere you go. Never leave home without it. A few sips in the car, in a meeting, or in a waiting room add up.

Wash your hands

Recent headlines claim that hospital-acquired infections are the fourth-largest killer after heart disease, cancer, and strokes. They cite lax hand washing compliance as a major contributor. Health officials at the Centers for Disease Control and Prevention (CDC) have long recognized the importance of good hand hygiene. When anthrax showed up in the mail, the U.S. Postal Service jumped on the soapbox and recommended people wash their hands after handling mail as a precaution against skin-borne anthrax. Likewise, the CDC suggested that simply washing your hands might be the best defense against SARS, the severe acute respiratory syndrome. A study published in the *Journal of Preventive Medicine* found that when the Navy ordered recruits at the Great Lakes Recruit Training Command Center in Illinois to wash their hands at least five times a day, respiratory illnesses dropped 45 percent.

Every time infection control nurse Sue Sebasco appeared on *Health & You*, the hospital's health information TV show, she stressed hand washing. Sue's mantra: "Wash your hands vigorously with warm, soapy water to prevent the spread of germs." Vigorously is the key word. If you're rinsing something sticky off your fingertips a quick swish works. For germ fighting use plenty of soap, get between your fingers and around your nails.

You are much more likely to be exposed to common germs than to a deadly disease. And since 80 percent of common infections are spread by hand contact, simple hand washing can greatly reduce your exposure. When hospitalized, if you don't see your caregivers wash their hands, remind them.

Notice how often you put your hands on your face. Many times a day, we unconsciously rub our eyes, scratch our nose, or put a finger to our mouth, giving germs easy access. Sharing a computer or telephone with a family member who has a cold increases exposure. And if the sales clerk handling your purchase and credit card obviously has a cold, you may be too sick by the weekend to enjoy the new party outfit.

The grocery store cashier handles dozens of transactions, and numerous shoppers have gripped the handle of the shopping cart. I don't wear a mask and gloves to the grocery store, but I do try and keep my hands away from my face, and I give them a good washing before I put the groceries away.

Alcohol-based hand sanitizers are available in purse-size bottles and pre-moistened individual packets for use away from home. They're great for our Jeep trips. When the group stops after jostling over rocks for several hours, the men head in one direction and the women in the other, looking for the nearest bush — or large cactus. After a welcome pit stop, we pop down the tailgate and bring out the finger food. I enjoy the fresh Arizona oranges much more after a couple of squirts of waterless sanitizer on my hands.

Beware of using too many antibacterial products, though. Americans spend about $1 billion a year on antibacterial products when plain soap works as well. Overuse of antibacterial chemicals creates resistant bacteria in the same way overuse of antibiotics does. Even some strains of E.coli have become resistant.

When someone in the household has a cold or other viral infection, you may want to purchase an antiviral product, since antibacterials don't kill viruses. When it comes to washing fruits and vegetables, plain water works as well as those special washes and is certainly cheaper.

Alabama researchers say most raw chicken in grocery stores is contaminated with some fecal bacteria — so in addition to thorough cooking, the best defense against food poisoning is washing your hands and everything you touch after handling raw meat and poultry. Cutting boards, faucet handles, utensils, and plates used to transport the meat to the stove or grill should be washed with hot soapy water. These precautions are especially important when cooking for the very young and very old, who are at greater risk of dehydration from vomiting and diarrhea.

Pay special attention to kitchen towels, dishrags, and sponges that can become contaminated while cleaning up. Using paper towels and sponges you run through the dishwasher or sanitize in the microwave for a minute reduces the wash load.

According to the CDC, 76 million Americans — that's one in four — get some form of food poisoning each year. Since it's estimated that hand washing could eliminate almost half of those instances, it's worth remembering a John Wesley sermon topic: "Cleanliness is, indeed, next to godliness."

Watch your mouth

Our moms were more concerned about what came *out* of our mouth than what went in. Sassy daughters weren't allowed. "You better watch your mouth, young lady," had nothing to do with food. Although I never got a good answer for how the food left on my plate could make its way to China, the threat of starving children and the promise of dessert assured a clean plate.

Now we're watching our weight, when we should be watching our mouth. Americans are always watching our weight — we're watching it grow faster than dandelions in the petunia bed — choking out sane solutions with desperation diets.

From one century to the next, the meaning of diet has changed as dramatically as the exuberance of the 1890s became the coming out of the 1990s. The description of what you usually eat has become what you shouldn't eat. Now diet means denial; and despite our best efforts, it's easier to calculate our losses in dollars than in pounds.

In the ultimate put-your-money-where-your-mouth-is scenario, we feed a $35 billion annual diet industry. Interestingly, the processed food industry spends about the same amount advertising their products. Do you think there may be a correlation?

Back to the weight-loss sales pitches: Would we fall for any other product with a 95 percent failure rate? Worst of all, there's no extended warranty. Most diets work short term. But we can't deny ourselves the foods we love forever, so in a year or sometimes only a few months, 95 percent have gained back the weight they lost, often plus a little more.

There's a good reason for this, and it's not a lack of will power. Researchers at the University of Washington and the Department of Veterans Affairs in Seattle have identified the yo-yo gremlin — an appetite-boosting hormone called ghrelin — which your body produces more of as soon as you stop dieting. This natural appetite stimulant, secreted by the stomach and small intestine, tells the brain you are trying to starve yourself and little "gremlins" set about making you hungrier, slowing your metabolism, and reducing your body's inclination to burn fat.

This efficient survival technique for early man is (along with our preference for Big Macs over Brussels sprouts) a major factor in today's epidemic obesity. Currently, gastric bypass surgery is the only way to reduce the hormone's production. No doubt the pharmaceutical industry is smacking its lips at the possibility of a magic pill that kills the appetite message before it reaches the brain.

Another hormone, PYY, may prove to be the anti-ghrelin by suppressing appetite. Dr. Stephen Bloom at the Imperial College School of Medicine in London, holds out the possibility that a pill form of this natural hormone may be possible within five years.

In the meanwhile, consider a lesson from Aesop's fables: A gullible ass heard grasshoppers chirping and wanted to know what they ate to produce such beautiful voices. When they told him they lived on dew, he decided to try it and died of hunger. We are dying of what we eat. Former Surgeon General David Satcher says that obesity may overtake smoking as the main cause of preventable deaths. Current estimates put premature deaths from obesity at about 300,000 a year. That's as many as 1200 deaths a day.

It's time to face the music. Obesity isn't about looks, it's about life; so tune out the fables of high-fat, low-fat, high-protein, low-carbohydrate diets, supplements, and crazy food combinations that promise results and deliver disappointment. No matter what the ads say or how good the before and after pictures look, keeping weight off is a long-term project, never effortless.

"The reality is that any diet that's successful in making you lose weight will lower your metabolic rate," say Dr. Scott Weigle, an associate professor of medicine at the University of Washington School of Medicine. He and other metabolism experts say it's the total number of calories consumed in a day, no mater their source, that affects metabolism. If you want to check your "burn rate," HealtheTech has a handheld device that measures your resting metabolic rate (RMR). Comparing your calorie intake with MedGem results — how many calories you burn in a day at rest — may explain why your diet isn't working.

Calories, fat or otherwise, are either burned with activity or stored. The only way to avoid the "from the lips to the hips" gain is to watch what goes across the lips and keep the hips moving. It's simple math — subtract the number of calories you burn through exercise from the number of calories you eat. Then "cook the books" until the ledger shows a balance of calories that *slowly* leads to a healthier weight.

Our eye is always on the target — the ideal weight. We want to hit that weight by the class reunion or by swimsuit season. What if we aimed for healthy habits instead of obsessing over pounds? Since diets aren't working, it's worth a try.

Some facts from the CDC and the American Obesity Association encourage the effort:

- Obesity increases the risk of illness for about thirty serious illnesses.
- Half of all women are overweight; one-fourth are obese.
- The age group with the highest prevalence of overweight is between sixty and sixty-nine.
- Obesity is the second leading cause of preventable death in the U.S.
- Losing even eleven pounds may cut the risk of osteoporosis of the knee by 50 percent.

At the 2000 Olympics, Korea's women archers stepped up on the platform to accept the team's gold medal for the fourth straight Olympics. In addition to a long tradition of archery in their country, an *Investor's Business Daily* article offered some insight into their domination of the sport.

The article noted that Korean women learn by working on technique with no concern for where the arrow lands. They're praised for good technique. Americans aim for the bulls-eye from the beginning and are never able to go back and concentrate enough on basics.

J. R. Calvert, in his instruction column for *Inside Pool*, laments that most players never take the time to analyze their stroke. "The single most obvious reason that most players never analyze these ingredients is that they never shoot at anything except an object ball," he says. Calvert advocates improving your billiard's game by eliminating distracting variables like the cue ball and cue stick to practice your stroke. "Your mind can concentrate on technique without concern for pocketing the ball."

Do you see a pattern here? In both cases, coaches encouraged practice without a specific target in mind. Certainly the goal is to improve their score, but in practice they concentrate on technique.

Nutritious food, appropriate serving sizes, and regular exercise are the techniques for weight control. Like a three-legged stool, it takes all three to maintain balance. Achieving that balance may keep you from becoming one of thirty-five people who die each hour from poor nutrition and lack of exercise.

With continual practice over a long period, you may reach a target weight — or maybe not. The real goal is lifelong healthy habits without the frustration of reaching for an impossible "ideal weight."

Several measures of body composition are a better guide to fitness than weight. Body mass index (BMI), lean body mass, waist-to-hip ratio, and the newest from Israel — neck circumference.

Here's the formula for calculating your BMI with an example of someone who is 5 feet 5 inches tall and weighs 150 pounds. Multiply weight by 705 (150 x 705) and height in inches by itself (65 x 65); divide the weight number by the height number. In this example the resulting BMI of 25 is right on the cusp of normal. A BMI of 30 is considered high risk, 40 puts you at extreme risk.

After an honest effort at the three-legged stool approach for several months, have a body-fat test done by a professional. Unlike the Sprats, BMI can't distinguish lean body tissue from fat. And since muscle weights more than fat, you may have made more progress than you think.

A BMI of more than 30, a waist of over 35 inches, or a neck circumference of more than 13.4 inches are indications that your weight may pose a health risk. However, if you've given it your best shot to drop below the high-risk category, it's time to think "pleasantly plump," described by the dictionary as a full and rounded figure that's agreeable to the mind and senses. If you're eating healthy foods, exercising, have plenty of energy, and feel good about yourself, who's to say you aren't "fit as a fiddle" — even if you are shaped liked a tuba.

And there's some medical evidence to back up this fat-but-fit theory. An American Journal of Clinical Nutrition study (unfortunately done only on men) of more than 20,000 men, over an eight year period, found that those who were fit, yet obese, had lower death rates than the men who were unfit but lean. They found little difference between fit obese men and fit lean men, suggesting that being fat and fit is better than being thin and sedentary, so we need to rethink how we define healthy weight.

Doctors warn that the ups and downs of yo-yo dieting (those ghrelin gremlins at work) increase the risk of heart disease. A study by the American Geriatrics Society indicates weight stability (not at obese levels, of course) is associated with optimal mortality rates.

According to the National Institutes of Health (NIH) losing 5 percent to 10 percent of your body weight, or as little as ten pounds in six months, if you keep it off, reduces health risks.

Of the most popular weight-loss books, *Eat More, Weigh Less* by Dr. Dean Ornish is the only one to receive an outstanding rating from the Physicians Committee for Responsible Medicine.

If you prefer to design your own weight-loss program try Ian K. Smith's book *The Take Control Diet*. You may have seen Dr. Smith on NBC's *Today* show or read one of his columns in *Newsweek* magazine. He explains the how and why of weight loss and, as the book title suggests, empowers you with the knowledge to take control. An extensive appendix lists foods' calorie, fat, fiber, cholesterol, sodium, and protein content, glycemic index, and energy density.

Armed with this information, you're ready to enjoy cooking and eating healthy versions of your favorite foods with a new twist. Try books like *The Healthy Kitchen: Recipes for a Better Body, Life and Spirit* by Andrew Weil and Rosie Daley (yes, Oprah's ex-chef). They are all about healthy, tasty food, rather than weight loss.

Better Homes and Gardens cookbook *The Smart Diet*, also takes a "non-diet approach." In *Living Lean,* Larry North says, "It's not about perfection, it's about progress." Progress is choosing a way to eat for life.

Organizations like Weight Watchers and Take Pounds off Sensibly (TOPS) offer group support, peer pressure, and recipe suggestions to help you stay the course. Or you can go it alone using the USDA's 30-page free booklet, The Food Guide Pyramid. Supplement the guide with books, magazine, and newspaper articles devoted to healthy eating. Clip and file recipes, charts on fast-food calorie counts, tips on ordering restaurant food, and guides to reading food labels.

Knowing that some restaurant salads top 800 calories, that Haagen-

Dazs actually has a zero-fat product, and how to cut the fat calories in favorite foods helps you design an eating plan that works for you. For $5, the Center for Science in the Public Interest (202-332-9110) offers a slide guide of the food in more than 250 restaurants. Carry it in your purse and compare the good, bad, and awful choices before ordering. Actually, there are no good or bad foods. It's a matter of making the best choices and limiting the amounts of certain foods.

A switch in the "You are what you eat" maxim to "I am what I buy," works for me. If I don't buy it, I can't be tempted. I won't go buy a bag of chips or a carton of ice cream if there's a tasty alternative in the house. Tasty is the key — celery and carrot sticks don't qualify. Eating five to nine fruits and vegetables a day requires more than bananas and broccoli.

As you know by now, my mindset on money is tight. After years of paying $7 a pound for steak, yet balking at $4 a pound for out-of-season fruit, I've learned to loosen the purse strings. Buying tasty asparagus, blueberries, Bing cherries, and vine-ripened tomatoes — nutritious foods that are also delicious and satisfying — reduces the times I succumb to the chips and dips.

Aim for a little-engine approach. With one chug at a time and an *I-think-I-can* attitude, you can climb the hill to better health — the real target.

In 1992, the U.S. Department of Agriculture replaced the basic-four-food-groups model with The Food Guide Pyramid. You've likely seen the pyramid graphic outlining the suggested number of servings from each of five food groups. The broad base of the pyramid, grains, suggests up to eleven servings. As the structure narrows, each successive level (fruit, vegetable, milk, and meat) reduces the number of servings until you reach the small tip of the pyramid reserved for fats, oils, and sweets, which warns — eat sparingly.

Supersizing is out. Six small meals are in. That's three appetizer-size snacks and three meals served on plates, not platters. Which brings us to the second leg of that sturdy stool: portion size. Unless we let the air out of overblown portions, even eating the healthiest foods won't stop the ballooning of America.

The American Heart Association (AHA) recommends replacing the butter and animal fat in our diet with monounsaturated fats, such as olive oil, nuts, and avocados. They mean a thimble full of oil, a demitasse cup of nuts, and one-sixth of an avocado. In 2002, the Institute of Medicine's Food and Nutrition Board revised their guidelines to include more of these healthy fats.

Many, including myself, have switched to one of the margarines containing plant stanol ester to block dietary cholesterol. Cardiologist Sarah Blumenschein reminded me that you must eat the recommended serving size to gain the cholesterol-lowering benefits. "We find it more convenient to take the pill form. You don't have to carry around a tub of margarine when you travel or eat out," she says. A combination works best for me. Since Benecol and Take Control are healthier and have fewer calories, I prefer to use them instead of butter. I keep pills on hand for times I won't get my three servings a day.

In his book *The Fat Fallacy: Applying the French Diet to the American Lifestyle*, Dr. Will Clower suggests we could improve our mortality rates by doing away with faux food and eating real butter, cheese, chocolate, and wine as the French do. Clower says the only thing the Mediterranean diet recommends less than sweets is red meat, and he devotes a good section of his book to the number of servings and serving size. If you aren't obsessed with meat and can eat more fish and olive oil, it's a healthy alternative.

Americans are obsessed with all food; it's the national pastime. We gain an average of seven pounds between Thanksgiving and New Year's. The National Football League boasts that the Super Bowl ranks as the third-largest occasion for Americans to consume food.

Mike Barnett, director of publications for the Texas Farm Bureau, offers his own twelve-step plan for food addiction: "Take twelve steps for every calorie you eat." Now that's a plan sure to deter the supersizing trend.

There's nothing reasonable about the Competitive Eating Association. In 2002, forty contestants competed for $25,000 in *The Glutton Bowl* aired by FOX. A Japanese fellow brags that he can eat fifty hotdogs in twelve minutes. Of course, we wouldn't do anything like this. However, we might celebrate the Fourth of July with two hotdogs with all the trimmings, a bag of chips, a three-inch square of brownies, a chunk of watermelon, and a sixteen-ounce soda — one meal with as many calories as the year we're commemorating! Serving size counts!

Eyeballing serving size is tricky — our feelings about food get in the way. Think about spilling a cup of water, a half-cup of milk, and a fourth-cup of blood. I rest my case.

Nutritionists and trainers suggest comparing serving sizes to familiar objects. Two dominoes or four dice equals a serving of cheese (not the size cubes that once dangled from rearview mirrors). To continue the game plan, a deck of cards approximates a three-ounce serving of meat, chicken, or fish. A tennis ball equals a one-cup serving; a golf ball a quarter-cup serving.

If you prefer body part measures, (certainly handier than dice and dominoes) a fist is a half-cup, a palm-size chicken breast is about three ounces, your thumb is about the size of an ounce of cheese.

It might be fun to come up with your own serving size ideas. Send me some and I'll post the cleverest ones on my Web site for others to enjoy. Can you do better than the person who found the irony in an ounce of chocolate being the size of a package of dental floss?

Serving size requires a mindset change for special foods. Southerners, like myself, would never consider a half-cup of beans a serving. Likewise, for pasta lovers. But unlike the grapefruit, cereal, or sub-sandwich diet, healthy, common-sense eating is something you can do for life. And you can occasionally choose to have three servings in a bowl of beans or pasta — as long as the daily total remains within the guidelines.

My favorite serving size story comes from Billie. The people at the donut shop see her coming and have her order ready — one donut hole. No need for a bag, she takes it to the car, savors the two bites, and licks her fingers. "That satisfies my sweet craving, and I can stick to my diet," she says.

When we're looking at a food plan for life, there should be no forbidden foods. Small portions of foods we enjoy improve our chances of making healthy choices most of the time. A wealth of information for every age and ethnic group is available to help us make those healthy choices.

To accommodate the special nutrition needs of seniors, Tufts University researchers have modified the food pyramid for those over seventy. Daily servings are modified, grains are moved up to accommodate a base of eight servings of water, and a flag at the top acknowledges the need for vitamin supplements.

Georgia State University has translated the pyramid into more than thirty languages, and the guide is often tweaked to include ethnic and cultural food choices. The Southwestern Michigan Dietetic Association designed an Arabic pyramid that includes hummus, goat's milk, figs, and couscous. A Mexican guide includes menudo, chorizo, and cherimoya. The Association of American Indian Physicians distributes a guide designed by the Yakima Tribal WIC program and the Washington State Department of Health. Their guide includes tradition foods in the Native American diet. Filipino, Irish, vegetarian — you name it, it's available. There's no lack of information for those interested in healthy eating.

Walk, wiggle, and waggle

In January, resolutionaries swing into action. By March, the pendulum sputters, the promise goes up in sweat, and the paunch protrudes for another year. We've all been there.

"The Secrets of Aging," a traveling exhibit produced by the Boston Museum of Science in conjunction with the Massachusetts General Hospital's Geriatric Medicine Unit and the American Psychological Association, highlights the current scientific research about the aging process. Exploring the 6,000 square-feet of exhibits, you quickly discover the importance of exercise in the aging process. In almost every one, whether directed toward brain, heart, or bone health, exercise is a key component. One section points out that inactive adults between ages thirty and seventy lose 20 percent of their muscle strength, between seventy and eighty another 22 percent goes, for a not-so-grand total of 42 percent by age eighty.

In addition to the cardiovascular benefits, exercise lowers the risk for things as diverse as diabetes and gastrointestinal bleeding. It's estimated that 80 percent of health problems associated with aging can be prevented or postponed by staying fit.

A *Consumer Reports* survey found that eight out of ten successful dieters included regular exercise in their weight-loss plan. Oprah honored people who had lost hundreds of pounds, and every one of them considered exercise vital to their success. One of the women said she concentrated on exercise for a month before even trying to change her eating habits.

Mostly we concentrate on the wrong thing — like losing thirty pounds. Exercise is about more than losing the love handles and honing the hips. It's about being healthy. It's about holding on to that muscle strength that helps us get out of a chair or bathtub. At our age, exercise isn't likely to give us a fabulous figure, but it guarantees a healthier body.

Health experts claim that 250,000 deaths a year could be prevented by something as simple as exercising. The idea has been around a long time. A line by poet John Dryden, "The wise, for cure, on exercise depend," is as true today as it was in the 17th century.

Ponce de Leon failed in his search for the fountain of youth on the coast of Florida, but the Web and health organization publications leads you to the real fountain of youth — exercise. So, whip up your enthusiasm with a baker's dozen of reasons to exercise:

1. **Promotes a healthy heart** - Heart disease kills almost half a million American women a year, more than all cancers combined. Exercise helps your blood vessels stay young and as flexible as someone half your age; it reduces the risk of a blockage, raises HDL, and lowers LDL.
2. **Challenges colon cancer** - Colon cancer is the second leading cause of cancer deaths in the U.S., killing more women than men. Walking a couple of miles a day can cut your risk in half by increasing the rate body waste and cancer-causing substances pass through the colon. For the same reason, diverticulitis symptoms may improve.
3. **Battles depression** - Research by psychologists indicates that physical activity works at least as well against mild-to-moderate depression as any other treatment. A commitment to an exercise regimen works so well that many patients no longer need medication.
4. **Reduces breast cancer risk** - Experts believe that regular aerobic exercise helps women reduce their risk of breast cancer. For almost twenty years the American Cancer Society's ten-step program to prevent all types of cancer has included a regular exercise program.
5. **Eases arthritis symptoms** - With painful, stiff, and swollen joints, America's 40-million arthritis suffers (74 percent women) aren't likely to think of exercise as a remedy. Yet exercise reduces joint swelling and pain while increasing mobility. Take it easy on your joints by using self-help exercise therapies available from the Arthritis Foundation.

6. **Improves sleep** - It doesn't rhyme, but works better than counting sheep. As long as you don't exercise near bedtime, you can expect to fall asleep faster and get a better night's rest.
7. **Lowers gallstone risk** - A Harvard School of Public Health study indicates women who exercise several times a week cut their risk of gallstones by about a third compared to non-exercisers.
8. **Increases mental capacity** - Regular exercisers have better memorization and word association skills than non-exercisers. A study of the cognitive abilities of a group of women, age sixty-five and older, tested by the University of California and retested several years later, found the mental abilities of those who walked the least more likely to decline. British researchers found that even the small amount of exercise involved in chewing gum can improve memory. And the American Academy of Neurology reported a number that will make you work up a sweat — 13 percent. That's the percent of decrease in the chance for mental decline for every extra mile walked per week.
9. **Moves more than muscles** - By improving digestion, exercise is a natural laxative, particularly if the exertion also gets you to drink more water.
10. **Delays Diabetes** - Regular exercise dramatically delays the onset of Type II (adult onset) diabetes. The eight million women who already have the disease will find that a daily brisk walk lowers blood sugar levels and reduces or eliminates the amount of medication required to control their diabetes.
11. **Boosts energy, endurance, and libido** - Sounds like one naturally leads to the other.
12. **Guards against Glaucoma** - Aerobic exercise increases blood flow to the optic nerve, decreasing the eye pressure that contributes to vision loss.
13. **Now hear this** - The increased blood flow associated with exercise also offers protection from hearing loss.

So there you have it. From ears to elbows to toes — every part of our body benefits from exercise. And we didn't even mention burning calories to promote weight loss, the main reason most people consider an exercise program. No matter your age or what shape you're in, physical activity is the best weapon in the battle against aging.

One of the most compelling arguments for exercise comes from Dr. Steven Devoe, Assistant Professor of Sport and Exercise Science at Ohio State University. Devoe and his graduate students study the relationship between exercise and the need for long-term nursing care. "We know from our research that the No. 1 reason people enter nursing homes is not because of a disease, but because of an inability to perform the activities of daily living. The key is keeping older people physically active and maintaining the skeletal muscle mass that allows them to keep up with simple daily activities, such as getting up out of a chair or rising from a bed or bath tub, or carrying groceries," he says.

Don't have time? Look around and you'll find the busiest people make time to exercise. That's what gives them the energy to meet a demanding schedule. President George W. Bush says his rigorous workout regimen "helps him clear his head" and credits running with helping him quit smoking and drinking.

By mid-century the medical profession began ordering exercise instead of bed-rest. During the Eisenhower administration, doctors had Ike back on the golf course shortly after his heart attack. Anyone who's had heart surgery will attest to the change. Jan said, "I think they had me up and walking before the anesthetic wore off!"

Even during convalescence, exercise is essential. Barbara woke up from knee replacement surgery to the whir of a machine moving her leg up and down to exercise the new joint until she could get out of bed. Joy Marie was walking up and down the street days after her knee replacement surgery. Diligent adherence to an exercise program paid off. They're both delighted with the surgery results.

Painful leg cramps caused by peripheral arterial disease respond better to walking than to staying off your feet. After a supervised walking program, patients who otherwise might be housebound were able to walk for almost an hour several times a week.

Back pain also responds better to exercise than to traction or bed rest. In an interview some years ago, Warren Potash, author of *Your Lower Back,* explained how after years of pain, surgery, and physical therapy, he and his doctors designed an exercise program for long-term relief of his lower back pain. Now physicians and back institutes around the country use exercise as the first line of defense against back pain.

Just six months of regular exercise can reverse the effects of sedentary living. You can stop your biological clock and possibly set it back a decade or so. Want to feel better at eighty that you did at seventy? Consider Leonardo da Vince's thoughts on inactivity: "Iron rusts from disuse; stagnant water loses its purity and in cold weather becomes frozen; even so does inaction sap the vigor of the mind." So get moving!

Choose bicycles that go nowhere, stairsteppers that never reach the second floor, landlocked rowing machines, or do it the old fashioned way — one foot in front of the other. Research indicates that walking carries the same health benefit as running, is easier on aging joints, and the only equipment required is a good pair of athletic shoes.

Good means well-fitting shoes designed for the activity you plan to pursue. If you plan on activities other than walking, look at shoes specifically designed for that type of motion. Cross trainers that provide side-to-side stability may work best. The new "Fit Print" system at Athlete's Foot stores digitally scans your foot for pressure points, arch depth, and specific quirks to your walking style to help you choose the best type and brand of shoe.

Getting started is easy. You know the drill. If you don't, there are hundreds of books, magazines, videos, television shows, and Internet sites to tell you how. Eight of the top twelve magazines, by circulation, listed by the National Directory of Magazines, devote large sections of their copy to health and wellness. Women's magazines give equal time to recipes for a healthy heart and heart-shaped cookies. You'll find exercise tips in almost every issue. However, beware of deceptive advertising messages sometimes carried in reputable publications. Rely on common sense to weed out the ads for supplements and devices that promise instant results — and, as always, check with your doctor before changing any long-term habits.

In a nutshell, start slow and stay with it. Staying with an exercise program is the tough part — about 80 percent of those who join a health club last two months or less.

Experts say forming a habit takes three to four weeks of total commitment. Remember dragging yourself out of bed the morning after cramming for finals or walking a sick baby all night? It wasn't easy, but aren't you glad you did it? It takes that kind of stamina to stick with an exercise program until it becomes a habit.

When you become a regular exerciser, you join an elite group. Only 25 percent of American adults exercise regularly, and that includes all those young folks who rock climb and mountain bike.

Before you get a head bigger than the muscles you're building, I'll give you the bad news:

It's easy to fall off the wagon — even when it's become a habit. I not only fall off the wagon, I tumble all the way down the hill. After faithfully exercising for years, a respiratory infection or a family crisis will sideline me for a week or so, and then I procrastinate for months before getting back into the routine.

I have lots of company. Rosemary, a CPA, walked five miles a day using Kathy Smith's Walkfit tape. Then tax season rolled around, and she was too busy. "I felt better, had more energy, and slept better, yet can't seem to get back in the habit," she lamented several tax seasons later.

As Somerset Maugham said, the unfortunate thing is that good habits are so much easier to give up than bad ones. Next to flossing, exercise seems to be the most difficult habit to cultivate. It takes constantly reminding ourselves of the benefits of exercise, setting goals, and planning creative rewards.

Just as you wouldn't expect to eat enough today to sustain you for a week, you can't stockpile exercise. While studying the effects of weightlessness, researchers at the University of Texas Southwestern Medical Center at Dallas confirmed the theory that people on complete bed rest lose about 10 percent of their body strength a week.

The good news is a few weeks of idleness (short of bed rest) doesn't wipe out months of exercise benefit. Fitness experts say you can regain the lost ground in about a month. It's a lifelong commitment, so create a discipline that works for you. Exercise indoors, outdoors, at the mall, in the mountains, in the water, on the dance floor — just keep moving.

Walking outdoors offers the additional benefit of observing the sights and sounds of nature: birds and squirrels chattering, trees changing color, the first bloom of spring, and the proverbial last rose of summer signaling winter is on the way. Or, if you live in an urban area with high pollution levels, you might opt for indoor exercise.

A Texas summer or Wisconsin winter also ends outdoor options, so have a backup plan. Across the country, shopping malls and health facilities sponsor walking programs. Registered participants walk in the mall before stores open. Sponsors often provide programs, health screenings, and a variety of prizes for reaching mileage or attendance milestones. It's a good choice unless the smell of warm cinnamon rolls is too tempting.

Lots of home exercise machines become clothes racks, but Barbara's treadmill hasn't. "It's so convenient to have it right here on the veranda. I can look outside or watch TV while I walk," she says. Her petite figure attests to her dedication. After a ruptured Baker's cyst, Betty purchased a recumbent bike. It doesn't do much for the decor, but it's the only exercise I can do that doesn't hurt my knees," she says.

Claire has always been a determined lady. After raising seven children, she got her college degree and began a career. Now she's retired and cares for her husband in their home. Every morning she's out doing her two miles. "At my age, I know if I don't walk, someday I won't be able to walk. I do about twenty minutes of yoga to warm up before I walk." Since she looks and acts ten or fifteen years younger than she is, she asked that I not publish her age. "People treat me differently once they know," she says. Since I know her age, I'm treating her with renewed respect and hoping exercise will do for me what it's done for her.

An outdoor person all her life, Judy rode, trained horses and riders, cleaned barns, and kept a big house. Weight was never a problem until she and Sid retired. "The weight just crept up on me when I stopped being active." Now dancing and hiking are keeping the pounds off. Their new home, which they participated in designing and building, backs up to the Tonto National Forest in Arizona; so hiking the Superstition Mountains has become a regular activity. "Between working on the house, dancing three or four times a week, and hiking, I get plenty of exercise now. Sometimes more than I want," she says.

Following their body-is-a-temple beliefs, many churches offer exercise classes. Marie, seventy-six, starts her weekday mornings at Fort Worth's East Meadows Baptist Church pumping her arms and legs in a chair exercise program designed for seniors. "It keeps me mobile. I can tell if I miss several days in a row," she says.

Calvary Baptist Church in Lexington, Kentucky averages 400 exercisers a day in their Recreation Outreach Center. At East Lake Methodist Church in Birmingham, Alabama, eighty-year-old Elvada teaches an exercise class for retired persons. "You people who can't get on the floor, find a chair," she says.

With 5,000 locations worldwide, Curves has become one of the largest women's fitness chains in the world. Franchise owner Muriel

Beck says their locations in small towns, their affordable prices, and their women-only policy contributed to the rapid growth. Curves' sixteen-machine workout circuit works all major muscles in a thirty-minute session. Recorded music tells you when to move and when to check your heart rate.

"I lost my weight through Weight Watchers, but to maintain it and tone up, I knew I had to exercise," says seventy-year-old Helen. "I've joined a lot of gyms and health clubs in my time, but I'm a firm believer in Curves. It's a pleasure from the minute you walk in. I especially like it because I can be in and out in thirty minutes."

Don't set yourself up for failure by setting unrealistic goals. Measure the effort, not the result. Helen's goal was to work out at least three or four times a week — not to lose a certain amount of weight or inches, but for its own sake — yet her six-month effort has paid off with the loss of eight to ten inches.

Forget the scale and tape measure and look to the calendar and clock for your goals. You don't know how long it takes to lose five pounds or take an inch off your waist. You do know if you're meeting the exercise goals you've set for yourself. That's success — just showing up. That's what you reward.

When someone dies, we take a dish. To celebrate a birthday, we bake a cake. When someone's sick, we make them soup. We console and celebrate with food. It's time for a change. Plan creative exercise celebrations — rewards *not* associated with food.

When you meet a long-term goal, treat yourself to a facial, a pedicure, or a new outfit; hire a cleaning service, order fresh flowers, or get brochures from spas and splurge on a day of pampering. Another option is to put money aside each week of success, then treat yourself to something really special in six months.

Syndicated columnist Marilynn Preston writes excellent fitness articles. With her permission, I'll share one of her motivational ideas.

"If you're getting a little bored walking the treadmill or running the path, there's a good way to renew your enthusiasm. Pick a place you want to visit. It could be a friend's house, the Grand Canyon, or maybe Vegas. Then figure out exactly how far away the place is. If, for instance, you've got a hankering to visit your sister and she lives in, let's say, Gainesville, Florida, figure out the number of miles, chart your route using real maps, and then hit the road. For every three, or five, or ten miles you walk, move yourself the same number of miles closer to your goal. For every thirty minutes of strength training, move yourself ten or fifteen miles ahead. Make a game of it. Track your route on the map, and when you finally arrive, reward yourself with something meaningful, such as a real visit to that very place."

If you're looking for a big challenge, follow the example of Joe Fisher, who tracked his walking for sixteen years before reaching his goal at age seventy-seven. He walked around the world — 24,901 miles — without ever leaving his home in Lawrenceburg, Tennessee.

A perfect reward that combines fun and fitness is a trip to Mackinac Island, Michigan, a quaint island that bans the state's best-known product — the automobile — and all other motorized vehicles. A brown horse and wagon makes UPS deliveries. You can rent a bicycle, horse, or carriage, or better yet, explore the island's eight miles of paved road and numerous trails on foot.

Stay at the Grand Hotel and bask on the veranda overlooking Lake Huron; order High Tea in the parlor; or book a relaxing massage at Astor's Salon.

To assuage any guilt over the irresistible cuisine, like the 100-foot-long luncheon buffet, plan your trip over Labor Day and participate in the Mackinac bridge walk. Every year more than 50,000 people walk the five-mile span that joins Michigan's upper and lower peninsulas between Lake Huron and Lake Michigan.

In the interest of full disclosure, I'll tell you my ultimate reward for getting into shape. After getting to what I consider an ideal weight — for me that's an off-the-rack dress size that doesn't need altering — I still had to buy clothes to fit my stomach. When at age fifty an empire-waist dress starts a pregnancy rumor, you know you have a problem.

Although zippers strained to hold in my middle, waists were too big, and pants bagged around my legs, so when I had to have surgery to replace leaking silicon breast implants, I treated myself to liposuction. Even a high-powered medical vacuum can't undo an inherited body type and half a dozen surgical slices through the abdomen, but the two pounds of fat sucked out of my middle are a definite improvement and worth what I paid for the cosmetic procedure.

After exercising at the gym and riding bikes together for several years, Sandy and her friends treated themselves to a trip to France. They bicycled through the French countryside, stopping for leisurely lunches and spending evenings gathered around the fireplace sipping wine at country inns.

A group of local walkers fondly known as the Three Musketeers treated themselves to a personal trainer to prepare for a trip to New Zealand. They'd studied the customs and were prepared to rub noses with Maori villagers, but were concerned about their endurance. "We want to hike at least a portion of the Melford Track," they said. Patty Stratton, a certified trainer, worked with them at the condo clubhouse for two months in preparation for the trip. "I work on building muscular strength, endurance, and flexibility. You don't have to have a fully equipped gym. With dumbbells, tubing, and Therabands, you can get a few folks together in your home and have a trainer work with you," she says.

If cycling in France or hiking in New Zealand aren't in your future, the Cooper Institute for Aerobics Research in Dallas found that you can stay healthy doing everyday activities. If you walk the golf course or walk through the woods in search of a yellow-bellied sapsucker, you're already exercising.

Weight loss and maximum health benefits require more intense sessions — about an hour a day of moderately intense activity. For general fitness, consistency is more important than the pace. A brisk walk works as well as a sweaty session on the treadmill. Raking leaves and mopping floors qualify.

A joint study by the Chinese Academy of Preventive Medicine in Beijing and the University of North Carolina found a direct correlation between motorized vehicle ownership and obesity. It seems it's not the diet that keeps the people of China slim, it's walking, riding bikes, and pulling rickshaws. The odds of being obese were 80 percent higher for those who owned a motorized vehicle, and those who acquired a vehicle during the study were twice as likely to become obese as those without the convenience of modern transportation.

If you're depending on daily activities for your entire exercise program, buy a pedometer. Strap it on and check your mileage. Figure the number of steps you take in the course of a week and consider meeting or beating your average. To lower blood pressure and take off pounds, shoot for 10,000 steps a day. That's about five miles.

The American College of Sports Medicine recommends low-to-moderate exercise for a longer time rather than exercising at high intensity for a shorter period of time.

To gain lasting cardiovascular benefits, *The Mayo Clinic Health Letter* suggests breaking down exercise to thirty minutes a day, forty minutes five times a week, or an hour every other day for a total of 200 minutes of exercise per week.

And if you can't find thirty minutes a day, break it into three ten-minute sessions. Anything is better than nothing. Walk in place while brushing your teeth, take the stairs, park at the back of the lot. Hey, even shopping counts if you spend more time walking than buying — a-two-for-one bargain.

If you're motivated by organized activities, the options are unlimited: tai chi, yoga, Pilates, chuan, gigong, dancing (belly, ballroom, or disco), and more. Going with friends increases commitment, so find an exercise buddy.

TV is my exercise buddy. I time my treadmill walk during the thirty-minute evening news slot. If you're not a news junkie, make a bargain with yourself that the only place you'll watch your favorite TV show is from the treadmill or bike. For me the payoff is maintaining the stamina to walk long corridors to airline gates and up the steps to ancient ruins and modern museums at my destinations. I also want to stay flexible enough to clip my toenails and fasten a back-opening bra.

Find a program that is practical for you. Take a class first and, after you're comfortable with the routine, buy a video for home use. Preview books from the library and rent videos before shelling out $20 or more for something you won't use. A program that advocates drinking two glasses of ice water and running five miles before dawn is a wasted purchase no matter what it promises.

Recognizing the importance of regular exercise for older people, the National Institute on Aging offers a forty-eight-minute video and an eighty-page companion booklet of aerobic, stretching, balance, and strength-training routines. At $7, it's a bargain.

The www.collagevideo.com site gives detailed descriptions of more that 700 exercise videos. Check it out if you're having trouble finding something you like. The Parkinson's Association of Southwest Florida (239-984-5303) offers four videos designed for Parkinson's patients:

water exercise, chair exercise, flexibility, and posture and balance. Dr. Abraham Lieberman's books, *Shaking up: Parkinson-Fighting Like a Tiger, Thinking Like a Fox* and *101 Questions & Answers About Parkinson's Disease*, are also available.

The American Geriatric Society says 96 percent of fractures result from a fall, and half of those are from poor balance, so an exercise program that improves your balance is a wise investment. Building core muscles (back, hips, and abdomen) improves balance and posture. Several books and videos that target these muscles are available. They include, wobble boards, bosu balls, stability balls, and core boards; but be careful. Used incorrectly, they may do more harm than good. One downside to exercising to a video is the lack of an instructor to assure correct use of the equipment. Health clubs offer instruction in the proper use of treadmills, stairsteppers, rowing machines, and weight machines. If you order something through the mail, be sure that the equipment may be returned. Beware of gadgets you don't know how to use.

Choose something you enjoy, and when enthusiasm lags, change the routine. Subscribe to a fitness newsletter and read newspaper and magazine articles for new ideas. A thorough search turns up something for everyone.

I'm fascinated with some new workout gadgets — a Flexing FootRest (FFR) and WorkOutWhizzer (WOW) designed around the principles of dynamic isometric/isotonic and oscillating resistance. Jack Wilson, motivated by life-altering accidents, founded Innovative Fitness Inc. (877-222-8173) and engineered products that provide a bona fide workout for the whole body while seated or standing.

Kathy Brazaitis, a physical therapist in Wausau, Wisconsin, told me how excited she is about the results she sees with patients. "You can make the workout tough or gentle, so it works for a wide variety of injuries and levels of fitness," she says. After speaking with Kathy and Dr. Mary Berry, a chiropractor trained in neurology and rehab, I decided that since the equipment works for people with disabilities *and* professional athletes, it would be ideal for keeping up my fitness routine while traveling.

The FFR burns calories and gets the blood circulating while sitting at the computer, watching TV, or riding down the road in a motorhome. The WOW — a disk suspended on cords between two handles — is small enough to tuck in the glove compartment, a travel bag, or your purse.

Dr. Berry, who's studying the benefits of the gear, measured our current fitness level in her Arlington office and established an exercise routine for our six-week motorhome trip. By applying ourselves to Flex and Whiz routines, she expects that we'll have fun while improving neurological, muscular, and cardiovascular function. Although my publishing deadline prevents me reporting more definitive results, I can tell you that this mini-gym will always travel with me. With recent scares about deep vein thrombosis, the Flight Flexor is ideal to carry on an airplane and the WOW can easily be used in a hotel room. Using the Flexing FootRest my ankles didn't swell after a long day on the road — a first for me. The Whizzer provided an invigorating workout in the confines of the motorhome or attached to the outside door handle or back ladder for expanded applications.

With rare exceptions, water aerobics can be practiced by anyone. It's easy on aging joints. Ninety-year-old Olga approaches the pool, cane in hand, one slow step at a time. Then she eases into the warm water and gracefully glides to her spot alongside Al, her ninety-three-year-old husband. I met Al and Olga at Valle del Oro, the RV resort in Mesa, where we spend part of each winter.

At 8 a.m., as the early class makes their way to the hot tub or showers, about forty people drop their rubber shoes at poolside and step into the warm water. Harvey, who teaches the early class, says if it weren't for water exercise he wouldn't be walking.

Like the Energizer bunny, this group just keeps going and going. Mostly they're the generation that Tom Brokaw wrote about in *The Greatest Generation.* They volunteer, work hard, love their country, and earn their own way. They know that exercise is the price you pay for an active life, and water aerobics is just the ticket.

My first attempt at water aerobics was pretty embarrassing. We began with jumping jacks, and klutzy me missed the intended 'X' of outstretched arms and legs — though, with my legs under water, no one notices my 'Y.' Fifteen minutes into the routine, with great concentration, I started getting the hang of it. My eyes never left our instructor, Winnie, as she counted out the repetitions. Next came arm stretches, and I followed along as she reached her right arm toward the sky then switched to the left arm with elbow bent, barely reaching the top of her head. Halfway through the reps Bette, the co-leader, caught my eye, and I realized my mistake. I'd been mimicking the teacher's bum left shoulder.

I discovered a pool full of people exercising their way through chronic ailments, such as arthritis, and recovering from heart surgery or joint replacements. Some go merely to stay limber to improve their golf or tennis game. Age and ailment-related jokes keep us smiling — and sometimes laughing, like when my lick-n-stick nipple rolled out of the shower stall.

Every class needs a clown. Ours is eighty-one-year-old Scotty. He thinks the numbers are reversed and behaves like the high-school students he coached in southern Illinois. He sputters and splashes as Fran, his wife of sixty years, looks on with good humor.

Buoyed by the water and camaraderie of friends, water aerobics is the perfect exercise program. Barbara's backyard pool keeps her exercising in the summer, but she makes the effort to drive to an indoor aerobics class in the winter. "I hate making the effort; but once I get there, I love it," she says. It is fun, so if it's available in your area, try it.

People who say, "I get enough exercise pushing my luck," gamble their independence. If your get-up-and-go has done got up and left, it's not too late.

Go for it! You're never too old to exercise. In fact, the older you are, the more essential it is to exercise. If you can't walk, then wiggle your toes, swing your ankles side to side, bend your knees, or raise your legs.

Weight train twice a week

Weight training is the icing on the exercise cake and offers some especially sweet benefits — like strengthening your bones to fight osteoporosis. Calcium, vitamin D, and weight-bearing exercise are the three major factors that affect bone health.

In our thirties we begin to lose muscle mass — as much as half a pound a year. Didn't notice that fifteen-to-twenty-pound loss did you? That's because as lean muscle tissue disappears, an equal amount of fat replaces it.

Unfortunately, lean tissue burns calories, while fat doesn't. Mystery solved. Now we know why, with each new candle on the birthday cake, we have to exercise more and eat less. It's the old "the faster I go, the behinder (literally) I get" theory.

To add insult to injury, at the same time we're losing muscle, our bones are deteriorating. Almost half of all women will have an osteoporosis-related fracture in their lifetime. By age seventy, a woman may lose as much as a third of her bone density. At eighty, one in three women has broken a hip — and 20 percent of those who fracture a hip die within a year. Caucasian, Asian, and small-boned women are especially at risk; yet polls show that two-thirds of women are doing nothing to slow or prevent osteoporosis.

Archaeologists find that our ancestors didn't have the number of broken hips we do today, and it's not because we live longer. All those labor-saving devices trip us up. We're not dragging wood to build a fire and waving a heavy wet blanket to send our neighbors the news. Instead, we flash the news around the world by pressing a button on the cell phone speed dial or tapping a few keys on the computer. As a popular telephone company slogan suggests, we let our fingers do the walking. And for 75 cents, the same company will redial and call you back when a busy line is freed up, saving us even those few finger movements.

No more lifting a heavy saddle and heaving ourselves upon a horse, pounding clothes against rocks; or toting water from a river or well. We don't even walk across the room to change the TV channel. We turn a key, flip a switch, twist a knob, or press a button. We're killing ourselves with convenience!

Our whole body needs to lift and push and pull. We have to create ways to use our muscles — referred to in the fitness world as weight, resistance, or strength training.

Dr. Miriam E. Nelson of Tufts University explains the benefits of weight training in her books *Strong Women Stay Young* and *Strong Women, Strong Bones.* Both are excellent sources for women who want to remain strong all their life.

You'll be convinced that pumping iron does as much for your body as pushing a steam iron does for your clothes. Unfortunately, you can't send it out to be done — it's a do-it-yourself project. And it's a project that becomes even more important as we age, since most women have stopped taking estrogen replacement, which offered some protection from bone loss.

Here's why weight-bearing and resistance exercises are a win-win equation. Ninety percent of the calories your body burns come from muscle use; so adding muscle burns more calories with an equal amount of exertion. Fitness pros say muscle burns up to fifty calories per pound, per day. Do the math; you'll like the exchange rate. By gaining just two pounds of muscle, you burn an extra 100 calories a day.

A weight lifting routine burns about 100 calories more than a thirty-minute walk. Although walking builds bone density in the spine, it does nothing for the hips. Strength training helps both and increases your endurance for aerobic exercises. Moderate weight training burns fat, builds bone density, improves heart rate and blood pressure, reduces arthritic swelling, and increases metabolism to control blood-sugar levels. It's the best way to boost metabolism.

Strong muscles protect joints and improve balance and agility, all in twenty to thirty minutes a few times a week. You are never too old. Several studies, including one by Dr. Nelson, concluded that eighty and ninety year olds benefit from weight training. *The Journal of Applied Physiology* reports than even older women with chronic heart failure benefit from strength training.

Major universities around the country cite studies showing that frail elderly people, some in their nineties, who participate in strength-building and balance exercises gain mobility. Such exercise has even freed some from their wheelchairs.

We're not interested in being body builders; however, there is a direct correlation between the amount of weight lifted and the increased bone-density realized, so give it your best effort. By lifting 100 pounds and winning body-building awards at seventy-eight, Morjorie Newlin proved it can be done.

My goal is to lift enough to get me where I want to go under my own power for as long as I live. I intend to walk to the front of the church at my grandchildren's weddings; stride across the lawn at their graduations; lift my great-grandchildren; climb the stadium steps to watch a game; walk along the 18th hole to see a grandson's winning effort; and (if I have any hair left) hold the hair dryer over my head long enough to look decent for those events.

Think you're too old to worry about these things? Consider that there are currently 75,000 Americans who have reached or exceeded 100. Most of these are women. If I should be so lucky, I want to be able to stand up on the first try. Remember those funny Carol Burnett and Vicki Lawrence skits? Well, it's no laughing matter when your legs and arms combined won't get you out of a chair. Daily living takes muscle power.

One study indicated that only 35 percent of women between seventy-five and eighty-four have the strength to lift a ten-pound object and place it on a shelf above their head. And women twenty years younger weren't much better off — 40 percent of them wouldn't be able to put a ten-pound bag of flour on an upper pantry shelf.

Many of the same cautions apply to weight training as to aerobic exercise. In addition, muscles need to rest at least twenty-four hours between sessions. (That's good news. At most you can only train three times a week.)

The local YMCA or senior center may offer facilities and equipment for weight training. If you already belong to a fitness center, take advantage of the machines designed to strengthen each muscle group, or do squats, lunges, heel raises, curls, and kickbacks with hand weights in your living room. Some say soup cans, water bottles, and milk jugs work, others advise the proper grip of dumbbells. A fold-up mat is nice, but a thick blanket or beach towel on the carpet works just as well.

As vice-president of risk and quality management for Parkland Hospital, Ann happily took the golden umbrella offered by early retirement. Managing risk for a county hospital that delivers 14,000 babies a year — more than any other hospital in the country—carries its own health risks.

Over lunch, she told me what a relief it was to leave the stress behind. But she wasn't ready to rest on her laurels or her buns. "I've always struggled to keep my weight down and I knew what would happen if I just sat around."

Instead, she took a part-time consulting job and hired a personal trainer to keep in shape professionally and physically. "I find it takes someone expecting me to be there at 7 a.m. and pushing me to do my best. I plan my week around workouts. When I travel, I always choose hotels with fitness facilities. I'm in better shape and have more energy now than when I was thirty."

That's an excellent plan if you can afford it. If not, library shelves offer a plethora of books and tapes to review and try before purchasing. If you don't find what you want, try the 1.3 million Internet sites on weight training.

Look for the programs written for beginners, those over fifty, etc., and notice the date of publication. Guidelines change. For instance, older books may suggest more sets of each exercise. The current belief is that fewer sets give you almost the same benefit and are easier on the joints. Programs designed for seniors often suggest slower repetitions with smaller weights.

Most programs suggest eight to ten exercises for the large muscles. Don't forget exercises for ankles, wrists, and neck, especially vulnerable areas as we age. The skills are easy to learn and a bone-density test, covered by Medicare, may be all the incentive you need.

A Yale University School of Medicine study of frail people seventy-five and older adds more incentive. Based on activities of daily living — bathing, dressing, using the toilet, transferring from a chair — the participants showed a 45 percent reduction in disability after seven months of strength and balancing exercises. These are the activities that keep you out of a nursing home.

Watch the numbers, and letters too

It's a numbers game. Learn the rules and follow the clues printed on every food and medicine package. How much fiber? How many fat grams? How much sugar and salt? How many calories? How many milligrams (or is that micrograms)? Is it a nutritional winner or loser?

To police the food you eat, remember Sgt. Joe Friday's advice, "Just the facts, ma'am." Arm yourself with the facts and you won't be ambushed by a 905-calorie taco salad with fourteen teaspoons of fat.

Use your present weight or wishful weight to calculate what it takes to reach your desired weight. The formula hasn't changed — eat less, exercise more. (A piece of pie isn't nearly as tempting when you know it takes four miles to walk off.) It's calorie count limbo. How low can you go — for life? Researchers find that people who establish realistic goals stick with them.

Arm yourself with lists of the calories and fat counts from fast-food chains and gourmet restaurants, as well as for your normal grocery items. New cookbooks and magazine and newspaper recipes list nutritional values, and it doesn't take a whiz kid to decide some favorite family recipes (loaded with oil, butter, cream, sugar) are for special occasions only.

Low-fat foods have improved, and some actually taste pretty good, though I'm more satisfied with a smaller portion of the real thing. On the other hand, with mustard, relish, ketchup, and onions, who notices the taste of a one-gram-of-fat hotdog?

Think of the second half of the nutritional duo — high fiber — as a game of blackjack. The magic number for this game is twenty-five instead of twenty-one, and you can't go bust. See what combination of grains, fruits, and veggies get you to twenty-five grams of fiber, and eat it every day. Minor changes make a major difference. Switching cereals can triple your breakfast fiber.

It's recommended that you increase fiber intake slowly and try one of the products that cuts down on flatulence. Foods high in fiber, especially beans, are what the little ditty refers to as "magical fruit" (the more you eat the more you toot).

On that note we'll move on to some important letters: HDL, LDL, BP, T-score, SPF. Do you know your cholesterol numbers and what they mean? How about your blood pressure and the amount of protection in your sunscreen? How about eye pressure and blood sugar levels?

Gladys bragged, "I haven't been to the doctor in years," while an elevated blood pressure silently destroyed her kidneys. Dialysis extended her life by a few years, but was too little, too late. The AHA reports that fifty million Americans have high blood pressure and a third of them don't know it.

As Yogi Berra warned, "If you don't know where you're going, you might get there." Knowing these numbers and your personal risk factors puts you in the driver's seat. Lifestyle and pharmaceutical remedies provide the road map.

Knowing your A, B, Cs

The vitamin alphabet grows longer and more complicated with each new study. Few of us eat the quantity and variety of foods needed to meet the recommended daily allowance (RDA), and it's no surprise that our aging bodies don't absorb nutrients as efficiently as they once did.

There's no question that vitamin and mineral supplements increase the nutrients in the average diet; but are they as good as the foods containing the nutrients? Clinical trials are now underway to determine whether we get the best results from the vitamins in food, in supplements, or when they are taken together. Since a National Institute on Aging study suggested that vitamin E may protect against Alzheimer's, I'm hedging my bets — adding a few nuts to salads and veggies *and* taking supplements.

The next question is what to take, how much to take, and when to take it (morning, night, with food or on an empty stomach)? Add absorption and safety issues to the mix before deciding on the best recipe for you.

A multivitamin formulated for older people provides less iron, more B-12, and most of the RDA in one daily tablet. The U.S. Pharmacopoeia (USP), the federal agency that sets standards for drugs and vitamin supplements, tests products for quality and composition. Look for the USP stamp.

A is for antioxidants

These free-radical fighters do exactly what their name implies — challenge the oxidation of hydrocarbons. Scientists talk about positive and negative valences, atoms, and ions. Think deterioration and corrosion — think rust. Free radicals are like the rust spots that formed on iron swing sets of the past. These unstable molecules spot our eyes with cataracts and our hands with 'liver' spots; they cloud our memories and clog our arteries. Oxidized LDLs don't create the pleasant patina of oxidized copper on cathedral spires, they coat our arteries and narrow the blood path.

Antioxidants to the rescue with vitamins A, E, C, and K. Vitamins A and C, dressed in the sunset colors — tomatoes, strawberries, sweet potatoes, oranges, cantaloupes, carrots, pumpkins, red peppers, and mangoes — lead the charge.

The feather in their cap is vitamin K. Dark, leafy and green, like spinach, kale, cabbage, Brussels sprouts, and broccoli. "Surprise, surprise!" as Gomer Pyle would say. As usual, the Green Berets in the battle for good nutrition are the green leafy vegetables (GLVs).

On another front, eggs, rich in vitamin E, are back on our plate — four a week, though without the bacon and biscuits.

More good news: Although it's still loaded with calories, chocolate has higher levels of antioxidants than prunes. It increases prostacyclins, which inhibit blood clots and sooth coughs and sore throats. Wow, what a balm for the guilt of chocolate lovers! We can adopt a new slogan: "A Snickers a day keeps blood clots and coughs away."

Other than GLVs, it's hard to increase vitamin E intake without adding inches and pounds. Vegetable oils, sunflower seeds, Brazil nuts, walnuts, and hazelnuts (does frangelico count?) are as rich in fat and calories as they are in nutrients.

Researchers have backed off on some of the earlier claims that supplements prevent stroke and heart attack, but evidence mounts that vitamins boost the immune system and lower the risk of blindness and prostate cancer.

Relying on anecdotal evidence, for years Ophthalmologist Alfred Humphrey urged his patients to take vitamins with antioxidants. National Eye Institute studies have now made it official. Antioxidants slow or halt cataracts and age-related macular degeneration (AMD), the leading causes of impaired vision and blindness in the United States. "All the studies show the benefit of vitamin and mineral supplements in lowering the progression rate of macular degeneration. Because it's hard to get all the antioxidants you need in foods, vitamins are being specially formulated for the eyes. The second thing I tell my patients is to quit smoking. Smoking, even second hand smoke, accelerates AMD," he says.

B is for folate?

Women of childbearing age have already discovered the benefits of folate in reducing the risks of birth defects. The CDC says the rate of spina bifida has dropped 32 percent since doctors began recommending folic acid before and during pregnancy.

My introduction to folate came when my brother-in-law had a heart attack. High levels of homocysteine, an amino acid that builds up in blood vessels, were the culprit. Like many post heart-attack patients, he's on heavy doses of folate and B vitamins. Early indications are that angioplasty and bypass surgery patients taking folate, B-6, and B-12 lower their homocysteine levels and help their reopened or new arteries stay open.

How do you get your homocysteine level down? Folate (folic acid), B-6 and B-12 supplements, folate fortified breads and cereals, and foods such as GLVs, citrus fruits, grains, chick peas, sunflower seeds, and more of those musical fruits — navy, pinto, kidney, and black beans.

The AHA is reserving judgment, but researchers from Boston to Belfast suspect that elevated levels of homocysteine also play a role in heart attack, stroke, dementia, and Alzheimer's disease. On another front, a study of Parkinson's disease in mice found that those fed adequate amounts of folate were able to counteract the adverse effects of homocysteine. "This is the first direct evidence that folic acid may have a key role in protecting adult nerve cells against age-related disease," says Dr. Mark Mattson, chief of the NIA's Laboratory of Neurosciences.

Another bonus comes along with a high-folate diet. *The American Journal of Clinical Nutrition* reports that women with hearing loss were deficient in folate and vitamin B-12.

The FNB says a third of people over fifty aren't getting enough vitamin B-12. A deficiency in this vitamin causes tingling and numbness in arms and legs, poor balance, and mental confusion, any of which might cause a fall and fracture. Along with calcium supplements, just a half-cup a day of GLVs, like spinach or collard greens, can reduce this risk.

With heart disease the number one killer of women, Alzheimer's even scarier than death, and Parkinson's afflicting about 50,000 Americans a year, I'd say a breakfast of fortified cereal and orange juice, containing enough folate to satisfy the 400 microgram daily requirement, may be the way to start your day. Then take Popeye's advice and stay strong to the finish with a serving of spinach for dinner.

C is for Calcium

Since 1984 the NIH has recommended calcium for post-menopausal women. Do you know how, when, and what kind to take. I didn't. For several years, after lunch every day I popped down a multivitamin and two calcium tablets thinking that 1400 milligrams plus a little calcium from food reached the National Osteoporosis Foundation recommendation. Wrong. The body can only absorb 500-600 mgs at a time.

Since I have most of the risk factors for osteoporosis and less than wonderful bone-density, I immediately began spreading my calcium intake throughout the day. A few years later, I read a study by the University of Texas Southwestern Medical Center at Dallas that says

I'm taking the wrong *kind* of calcium. It seems that calcium citrate gives you more bone for your buck by absorbing 25 percent better than calcium carbonate. If you want to check your brand, drop a pill in six-ounces of vinegar and stir every five minutes for half an hour. If it hasn't dissolved by then, look for another brand. I've switched brands; I take them with meals to boost absorption, and I watch for new developments.

Damned if you do, damned if you don't

To get enough vitamin D, you can eat liver (notice I said you, not me). The day I left home, I swore that liver would never be eaten or served in my house. I delighted in the news that organ meats were high in cholesterol and shouldn't be eaten anyway. Now they say liver is a good source of vitamin D (folate, too).

If you can trust the amount of vitamin D fortified milk contains (which according to the feds is no sure thing), it takes thirty-two ounces a day for the RDA. Fat chance.

Fatty fish like salmon are a good source of vitamin D, although, for me, fish should be white and the "fatty" should come from batter and frying. I go along with the Polish proverb: "Fish, to taste right, must swim three times — in water, in butter, and in wine." Albacore tuna is a tasty choice unless you add equal parts mayo, as I prefer. Thankfully, new studies indicate you can cut your stroke risk by eating seafood, regardless of omega-3 content, even once a month. That I can handle.

Our grandparents got plenty of vitamin D eating eggs for breakfast and working and playing all day in the sunshine. They didn't live long enough to worry about melanoma. We're working and playing indoors. It takes a minimum of ten minutes a day of sunshine to produce the vitamin D you need, so slather on sunscreen and spend some time outdoors.

Vitamin D is too important to ignore. The FNB upped the recommendation to 600 international units (IUs) for those past seventy. Vitamin D is essential to build strong bones and teeth and maintain the nervous system. I'm not likely to get enough from food sources, so I take a multivitamin and calcium with 200 IUs of D.

Too much of a good thing

If a little is good, a lot is better? No. You can overdose on almost anything. Sometimes you're just wasting your money on mega-doses of supplements because the body is unable to absorb the additional amount. Other times, the results are toxic.

High doses of vitamin C increase the risk of kidney stones. Excessive amounts of vitamin D can cause life-threatening kidney damage. Be safe. Consider all the sources of a vitamin — those occurring naturally in foods, those added to fortified foods, and those supplied by supplements. Don't exceed the upper limits.

We all know we eat too much salt. Processed foods are loaded with sodium then we add salt during the cooking process and sprinkle more on at the table. You've probably heard that a potato simmered in an over-salted dish absorbs the salt. Well, it seems the same thing happens in the body. Loading up on potassium rich potatoes and bananas is no better than putting too much salt in the stew, but it may ease the guilt when you can't resist a little extra salt.

As young women, we had to worry about anemia. Now our bodies hoard iron, sometimes to dangerous levels. A friend of mine died of hemochromatosis, a rare form of iron overload that affects a small percent of the population. A University of North Carolina Medical School study found that the 15 percent of the population with gene mutations associated with high iron levels were 40 percent more likely to develop colon cancer.

Scientists know that an elevated iron level, along with elevated LDL cholesterol, is risky. Now they suspect there may be a link between iron deficiency and brain cell degeneration; so unless you know you have an iron deficiency, a multivitamin and natural food sources are adequate.

Aspirin is neither vitamin nor mineral. It's also not acetaminophen, naproxen, or ibuprofen — medications too often used interchangeably. Anyone at risk for a heart attack — and that's *every* woman over sixty — has been advised to take an aspirin a day. A University of Minnesota study suggests that aspirin may also reduce the risk of pancreatic cancer, and other studies show aspirin therapy reduces the risk of colon, esophageal, stomach, and rectal cancer.

Early studies suggest that aspirin, ibuprofen, and naproxen may help dissolve the plaque that causes Alzheimer's. The catch? Prolonged used of these drugs may cause intestinal bleeding and kidney damage. Ibuprofen taken throughout the day for arthritis pain may sacrifice the blood-thinning effects of aspirin; however, switching to one of the COX-2 inhibitors for arthritis relief can be a major financial sacrifice. What's one to do? Check with your doctor and consider your particular risk factors.

Unless your doctor advises high doses, a daily low-dose aspirin tablet is the ticket. Taking Tylenol, Advil, or Motrin relieves pain, but doesn't do anything to prevent clot formation. For best results, take a product specifically designed for the type pain you have — aches, fever, muscle pain, headache, etc.

For several years following a stroke, eighty-year-old Bonnie faithfully took a daily aspirin as prescribed. She bought the cheapest thing she could find with no concern about the strength. One day while staking the tomatoes, she toppled over and gashed her arm. "I bled like a stuck pig, so I quit taking those aspirin. My blood is already too thin." Two months later she had a second stroke — a dramatic reminder that even over-the-counter drugs can be dangerous if improperly used.

When you're prescribed a new medication, make sure the prescribing physician knows all the other medications you take. Some combinations are dangerous. For instance, combining statin drugs with steroids risks muscle damage. If you need steroids on a short-term basis, ask about temporarily discontinuing your cholesterol-lowering medication. It's also a good idea to check with the pharmacist about drug interactions.

In many cases, a small change suffices. Since learning that grapefruit affects Lipitor (possibly becoming 15 times more potent), I've replaced salty-dogs — fresh squeezed Arizona grapefruit juice with a splash of Vodka — with equally tasty fresh orange juice drinks as my wintertime happy-hour indulgence. Also, the new drinks, sans salt around the glass rim, are blood-pressure friendly.

Supplements — safe or sorry

The jury's still out on herbal supplements. Some, like those with ephedra, have significant, sometime life-threatening side-effects. The U.S. poison-control centers report that ephedra accounts for 64 percent of all adverse reactions involving herbs. Further research and possible regulation of supplements may make for safer choices. Until then, use caution and check ingredients.

Some friends swear that glucosamine and chondroitin are effective arthritis remedies. Another friend lost the feeling in his hands and feet from the arsenic in herbs he used to supplement traditional treatment for prostate cancer. Thankfully, he's past the five-year mark and doing well.

Phyllis is convinced that ginkgo biloba would help her memory, but she keeps forgetting to take it. That's all right; new studies question its value in reducing memory loss — although, if she has pains in her legs from a lack of blood flow, ginkgo biloba might bring relief.

Selenium, a trace mineral found in enriched grains, pasta, walnuts, beef, tuna, and brewer's yeast, may help asthma sufferers and may reduce the risk of prostate, lung, and colo-rectal cancers. Stay tuned. A seven-year study is underway to determine the prostate benefit.

A U.S. Pharmacopeia's certification program, the Dietary Supplement Verification Program, has established standards to ensure that dietary supplements don't contain dangerous levels of heavy metals, pesticide residue, or other toxic components. Their certification does not guarantee the supplement will work, only that it contains the ingredients listed on the bottle.

Even supplements that are safe may interact with prescription medications. Mostly, figuring out which alternative medicines are safe and helpful is a pain in the neck amounting to a $4.2 billion-a-year pain in the pocketbook.

A cheaper and safer alternative to trial an error is a book edited by Dr. Les Paul and Dr. Becky Nagle. *The Essential Medication Guidebook to Healthy Aging* covers prescription and over-the-counter medications, specifically addressing drug interactions and the way drugs affect older patients.

Wake up to the wonders of sleep

When they passed out perfect pitch and equilibrium, I must have been sleeping. As earlier noted, my bucket is more apt to be filled as a result of motion sickness than holding a tune; but I do have a talent for sleeping. Others so gifted may laugh, but chronic insomnia is a woolly problem affecting our physical and mental well-being.

Our forbearers went to bed with the chickens and woke to the cock's crow. Before Thomas Edison's incandescent light bulb, people got enough sunshine and exercise during the day to sleep from sundown to sunup. Since then, we've burned a century-long electrical path to a 24/7 world. Our circadian clock longs for the rhythms of the sun, while our alarm clocks tick to the cadence of commerce. Like the rest of the broadcast media, the CBS eye never closes. The ATM never sleeps. Likewise, 130 million of us have trouble sleeping — 60 percent of those sixty-five and older, according to the National Sleep Foundation.

Restful sleep restores our mental agility and boosts our immune system. Dr. William C. Dement, considered the father of sleep medicine, believes sleep is an important predictor of how long you will live — maybe more important than diet and exercise! He says our brain keeps track of lost sleep like a loan shark, expecting to be repaid "with interest."

In *The Promise of Sleep,* Dr. Dement says stress-induced insomnia is probably the most common sleep problem. Sleep debt adds up until we are chronically tired. Women who have trouble falling asleep or who fall asleep easily only to wake up a few hours later are naturally going to wake up feeling tired.

You'd think that with no more infants crying for attention, no reason to lie awake wondering if little sperms are wiggling their way into our wombs, and no more worrying about teenagers out for a hot night on the town, we'd be able to sleep. Alas, old age brings its own set of sleep-breakers. Now it's hot flashes, bladders crying to be emptied, and snoring (his or your own) that keep us awake. Add arthritis pain, leg cramps, and Restless Legs Syndrome (RLS) to the mix, and it's a recipe for insomnia.

You may have trouble falling asleep if you have one of those extra-firm mattresses touted a few years ago as good for your back. If so, trade in your hard-as-a-rock mattress for one of the new ones that adjust to your body's weight and shape. Space-age memory foam (developed by a Swedish company from NASA's early anti-G-force research) and dual-control mattresses with air chambers and moveable springs are new alternatives. They're not cheap, but when you consider that you spend more hours on your mattress than on any other piece of furniture in the house, it's worth the cost.

Our memory-foam mattress proved to be one of our best purchases. It's very comfortable, and movement on one side of the bed doesn't rock the other side, so we never wake each other up by turning over. And since I began toting my funny-shaped ergonomic pillow everywhere, I haven't woken up with a stiff neck.

Add to the comfort by wrapping your mattress in luxurious linens and your body in your favorite sleep attire — silk, satin, or flannel. For me, nothing beats the comfort of my birthday suit, so my nightclothes lie next to the bed in case of a fire or tornado.

Sleep experts suggest the bedroom be reserved for two purposes. All other activities, such as reading and watching TV, should be done in another room. Restful sleep requires a dark, cool, quiet place. Room-darkening shades, a ceiling fan, and a lowered thermostat satisfy the first two requirements. If you are a light sleeper or live in a noisy neighborhood, try "white noise" to mask the nocturnal clamor. Numerous radio-like devices broadcast the soothing sounds of rainfall or ocean waves to lull you to sleep. Some sound machines infuse aromas into the air and swirl soft light on the ceiling.

Although a heavy meal is not advised, you may want to add a light snack to your bedtime routine. In her book *A Woman's Guide to Sleep: Guaranteed Solutions for a Good Night's Rest*, Dr. Joyce A. Walsleben suggests including foods that contain the sleep-inducing amino acid, tryptophan — bananas, cheese, turkey. (This explains the Thanksgiving Day naps.)

Dr. Walsleben, director of the Sleep Disorder Center at New York University School of Medicine, offers a comprehensive look at women's unique sleep problems, the causes, and the cures. It's a must-read for women struggling with sleep deprivation.

Early to bed, early to rise

Ben Franklin promised health, wealth, and wisdom to those who retire early, but going to bed late and rising late works as well, so long as you get seven to eight hours of sleep each night. The experts say you do not need less sleep as you get older.

Carole is a very early riser, often walking through her Calgary neighborhood before dawn. Rather than toss and turn on the occasional nights she can't sleep, she does as the specialists advise and gets up. She puts a prerecorded tape of a soap opera in the VCR and watches until she feels sleepy. I suspect this busy lady seldom takes time to watch soaps during the day, so her nocturnal interruptions become a guilt-free indulgence before returning to bed. The NSF offers these tips for a good night's sleep:

- Drink less fluid, especially alcohol and caffeine, close to bedtime.
- Avoid heavy meals near bedtime.
- Exercise regularly, preferably in the afternoon.
- Establish a relaxing bedtime routine — a hot bath, soothing music.
- Maintain a regular schedule, going to bed and getting up at the same time every day.

If none of this works, you may be one of the 18 million Americans suffering from sleep apnea, a disorder that can be life-threatening. Loud snoring every night and pauses in breathing are signals that the tongue and soft palette are blocking your airway and you aren't getting enough air. If that feels familiar, consider it a wake-up call to seek medical advice.

Write it down

It's the umpteenth time you've heard this, right? That's because it works. It even has its own verb — journaling. A beautifully bound book with notes to inspire you, lined notebook paper, notes jotted on the calendar, or a magnetic pad slapped on the fridge all work equally well. It's not the paper; it's the pencil-and-pen work that counts.

Writing down goals increases the possibility of achieving them. As Confucius said, "The strongest memory is not as good as the weakest ink." A journal reveals patterns of behavior that will help you create situations that produce the best results and avoid those that don't work. If a brisk walk makes you feel really good, write it down. If a big, heavy meal makes you feel sluggish and bloated, write that down too.

Florence Nightingale's habit of observing and recording in her journal helped her discover the importance of good hygiene. Long before bacteria was discovered, she noticed that infection spread in dirty surroundings and among soldiers who ate from the same pot. When she began washing soldier's clothes and linens, cooking individual meals, and opening the field hospitals to fresh air, the death rate dropped.

"It's a dream until you write it down. After that, it's a goal," says

Emmitt Smith, who broke Walter Payton's record to become the NFL's all-time leading rusher. It certainly works for him. His to-do list included gaining a thousand yards, making Rookie of the Year, and going to the Super Bowl. He achieved them all and more. I suspect induction into the Pro Football Hall of Fame appeared on his list long before it was a sure thing.

Beethoven puts another spin on writing things down. He said he had to write ideas down right away or he forgot them. When asked why he never referred to his notebooks when writing compositions, he's reported to have said, "If I put it into a notebook, I never forget it and I never have to look it up again."

Don't go off half-cocked and set unrealistic goals. I did before I found that the best news release doesn't guarantee front-page placement or even that you will make it into print. Nor does a beautiful invitation guarantee attendance. A tornado rips through town, the school burns down, or the police chief is arrested for fraud, and your wonderful story slips to the back page.

I was measuring success with my eye on the target instead of on the only thing I could control, which was the planning. I learned that after checking the local sports, church, and civic calendars, setting a date without a lot of competition, and sending a timely, accurate, and enticing invitation, there was nothing to do but hope the unforeseen didn't rain on my parade. (Maybe this was the beginning of my *Umbrella* philosophy.)

Measure success with goals you can control and promises you can keep. List what you "will" do, not what you won't eat or how many pounds you'll lose. Fill your scorecard with lifelong healthy habits.

If insomnia is a problem, make a sleep calendar that lists your bedtime routine, when you go to bed and wake up, the number of times you get up during the night, and the quality of your sleep. Only if it's written down can you see what pattern of behavior works best.

Write weight training and exercise times on the calendar and check them off or draw a line through them as you complete them. (Having to confront missed dates is an incentive not to miss a day.) Start slow and up the ante each month until you reach the goals you've set for yourself.

For at least a week, write down *everything* you eat for a base line.

Although the food pyramid has come under fire as based too heavily on carbohydrates, making people think only fats cause weight gain, it's still a good place to start. Using it as a guide, design a food plan for yourself that combines calories and serving size and replaces unhealthy fats with nuts and vegetable oils.

If the plan includes eating breakfast every day, write it down. Are five, seven, or nine fruits and veggies a day the goal? Make a numbered list and fill in the blanks each day. In this case serving size is a plus — a cup of vegetables may be two servings. And don't forget water. You get the idea. If there's one blank left on your list, you may opt for an apple instead of a turnover for a bedtime snack. (Come on, there's a chance isn't there?) Want to up the odds? Make a grocery list of healthy foods and stick to it. That apple looks a lot better when a turnover isn't handy.

While you're at it, write down all the medications (prescription and OTC) you take and carry it in your purse. It's easier than carrying a bag of medicine bottles around, it's handy for completing forms in doctor's offices, and in an emergency it could be a lifesaver. Read the fine print on your medication inserts and write down any change you feel while taking a new medication.

There are some really weird reactions to drugs. Believe it or not, a dry cough, a nasty sunburn, and a torn Achilles tendon could all be the result of medication. A metallic taste could be caused by diabetic medication. If you don't write it down, you may not know that it's the extra fiber in a new pill that's causing embarrassing flatulence.

For the same reason, it's wise to have a personal medical history of illnesses, surgeries, allergies, etc. The mastectomy date you don't forget, but others are harder to keep track of. (And I'm always afraid I'll misspell hysterectomy or tetracycline.) File with important papers and retrieve when needed.

Go a step further and purchase *How Healthy is Your Family Tree?* written by Carol Krause and subtitled *A complete guide to tracing your family's medical and behavioral history.* Krause's practical genogram workbook offers a step-by-step guide to tracing your family's medical history. A family with a history of breast cancer or colon cancer can begin screening and taking preventive measures at earlier ages than normal. A pattern of addictive behaviors or depression alerts family members to their risk, and early intervention and treatment may avert serious consequences. Tracing your genealogy is interesting, and emphasizing the "genes" in your family history could be a live-saving gift for your children. (Another ATB project for me.)

Worship

In her research, Lynn Peters Adler, founder and director of the National Centenarian Awareness Project, identified spirituality as one of seven pillars of successful aging. She includes faith as one of the qualities shared by those who reach and pass the 100-year mark. Adler and other researchers find that faith — along with attitude, diet, exercise, genes, and a sense of humor — plays a role in longevity.

Studies show that people with spiritual or religious beliefs, those who pray frequently, and those who enjoy the social interaction of a family of believers are less anxious and suffer less from depression than others. Beliefs that discourage unhealthy habits like smoking and drinking also contribute to overall good health.

More than our outward appearance, our spirit defines us. When the years cool our physical abilities, faith — the fire that burns within — warms our heart and lifts our spirit. That spirit can be found in churches, temples, mosques, and the wonders of nature.

It's impossible for a single religion, doctrine, or creed to define our various beliefs. Worship comes from the word "worth" as in honor, dignity, reverence, devotion, love, and admiration — hardly the vocabulary of charlatans, sinning priests, and the Taliban, who think they alone hold the hand of the Almighty.

The way people argue religious doctrine you'd think they based their faith on years of comparative study. In my opinion, it takes little study to conclude that our view of God forms at the same time our eyes develop — in our mothers' wombs. The dictionary says faith is an unquestioning belief that doesn't require proof or evidence. Few need more proof than the belief of their parents. Demographics seem to confirm the familial, geographic, and cultural basis of religious belief. Recent human genome studies on identical twins raised separately shows there may actually be a genetic connection in our religious choice. In any case, whether we march to *Onward Christian Soldiers*, chant the Kaddish, or bow to the East is usually determined at birth.

Each new discovery — a far off universe or the human genome — attests to a force greater than ourselves. Deciding who gets credit is the sticky wicket. And the wicket gets stickier when a certain group tries to claim that Jesus, Buddha, or Allah is the only gate to salvation. It's amazing how many people believe the Lord works in mysterious ways, yet think they alone have all the clues to solve those mysteries.

Intolerance consumes the moth egos of zealots, while those of quiet faith carry a flame for all to follow. Their kind of faith makes life worth living no matter the number of years.

The inner peace that makes for successful aging is a confidence that we are not alone, that our life has purpose, and that we'll be given the strength to overcome adversity.

My religion is best described by Abraham. Not Abraham, the father of Judaism, Islam, and Christianity, but Abraham Lincoln. He said when he did good, he felt good and when he did bad, he felt bad. He claimed no particular denomination, but often referred to the goodness of God and the will of God. He thanked people for their prayers, and, in acknowledging women's efforts during the Civil War, closed a speech with "God bless the women of America."

I'm a Protestant by birth and a skeptic by nature. I believe in a deity of inclusion and prefer the Golden Rule to strict dogma. I've certainly lived under the wings of a guardian angel. Those who love me, forgive me, and stand by me in spite of my faults nourish my spirit. The miracles of a creator who gave me the senses to appreciate a fragrant rose, the majesty of snowcapped mountains, the taste of a fresh peach, the song of the human voice, and the touch of a loved one make my spirit soar.

Following your own spiritual path leads to a healthy attitude toward aging, so if you've gotten away from your religious roots, this may be the time to renew your spirit. It's good for body and soul.

A matter of choice, not chance

We live in a wonderful age. In early stages, 90 percent of cancers are curable; joint and organ replacement is commonplace. Our clogged arteries are reamed, propped open with stents, zapped with radiation, or replaced. Bioresorbable stents that dissolve once the wall of the blood vessel heals are in the research pipeline. Every year brings new advancements — pharmaceutical, surgical, and therapeutic remedies that add years to our lives.

Bad genes and bad luck account for some of life's maladies, but we can change the odds. Dr. Thomas Perls, who designed the "Living to 100 Life Expectancy Calculator," says good genes can take us to age eighty-five and that preventive steps may add another decade. The calculator's questions add up to a prescription for preventive care. Improve your luck by visiting www.livingto100.com or buy the book of the same name to check out your longevity potential.

See how your lifestyle measures up at Northwestern Mutual's quiz at www.LongevityGame.com. And just for fun go to www.deathclock.com, a site that calculates your death date based solely on your age, sex, and attitude.

It's easy to say you don't have any interest in living to 100 or making the round-the-clock effort it takes to beat the biological clock. The truth is, there are 60,000 Americans, mostly women, who are more than 100 years old. If you're genetically blessed, you may find yourself at eighty-two or ninety-two sitting in a wheelchair, tethered to an oxygen tank, waiting for someone to change your diaper. Forget those before and after pictures in the weight loss ads! This is the mental picture to hold on to when you want a cigarette and would rather skip the workout and go for super-sized takeout. It boils down to taking care of yourself — to finding the courage to replace bad habits with good ones. Healthy habits lengthen life; more importantly, they postpone disability.

Fighting the symptoms of old age takes courage, a battle plan, and commitment. *Umbrella* offers an outline. The words of honest Abe may help with the courage and commitment: "And in the end, it's not the years in your life that count. It's the life in your years."

Reflect, Don't Regret

"... fill the cup that clears today of past regrets and future fears. Unborn tomorrow, and dead yesterday. Why fret about them if today be sweet."

— Omar Khayyam

When life's predicaments make your blue, put on rose-colored glasses. Look for the good, savor the best, forget where the other road might have led. Time spent regretting and focusing on the past is like driving looking in the rearview mirror. Look ahead with only an occasional glimpse at the past to be sure you aren't broadsided by history repeating itself.

When asked about regrets, Helen Hayes said she wished she'd ridden a bicycle. The first lady of the American theater died on St. Patrick's Day 1993 with this one regret. Her daughter died of polio at age nineteen, Ms. Hayes was a widow for almost forty years, and allergies forced her retirement from the stage. Yet, when asked about regrets, she said nothing of the tragedies of her life; in fact, she recalled how fortunate she had been.

Walter Cronkite (a San Jacinto High School graduate) reached the pinnacle of his career without scaling any peaks. At eighty-three, he said he regretted never climbing a mountain. How interesting that both Hayes and Cronkite, each with hundreds of honors, point to some small physical endeavor they wished they had tried at a younger age.

Until asked, neither probably gave much thought to regrets because successful people seldom do. Pot of gold or faux pearls, they count the treasures. We can treasure the past with selective memory or let the hurt inflected by parents, ex-husbands, or whomever, weigh us down. If we allow it, time fades life's harsh realities, great hurts become soft aches seldom revisited, and we learn to adjust — unless of course, we hold onto every regret and let it fester like a great oozing sore on our psyche.

If it's possible to work yourself to death, my father did. He did whatever needed doing. Sweeping the sidewalk in front of the dime store where his mother clerked was the first of a string of jobs. He was nine years old. For the rest of his life he worked, shunning vacations.

During the war, his country needed war materiel so he worked eighteen-hour days. On occasion, Mother would get a call that he wasn't coming home for a couple of days. When the Navy needed a part to get a ship back to sea, the company would actually bring in cots. The men slept a few hours, ate a quick meal, and went back to their machines.

When Mother needed the car for the day, we'd drive across town before dawn to drop Dad off, then go back again in mid-afternoon to wait in the parking lot. Although the whistle blew promptly at three, we knew he would be the last to emerge from the corrugated metal building. Whistling, his wavy dark hair still wet from the shower, he'd saunter toward the car with an empty lunch box in one hand, dirty clothes tucked under his arm, and sometimes a box of metal shaving to scatter around the rose bushes. With blue eyes twinkling and a smile that accentuated his dimpled chin, he'd tell us about the latest prank. Once he got back at a man who was stealing gum from his locker by replacing it with its laxative-laced cousin. At other times the jokes were on him. Once, his pants legs were stapled together.

He built our family's first house from the ground up and maintained and remodeled every house we lived in after that. We had one bath, one phone, and one car; but we always had a two-car garage. My father's job as a machinist fed the family, but it didn't feed his curiosity. Immediately after dinner he would disappear into the garage, often working into the wee hours, seldom getting more than four or five hours sleep.

Boxes and shelves lined the walls. It was a virtual hardware store of electrical, plumbing, and gardening supplies. As he moved from one interest to the next, the shelves became filled with the tools of the trade until, finally, he had to dangle some from the ceiling. He built a greenhouse and grafted strange trees with different blossoms and fruit on various branches. He built a fishpond that spawned more frogs than fish. He built box fans from wood and chicken wire and fashioned lamps from cypress knees. And when things disappeared from the garage, he rigged a camera to get a picture of the neighbor-boy thief.

He was an engineer without a high-school diploma, who lived the scout oath without ever wearing the uniform. He went to church for funerals and my wedding, although the price of his suit gave him pause. He claimed it was foolish to spend so much money for something he would never wear again. Three years later as he was dying, it probably pleased him to know we wouldn't have to buy him a suit.

By today's measure, he was not a good father. He never hugged or kissed his daughters or told us he loved us. He expected me to marry and raise a family. He never mentioned college or a career. He also never hinted that he would have preferred a son. Neither pushed or coaxed, I was welcome to work along side him, wrapping bright colored thread around fishing rods, carefully pouring hot lead into molds for fishing weights, or helping with any of a dozen projects he had going.

Today, child psychologists talk about building self-esteem and accepting consequences. Little praise, but equally sparse criticism, took care of my self-esteem; and there was no question about accepting the consequences of my deeds. When I was growing up, neither children nor adults expected to be rescued from "beds of their own making."

I have no regrets. In his own way, my father loved me. He provided food and shelter, and somehow I inherited a healthy dose of self-worth and initiative that makes up for any lack of talent or education.

Likewise, when thinking about my husband Fred, I choose to remember his good qualities. The children have inherited his sense of humor, his competitiveness, his love of golf and games. I see the resulting laughter and joy in my grandchildren. The oldest, now teenagers, delight in outscoring their parents.

A brief moment of sadness still interrupts the graduations, weddings, and births when I wish the children could share their joy with their father. When I held Chelsea for the first time, when Blake won his first golf tournament, I thought of what Fred missed. He would be so proud of his children and grandchildren.

It was senior prom night 1955. Mama and I had made the dress from yards of lavender net. I measured, pinned, and cut layers of material into 2-inch strips and rolled them into balls. For days the old Singer hummed as row after row of scallops circled the skirt. Strapless was in, but my breasts were not, so more ruffles enhanced the décolletage.

Fred arrived with the obligatory florist box, and Mama proudly pinned the white orchid on her oldest daughter, bragging how the flowers' purple center complemented the dress. The mingled fragrance of Old Spice and Prince Machiavelli escorted us across the lawn to the car.

Neighbors smiled and waved as we drove off with ruffles billowing out the passenger window. Fred asked if I minded making a quick stop before the prom. Of course I did, but I never said no to this handsome young man I loved. Not then or later.

The neon Bill William's Drive-In sign beckoned to teens in '39 Fords, '47 Chevy's, and a few Plymouths. Late-model cars belonged to dads, and farm boys left their pickup trucks beside the barn.

On weekends, teens drove up and down the parking lot looking for a space near friends. Like all the girls, I sat in the middle of the bench seat. (It was before bucket seats and seat belts, but we wore enough crinolines to prevent any thigh-to-thigh contact.) Full skirts, bobby socks, and saddle oxfords or penny loafers were date-night attire. Red and white Lucky Strike packs or Camels showed through boys' carefully rolled, white T-shirt sleeves. Cuffed, tight, low-slung Levis fell above their white socks and brown loafers.

Costumed carhops, glistening in Houston's humidity, clamped trays of greasy hamburgers and thick milkshakes on rolled-down windows. Before midnight, cars peeled off for the submarine races at Memorial Park and a little necking before curfew.

This place where we had spent so many evenings was the stop Fred had in mind. I remember his blue eyes, his blond flattop perfectly spiked with butch-wax, and how good he looked in his rented tux. I don't remember what he said when he pulled a velvet box from his pocket and slipped a diamond ring on my finger.

My engagement overshadowed any memories of the prom, but I do recall stopping by home to change clothes and show my mom the ring before we joined other graduates for the traditional beach celebration in Galveston —roasting marshmallows and watching the sunrise.

We married six months later, and Fred joined the Army. After boot camp, we loaded our '54 Ford for our first trip east — a five-day adventure that began my love of travel. We drove through New Orleans, past gulf-facing mansions framed by moss-dripping oaks, and then we curled through the Smokey Mountains of Tennessee and into the blue grass of Kentucky. We stopped for a half-day's history lesson in D.C. before crossing the George Washington Bridge into New York City. We wormed our way around the outskirts and left, satisfied with a small bite of the big apple. The last leg of the trip took us up the seashore through three states before noon — quite a trip for two Texas teens.

I was a slice of southern white bread among Boston bagels. In New England, they let apartments, chilled tonic, and drank tea without ice. Back home we didn't let anyone stay without the rent, and we applied our hair tonic at room temperature. The locals were as confused by my fixin' to make a pallet as I was when told I had dropped my babushka.

The Fort Devens' dog faces fed the local economy, but the small townspeople reversed the role and bit their benefactors at every opportunity. Well, if they didn't appreciate this soldier's wife, I wouldn't give them the satisfaction of letting them know. I had better things to do. On my own for the first time, I did all the things my mama wouldn't let me, like eat all the chocolate chip cookie dough without baking a single cookie and drinking iced tea all winter long.

The winters in Massachusetts are long and cold. Without a car, television, or telephone, and with Fred gone for long hours, I was lonely. On a private's pay, there was no money for entertainment. One day on a walk, I discovered the library.

My friend, Rosemary, read all the time, but I was always too busy. My family took the Houston Press, the yellowiest view of the time, but I don't recall reading it. As a conscientious student, I read what was required, but nothing more. Then Pearl Buck's *The Good Earth* opened up a whole new world to me, and I was not lonely any more. Reading became my life raft.

Then, and many times since, I've seen the truth in Tom Stoppard's line in *Rosencrantz and Guildenstern Are Dead:* "Every exit is an entry somewhere else." Aging gives us a heavy key ring to carry. It's up to us whether we stare at the closed doors with regret or open our mind to new opportunities. And if opportunity doesn't knock? Take Milton Berle's advice and build a door.

When those exits doors swing back and slap you in the face, think about Hall-of-Famer Reggie Jackson. Every time he came to the plate, he expected a hit. It didn't happen, but he persisted and kept on swinging. In fact, he holds baseball's career strikeout record (twice as many as second place Babe Ruth). He was also the 1973 Most Valuable Player in the American League and the World Series. Thirty years later, he remains among the all-time leaders in home runs and runs batted in. After a successful baseball career, he could have sat on the sidelines. Instead, he's using his reputation and resources to bring African-Americans into auto racing as owners and drivers.

Marie, the nurse assigned to care for a seriously ill celebrity with a distraught and demanding husband probably thought she had drawn the short straw. Loving husbands, especially powerful men accustomed to being in charge, often take their frustration out on hospital personnel. Charles Bronson was no exception. Over time though, Marie's frank demeanor and uncompromising care won him over and changed her life. She could have reflected on the years she'd built toward a nurse's pension and missed an opportunity, but she didn't. Instead, she accepted his offer to go home with them and care for his wife. After Jill Ireland's death, he kept his promise and found work for her with his celebrity friends. Her brave decision and kind heart took Marie to Australia and exciting destinations around the world as nanny for the seven children of another star.

We can sit on the sidelines praising the past and let the present race by or we can choose to stay in the game until the last out. In *Resilience: The Power to Bounce Back When the Going Gets Tough*, psychiatrist and author Frederic Flach says the key to persistence is resilience. "When you go through any kind of stress or change . . .there's a certain level of disruption. The resilient person adapts, recovers from the impact and learns from it."

Every door of opportunity doesn't open to easy solutions. Let me tell you about a woman who suffered a revolving door of tragedy, but whose misfortune opened doors for thousands of American children.

Alma was pregnant with her fourth child when her two oldest were diagnosed with phenylketonuria (PKU). Although this rare, inherited metabolic disorder was first described in 1934, even as late as the 50s, it was seldom diagnosed in time to prevent mental retardation and other neurological problems.

After several major medical centers offered little help, Alma and Jim moved across the country to be near a medical facility doing research on the disease.

When this disease is not treated within the first year of life, irreparable brain damage occurs. It was too late for the older children; a third child beat the odds and was disease free; and the fourth became the subject of tests and research, confirming the benefits of a special low-protein diet.

A scientific explanation of the disease includes gene mutations, metabolic error, chemical imbalance, and amino acids. As Alma explained, "The more protein she eats, the less brain she'll have." This was on a day our children interrupted their play for snacks. As each one picked a favorite munchie, Alma's five-year-old happily accepted a lollipop. Of the numerous sugary snacks, Alma said, "She may not have any teeth, but she'll have a brain."

Rather than allowing her life to be overwhelmed with regret that two of her children would spend life in an institution, Alma worked full-time for a mental health organization and volunteered untold additional hours. She and Jim joined a grass-roots effort that lobbied for mandatory testing for PKU. Concerned parents and mental health organizations battled lawmakers and healthcare providers for years. Their persistence paid off. Today, the four million infants born in the U.S. each year are tested. The incidence of one case in every 8,000 births may seem statistically insignificant, until you think of 500 or so babies that mandatory screening identifies for early dietary treatment.

A few summers ago I visited Alma in her Denver home. We sat in her cozy kitchen and, in the course of a few hours, tried to fill a thirty-year gap of lost contact. Her parents had died, her children were middle-aged, and she and Jim had retired. The photographs that filled every wall recorded the courage of a family determined to find joy in all things. Pictures of picnics, the family gathered around a Christmas tree, and gapped-tooth youngsters blowing out birthday candles showed loving parents smiling at happy children.

After lunch Alma calmly discussed their latest concern. The baby who was poked and prodded to further PKU research had once again become a guinea pig for science. They had been told it was okay to stop the low-protein diet once the brain was fully developed. It wasn't okay, so the little girl with the lollipop, now in her forties, lost several IQ points before realizing she had to return to her restricted eating regime.

After a half-century struggle, you might expect Alma to be a bitter old woman, regretting all the things her life could have been without PKU. She could blame her religion's ban on birth control, the medical profession for not acting sooner, or some ancient ancestor (in Ireland one in 4500 babies is born with PKU). Instead she's as bright and cheerful as her flower garden, blooming with hope. Her home is one of warmth and love.

In a 1965 Rocky Mountain News' article, she said, "We only hope that our misfortune may help other families." Because she and others chose hope over despair, we now have mandatory testing that provides early detection.

If you're regretting that your child or grandchild has to be on a restrictive diet, take daily insulin shots, or use a wheelchair for mobility, reflect on the alternative and find hope in your heart.

If you're having trouble finding any positive reflections of the past or present, you may be suffering from depression. A generation raised on the "pull yourself up by your boot straps" philosophy is less likely to seek help, unaware that in many cases their feelings of hopelessness are the result of a chemical imbalance in the brain. The American Psychological Association says that women are twice as likely as men to suffer from depression. Almost all depression can be successfully treated, either with something as simple as daily exercise or with antidepressants; yet few seek treatment.

It's often a chicken-or-the-egg situation. Which came first? Did depression suppress the immune system and cause health problems or did failing health cause the depression? In either case, medical help is advised. The suicide rate among seniors is 50 percent higher than for the nation as a whole and rising. Untreated depression takes the majority of the blame, but statistics don't tell the devastating story.

"We'll never know why Mother chose suicide," Donna says. Mary showed none of the signs of depression. At eighty-seven, she was very active, a snappy dresser, had her nails done every week, and never mentioned being despondent. In looking back, her behavior the week before was unusual. She withdrew cash from the bank, destroyed important papers, had a long reminiscing phone call with a daughter, and declined a regular weekly excursion. "At the time we didn't think much about it," Donna explained. "And we didn't know about the $100 she withdrew from the bank. We never did find out what she did with it.

"That evening my husband Frank made grilled cheese sandwiches, and the three us ate together. We changed into pajamas and watched TV. I went to bed first. During the night Frank got up and found her hanging from the patio rafter. She had changed into a silk jogging suit and used an old rope we had never seen. She didn't leave a note or any clue. I thought I could read people pretty well. Maybe because she lived with us and we were so close . . . I guess we'll never know, but twelve years later it's still difficult."

Researchers say elderly people often hide their intent to commit suicide. Shortly before they jumped to their death, the maintenance man at a Florida high-rise apartment removed the screens from the windows so an elderly couple "could better enjoy the ocean breeze." Lack of social support, poor sleep patterns, terminal illness, chronic pain, and frustrating memory loss are enough to cause depression. Treatment may relieve the mental stress that too often leads to suicide.

Little things mean a lot

The Chinese philosopher Lao-tzu wrote: "The journey of a thousand miles begins with a single step." Likewise, life's journey is the sum of a thousand small decisions we make every day, in good times and bad.

If you put all your energy into a few large expectations that don't work out, you set yourself up for disappointment. If the cruise to Alaska falls through, sign up for a class at the local college or visit a friend or relative during the week of the cancelled trip. Somewhere between "too many irons in the fire" and "putting all your eggs in one basket" lies a middle ground to turn acorns into trees.

When great life changes occur, people find that it's the little things they miss more than they expected. After the loss of a spouse, widows catch themselves in mid-sentence commenting about a TV show or asking the answer to a crossword puzzle. Anticipating the times and places that make you blue and changing little routines eases the pain. Don't leave his favorite cup sitting at the front of the cabinet as a constant reminder of your loss. If you always read the newspaper together at the kitchen table, take your coffee and paper to a different room. If you always went out to dinner on Friday evenings, make plans with friends in advance. To get back on track, change the little things, and with time you'll see the wisdom in David Everett's poem: "Large streams from little fountains flow; tall oaks from little acorns grow."

Tip the scales in your favor by keeping up with the little things — technological, medical, and safety — that improve your health and environment.

Visualize the best

No one would deny the determination it takes to overcome the great sorrow of losing a loved one. It takes courage to learn to speak again after a stroke; to give yourself insulin shots when oral medications no longer control your diabetes; to struggle through chemotherapy; or to learn to walk on artificial joints. Those are the times to reflect on this Japanese proverb: "The sharp point of the treasure sword was honed on the grinding stone. The fragrance of the plum blossom was conceived in bitter cold."

When you're stuck in a chair or the bed, try taking a mental vacation. Choose what suits you — skip through the sunshine or slosh through the snow. The lovely words from the last verse of Robert Frost's *Stopping by Woods on a Snowy Evening* were written on a hot July morning. Our minds can carry us anywhere. And you, too, have "promises to keep and miles to go" before you sleep.

Whatever you call it — visualization, day dreaming, positive imagery, guided imagery — it works for geniuses and grunts alike. Albert Einstein discovered the theory of special relatively while visualizing himself riding a light beam. Athletes have switched to equal parts physical and mental preparation to hone their competitive skills.

One of our greatest champions, Muhammad Ali, offers this insight: "Champions aren't made in gyms. Champions are made from something they have deep inside them — a desire, a dream, a vision. . . They have to have the skill *and* the will. But the will must be stronger than the skill." Tiger Woods displayed that kind of desire and vision while battling food poisoning during a tournament. Despite throwing up every few holes and doubling up with stomach cramps, he won the Bay Hill Invitational for the fourth straight time.

I've been daydreaming since my days under the Chinaberry tree. I've gone to sleep so many nights visualizing signing this book that it's amazing I don't wake up with writer's cramps. Interestingly, with no other explanation, it seems I've regained the strong easily manicured nails that disappeared when my cholesterol went from above 300 to below 200. I'm told there's no medical indication that the goo that clogs arteries strengthens nails, but I'd tried every internal and external cure for peeling, splitting nails without success. Recently, however, for no apparent reason other than those nocturnal visions of my hands with lovely manicured nails autographing *Umbrella,* the nails are back. Coincidence? Maybe, since the liver spots and protruding veins are still there; but I'm not discounting the value of positive visualization.

Olympic swimmers, runners, and skaters all relate stories of victory based on visualization. Tenley Albright first visualized success when she was a victim of polio. Lying in her hospital bed, she visualized the three steps she needed to take to convince herself and her doctors that she would walk again. Those first successful steps eventually lead to a gold medal in figure skating in the 1956 Winter Olympics. She followed an outstanding athletic career with an outstanding medical career. In 1999 she was inducted into the International Scholar-Athlete Hall of Fame.

Another Olympian, swimmer Dara Torres, cheated the biological clock by making a comeback at age thirty-two (a granny in swimming circles) after a seven-year absence from competition. She visualized success and did everything she could to make the team. Her dreams became reality when she became the first American to swim in four Olympics. In the process, she won two gold and three bronze medals. Now she's setting records swimming for charity, recently becoming the first woman to win the Toyota Pro/Celebrity Grand Prix Race in Long Beach, Calif.

Dr. Joyce Brothers says, "Before your dreams can come true, you have to have those dreams." So step up to the starting line, reflect on how you want to spend the rest of your life, and write the perfect script.

Although pretty pictures help you get there, it does take a plan. A mock-up of the *Umbrella* cover sits on my desk. Obviously, it will take more than visualization for that cardboard filler to become interesting and attractive pages; but the visual reminder of the goal spurs me to keep at the task.

Choose a model for successful aging, visualize yourself in that role, and set about making the dream come true. As you might expect, I recommend going to the library and getting some books on visualization.

There is one catch to visualization. Remember when your mother would say, "If you don't have anything nice to say . . ." Well, that goes double for self-talk. This visualization stuff works just as well in reverse. If you imagine yourself old, tired, and lonely, that's probably what you'll become. In his writings on "Psycho-Cybernetics," motivational guru Dr. Maxwell Maltz says, "The mind cannot tell the difference between an actual experience and one vividly imagined." One devastating experience, visually relived over and over, takes an emotional toll with each recall.

Charles Platkin's book on behavior modification, *Breaking the Pattern*, suggests creating life preservers to maintain the will to work toward your goals. Picture yourself as you want to be in the future, and throw yourself a prerecorded life preserver when you're drowning in doubt.

When bad thoughts creep in, replace them with good ones. The most powerful visualizations use as many senses as possible, and this one has it all. She's a teenager now, but one of my favorite life preservers pictures Chelsea at three seeing the ocean for the first time. I can feel the gritty sand under my feet, smell the salt air, hear the waves crashing, see her chubby legs splashing in the foam, and picture the look of amazement when she tastes the salty spray. On the many occasions that her immune deficiency induces a medical crisis, I wash away the dark thoughts with this memory and staunch the tears with a smile.

Lights, camera, action

When bad images of aging confront you, fight back by casting yourself in an epic movie as the heroine who finds the pot of gold at the end of every rainbow. Move the plot toward a happy ending by setting goals and committing to follow through. That's the price of the ticket. Reruns are free, so wear out the film replaying a "happily every after" scenario.

While you're visualizing, take a hard look at the "good old days." Was the grass really greener? What about all the watering, fertilizing, and mowing it took to keep it that way? An equal investment in keeping up with medical advances and changing technology improves the grass color on the downhill side of the fence.

Styles, definitions, and communications change. Though surely nothing written today is any more nonsensical than "Mairzy Doats" or the jitterbug, like every generation we complain about the movies, music, and dance of the next generation. They've taken the "men only" sign off the tattoo parlor, and both genders are piercing places we can't imagine (and frankly, I don't want to). Still, we discover that boys with long hair and earrings and girls with toe rings and black fingernail polish are equally loved when they are ours.

Updating our vocabulary brings us closer to younger generations, so I try to understand the language of my grandchildren. I thought I kept up pretty well until my granddaughter surprised me by talking about her dad getting buff. I couldn't image my reserved son-in-law walking around the house sans clothes. Luckily, before asking any embarrassing questions, I discovered he had a new gym membership and was buffing up his physique.

Knowing that a CD may provide financial gain or music, that Spam isn't just a fatty food, that coming out doesn't always refer to a debutante ball, and that snail mail isn't slimy avoids some laughable mix-ups, but is of little consequence.

The important thing is that we accept the conveniences and technology the language describes. My mother called her refrigerator an icebox into the '70s; I still claim to "dial" the phone although I haven't had a rotary phone in twenty years. Before Gulf War II, none of us had a clue what embedded reporters were, but we quickly came to appreciate their dangerous assignment and the technology that gave us a front-row seat in the battle for Baghdad.

From outhouses to smart houses

No other generation has seen the dramatic changes that have occurred in the past century. We've come from horse and buggy to spaceships, from the box camera to the digital camera, from modesty to nudity, from the outhouse to the smart house that electronically turns the lights on and off, heats, cools, and cooks on a pre-programmed schedule. Machines wash and dry our clothes and dishes. Disposables — aluminum foil, zip lock bags, diapers — save time and energy. Satellite dishes replace rabbit ears and beam 300 television channels into multiple TV sets.

I'm thankful I grew up when we could safely play outdoors, and I enjoy the good-old-days' stories that come across the Internet; but without even touching on the lifesaving medical and pharmaceutical advances, an honest look at the good old days shatters any idyllic images. Even low-water toilets are better than chamber pots and outhouses. Recall what life was like before:

- Air conditioning
- Frost-free refrigerators, self-cleaning ovens, microwaves
- Cars with seat belts, air bags, heat, air conditioning, turn signals
- Blow dryers, curling irons, and Velcro rollers
- Washers, dryers, and perma-press clothes, fitted sheets with deep pockets
- Computers, e-mail, the Internet, copy machines
- Speed dialing, call waiting, caller ID, and cell phones
- Contact lenses, hearing aids that fit in the ear canal, dental implants
- Moistened wipes that clean everything from a baby's bottom to the bathroom sink
- Convenience foods — packaged, frozen, microwavable
- ATMs, automatic deposit, credit cards
- Cellophane tape, duct tape, glue guns

At first women shunned cake mixes and prepackaged foods, but each generation moves toward more convenience. Nothing was instant about Sunday dinner at MamMaw's house—a weekly ritual for my family. My dad's parents lived on a small farm and raised most of what they ate. In hindsight, I marvel at the effort it took to prepare those delicious meals. Tilling and weeding the garden, feeding and watering the animals, then churning the butter, kneading the bread, shelling the peas, canning the excess —it's now hard for us to imagine living that way.

My grandmother bought fertilized chicken eggs, hatched the chicks under a naked light bulb, then moved them to the chicken yard where she fed them and cleaned the coops. For Sunday dinners she rang a chicken's neck, plucked the feathers, cut it into servings, and stood over a skillet of popping grease frying it.

My mother bought a whole chicken and cut it up. I buy skinless, boneless chicken breasts, and my daughters buy ready-to-eat chicken. My granddaughters pop chicken fingers into the microwave.

Regrettably, none of it tastes as good as MamMaw's free-range chicken fried in lard and bacon grease. However, it takes little refection on my part to know that if it were up to me to wring a chicken's neck, neither taste nor fat content would be the issue.

In fact, the best foods from our past are usually loaded with fat and calories, so I prefer to wow the family with made-from-scratch originals only on special occasions. Most of the time, I appreciate the premixed, precooked, just-add-water convenience foods that allow me to save my energy for more interesting activities.

My friends who winter in Arizona have the right idea. Kudos go to the hostess who entertains with the least effort. Instead of dicing and slicing ingredients for a ten-step recipe, they spend their days reading, crafting, playing cards, and on the golf course. When guests come, they nuke frozen entrees, toss salad from a bag, serve simple desserts, and depend on camaraderie to be the highlight of the evening. No one is disappointed.

We won't be disappointed if we embrace today's technological advances designed for our comfort, convenience, and safety, although, I do find myself longing for a TV with a simple on-off button. I'd be happy to walk across the room to use it. I can navigate the Internet and drive the motor home along the interstate highway system, but I cannot get the hang of three remote controls with close to fifty buttons on each. I fantasize about a robot that responds to my voice command. I name the TV show I want to watch or record, and it chooses cable, antenna, satellite, DVD, surround sound — whatever the optimum setting are — and does *not* tell me how easy it is.

As the baby boom becomes the senior boom, manufacturers cater to our needs. Devices — electric-lift recliners, extenders for hair brushes, bottle attachments that help shaking hands apply eye drops, ergonomic keyboards for those whose arthritis prevents using a regular keyboard — extend independent living.

The American Society on Aging sponsors "Product Design for an Aging Society." Last year's winners included a protective, padded girdle to prevent hip fractures, a utility knife with a retractable blade, an underarm thermometer, and more.

Moisture-enriched pantyhose and moistened wipes to clean the silver and toss are now on the market. House paint that warms the house in winter and cools it in summer and electronic fruit bowls designed to optimize freshness are coming soon.

I'm hoping the engineers and inventors turn their genius to things like microwave popcorn that doesn't leave husks in my teeth; plastic packaging that doesn't take a machete to open; mascara and fingernail polish that comes in containers small enough to be used up before they go bad; a shower with a thermostat that flashes green when the water temperature reaches a pre-programmed setting and maintains that temperature until I turn it off. What's on your list?

The Bible says, "Ask and you shall receive." We need to use the baby boomers' buying power to ask for products and services that benefit the aged.

Keeping up sometimes involves more than convenience. We wouldn't buy a carton of milk without checking the date, yet we often base decisions on outdated information. Medical practices that changed little over decades now change in a matter of months.

We've come a long way since the best medical minds of the day drained almost five pints of blood from George Washington, probably killing him in an effort to save him. Viennese psychiatrist Franz Mesmer treated his patients by playing a glass armonica. He used Ben Franklin's invention (a refinement of rubbing fingers around wine glass rims) to "mesmerize" his patients and relieve depression and nervous disorders.

By the middle of this century, today's medical advances will be as outdated as those of earlier centuries. Scientists working on the Human Genome Project are identifying the three billion letters in the human genetic code that predict an *average* age of ninety years, so prepare for rapid changes in medical practice.

Patients and doctors alike are slow to change. It's taken years for women to realize they are at a greater risk for heart disease than for breast cancer. Twenty percent of the population still puts butter on burns, a bad idea. Butter, however, may be better on your bread than hard stick margarine. Check it out.

After a twenty-year drift to more complex and costlier drugs, clinical trials sponsored by the National Heart, Lung, and Blood

Institute show that diuretics, medically and economically, are the best choice for treating high blood pressure.

Cardiologists are looking at stress tests in a whole new way. A study at the Cleveland Clinic Foundation found that what happens in the minutes *after* you step off the treadmill is an important risk predictor.

C-reactive protein (CRP) has been added to the list of usual suspects in the fight against heart disease. A study at Brigham and Women's Hospital concludes that high levels of inflammation are twice as likely to cause a fatal heart attack or stroke as high cholesterol and may explain why 77 percent of the women who have a heart attack have normal cholesterol levels. High blood pressure, smoking, and chronic infections anywhere in the body can produce inflammatory proteins, which damage blood vessels. Inflammation of the lining of an artery wall can break away and obstruct the artery. The same things that lower cholesterol — diet, exercise, statins, aspirin — lower CRP, so you may already be doing the right thing. If not, ask your doctor about an inexpensive test for CRP. It may keep you from needing CPR.

We're learning that fever helps the body fight infection and shouldn't be suppressed except in the very young and very old. And don't be surprised if the baby boys in your family are no longer circumcised. That's the recommendation of the American Academy of Pediatrics.

Did you know that if you're over seventy you may not need PAP smears? If you're not sexually active, it's possible you can stop having them at a younger age. Check with your doctor. The new guidelines, however, do *not* mean you can stop having an annual physical that includes a gynecological exam.

A healthy lifestyle includes being a health-conscious consumer who keeps up with changes and seeks out the best practitioners and health facilities.

Practice prevention

Play it safe by getting a flu shot every year, a pneumonia shot every five years, and a tetanus shot every ten years. The CDC says 80 percent of the more than 20,000 flu deaths and more than 40,000 bacterial pneumonia deaths are preventable with vaccination.

What was merely hinted at a few years ago is gaining credibility: There is a link between Alzheimer's disease and lifestyle, possibly more than genes. The same risk factors for heart disease — diabetes, high blood pressure, excess weight, high cholesterol, and lack of exercise — are risk factors for Alzheimer's.

Studies are currently underway to determine if a new form of chickenpox vaccine prevents painful shingles attacks that affect a million Americans every year, most of them elderly. Until a vaccine is available, seek immediate medical attention at the first signs of a rash or skin sensitivity. An antiviral agent given within three days of the onset may decrease the length and severity of the disease.

Schedule mammography, colon, and skin cancer screenings. Visit your doctor annually for an exam that includes blood and urine analyses to identify potentially deadly diseases in their early and most treatable stages.

Thoroughly cook eggs, meat, and poultry. Promptly refrigerate leftovers and doggie bags from restaurants. Cut raw sprouts from sandwiches and salads. Review the food handling tips in Chapter 3.

If you're still smoking, no matter how many times you've tried to quit, it's worth another try. The fatality rates from lung cancer and a fist full of other diseases caused by smoking make quitting the most positive thing you can do for your health. On top of that, the National Fire Prevention Association says more fatal fires start from smoking than from any other cause.

Get a medical alert bracelet or necklace for yourself or family members with diabetes, severe allergies, or Alzheimer's.

Go to the hospital by ambulance to increase the chance of receiving lifesaving therapies within the "golden hour." Call 911 so the hospital can anticipate your arrival and be ready to administer treatment immediately. In some areas, ambulance crews are qualified to begin treatment before you reach the hospital, decreasing the extent of permanent damage from a heart attack or stroke. Make sure your address is clearly visible to assist emergency personnel in finding your home quickly.

Take advantage of the newest therapies by seeking a second opinion and doing your own research. We hated losing the Dr. Welby's in our life — but do we really want to return to the days when the doctor patted us on the head and said not to worry? I don't. However, more choice means more responsibility to education ourselves. Don't count on your doctor to send you a reminder that it's time for a checkup, a flu shot, or a mammogram. If you want to be a partner in your own healthcare decisions, be prepared to make some tough choices.

Lumpectomy or mastectomy? Caught early, a tumor under three centimeters may be treated with a lumpectomy and a new five-day internal radiation procedure instead of radical surgery, chemo, and six or seven weeks of radiation. It is not a choice to be made lightly, but it is one worth checking into.

It's the "practice of medicine" and we all know that practice makes perfect (or almost). For complicated procedures, to the extent your medical coverage allows, find the hospital and surgeon with the most experience. Information is available if you ask.

Doing 300,000 hip replacements a year (a number expected to double within twelve years), has given doctors plenty of practice and brought improved techniques. Before having surgery, check out new minimally-invasive procedures that reduce pain and recovery time and the metal-on-metal implants, which last decades longer. Severe back pain? See if you're a candidate to have acrylic cement injected into deteriorating vertebra to stabilize your spine.

In a few years you may be able to swallow a tiny camera or inhale helium to allow your doctor to view internal organs. A synthetic version of Gila monster venom may replace insulin injections for the 17 million Type II diabetics. Brain cell transplants for stroke victims and "pacemakers for the brain," which will treat depression, are on the drawing board. Just remember. None of these medical advances can prevent simple home accidents. That's up to us.

Take falls out of your future

Falls, including a thousand hip-fractures a day, are the sixth-leading cause of death in older adults. The American Geriatric Society says 40 percent of falls are caused by something in the environment. More than 200,000 injuries a year — 500 emergency room visits a day — occur in home bathrooms, so put up grab bars, get bath mats with nonskid backing, and apply rubber adhesive strips to the tub or shower floor. If it's difficult to stand long enough to shower, get a shower stool and a hand-held shower head.

Eliminate tripping hazards like throw rugs and magazines stacked on the floor. Avoid using a ladder or step stool by putting everything within reach. Rearrange cabinets and make your next refrigerator a side-by-side model that puts more food in easy reach.

For additional tips call 1-800-824-2663, for the American Academy of Orthopaedic Surgeons' brochure *Don't Let a Fall Be Your Last Trip.*

Homeland security

The Department of Homeland Security has made suggestions for preparing for a terrorist attack. Having an evacuation route plan, a supply of bottled water, a battery-operated radio with extra batteries, canned food and a can opener, etc. are good ways to prepare for terrorists, tornadoes, or other natural disasters.

The truth about terrorism, however, is that you're much more likely to experience a disaster in your own home than from an attack. Take the time to create a personal home security plan. Read and reread articles on safety, and build a moat of security around your home.

Deadbolts on the doors, windows that lock, motion-detecting outdoor lights, and monitored alarm systems promote security. However, only you can assure your safety. Keep your valuables in a safe or safe deposit box. Install a peephole large enough and low enough for you to see out, and *never* opened the door to a stranger.

Don't answer the door or let anyone you are not expecting or don't recognize come into your home. Having a uniform — police, utility company, or business — doesn't mean someone is legitimate. With the door locked, ask for a name and phone number to call and verify their story. Women have lost their lives by letting an official-looking person in to "check for a gas leak." Don't hide keys under doormats or flower pots — thieves know all about those places. And no matter how distressed a person asking for help seems, don't let them in. Offer to call 911.

To prevent accidental scalding, reset the hot water heater to 120 degrees. At this temperature it takes ten minutes to get burned. At the manufacturer's setting of 140 degrees, third-degree burns occur in six seconds. As an added bonus, you'll save on water-heating costs.

Smoke detectors and carbon monoxide alarms are inexpensive lifesavers. Change the batteries each fall when you set the clocks to go off daylight saving time, and replace alarms every ten years. Avoid space heaters. If that's not possible, buy the type that automatically shut off when turned over. Have a fire extinguisher handy and know how to use it.

If you know you've gotten forgetful, keep a book to read or some project to work on in the kitchen, and never leave the room while you're cooking. Avoid wearing clothing with loose floppy sleeves that may ignite if you get too close to the burners.

Take care with candles. Almost 13,000 fires and 150 deaths occur annually, mostly when candles are left unattended and near combustible materials. Burn non-paraffin candles with lead-free wicks, especially if you have respiratory problems. Better yet, opt for good smelling potpourri.

Always wear a seatbelt in the car and a helmet when biking. More adults than children die from bike-related accidents. Park in well-lighted areas and have your key ready to open the car door. Store packages out of sight.

The risk of Deep Vein Thrombosis (DVT), often associated with long-distance travel by car, plane, or train, increases with age. An Oxford-based Aviation Health Institute survey found that 64 percent of the DVT airline incidents occurred in women. DVT, the formation of a blood clot in a deep vein, usually in the leg, is not life-threatening unless the clot breaks loose and travels to a lung or the brain. Airline travelers are encouraged to wiggle their toes, feet, and ankles while seated and occasionally walk the aisles. The Flight Flexor (www.InnovativeFitness.tv) is ideal for long flights. When traveling by car, it's advisable to make frequent stops to get out and stretch your legs. If you're at high risk for blood clots, consider wearing compression stockings, taking aspirin, or getting a blood-thinning injection before long trips.

Even scarier than a blood clot is having your gas tank explode, so avoid getting back in your car while pumping gas warns the Petroleum Equipment Institute. What seems sensible — getting back in your vehicle during cold weather — can cause a flash fire sparked by static electricity when you get out of the vehicle to remove the nozzle. Play it safe and brave the heat or cold while fueling your car.

Grandparenting is hazardous duty

Can you think of anything more regretful than having a grandchild get seriously injured or die while in your care? Most grandparents conscientiously buckle their charges into car seats, strap on their helmets, and attentively watch while they swim, but they aren't always aware of new hazards. Small changes, such as children properly restrained in the back seat and putting infants to sleep on their backs, have a big impact.

Child safety seats have more than halved infant death rates. A national campaign on airbag safety alerted parents to the danger of putting infants and small children in the front seat, and deaths declined by 90 percent while the number of airbag-equipped cars increased.

Sudden Infant Death Syndrome (SIDS), the leading cause of death in babies after one month of age, has declined by as much as 80 percent since mothers were advised to place babies on their backs to sleep. For years, we were told to put babies on their stomachs. Since the American Academy of Pediatrics' guidelines changed, there has been no increase in the number of choking deaths; and the flat spots on the backs of babies' heads are temporary. This simple change prevents several thousand crib deaths a year.

Studies show uninflated latex balloons or pieces of popped balloons are the leading cause of choking deaths among children under six years old. If a piece of latex is sucked across a child's airway it's usually impossible to reach medical help in time to save the child. The Heimlich maneuver doesn't work. In our sue-happy society I'm amazed to see businesses that put themselves at risk by passing out balloons. In fact, a major network news magazine gave balloons to young septuplets celebrating their birthday. At least fifteen years ago, hospitals discouraged balloon bouquets in pediatric units and requested the substitution of Mylar balloons. Now many hospitals forbid latex balloons, citing the choking hazard for children and allergic reactions for people of all ages.

For years, the Window Covering Safety Council has issued warnings about the hazards of the cords on blinds and offers free repair kits (800-506-4636) for old-style installations, yet children continue to strangle to death when they become entangled in the loop-style cords.

Seven years ago, the FDA warned that Lindane, a drug used to treat lice, could cause brain or nerve damage when overused; yet it still happens. Why take a chance when there are safer products on the market?

Small toys, whole grapes, hot dogs, chips, and raw vegetables in chucks large enough to lodge in a child's windpipe are just a few of the things that cause choking deaths each year. And who would have thought that children's favorite sandwich ingredient could be the world's most allergenic food? Peanuts lead the list of fatal food allergy reactions, and researchers suggest babies not be exposed to these healthy legumes until their immune system fully develops.

Doing the little things that keep ourselves and those around us safe reduces the possibility for regrets and allows us to reflect on the possibilities for the future.

André Gide offers this bit of wisdom about letting the past get in the way of the future: "Though loyalty to the past, our mind refuses to realize that tomorrow's joy is possible only if today's makes way for it; that each wave owes the beauty of its line only to the withdrawal of the preceding one."

You can withdraw to your recliner and wait for death to end your misery or you can consider your problems like those of Henry Kaiser — "opportunities in work clothes" — and role up your sleeves and get to work.

Exercise Your Options

Do not let your chances like sunbeams pass you by,
For you never miss the water 'till the well runs dry.

— Rowland Howard

Don't squander the last quarter of life pondering the possibilities. You can stew about something until the cows come home, but tough decisions aren't like cheap cuts of beef that soften with lengthy cooking. Conventional wisdom suggests long-term planning, with a careful weighing of options before making decisions — a tough choice at an age when long term is shorter and options are fewer.

The dictionary describes conventional as *not original or spontaneous* and wisdom as *knowledge* and *good judgment*, making conventional wisdom an oxymoron worth rethinking. From Mae West, the exemplar of the unconventional comes, "He who hesitates is last." Like Cinderella in Stephen Sondheim's musical *Into the Woods*, West knew that "Opportunity is not a lengthy visitor."

Analysis paralysis denied American companies the early lead in global electronics markets. We delayed production to enhance products with cutting edge technology. While we sliced, diced, and fine-tuned, Japanese manufacturers roared past us for the lion's share of the market. U.S. companies recouped their losses by going to market with the best they had and adding innovations to each new model — the "new and improved" sales pitch Proctor and Gamble has used for years.

Apple Computer developer Guy Kawasaki increased sales with "raging, inexorable thunder-lizard evangelists." I don't know what a thunder lizard is, but it sounds like a reptile that counts his money while the wise old owl sits on his perch pondering.

And here's what Abe Lincoln had to say about waiting to act while pondering the future: "Things may come to those who wait, but only the things left by those who hustle." A fictitious peek at 1900's Dodge City, demonstrates that even hustlers have trouble predicting the future.

A visiting salesman convinces the town leaders that the world's largest cattle market is going the way of River City. The monster isn't pool with a capital "P." It's manure with a capital "M." A steady flow of cattle herds, horses, and buggy traffic predicts knee-high manure in twenty years. At least that's what the entrepreneur selling shovels and swampland on the edge of town said. But he didn't count on Henry Ford and the horse-less carriage. By the beginning of this century, we had forgotten the effects of twenty or so pounds of manure dumped on the streets by each four-legged transport. Our four-wheeled vehicles have become the pollution villains. Now on our side of the ocean, President Bush launches an initiative to produce hydrogen-powered cars; and in rural South Africa, women cook on gas stoves using biogas generated from cattle dung. Who knew!

In 1979, attempting to solve its exploding population problem, China initiated a one-child-per-family policy. They didn't count on the cultural bias that favors boys, and sex-selection practices led to a new crisis — millions of marriage-age men with no one to marry.

The aerospace industry's long-term plans didn't count on the end of the cold war. The savings and loan deregulators prepared for prosperity. They couldn't foresee fraud and Keating-type cheating; and who among us could have predicted that terrorists and a slumping economy would turn our nest eggs into chicken feed?

Many successful people have had the door slammed in their faces before they found the key to success. Fred Astaire was told he didn't dance well enough to be in the movies. Dorothy Harrison Eustis was told that expecting blind people to trust dogs was outrageous. John Kilcullen was told people wouldn't buy books that called them dummies. Siegfried and Roy were told magic wouldn't work in Las Vegas; and television network executives told National Football League Commissioner Pete Rozelle that people wouldn't watch *Monday Night Football.*

For a more recent example, consider the post-September 11 prediction that Americans would stay home watching TV and videos rather than go out to movies. Wrong. Within the next year, Hollywood was setting box-office records.

Individuals, companies, and countries fail at predicting the future, so why should we expect our perfect plans to stand the test of time? Is it all a matter of luck?

Lucille Ball said she didn't know anything about luck. "I've never banked on it, and I'm afraid of people who do. Luck to me is something else; hard work and realizing what is opportunity and what isn't." Numerous others echo the "luck is preparation meeting opportunity" message.

When a football player grabs a fumble and races down the field for a touchdown, it's called a lucky break, yet it is equally his preparation and alertness. Joan is that kind of lucky — prepared for whatever life brings.

As a rebellious teenager, her life in the fast lane led to a car crash that landed her in a hospital bed for six months, lucky to be alive. After months of therapy, one leg was still two inches shorter than the other. She felt lucky to walk without a limp and smiled so big that no one looked at her feet. Joan finished medical school, married, and set up her practice. Her mother managed the office and the space behind the reception area became her four-month-old daughter's nursery.

Luckily, her second daughter was born the week before boards. Joan and her week-old baby flew to Chicago for the test to become a board-certified obstetrician/gynecologist. A third pregnancy and delivering twenty babies a month took its toll. Joan's back couldn't stand the strain, and doctors said she needed surgery to lengthen her leg. As luck would have it, a surgeon in Dallas recommended shortening the longer one instead. "Besides, he explained, "short people live longer." Now she wouldn't have to hear her three-year-old say, "Mommy, you have funny shoes."

Joan didn't depend on luck at the hospital. She marked "wrong leg, wrong leg" all the way down the shorter leg and; after a successful surgery and several months of therapy, she was standing tall.

Now another problem surfaced. Three children under age five made it impossible to continue delivering babies and be the mom she wanted to be. Against the advice of colleagues, she limited her practice to gynecology and spent more time with her young family, returning to obstetrics when they were older.

Wanting to share her good fortune with the community, she ran for a spot on the school board. When a runoff election resulted, she had the option of canceling her trip to France for her brother's wedding celebration. Instead she campaigned until the day she left and trusted her family and friends to handle the last minute details. Four days later, in Paris, she learned she had won with 66 percent of the vote.

Each time she got lucky, Joan had an opportunity to say, "I can't." Instead, she was prepared to exercise her options in spite of the obstacles. No waiting until the baby was older to start her practice. No postponing boards until a more convenient time. No neglecting her family or disappointing her brother.

In addition to heading a group practice, she and her family took the opportunity to join a downtown revitalization effort and opened a bed and breakfast and later a spa. Of course, when the businesses flourished, some said that she was just lucky.

The odds of being struck by lightning are greater than the odds you'll get a knock on the door by the prize patrol. It's a nice fantasy, though, dreaming of far away places, luxury cars, and endowing a favorite charity. Even those in the lap of luxury, however, have to stand up and do some things — like exercising and flossing — for themselves. Although a personal trainer helps, only our own sweat gets results. High-dollar dentures are still false teeth.

The truth is we have to make our own luck. Remember the crossword quiz in Chapter 1? Often the same word takes on a different meaning depending on whether it's used as a noun or verb. People are like that. Some choose to be a thing and wait for something to happen to them; others take action and make things happen.

Donna Gold is a verb — she discovered early that there's more than one way to (cat lovers please note my discretion) do things.

In elementary school, Donna wanted to run for school treasurer, but drew the short straw for a ballot with room for only four names. Not one to leave something this important to chance, she complained to the principal and got permission for a write-in campaign. With a clever campaign slogan, "Let Gold take care of your gold" and a creative volunteer job, she beat her four male rivals in a landslide. The volunteer job? She helped young students with their handwriting — including teaching them to write her name.

One of my volunteer jobs brought a similar turn of fortune. In 1970, as president of the Irving Republican Women's Club, I was responsible for opening and staffing our small campaign headquarters. Wanting to make a big splash with my first assignment, I wrote a letter inviting the first lady to our grand opening, not knowing local organizations are expected to pay campaign-trip expenses. (My Jewish friends called it chutzpah; I prefer to call it enthusiastic ignorance.) Fortunately, after a few sleepless nights, a reply came from the White House saying the first lady was unavailable. Whew!

Undaunted, I invited the wife of a Texas congressman running for the Senate to do the honors. Since he was speaking at a rally in Dallas, travel expenses for his wife weren't a problem. She graciously agreed.

Red, white, and blue bunting and balloons welcomed our special guest. While we waited for the photographer to arrive for the ribbon cutting, she and I chatted about our children and schools. A typical mother, she discussed the concerns she had about her children changing schools. Texas schools taught state, national, and world history in one order; new schools might be on another schedule, so she worried they might miss something.

The photographer arrived, and I posed candidates with our guest, missing my own chance to have my picture taken with a first lady — just twenty years ahead of her time. And she needn't have worried about her "boys" missing a history lesson. They are making their own history.

"You just don't luck into things as much as you'd like to think you do. You build step by step, whether it's friendship or opportunities," Barbara Bush says. Although her long-range plans probably didn't include stints as first lady and first mother, her philosophy explains why she excels at every role.

So if it isn't a question of how well you plan or how lucky you are, what's the solution? Like the former first lady says, it's a step-by-step process — a theme that begins with this book's title and continues from one chapter to the next. Forecast sunshine, prepare for rain. If you forget your umbrella, you may get lucky or you may get wet.

Preparing for a variety of possibilities improves the odds that you'll be prepared when opportunity knocks.

Prune in winter to enjoy roses in the spring

Simplifying and pruning some of the *stuff* is the first step in finding time to smell the roses. The KISS (Keep It Simple, Stupid) principle doesn't mean kissing everything good-bye. It means concentrating on what's important — pruning the unnecessary.

Business leaders, politicians, scientists, and naturalists equate the KISS principle with success. James Carville credits the 1992 Clinton campaign victory to focusing on one simple message — the economy. British scientist John Dalton, reduced complicated data into its simplest form to discover the atomic theory of matter. On fulfilling dreams, Henry David Thoreau said, "As you simplify your life, the laws of the universe will be simpler." And motivational author Stephen Covey says, "The main thing is to keep the main thing the main thing."

For me, and probably for most of you, the main thing is living to an independent old age, which means every option should be based on that goal. One-third of our day is consumed with sleep; another third is eaten up with buying and preparing our food and dealing with clothing, shelter, and transportation.

Repairing, cleaning, and moving our stuff from one place to another eats up much of the last third. Organizing, simplifying, and downsizing eases the burden. Watching my mother and mother-in-law suffer through moving to a retirement facility after a health crisis convinced me to begin the process while in good health.

My mom went from teenager to wife during the depression and, like many of her generation, kept *everything* — just in case. Jack (whom she married after my father died) and his eight siblings truly knew hard times. They stuffed paper in their shoes, went hungry, and nearly froze when blue northers swept across their Texas farm. Riding the rails to California to pick cherries at age thirteen made Jack a lifelong hoarder.

For more than twenty-five years, these garage-sale soul mates enjoyed a Peter and Paul life. They even had two old motor homes so they could rob parts from one to keep the other running. The house and outbuildings bulged with bargains that stretched their small pension into the good life. When Jack died suddenly, the bargains became a burden. Over several years and many tears, Mother gave away, sold, and buried their treasures, then moved from the acreage on the river to a small place in town.

After her second stroke she could no longer live alone 200 miles from me. The move to a studio apartment in a retirement home meant giving up more memories. She kept pictures, scrapbooks, and needlework projects, but rods, reels, tackle boxes, and old fishing hats had to go. She and my father had wrapped rods, poured weights, fashioned lures and flies, and hand-tied crab nets. Fishing was a favorite hobby for her and Jack too, so saying good-bye to a half-century of fishing and all the attached memories was heart wrenching.

My mother-in-law happily gave her lovely crystal, china, and antique furniture to family members. For her, closets full of clothes — some from the '30s — were the problem. Worn-out raincoats, appropriate for Seattle weather, mingled with wool coats from the Minneapolis winters of her younger years. We deviously filled bags for trash or charity while she napped. I slyly buried a once-fashionable stole — beady-eyed foxes staring up from moth-eaten bodies — in the bottom of a garbage bag. Expedience required destroying her memories without knowing which might bring pain or pleasure.

I wanted to make my own painful trash and treasure decisions. If you haven't had similar motivating experiences, pretend a fire or flood destined to destroy everything you have is imminent. You have ten minutes to load what will fit into your car. Tick off the treasures in your head, then take a slow walk around the house looking in closets and drawers to see what you missed. Pretty scary? Well it's not nearly as scary as trying to make these decisions while lying in a hospital bed, drugged and disoriented.

The first obstacle may be your spouse and children. Put grown children on notice when you begin the downsizing process. Cheerleader costumes from high school and wedding gifts waiting for the bigger house are their responsibility. If your spouse is reluctant, at every opportunity point out the advantages of less stuff, a smaller place, or whatever is your goal.

After an ice-skating career and 34 years of teaching dance, Mary Gordon closed her studio and began planning for a more relaxed lifestyle. It took years to convince her husband to sell their big house for the convenience of a smaller place. She got her foot in the door when Bill reluctantly agreed to fix up the house and put it on the market while they looked for something smaller. She took the drapes off the walls, removed the pictures, and packed the china in preparation for painters and the impending sale.

When everything was finished, the place looked so nice Bill decided he didn't want to move. She refused to give in, so for years they lived without drapes on the windows and borrowed dishes from a neighbor when cooking for a crowd. Bill wasn't interested in going to look at some new condos under construction, so Mary Gordon went alone. She fell in love with them and reserved a prime location. Without telling Bill she would forfeit her deposit in forty-eight hours, she and her daughter dragged him (almost literally, she says) away from a televised football game to see the homes. He approved and after a ten-year wait they are both enjoying condo living.

Your move to a smaller place may be years away, but it's never too early to sift through the stuff in the attic and basement. We discovered unpacked boxes from when we'd combined possessions twenty years before. Over the years haphazard spring cleaning and an occasional garage sale had weeded out a few things, but nothing of the magnitude required for giving up a 1000 square feet of space.

I adopted the "use it or lose it" philosophy of friends Roger and Jan, who begin each year by ridding closets and drawers of anything not used in the past twelve months, and imposed my own "functional or fashionable" litmus test on the downsizing.

Don't throw out the baby with the bath water

A word of caution before you begin sorting the trash from the treasure: Don't throw out a combination lock worth several hundred dollars or a vintage perfume bottle worth several thousand. Check with the experts. A trip to the bookstore and the library turned up several good books on collectibles and antiques. Listings include every type of collectible — bottle openers, swizzle sticks, calendars, souvenir spoons, and more. A virtual browse on the Internet reveals the ordinary as well as offbeat items people collect.

Would you believe people collect dirt? Not the kind that sticks to the bottom of your shoes, unless of course you've been traipsing though a celebrity's flowerbed. If so, you can display it in some clever container and sell it or submit your soil sample to the Museum of Dirt at www.planet.com/dirtweb/dirt. I stopped laughing when I realize I had some common ground with these folks. I have not one, but *two*, dirt collections. My Sanibel Island seashells rest on a bed of Florida's white beach sand, and a colorful glass bottle made from volcanic ash holds Mount St. Helen's ashes swept from my mother-in-law's Portland porch.

Our attic produced a World War II army blanket and a box of old newspapers commemorating long past presidential elections and space flights. Remember when we got up before dawn and held our breath watching those early ventures into space? Surely the grandchildren will prize these bits of history, I thought. Wrong! In this day of space stations and missions to Mars watching John Glenn puddle jump into the Atlantic held little interest for them. They were as interested as I would have been at their age if invited to watch someone crank a Model-T. Besides, they can see the flight in living color on the evening news and hear Mission Control's conversations with the astronauts on their computer. I checked a popular online auction house and found my brittle yellowed treasures worthless.

It would be easy to chide my mother-in-law for the forty coffee cans she saved, except for the large plastic bag of tea tins I had in the attic. We save these items expecting to someday use them to organize our stuff, but they just become more stuff. I kept those tins for twenty years, envisioning them painted in bright colors sitting in a row with labels on each one. I must be the only one who didn't realize their only practical use was holding tea because we couldn't even give them away in a garage sale.

Although I'm not a value-minded collector (somehow I think you knew this), *you* may have some treasures hidden in your attic.

Pat and her husband, Dick, do appraisals and hold estate sales and auctions. Pat advises calling a professional first. She says that often a family has already thrown away valuable items before they call her. I can believe that. I expected to haul off a rusty wheelbarrow after my mother's yard sale. Fortunately we hired a professional to help—Janie retrieved the wheelbarrow from the trash pile and sold it for $100!

Even the professionals are sometimes surprised. About five years ago Pat bought a box of Madam Alexander doll clothes for $12. When her granddaughters outgrew dressing dolls, she sold the used doll clothes for $3,000! Antique dealer Walt Brygier rescued a wealth of documents when a box on its way to the trash fell apart scattering letters, drawings, and manuscript revisions. A fortuitous accident that brought $80,600 at auction for the papers that belonged to the late author and poet Carl Sandburg.

Digging through a box of dusty books in her Kentucky basement, Cherry found a recipe for fried chicken with eleven herbs and spices tucked in an old ledger. Not surprising to her since the house once belonged to Harland and Claudia Sanders, but apparently a surprise to KFC, who thought it belonged to them. When a judge ruled otherwise, KFC denied it was the original recipe (sure!). With the recipe safely locked away, Cherry and her husband, Tommy, continue operating the restaurant named for the Colonel's wife while they consider their options. They're more excited about the number 202 than eleven. Claudia Sander's Dinner House made *Southern Living's* best 202 things to do in the south list — and became another place to visit on my ATB list.

Your family may not have a famous recipe, but it's worth checking through any boxes of old books and magazines. Thinking old magazines couldn't be worth much, heirs sold a whole box full for $5 at an estate sale. It turns out many of the ads in the magazines were worth more than $5 each, but the real find was a celebrity golf tournament program autographed by most of the participants — names like Mickey Mantle, Joe DiMaggio, and Joe Namath.

You may not find any cash under Mom and Dad's mattress, but they may have bought one of the soup can look-a-like mini safes or stashed a diamond ring in a medicine bottle under the cotton. It's happened, so don't be too fast in sorting through their belongings.

Now back to your own salvage operation. When you've sorted the keepers from the rest, it's time to maximize the storage space.

Stretch the space

In an *Investor's Business Daily* article, Hunter Jameson describes how Westinghouse Electric Corp. reduced costs by 30 percent by standardizing and changing the shape of fuel-storage tanks. Rectangles became cylinders with fewer seams and one-size caps for all heights. Hewlett-Packard Co., by setting guidelines for length, width, and breadth of printers, requires one-third less shipping space. New printers have twenty-five parts compared to more than 200 in the original models.

These value management techniques are particularly applicable to the kitchen. Optimize cabinet storage by trading all the odd sized mixing bowls for one set of five to seven nesting bowls and stacking casserole dishes with lids inverted.

A small pan, a large stockpot, two or three sizes in between and a couple of skillets are more than can fit on the top of the stove at once. Retire the rest. A microwave steamer or a pot with a lid and removable steamer rack can replace the vegetable steamer, rice cooker, and several other appliances. Do you have a deep fryer that hasn't held grease since lard became a four-letter word? And when did you last use the slow cooker, individual salt and pepper shakers, or fondue pot?

Take inventory and keep only the things you use. This exercise resurrected several items I hadn't used in years. A few I've kept, others were more trouble to clean than their convenience warranted.

A good set of knives, a grater, and one chopper can do the job of a gaggle of gadgets like an egg slicer, nut chopper, cheese slicer, and garlic press. Sharpen the keepers, cut the others. Food processors and blenders are great if you use them. If not, pass them on to someone who will.

Purge the plastic

Most refrigerators can't hold our stash of plastic containers for storing leftovers. Lidless, pitted, and stained containers clutter cabinets. Fond reminders of long ago Tupperware parties mingle with salvaged butter tubs and cottage cheese containers, all stuffed together Fibber McGee style. Six stacking containers for leftovers and a few larger ones that go from freezer to microwave for make-ahead recipes will suffice.

Freezer bags save even more space. Place a bag inside a microwave-safe container, pour in soup, sauce, or stew. Put it in the freezer until thoroughly frozen, remove the dish, label the bag, and store frozen. The contents fit perfectly in the microwave dish for heating later.

Full-time RVers Joe and Dee were a great source of downsizing ideas. An outside compartment under their coach holds cake pans, the turkey roaster, and large serving bowls used occasionally, leaving the limited indoor space for frequently used items. I adopted their idea in my condo, with floor to ceiling shelves in a laundry room closet. Middle shelves hold things most often used, higher and lower shelves accommodate the mixer, blender, and things used less frequently. Cabinets in your garage or basement work as well.

If you're overwhelmed, start with things you aren't emotionally attached to — linens for example. You need only one set of sheets for each bed. A linen closet stuffed with extra sheets and pillowcases waiting for the once a year upchuck wastes space. One spare set to fit the largest bed works for emergencies, unless you have a family prone to stomach upsets or bed-wetting. In this case, medical advice is more appropriate than more sheets. Wash the bedding once a week and immediately remake the bed. Voilà — fresh linens without having to fold contour sheets.

The same principle applies to towels. Buy pretty towels that match your decor and have plenty of racks to hang one for your body, one for your hair, and several hand towels. Wash and return them to their racks weekly. We put the same toothbrush in our mouth twice a day for six months; surely we can use the same towel seven times. To cut down on the number of washcloths you need, try a personal bath sponge. It dries between uses and lasts longer than a washcloth.

Antique indicates something from an earlier time that may have some value. We had mostly "antechs" — items of no value antiquated by technology. Why, I wondered, do we have liquid paper, carbon paper, and a typewriter eraser (the kind with a brush on end) when we have two computers and no typewriter? Calculators, slide rules, even an abacus jockeyed for space among India ink, dried-out pens, and ink cartridges. And why save stencils when the computer prints any size and style letter we desire? Other than the slide rule Vince began his engineering career with, the antech gadgets succumbed to high-tech gismos that no doubt will be obsolete by the time I learn to use them. That's progress.

Cracked, crazed, and generally ugly pots, along with every floral vase I ever received, were rooted in cabinets all over the house. Half of a 200-year-old bud vase collected dust as if someone was expecting it would magically regain its broken top. An antique dealer paid $50 each for a couple of vases. Others were given to family members or sold at a garage sale. The few pots and vases we kept for aesthetic and sentimental reasons are displayed or used several times a year, making the "use it or lose it" policy a nice justification for buying fresh flowers.

Hang it, hook it, or hide it

Hang it from the ceiling, store it under the bed or over the door, stash it under a skirt. For an uncluttered living area, stow a stack of magazines or videos under a skirted table or swap the coffee table for ottomans with storage. Add sofa tables and end tables with drawers and shelves.

Hang the iron and ironing board, dangle cups from hooks, store stemmed glasses upside down. Put risers in the pantry and use spice racks that lie in a drawer. Hang potholders on the inside of cabinet doors. Racks that hang over doors neatly store paperback books or tapes. Free up counter space while you cook by attaching a small square of corkboard or magnetic strip to the inside of a cabinet door to hold a recipe at eye level.

Clear plastic boxes on rollers and risers that lift the bed a few inches make putting stuff under it easier than ever. A cedar chest at the end of the bed is perfect for storing blankets and sitting on while putting on your socks and shoes. You may find narrow stacking drawers that fit next to the pipes under kitchen and bathroom sinks, an often-neglected storage area.

Plates, plants, and baskets are only the beginning of ideas for things to put on high shelves. Sandy enjoys her Christmas village collection year-round on her kitchen plant shelf. Pam's collection of Native American dolls peers down from her kitchen shelf; a glass case in the dining room holds more than 200 Hummel figurines; one bedroom sports Dallas Cowboy keepsakes and Superbowl souvenirs; the computer room holds trophies and plaques honoring personal sports and professional achievements — floor to ceiling treasures. The bathroom corrals the Texas memorabilia and salutes the Lone Star State with boots, bluebonnets, and the state flag emblazoned on towels, the rug, a soap dish, and more.

Phyllis, having gone through a similar experience to mine with her mother-in-law, chose to leave behind anything that had to be packed away when she downsized. She chose a suitable western theme to display her and Mike's Texas heritage. Her plant shelf holds his dad's handmade cowboy boots from the 1940s, her tiny childhood chair draped with chaps, a kerosene lantern, and several pieces of Mexican pottery. A quilt hangs on one wall, and a collection of family pictures adorns the adjoining dining room walls.

Phyllis plans to get the last of the small keepsake items, like a few odd pieces of silver, out of their boxes by attaching them to a grapevine wreath that fits ideally into her decor.

Bundle it, basket it, put it under glass

Creative decorating saves memorabilia and makes family keepsakes special. Mementos rescued from musty boxes and attractively displayed collections are great conversation pieces. Knowing that at some point in your life you will likely live in one or two rooms, enjoy your keepsakes while you can. If you can't find a way to display them it's time to part with them, so be creative.

Fill ballet slippers, cowboy boots, or athletic shoes with plaster of Paris and use as doorstops or bookends. Use a commemorative mug as a pencil cup. Glass domes, bowls, tall cylinders, and jars corral collections and decorate the house. Fill an old Mason jar with antique buttons, a fish bowl with seashells or matchbooks, a crystal goblet with a broken string of crystals.

Natural or painted baskets make pretty and practical containers. Try a basket to stack hot pads and kitchen towels. For a more formal setting frame grandma's cameo on a velvet background or fill a beaded evening bag with potpourri. Do you have a scarf you haven't worn in years but think you might someday? Enjoy it draped over the top of a skirted table or hanging from a circular towel hook ready to wear if you choose.

Visiting relatives appreciate the family antiques in our combination guest room/family museum, while other guests are content with a comfortable mattress under Grandmother's crocheted bedspread. Old pictures and shadowboxes cover the walls. A plant shelf displays items from parents and grandparents. A lock of hair and a dainty heart-shaped gold locket mirror the curls and locket in a childhood portrait. Another shadow box holds a dance recital picture, program, and the blue angora sweater with crystal buttons seen in the picture.

Displaying our past begins a dialog between the generations. My grandchildren are fascinated with the portrait of my mother sporting her new bobbed haircut and 1920s fashions. The Thomas Edison windup Victrola (actually an Amberola patented in 1903) that plays cylinder records begins a "before electricity" conversation. I assure them their gray-haired grandma really is that little girl with the blonde Shirley Temple curls.

Craft stores have ready-made shadow boxes in several sizes. Use velvet, felt, or satin for a background or create an original design with a piece of quilt, needlework, sheet music, or map. Try an overall bib or the back of worn jeans with a memento peeking out of the pocket for a casual look. If you prefer, a professional framer will complete the project with an interesting arrangement and matting technique. Jump-start your creativity with these three-dimensional ideas.

- A pocket watch, pocketknife, and sepia photograph.
- A picture of a veteran in uniform, medals, and letters.
- A special occasion commemorated with ticket stubs, a program, and a napkin.
- A beach vacation collage of pictures, postcards, and seashells
- An album cover and autographed picture of a favorite musician.
- A golf metal, score card, worn glove, and colorful tees.

Floating frames are ideal for sandwiching flat items between two pieces of glass — the lace handkerchief grandmother carried in her wedding, a crocheted doily, or a special letter you want to see both sides of. A few standard size frames are available or a frame shop will customize one.

If a floating fame doesn't interest you, fashion throw pillows from antique handkerchiefs, scarves, and fabric from special occasion dresses. Pull them all together with matching backs. Mount antique costume jewelry on a wall hanging, decorate switch plates, or make pushpin heads for the bulletin board or magnets for the refrigerator.

Stash old letters and special greeting cards in a mailbox — antique, modern, or decorated. Our collection includes several old postcards, including my birth announcement, touching World War II letters from Vince's father (V-mail from Africa with the censor's stamp) as well as one from an uncle who died in battle a few days after he wrote the letter, and a postcard postmarked Nov. 22, 1963 from Dallas, printed by my then five-year-old son, telling his grandmother of the day's tragedy.

The letters and cards are only valuable to our family, but they deserve a place of honor.

Control the clothes closets

Often we retire from the corporate world, but our clothes are still on call. We hire the house painted, plumbing fixed, and trees trimmed, yet hold on to faded old clothes for those dirty jobs. Then there are those clothes we will never fit into again. Change your mindset. Getting rid of those clothes isn't conceding to weight gain; it's an incentive. When you lose weight you deserve a new wardrobe.

Are you a wannabe Imelda Marcos with a pair of shoes to match every outfit? If so, part with a few or get creative with storage options. I have few pairs of shoes since they all hurt anyway, but I'm a jacket junkie. Generic coats are fine, but I'm a sucker for lightweight wraps that become part of the ensemble for cool evenings, chilly restaurants, and theaters. My creative option is to fill the coat closet with my jackets and put guests' coats on the bed.

It may take an objective friend or a professional closet organizer to realistically ferret through your wardrobe. Many stores offer consulting assistance when you buy racks, hangers, and storage boxes. Naturally, a do-it-yourself approach is less expensive.

Barbara organized her packed walk-in closet with colored plastic hangers, double rods, and plastic containers. She hung short-sleeve cotton blouses on red hangers, long-sleeve silks on blue hangers, etc. Dozens of T-shirts are folded and stacked by color and type. Her neat and orderly closet makes finding things easy and postpones parting with her extensive wardrobe.

If you're closet is phone-booth size, try other strategies. Box up those hard to part with items, tape up the box and store *inconveniently.* If you want to wear something bad enough to get a ladder to reach the box, remove the tape, and press the item, put it back in the closet. If the box is unopened after a year, donate the clothes to charity.

A picture is worth 1000 words and maybe a few dollars

Once you've organized the closets and run out of ideas for displaying your treasures, consider taking a picture before discarding or selling an item. In my case a few small running trophies won in the over-fifty age group were not worth displaying or storing. A quick picture made for no regrets when they clanged into the trash bin.

Donna's father, on the other hand, had baseball memorabilia worth several thousand dollars. He constantly worried his collectibles might be stolen, especially his Babe Ruth autographed ball and "Yaz" bat, autographed by Carl Yastrzemski. Now he can look at the pictures of his treasures anytime and enjoy the profits his longtime collection brought — a double play.

His son-in-law thought it was such a good idea that he donned his tennis clothes, had his picture taken with all his trophies, removed the name plates, and donated the trophies to the local Boy's Club.

If animal rights' concerns have relegated your fur coat to permanent storage, why keep it? Are you insuring valuable jewelry you're afraid to wear? If so, how about having your makeup and hair done for a glamorous portrait wearing the coat and jewelry? Now you may sell the items or surprise family members with an early inheritance. In either case, you save storage and insurance costs and likely will see more of the luxury items in the portrait than you have seen of them in years.

Ideally this downsizing process is the first of several steps you will take as you prepare for a smaller, low-maintenance home, while considering a future in a very small, no-maintenance retirement home or possibly one room in an assisted-living or skilled nursing facility after that. Feeling in control of this transition eases the process.

Once you've found a place for the functional and decorated with the fashionable, it's time to unload the rest.

Give it away, sell it, or trash it.

Naturally, you want to give things to your family first. As we sorted through things, small items went into boxes labeled for each child. Few items were of any great value. Most were keepsakes or fun remembrances from their childhood. The son in his mid-forties got the bottom half of that 200-year-old vase, which he broke with his ten-year-old horseplay. The family that just bought their first home got the yard tools and outdoor Christmas lights. Another daughter got the living room sectional, another her grandmother's treadle sewing machine.

Be sure your children know the value of the things you give to them now or that they will inherit later. Gloria's little woven baskets didn't look too impressive, but at the suggestion of a friend she had a local museum look at them. It turns out the Yakima Klikitat Indians wove the cedar-root baskets in the mid-1800s and they are valued at $500 each. Now the heirs know.

Darline offers this advice on giving things to your children — It should be a gift with no strings attached. "I've decided when I make a quilt and give it away that I've enjoyed making it, and if they let the dog sleep on it, so be it." If it will create friction in the family if children don't keep the silver polished, the antique wood oiled, and generally don't take care of things as you have, it may be better to find another home for your treasures. Consider selling them and using the profits to take the whole family on a trip.

Sell things at a garage sale, through newspaper advertising, at resale shops, or through an Internet auction. Not sure how to sell a few odd pieces of china? Replacements, Ltd. buys and sells old china, crystal and collectibles. They advertise an inventory of 100,000 pieces — some 100 years old. Someone may need your one odd cup to complete her set.

Appraisals are advisable for valuable items you plan to insure, but may be costly and unrealistic for selling things. I got some great advice from a longtime Fort Worth antique dealer, who reminded me that something is only worth what someone is willing to pay for it today. I took her advice, got three bids on my antiques, and sold to the highest bidder. If the price didn't suit me, I gave it away.

Goodwill Industries, the Salvation Army, and local community charities are anxious to have things you can no longer use. Women's shelters and homeless shelters need linens and gently used clothing, games, and toys. The Lion's Club collects old eyeglasses to distribute. Retirement homes and nursing homes appreciate books and magazines. Local youth organizations welcome sports equipment and craft supplies.

At this point, you shouldn't have much left. It's time to trash the faded, dust-covered plastic flowers, antechs, and the stuff that didn't sell at the garage sale.

Admittedly, we didn't do a perfect downsizing job — there are a few boxes in the garage — but our smaller quarters are comfortable and uncluttered. It's like a great weight has been lifted.

Unfortunately, like the weight around our middle, stuff has a habit of creeping back. Most full-time RVers don't buy anything without knowing in advance what it will replace. If something comes in, something goes out. This "in and out" rule allows them to crisscross the country year-round without strangling on souvenir T-shirts, a good rule to adopt once you downsize.

Eat, drink, and merrily collect memories

Now's the time to make our favorite things the ones Maria sings about in the *Sound of Music* — sights, sounds, and tastes enjoyed for the moment. Phyllis, who owns and operates a tour company, doesn't feel so bad about passing up the temptations on her travels knowing she's coming home to a cozy and uncluttered home. "If I can't wear it or eat it, I don't buy it. I enjoy it when I see it, and that's enough," she says.

If you must buy something, know what it's replacing or fall back on the fashionably functional. If you're ready to swap an old sweater for a new one of Irish wool seen while visiting the Emerald Isle, fine. If not, pass it up. When visiting a gallery consider a pillbox with an impressionist painting on the lid to replace the plastic one with a pharmaceutical ad on the top, and leave the coffee table book behind. Insulated cups and glasses, key chains, and spoon rests make good remembrances *if* you plan to use them. For me, a spoon rest covered in bright colored fish recalls a sunny day at an Oregon aquarium.

From downsizing to upscale living

Once you've launched the children and jettisoned the excess baggage, you're ready to consider your next home. Picture your lifestyle taking the most optimistic and pessimistic views in five-year increments. Then be prepared to exercise your options.

A lifetime of healthy habits increases the odds for good health into your later years; but like the roll of the dice in Monopoly, sometimes you draw the "Go directly to jail" card and miss the good properties along Boardwalk. There are people in their seventies living alone and pulling their golf clubs around the course several times a week, while others the same age are unable to navigate their wheelchair down the nursing home corridor.

In either case, bigger isn't better. Think small and increase your options. If the laundry room is ten steps from the kitchen sink, why do you need a sink in the laundry? Soak stained garments in the kitchen, drip-dry things in the shower. Fewer commodes and sinks to scrub and less carpet to vacuum mean more time to play.

Do you need an extra bedroom for overnight guests a few times a year? Unless your grown children and their families visit often, consider a top-of-the-line queen-size inflatable mattress with a built-in electric pump. Overnight guests can sleep comfortably anywhere you have floor space. When the guests leave, the deflated mattress and linens can be stowed in a small bag.

For the money you save on the purchase, upkeep, and taxes for an extra room, you can treat people to a night at a bed and breakfast in town and leave yourself refreshed and ready to show them the sights. Or consider treating the parents of young children to a night in a hotel while you keep their offspring at your house. If practical in your area, a tent and sleeping bags for the grandchildren makes their visit an adventure.

For the few times you entertain a crowd, you can rent a punch bowl, coffee urn, tables and chairs, or plan the event away from home at a restaurant or reception hall.

Take stock

Whether your dream house is a condo on the golf course, a townhouse in the city, or a farmhouse near your rural roots, the real estate mantra, location, location, location applies. Will you be near the children most likely to see to your care? If not, be prepared for another move later in life.

More importantly, when you move will you be able to find a doctor? According to an American Medical Association survey about 25 percent of physicians have limited the number of Medicare patients they accept. Patients in about half the states are having trouble finding a physician who will take them. If Medicare continues to cut reimbursement to physicians, expect the trend to continue. In many parts of the country, unless you are established with a physician before you turn sixty-five, you'll have difficulty finding one.

Transportation, HMO requirements, and supplemental insurance coverage may further limit your choices. Burlene has to arrange private transportation for doctor's visits and can't use the most convenient hospital because there aren't any doctors taking new Medicare patients within the area where her retirement home provides transportation.

As with buying stocks, at the time of purchase you should have an exit strategy based on your health and safety, not your age. Is the investment for a boat and cabin on the lake worth it for the number of years you can enjoy that lifestyle? Is an A-frame in the mountains, far from medical care, a good short-term buy? Would you like to diversify your nest egg and migrate with the birds — south in the winter and north in the summer? All are outstanding options if you accept the idea that this won't likely be your last home.

Trailer trash and other treasures

Once only wealthy Americans who had servants to look after several residences could follow the winter sun south or hang out at the beach in the dog days of summer. Now manufactured homes on wheels or on the ground offer the flexibility for everyone to take their retirement on the road if they choose.

Recreational vehicles bear little resemblance to Lucy and Desi's trailer. RVs come in every size and shape — from comfortable and affordable to luxurious motor homes with hot tubs, big screen TVs, fireplaces, and $1 million price tags.

The places to park them are as diverse as the vehicles. If "double-wide" conjures up knee-high weeds and junk cars, you haven't seen the active adult resorts dedicated to RVs and manufactured housing. Pool halls, tennis courts, softball diamonds, shuffleboard courts, heated swimming pools, and more are surrounded by spacious lawns and beautiful flowers. Residents, winter or year-round, join craft classes, card games, music programs, dances, and participate in activities for every interest, including computer facilities for techies and fitness centers for the health conscious.

Park models, about 400 square-feet, and manufactured homes of several thousand square feet are more affordable options than homes built on site. Manufactured housing developments are particularly popular across the Sun Belt.

From her spacious deck, Marjorie says of her park model, "I didn't know they built little houses like this. It's like a honeymoon cottage. When my granddaughter came to visit and heard everyone asking one another if they had a good summer and what classes they planned to take, she said it was just like returning to college in the fall."

For years Don and Phyllis spent summers in the Colorado home they designed and built and traveled to Arizona for the winter, first staying in an RV and later buying a park model in the same Mesa RV resort. In their seventies, they had had enough of packing and moving four times a year, so they bought a larger manufactured home in an active adult community and made Arizona their permanent residence.

They picked their favorite features, colors and amenities from twenty floor plans. Now to escape the heat, they travel in the summer or spend their time in the pool and enjoy indoor activities in the spacious clubhouse. Their busy days include workouts in the fitness center, watercolor classes, games, dances, dinners, teaching life-story writing, and more.

Molly and Gale solved the packing and moving dilemma by living in their RV year-round. When the weather gets too warm in Yuma, they unhook the water, electric, and sewer service and make the one-day drive to Payson. They have breakfast in the desert and dinner that evening in the mountains. Before the snow flies they make the trek south to rejoin their winter friends.

Before social security, widowed women like Bev's mom eked out a no-frills existence, so a trip to Chicago to visit her young aunts was a great adventure for twelve-year-old Bev. "My aunts had jobs and were supporting themselves. One joined the Navy. Three weeks in the big city and I thought, "If they can do this, so can I." She knew someday she would travel and hasn't let "things" or the lack of them deter her from her dreams.

"Once my dream was to have a hutch for the Rosenthal china Frank brought home from Europe after the Korean War. Now I don't even care about the china," Bev told me. When forced into early retirement, they gave away everything, including the china, to their daughters and left Oshkosh the day after Christmas in a thirty-two-foot trailer.

Bev and Frank spend their winters in a park model in Arizona and do volunteer work in exchange for their summer campsite in Wisconsin. At least it started out that way. After a few years, Bev became a valued paid employee. At the Oshkosh Air Show, she coordinates transportation for the VIPs among the 850,000 people who attend each year. In the spring and fall, you'll find them at Peninsula State Park in Door County, Wisconsin. They began as volunteer campground hosts. Now Bev is salaried, and Frank enjoys volunteering in the carpenter shop.

"We've never regretted our decision; we treasure every moment. The only thing our grandchildren ask is, 'Will you have enough room for me to sleep?'" And indeed they do — sometimes in a tent outside.

Joe and Dee planned to spend a couple of years traveling the country, seeing the sights, and looking for the ideal retirement spot. Well, two years turned into six. By planning their trips around weather and events, they've witnessed New England's glorious fall, taken in the Derby in Kentucky, followed the square-danced circuit across the country, and visited every major natural and cultural site.

After living on the road for that long they didn't ever want to be burdened with "stuff" again, so an 1100 square-foot house is just right. The motor home is gone, and they've embarked on new adventures, like a recent cruise to Alaska. Europe and Asia are next.

Empty nester housing

The 55-plus market, 72 million strong and healthier and wealthier than previous generations, has developers around the country responding by catering to every interest. Over the next few pages we'll look at the some of these choices and the lifestyles they offer.

Florida, with almost three million residents over the age of sixty-five, has created "elder ready" communities providing special services and an infrastructure designed especially for elderly residents. Longer signal lights allow more time to cross the street, and easy-to-read signs with large letters are a few of the requirements to be certified "elder ready."

A trend that began in the Sun Belt and has spread around the country offers active seniors home ownership in a resort setting. A monthly association fee covers outside maintenance and community amenities in active adult communities (AACs).

People rarely retire to rest and relax in a rocking chair, and those who do shorten their lifespan considerably. Retirement means twenty or thirty years of freedom to be a kid again — a perfect opportunity to exercise your options. As the grandchildren say, "Retirement is like summer camp all year." True. And like choosing a summer camp, choose a place where you can grow mentally and physically; a place to have fun and make new friends. Don't feel guilty! Neurological studies show that people with a high level of leisure activities reduce the risk of developing dementia by 38 percent.

Do your college days hold more fond memories than summer camp? If so, consider retiring to academia. Today's university retirement communities are nothing like the dorms of fifty years ago. Leon Pastalan, professor of architecture and urban planning at the University of Michigan says, "People are realizing that a warm climate is not enough — retirement has got to add some sort of value to both society and the individual."

College/university-based retirement communities are valuable partnerships providing residents with access to lifelong learning and campus activities, while providing the university with boosters, volunteers, and contributors. More than fifty North American institutions have varying arrangements — from on-campus facilities owned and operated by the university to informal partnerships with nearby retirement communities. Iowa State, Penn State, the universities of North Carolina, Notre Dame, Indiana, Virginia, Duke and many more have retirement communities. In Canada, the University of Guelph in Ontario owns an outstanding 600-home active adult community, The Village by the Arboretum.

"I think of AACs as cruises on land. People want to be pampered just as if they are on a cruise vacation," says Linda Ernest, national product manager of *Mature Living Choices*. This pampered lifestyle lets you trade your rake and snow shovel for a tennis racket and golf clubs, lets you dance and play cards in a luxurious clubhouse, workout in a fully-equipped fitness center, take water aerobics, or loll around the swimming pool.

Although "active" is the key word, AAC builders incorporate universal design features into construction plans. Universal design means the products are flexible enough to be used by a wide variety of people of all ages and abilities and anticipate a time of changing physical abilities. In home design, the concept emphasizes anything that helps seniors live independently — wider doorways, kitchens, and bathrooms, ramps to replace stairs, and sometimes lower counters and higher toilets.

Although I would have preferred an AAC, the closest one is too far from my mother and daughters. Right now my mother needs my assistance, and later I'll need my daughters' help, so we made the next best choice. Our small condo in a gated community incorporates universal design, which will allow us to stay here until we need help with daily living activities. An association fee that covers grounds, clubhouse, and pool maintenance frees us to travel. The clubhouse, with a library, fitness equipment, a kitchen, and an entertainment area offers space for activities our small condo doesn't accommodate. A grocery store, hardware store, pharmacy, video rental store, fast food restaurants, and banks are within two blocks. The city offers transportation for seniors, and there are future plans for a shuttle to run between the park-and-ride across the street to a rail line running between Dallas and Fort Worth. For now, this offers all we require to age in place.

A stitch in time saves nine

How long can you live independently? Longer than you should. As earlier examples show, moving before you *have* to saves a lot of grief for you and your family. When should you consider some assistance?

1. When you are frightened and afraid to go out of your house.
2. When (not if) you give up driving, and transportation isn't readily available.
3. When cooking is such a chore that you snack rather than fix nutritious meals.
4. When you're overwhelmed with home maintenance.
5. When you're no longer going to ball games, plays, or symphonies.
6. When you could fall or have a stroke and nobody would know for hours.
7. When it's too much trouble to exercise.
8. When you're lonely.
9. When you don't have a reason to get out of bed, shower, and dress.
10. When you aren't able to keep track of your medications.

For several years her family and friends encouraged Pauline to move to a retirement home. She resisted until she fell in her garage and lay on the floor all day with a broken hip. She was in her nightgown when the paramedics, alerted by a neighbor, rescued her about 9 p.m.

If it had been an extra hot or cold day, she could have died. Instead, she went to the hospital for surgery, then to rehab, and finally an assisted living facility. It was up to her family and friends to sort through her things and sell the house.

It's not impossible to "age in place," it just takes more effort than most people are willing to expend. If you plan to stay in your own home, give it your best shot. Considering the cost of care facilities, you can pay for a lot of services to maintain your independence and make your home safe and comfortable.

Federal and state agencies, straining under ballooning Medicaid costs, are encouraging home and community services as an alternative to nursing home care. See what's available in your area.

AARP suggests you not wait until a crisis hits, but begin now to prepare your home for a time when your physical abilities change. Their Web site offers brochures and pamphlets on home modification. If for some reason you are unable to stay in your home, the "senior friendly" upgrades are an excellent selling point.

Up the wattage

As we get older our eyes' lenses gradually lose flexibility. By middle age, it takes double the wattage to light a room as sufficiently as when we were younger, and the decline continues. Some studies suggest we seniors need fifteen times as much light to see as well as when we were ten years old.

Good lighting may prevent a fall, so make sure halls and stairs are well lit and use nightlights in the bath and bedroom. Since safety often precludes simply adding larger watt bulbs to existing lighting, look for new solutions, such as metal halide technology and full-spectrum lighting invented by Dr. John Nash Ott. The superior light you experience in shopping malls and sports arenas and the Ott-Lite are now available for home lighting. Microsun's metal halide table and floor lamps, although not cheap, merit consideration. If you've had your eyeglasses' prescription checked and cataracts removed and still strain to read or see the stitches in needlework projects, these new technologies may be the answer.

Keep in touch

Make some arrangement to summon assistance in case you fall or have some other medical emergency and are unable to get to a telephone. Arrange for someone to call you twice a day and alert family if you don't answer, or work out a system with a neighbor to close a shade each evening or turn off the porch light each morning to signal them that you are all right. You can subscribe to a personal emergency response service or a computer telephone service for as little as $1 a day.

Personal help buttons are clipped on or worn around your neck like a necklace or around your wrist, so you can call for help at any time. Taking the idea a step further, Caring Technologies has designed a strap to be worn around the torso that detects a fall or cessation of chest motion and automatically calls for help even if you're unconscious.

The CarePartner Telephone has an emergency response component and can be programmed for up to six reminder messages — appointment times, when to take medications, or when your favorite TV show comes on. A Morning Reporter alarm clock/radio at $130 plays pre-recorded messages that remind you when and how to take your medications. A pager service offers a similar accommodation for about $40 a month. Either may be an inexpensive option considering that 10 percent of hospital admissions and 23 percent of nursing home admissions are the result of poor medication compliance.

Some municipal and civic organizations have initiated systems to monitor homebound residents. In Harris County, Texas, constables investigate if seniors on their list don't respond to an electronic phone message.

Over the next decade, expect to see more high-tech innovations to lower healthcare costs and link isolated seniors with their caregivers. Telemedicine, videophones, video conferencing, and even commodes that check urine and transmit the information to the doctor are on the drawing board.

Make it easy on yourself

Be comfy warm in winter and cool in summer by properly insulating your home and having heating/cooling units regularly serviced for safety and comfort.

Take a hint from retirement homes and replace heavy dining room chairs with ones that roll so you can easily pull yourself up to the table and push away. Firm sofas and chairs with arms and of medium height make it easier on arms and legs, as does a bed you don't have to climb into.

Replace the knobs on doors and faucet hardware with lever-type handles and add pulls or handles to cabinets and drawers with finger grooves. Many a fall occurs while stooping over to plug in an appliance, so raise often-used electrical outlets to twenty-seven inches above the floor. Plan for wheelchair use by lowering light switches to the same level.

All these safety precautions won't help if you lose your mental capacity. A MacArthur Foundation study designed to examine the factors responsible for the positive aspects of aging in America included a strong social support system, social connectedness, and a reduced feeling of isolation as contributors to maintaining mental function. The statistical evidence concluded that isolation is a powerful risk factor for poor health. A conclusion supported by numerous studies in the past decade is that the more people participate in social relationships, the better their overall health.

All this raises the question of social involvement when you choose to age in place. There's no bingo game down the hall or friends to join for lunch in the dining room. It's up to you to make the effort to maintain social relationships. Marie and Jackie, both single, prove it can be done.

Her friends call this retired nurse Saint Marie. She doubled up on house payments to pay off her home before she retired, and she drives a well-used car. Her fixed income covers taxes, home maintenance, and lots of fun. Once she had her purse snatched in her garage. Now she shuts the automatic garage door before getting out of the car and practices other safety rules, but she doesn't stay home. You'll find her on the road going to exercise class, her volunteer gig at the hospital, meeting friends for lunch and dinner, taking several trips a year, and mostly doing for others. She's the one who takes her friends and neighbors to the doctor, sits with them in the hospital, takes food when they get home, and visits them regularly if they're in a nursing home. Did I mention that Marie is seventy-seven and looking forward to a retirement home. Yes, she knows that when she can no longer drive, she'll have to move.

The day I called to ask Jackie about her schedule she had just returned from her workout, a four-to-six times a week routine. "The rec center is just about a mile from here, and if you're over sixty-five it only costs $10 a year. My neighbor and I go together. It helps if you have someone to go with. Neither of us wants to disappoint the other, so we go even when we don't feel like it.

"I love my townhouse, but I'm almost seventy, and I want to stay open to the possibility of moving to an assisted-living facility when I can't drive. You have to stay active. It's good for your body and mind."

Jackie's activities revolve around her church's 600-member adult singles group. She's held every office and done every job from president to peon. On alternating Tuesdays she goes out with the "Tuesday Lunch Bunch" or to a "Suds 4 Duds" meeting. One is purely social; the other combines lunch with charity by buying large buckets of detergent and separating them into four-cup bags for the church's downtown mission. Dinner often follows "Tuesday Gathering," a happy-hour gabfest.

On Wednesdays the "Fun and Feast" group goes to dinner, and once a month they go to a play. Thursday's "Friendship" group shares a covered dish dinner. Fridays are a day to relax, read (several books a week), and maybe go on a date in the evening. There's a dance every Saturday night, and once a month the group goes to the theater for a matinee performance. After church on Sunday, the group goes out to lunch together. Then in the evening, it's more dancing, often followed by a trip to a pancake house for a late-night snack. Mondays begin with a Weight Watchers weigh-in. "It keeps me on track and means I sometimes take my own food to events."

Knowing Jackie has had some serious health problems in the past, I asked about that. "Oh, I'm doing good," she says, then corrects. "Let's say I have a good attitude about my health." It is an understandable correction since she has had three heart procedures, including by-pass surgery, and her medications cost $2,000 a month.

That good attitude is why you won't find her alone and feeling sorry for herself on holidays. She joins her minister ex-husband, his wife, and their combined families so her children won't have to split their time between parents. Or you may find her sharing the joy of the season with the homeless — serving food at a shelter.

A joyful heart

Once again we see that attitude, not circumstances, makes the difference in how we age. As perfect as our situation is for now, at some time in the future I picture myself in a continuing care retirement community. Actually, spending my days playing bridge, taking painting lessons, being chauffeured where I want to go while someone else does the cooking and cleaning is a rather pleasant prospect.

Always the decorator, I already know which pictures and furniture I want to take, and I've saved ads for youth-size furniture that is ideal for a small assisted-living bedroom.

Not your father's old folks home

Once elder-care options were limited to losing privacy and independence by moving in with one's children or going to a nursing home. Twenty years ago that meant drab, smelly, and depressing.

Government regulations and several grass-roots advocacy groups are changing that. The Pioneer Network, a national resource center dedicated to changing the culture of the care of America's aging citizens, works to erase the distinction between home care and institutional care. The Eden Alternative, founded by Dr. William Thomas, is working to change nursing homes from places of "loneliness, helplessness, and boredom" into places where life is worth living.

Traditionally, nursing homes have functioned like acute-care hospitals, right down to the nursing stations and strict routines designed for maximum staff efficiency. Although desirable for treating critical ill patients, it's a stifling atmosphere for daily living. Pioneer Network's executive director Rose Marie Fagan says "When we transform our nursing homes into human communities, places for living and growing, we will ultimately change the very nature of aging in America."

Apple Health Care has adopted a "Better Life" philosophy, transforming their institutions into communities that let you maintain control of everyday decisions. "We are on the path to ensuring that the beds we provide are beds that we, ourselves, would want to lie in."

Nursing Home Pioneers in twenty-three states strive to make long-term care facilities places to live, not places to wait to die. Although colorful accents, planned activities, and pets, are part of these initiatives, the goal is to make institutions more homelike, giving residents more control over their daily routine — things like when to get out of bed, when to eat, and when to bathe.

At www.medicare.gov//Nursing//Overview.asp. you can get information on 17,000 nursing homes. Deficiencies found during government inspections, their use of physical restraints, and the percentage of patients with bedsores, help weed out the worst. To further your evaluation, compare demographic features, such as the number of beds and resident characteristics (average age, diseases, etc.).

Interestingly, some of the older facilities have taken to new ideas quicker than newly built ones, so look beyond the fancy facade when evaluating. And you don't have to live in a big city to find a progressive facility. Tiny Winnie, Texas, population less than 3,000, boasts an Eden Alternative facility — The Arboretum of Winnie. "Our census is at 100 percent, and we maintain a long waiting list," says administrator Cynthia Reber.

That's easy to understand. Even children like coming to this nursing home. The staff and residents grow flowers and vegetables and share the harvest with family and friends. Dexter, a large green and gold macaw, greets visitors with "hello" and "good morning," chats with 100-year-old Lola, or calls to Rascal, the Boston terrier, as Nick takes the dog for a walk.

Most of the dogs, cats, birds, and fish belong to the Arboretum, but they made an exception for Margie's nineteen-year-old Chihuahua — at night Pedro sleeps in the bed with his mistress on the Alzheimer's unit. During the day, he and Pierre, a cocker spaniel, parade through the unit collecting doggie treats from the residents. Several cats roam the halls of the regular unit. Lucretia, the dachshund, waddles along behind Cissy as she cleans. The housekeeper makes her way from room to room, while Lucretia goes from lap to lap.

Cultural change moves as slowly as cold molasses, so baby boomers should use their clout to light a fire under providers and heat up the process. It's time to storm the last bastion of elder housing that hasn't crumbled under pressure from the baby boom generation and join an effort in your community to promote change. Change will occur only when families demand that nursing home providers embrace a philosophy of concern for residents over rules. It's not an impossible task — money talks.

The senior market that moved the largest specialty apparel retailer to change the cut of their jeans can surely influence the focus of long-term care. Gap introduced a new line and ad campaign titled "For Every Generation" when their concentration on a young audience met with declining sales. They switched emphasis with a media campaign featuring some gray-haired folks. One ad pairs country old-timer Willie Nelson with up-and-coming Ryan Adams touting a multigenerational denim line to woo back baby boomers who shunned hip-huggers and glittery stretch tops.

Baby boomers shunned sterile obstetrics care, moved fathers from the waiting room to the delivery room, and have hospitals competing for the birthing business with cozy home-like settings. When we shun the current nursing home concept, we'll see the kind of changes that have occurred in other elder-housing choices. A smorgasbord of alternatives to satisfy every appetite and interest have a whole new look and feel — from private, individual apartments with a menu of services to twenty-four-hour nursing care, and from plush and expensive to adequate and affordable.

Naturally costs rise with the level of care. The least expensive option is a senior apartment or retirement home that furnishes meals, weekly housekeeping and linen service, transportation, and activities. Since no medical services are provided, you must be physically and mentally able to take care of yourself in your own apartment.

We all know it's the little things that become big irritants, so don't let plush carpet and beautiful furniture in the lobby overshadow the fact that you will spend many hours in your own apartment. Pretend to go about your daily routine of showering, dressing, preparing a meal or snack so you can notice any problems before you move in. Are there bright lights? Is it cozy or drafty? Do you have an individually controlled thermostat? If your apartment faces the west, is the air conditioning adequate? Is there enough storage space? Are the closets outfitted with a rod that hangers easily slide along or plastic coated metal racks with slots just big enough to fit one hanger and too small for you to see? Will the bathroom be warm enough? The heat source that supplies the rest of the apartment may not be enough to keep old bones warm in a spacious bathroom that accommodates a wheelchair. If you're a plant lover, make sure you have the light exposure to grow some of your favorites.

As mentioned earlier, don't sign a contract until you have established a relationship with doctors in the area that accept Medicare, your HMO, or other insurance. Most retirement homes offer some sort of transport, but it may be limited to a specific radius.

To get the most for your money, take full advantage of the services a retirement home offers. If all you plan to do is eat your three meals a day and play an occasional game of bingo, don't pay the higher rent for amenities you won't use.

Assisted living, the interim step between independent living and a nursing home, adds assistance with routine daily living activities to the amenities of a retirement home. From a base monthly charge, prices rise with each level of added care. Medication supervision, showering and dressing assistance, incontinence care, and assistance with meals all add to the monthly bill.

Nursing homes, the last rung on the elder-care ladder, are skilled facilities providing twenty-four-hour care. As discussed earlier, this is the only level of care paid for by Medicaid for those who qualify.

If you prefer to skip the assisted living phase and are determined to avoid a nursing home at any cost, consider a continuing care retirement community (CCRC) that offers a continuum of care from independent living to twenty-four-hour skilled nursing care on the same campus. A few of these facilities have lease arrangements merely requiring a deposit and thirty-day move-out notice, with monthly rent that escalates with each additional level of care. However, if a long-term lease and large deposit are required, review your assets to assure you can afford the rising cost of any additional care you might require.

Most CCRCs (sometimes called life-care facilities) require a large (possibly with five zeros) partial or fully refundable entrance fee *and* monthly rent. But don't let that scare you off. It may be exactly what you need if you're in that middle-class squeeze. Here's why.

If the proceeds from your home or the money you have in savings and stocks will cover a hefty entrance fee and you have a pension or other retirement income to cover monthly rent, you can live in the lap of luxury. The monthly rent is about the same or less than you would pay for a comparable apartment or home, and you're guaranteed lifelong care, plus the return of all or part of your entrance fee to your estate. The entry fee and monthly rent are determined by the size apartment you choose. A few list entrance fees as low as $65,000, with rents comparable to an apartment complex. High-dollar resort locations are triple that.

The possibilities are limitless. You may choose an oceanfront campus lined with palm trees, a golf-course community in the dessert, a cottage campus in the northwest woods, a high-rise enclave downtown, or a facility adjoining and affiliated with a college or university.

In addition to the basics — meals, weekly housekeeping, flat laundry service, scheduled transportation, and extensive activities — most offer amenities that include many of the following:

- Grounds and building security with an individual emergency call system
- On-site health clinic with a doctor on-call 24/7
- Fitness facilities with personnel to design individual wellness plans
- Pubs, ice cream parlors, formal and informal dining opportunities
- Pools: outdoor, indoor, and whirlpool spas
- Hair and nail salons
- Library, game rooms, arts and crafts rooms
- Billiards, shuffleboard, tennis, and bocci ball courts
- Well-manicured grounds with walking paths
- On-site banking
- Cable television
- Computers and Internet access
- Religious services
- Hotel-style gift shops
- Garages or carports
- Overnight guest facilities

An added benefit: CCRCs provide some assurance for couples so they can stay together in the same familiar surrounding, even if independent living isn't possible for both. Beginning at age sixty-five, the risk for Alzheimer's and senile dementia rises each year. By age eighty-five, half the population suffers from serious signs of mental deterioration, making it comforting to know that in a CCRC one partner can continue an active life while the other is cared for in a safe environment. One may be a short stroll away in the skilled nursing wing, making it possible for the independent spouse to visit frequently and share meals.

Climate and culture

If you've always lived in the northeast, even if you've taken winter vacations in a sunny, warm climate, don't assume you'll be happy living in a place like Florida full-time. Now that you've given up shoveling snow and don't have to drive on ice, it's not so bad to live in a place ablaze with color in the fall and covered with a serene blanket of snow in the winter. Experience at least one summer in the south before swapping changing seasons for yearlong heat and humidity.

Empty nesters, like birds of a feather, flock together, so consider your age and interest in your search for the ideal home. New places attract younger, more active seniors; the residents of a twenty-year-old place may all be in their eighties or nineties and less interested in activities. Notice the physical and mental age of residents when choosing a place.

Most CCRCs are nonprofit, and some are operated by a specific faith. Naturally, you'll be more comfortable with people of similar beliefs or in a nondenominational setting. If you celebrate your New Year with challah and honey, and the dining room is accustomed to celebrating the New Year three months later with black-eyed peas and corn bread, it may not be a good fit.

Retirement resorts specifically for retired military officers and their spouses or widows rank high with the spit'n polish folks.

Are you cool to pets or can't imagine living without something warm and fuzzy? On my way through a retirement home, I saw four ladies playing bridge in a lounge off the lobby — one had her Lhasa apso curled around her feet, while a tiny poodle slept in her partner's lap. I stopped to speak to the ladies and pet their pooches, thinking how nice it was for them to have their companions with them. The next week the facility sent out a notice that the health department didn't allow pets in public areas.

That's not always the case. As mentioned earlier, some homes have resident pets that roam the halls and visits resident's rooms. In most cases, a specific wing of the building is pet-friendly, with animals having only limited access to other areas. Check it out. If you have allergies or an aversion to four-legged friends, you may want to look for a no-pets-allowed place.

Meals are the main event at retirement homes and also the thing most complained about. After seven or more decades of eating what we want when we want, eating on someone else's schedule takes some adjusting. Look for a place with the most flexible meal plan. Does everyone eat at the same time from a limited menu or is there a two-hour window and lots of delicious foods to choose from? Are three meals included in the rent or may you choose one or two a day? If you get up at 5 a.m. ready for a hearty breakfast, and the dining room serves continental fare at 8 a.m., don't pick a meal plan that includes breakfast. The same applies if you're not an early bird and can't be tempted out of your room before nine no matter what is served for breakfast. (As my mom says, who wants worms for breakfast anyway.)

If you're a jeans-and-sports kinda gal and the folks at one place dress for dinner and the activities calendar lists trips to the opera and symphony, forget it. Look for a place where they play dominoes and throw parties to watch championship games on a big-screen TV.

Inquire about policies on smoking and alcohol use. Some places frown on both, while others sponsor regular happy-hour events and offer wine with dinner. For health and safety reasons, some don't allow smoking even in private apartments.

Now that you've looked at the options, before you plop down your life savings, do your homework. Find out exactly what "access to lifelong nursing care" means — nursing care in your residence, transfer to another location within the campus that has the appropriate level of care, or transfer to an off-site nursing home. Find out if there are additional charges for the more extensive care and what arrangements are made if the on-site facility is full when you need the next level of care. Most importantly, understand the requirements for the refund of your entrance fee and the financial stability of the organization.

Begin by checking with the Continuing Care Accreditation Commission. Do your own research, which includes lengthy visits on the campus, interacting with residents. Before you sign on any dotted line, have an attorney review the contract. Once you're satisfied with the financial and legal aspects, prepare to enjoy the good life. You've earned it.

If you've been reading this with parents in mind, don't delay in beginning a discussion of their plans. Armed with the list of ten warning signs and information on the exciting options available, you may get agreement on when it's time for them to give up their home for one of the senior-living options.

For many families, shared quarters breed resentment and discord; for others, it creates a warm opportunity. Freda, who was born two weeks before the Titanic sank, has her own tiny bedroom and kitchen within her daughter's Winnipeg home. While her daughter works, Freda sails through the household chores as if she were twenty years younger, leaving her daughter time to relax when she gets home. When we visited, Freda prepared a delicious five-course dinner, including homemade pie. She obviously thrives on this cozy inter-generational atmosphere.

But, then, people like Freda thrive in every circumstance. Last year her daughter had some health problems, so Freda chose to move. She writes, "I've moved into a seniors complex, and I love it. The days pass by very quickly . . . it seems I can always find something to do." She brags about her view of the city, the complex's hairdresser, and the entertainment opportunities. At almost ninety-one years old, she was baking her fourth batch of fruitcakes for gifts and "to serve to friends that drop in around Christmas." Her attitude keeps friends dropping by.

An Elder Cottage Housing Opportunity (ECHO) home falls between having parents share your home or go to a separate facility. ECHO homes, or Granny flats as they call them in Australia, are small, portable, manufactured homes designed to be installed beside or in the backyard of a single family home. They are removable and reusable. However, without the wide-open spaces they enjoy down under, lot size and local zoning ordinances prohibit this low-cost alternative in many areas.

If you have the space, an ECHO unit maintains privacy for you and your parents, yet keeps them close enough to care for without traveling great distances. When they no longer need the home, it can be removed and sold.

As you investigate other alternatives, get as much input from your parents as possible. Take some floor plans and let them arrange furniture. Knowing they can take familiar furnishing reassures some, while some enjoy buying new furniture and redecorating. Giving up overwhelming home and yard maintenance may be an encouragement.

Comparing current expenses with the services included at a retirement facility and promising not to sell anything until they've tried a new place for three months eases the transition. If your parents' home needs painting and repairs, it's an ideal time for a trial move. They can take a minimal amount of clothing and furniture to see how they like it. Most adjust and are happy to stay, and the house is ready to put on the market.

The U.S. Administration on Aging sponsors Eldercare Locator, the Assisted Living Federation of American, representing 7,000 providers. The American Association of Homes and Services for the Aging, represents 5,600 not-for-profit facilities. These agencies can assist you in locating the appropriate care.

Bridge the gap with a GCM

If you've made your best effort and feel your parents' resistance to a move is jeopardizing their health and safety, consider getting help from a geriatric care manager (GCM). Professional care managers are trained in gerontology, social work, and counseling. They assess the quality, cost, and services available to help older people and their families with long-term care arrangements. A GCM can serve as a short-term advisor, simply evaluating needs and available resources to help the family develop and initiate a care plan. Or they may take on the role of patient advocate, acting as a liaison with adult children who live far away by monitoring the well-being of their elderly clients in long-term care facilities.

Beware. As in any other field, there are unscrupulous individuals who take advantage of families during a crisis. Some are merely referral agents who charge the family exorbitant fees or shuffle clients between homes and collect finders' fees paid by the facilities.

The National Association of Professional Geriatric Care Managers, The National Council on Aging, and The Case Management Society of America set professional standards and can assist with lists of certified and licensed individuals and agencies. These organizations advise getting a written agreement outlining how fees are calculated and checking references, licenses, and certifications.

If all else fails, see if the newest innovation — a CCRC that provides services in a person's own home for their lifetime — is available in your area. Friends Life Care, available in five counties surrounding Philadelphia and slowly expanding to nearby states, offers several plans that vary in cost based on age and services. One plan, with a fixed benefit, features no monthly fee increases and a lifetime dollar maximum of $150,000. If it turns out to be successful for the company and clients, you can expect to see similar options nationwide.

This chapter devoted to exercising our options focused on how and where we will spend our last years. Ever since homo sapiens sought the shelter of caves, where we live has affected the quality of life. Our desires range from simply satisfying the necessities to creating comfort to living in luxury.

Over time, things like indoor plumbing move from luxury to necessity. Although it's not likely we know in our fifties exactly what our needs and desires will be at eighty, it's certain that our financial situation greatly bears on our options.

Financial security

Second to outliving our mind, our greatest fear is outliving our money. If we live long enough, no amount of money or insurance will keep us from being dependent on someone — usually our children. We have little control over physical dependence, but we don't have to be a financial burden.

The crumbling of the buy-and-hold, cut-your-losses, take-your-profits philosophies under the weight of terrorism and new international market realities has created scaled-back retirement expectations for many of us. Those of us who were flying high in the 90's, thinking we were savvy investors, saw our balloon burst in the new century — our profits *and* principle fizzled.

Without a reliable Ouija Board to calculate our life expectancy, with the 800 Internal Revenue codes that apply to seniors only, and with a volatile stock market, it's not surprising that we rely on certified financial planners and senior advisors for assistance.

Unless you're prepared to invest the time in educating yourself on various investment strategies, consider hiring an independent advisor whose fees are based on an hourly rate or percentage of your assets (typically about 1 percent). AARP offers a CD-ROM, "10 Steps to a

Better Financial Future," which is not biased toward any one financial product. Otherwise, the trust department of the bank is likely to advise trusts, savings accounts, and CDs, while a planner based in an insurance company will push life insurance and annuities, and a broker will want to sell you stocks and bonds. All these products have a place in your portfolio, and you can expect a less biased opinion regarding the balance of investment vehicles from someone whose compensation isn't based on commission and who considers the tax consequences, as well as your long-term goals.

Before choosing someone, seek the advice of satisfied customers, professional standards organizations, and the U.S. Securities and Exchange Commission. You'll find contact information on the brochures provided by the professionals you're considering. Get a written agreement that lists all fees, and carefully monitor transactions and statements.

With limited assets, a financial planner may suggest a reverse mortgage; a Qualified Income Trust (QIT), long-term care (LTC) insurance, or a combination.

Reverse Mortgage

For those who find themselves "house rich, cash poor," struggling to make ends meet, yet living in a home with a large amount of equity, a senior reverse mortgage may be ideal. If you are sixty-two or older, your home is paid for (or close to it), and you occupy the residence, you qualify for a Fannie Mae "Home Keeper" loan or FHA Home Equity Conversion Mortgage. An HECM, a concept supported by AARP, allows you to borrow a portion (usually up to half) of your equity without requiring that you repay the loan as long as you occupy the home. The loan is due when you move or die. You maintain the title to the house and may choose to take the equity in a lump sum or receive monthly checks. The payments are tax free and don't affect your Social Security or Medicare benefits.

"Reverse mortgages are a real good program for people living on a fixed income," said Betty. "Getting your equity out of your home helps with monthly living expenses. If my husband dies, I can continue to live here. If I have to go to assisted living and the house has to be sold, what's owed comes out of the sale."

In most cases, heirs sell the house, pay off the mortgage, and share any remaining equity. As a safeguard against a real estate bust, Betty says they took out insurance to make sure their heirs wouldn't owe more than the house was worth at the time of the sale. After two years, Betty's so comfortable with the program that she's helped a friend apply.

Scott Norman, president of the Texas Association of Reverse Mortgage Lenders, confirms the benefits of a reverse mortgage, but urges people to educate themselves and find a lender who is familiar with HECMs — "someone who can talk you through the process." In other words, make sure it's the right choice for your situation.

It's complicated and not the answer for every homeowner, so a few states have counseling requirements before taking a reverse mortgage. If yours does not, contact the National Center for Home Equity Conversion or AARP for a list of preferred lenders and counselors.

Qualified Income Trust (QIT)

Frank Spiro, a certified senior advisor who specializes in senior financial issues, suggests a QIT, sometimes referred to as a Miller Trust, for those whose monthly income from Social Security and pensions falls short of paying for nursing home care, but exceeds their state's maximum income for Medicaid assistance. For those who qualify on all counts except monthly income, a QIT may avoid the need to "spend down" until assets are exhausted before applying for assistance.

A brief overview gives you an idea of whether you or your parents could benefit from such a trust. Each month, income that exceeds the Medicaid cap goes into a trust with very specific, limited uses. It will be forfeited to the government upon death. The remainder of the income, except $60 a month for personal care, goes toward nursing home rent, with the government picking up the balance. In most cases, the portion paid by the government amounts to hundreds of dollars more than you're putting in the trust, so don't fret about the money reverting to the government. It's a more than fair deal.

Giving your assets to offspring to avoid spending down is dangerous business. Most of the loopholes have been plugged, so you may find yourself without assets and unable to qualify for Medicaid when you need it. From the other side, if your parent wants to give you more that the annual amount allowed as a gift, you will be paying taxes on the money and its earnings, probably in a higher tax bracket. Receiving such a gift usually means you've taken on the responsibility of your parents' life-time care, which may be a greater responsibility than you care to shoulder.

Long-term care insurance

If your assets and monthly income allow you to live the good life without the need for a reverse mortgage or QIT, you may want to consider long-term care insurance. Medicare provides only short-term nursing home coverage following hospitalization and provides no assisted living costs. With predictions that about half of Americans will require LTC in the future and AARP estimating the average cost of long-term care at $56,000 a year, it's surprising that only about 6 percent of Americans have purchased long-term care policies. With our portfolio headed toward the poor house and both mothers in care facilities, my husband and I decided to purchase policies before we turned sixty-five.

Our mothers' ages and health precluded purchasing LTC policies. Some families have seen the benefit of helping their parents obtain LTC insurance, even paying the premiums if their parents can't. Considering that Ivy League college costs compare favorably with LTC costs and may continue beyond four years, it's worth considering. If there are several children in the family to share the costs and your parents qualify, it's a wise investment that protects your inheritance.

Don't think nursing home insurance. Actually an LTC policy may keep you out of the nursing home. Benefits have drastically changed in the past few years and cover assisted living, Alzheimer's care, home care, adult day care, and even minor construction (ramps, widening doors, lowering sinks). Some policies pay part or all of the costs to train a family member to provide special care in the home. They also provide a substitute (twenty-one days a year) to give the caregiver a break, cover the cost of medical equipment rental, and more.

One of several companies represented by financial advisor Jerry Eastman recently introduced "shared care." For a small additional premium, a couple can gamble that they won't both need the same length of care and opt to share the total years. For example, each buys a three-year policy for a total of six years' coverage that can be shared as needed. Although the average stay in a nursing home is three years, this gives you a cushion if one partner's mental health declines faster than his or her physical health and several more years of care are required.

After two months of research and interviews with several companies, we chose policies, including shared care, which met our goals. Each situation differs, but this is one of the few cases when being single is an advantage. You don't have to worry about maintaining a household for yourself while paying for long-term care for a spouse at the same time.

Comprehensive guides outlining the features and pitfalls of LTC policies are available online:

- www.naic.org (National Association of Insurance Commissioners)
- www.unitedseniorshealth.org
- www.longtermcareinsurance.org offer

As when buying a car or an appliance, you can get the basic no-frills model or you can add enough bells and whistles to break the bank. The younger you are when you buy, the less expensive the policies, and many are discounted for good health. Most offer a premium reduction when husband and wife both purchase a policy and/or when payments are made annually rather than monthly. Those who wait until after the diabetes diagnosis, heart attack, or stroke probably won't be eligible for a policy at any cost.

The per-day benefit, the years of coverage, the elimination period (the waiting time before coverage begins), and inflation coverage set the base cost. Any extras add to the premium. Bottom line, if you are in your sixties, expect to pay $100 to $200 a month per person — a hefty chunk of disposable income. You'll have to decide if the cost is worth the peace of mind.

Well-known financial planner, Suze Orman says LTC insurance is "a foundation for your future financial security, comfort, and peace." Financial advisor Ray Martin suggests that anyone over fifty with more than $200,000 and less than $2 million in assets should buy the insurance. I understand that even Warren Buffet (a man with way more than $2 million) has purchased an LTC policy.

LTC insurance *does not* cover retirement home rent. To collect LTC benefits, you must be cognitively impaired or need assistance with Activities of Daily Living (ADLs), a level of care not provided in an independent living facility. The inability to do two or three ADLs —

bathing, continence, dressing, eating, toileting, and transferring (from wheelchair to bed or toilet) — as determined by your physician, commonly determines eligibility.

For us, it's worth the premium cost to know that we can travel, stay in our home, or choose a retirement facility without worrying about long-term care costs.

Safeguard your identity

After you've taken the advice of experts on the big-ticket items, consider other ways to protect what you've got, to stretch it where you can, and to outsmart the thieves who want to take it away from you.

Your identity is the latest target. Thieves use your personal information — date of birth, social security number and the like — to open bank accounts and credit card accounts. They change the addresses so you never see the bills and balances, then write bad checks and run up charges on the accounts. According to the Federal Trade Commission, it's often more than a year before the victims discover their identity has been stolen. Therefore, the FTC advises checking your credit report once a year.

Identity thieves target mailboxes. Since the red flag on your mailbox alerts the mail carrier *and* thieves, take outgoing mail to the post office or to a locked postal collection box to assure vital personal information isn't stolen.

Pre-approved credit offers, department stores discounts on first-time credit purchases, and perks for buying keep our wallets bulging with plastic. Choosing one or two cards with the best interest rate, annual fee, and awards program limits your exposure. If you're unhappy with your current contract, www.creditcards.com is one of several sites to assist you in comparing offers.

Once you've made your choice, reduce fraud opportunities by opting out of all of further offers. Call 888-567-8688 and have your name removed from the pre-approved credit card list. If you receive any unsolicited offers, shred anything that includes personal information.

Naturally, paying for everything with one card accumulates award points faster and saves the hassle of notifying numerous companies in the event your card is lost or stolen. In anticipation of this possibility, lay out your driver's license, credit cards, Medicare/insurance cards,

Social Security card (which shouldn't be carried), and copy both sides on a single sheet of paper. If everything won't fit, consider skinning down the contents of your wallet. Stow the information, along with a blank deposit slip from each bank account, in your safe deposit box or other secure location.

Avoid stand-alone ATM machines without security cameras, and never accept a stranger's assistance if you're having trouble operating the machine. Put your money away immediately.

Common sense tells you the health club, beauty salon, and video rental store don't need your SSN, but those who advise *never* giving out your Social Security number are mistaken. If you plan to use the services of a doctor or hospital, open a bank account, establish a brokerage account, apply for a mortgage, or attend a college class, you will likely be required to supply your SSN or forego the services.

Only buy things, sign contracts, or give credit card numbers and your Social Security number when *you* initiate the transaction. That means buy nothing at the door, over the phone, or on the Internet unless you made the contact and have had an opportunity to check references and business practices. To remove your name from the pre-approved credit card list, you must give your SSN, but *you* have initiated the call.

Apply the anti-drug campaign slogan — Just say no! Don't respond to surveys, send contributions, or accept prizes. As soon as American troops crossed the border into Iraq, scam artists were asking for donations for soldiers and refugees. Don't be fooled. Hang up the phone. By the time you read this, you will be able to register for the national "No Call" program sponsored by the Federal Trade Commission. You can register at a toll-free number or online to stop telemarketers from calling you. We've found a similar program in Texas to be quite effective. Charities and political candidates can still call, but it's stopped about 90 percent of the calls we were getting.

One other thing, while we're on the subject of phones. For safety, many single women use initials instead of their first name in the telephone directory. Some widows leave the phone listing in their husband's name for years after his death. That's not a problem unless you'll be upset when you get calls and mail addressed to him. If that's the case, add this to the list of things to put into your name after the death of a spouse.

Subscribe to the old "cash and carry" principle. Never give cash to someone — not anytime, not anywhere — unless it's in exchange for a product you are purchasing and taking with you. Walk away if someone offers to share money they found. There's always a catch.

According to a Justice Department report, an older American is the victim of a scam every twenty-two seconds. Aggressive security-system salesmen, home-repair scams, nonexistent charities, and bogus contests target seniors. Fraudulent telephone sales reap an estimated $40 million a year, so become a vigilant consumer and avoid the pitfalls of scam artists and their unscrupulous schemes.

Sometimes it is not schemes but carelessness that allows thieves to take advantage of us. That was the case when I left my purse in an unlocked file drawer in my office while I stepped out for a moment. As I returned, a young man met me at the door saying he was looking for someone. He gave me a name I didn't recognize, and I sent him to the information desk, never suspecting I had been robbed. An after-work stop at the grocery store revealed the missing driver's license, bank card, and several checks taken from the back of the pad.

I notified the police and planned to call the bank the next morning as soon as they opened, but they called me — at 3 a.m. It seems they were checking the ATM machine (during the night so they wouldn't disturb customers) and needed my pin number. Even in my groggy state I realized the thief thought I was *really* stupid. I squelched my urge to scream at him, gave him four bogus numbers, hung up, and called the police. The ATM kept the stolen card and the police arrived just in time to nab him before he reached the waiting cab.

Stretch your resources

Taking advantage of senior discounts for airline tickets, early-bird restaurant seating, and movie matinees stretches modest incomes. Well-supervised beauty school students and dental students take a little longer than pros, but do the job for less than half the normal cost. No matter how long you've been divorced, if you're sixty or older, you may be eligible to draw benefits from your ex-husband's Social Security when he dies.

Meals On Wheels delivers meals to homebound elderly and disabled citizens. Several telephone companies offer special rates to seniors. My mother pays about $5 a month for no-frills service. Low cost transportation is available to seniors in many areas. You never know what's available until you ask.

If you can't walk and are unable to push a wheelchair, Medicare will pay for an electric wheelchair. Most mastectomy patients are aware that Medicare covers the cost of breast prostheses, but may not know that prosthetic bras are also covered.

Medicare not only covers diabetics' regular visits to podiatrists, but also pays for therapeutic shoes for patients who continually suffer from foot infections. Bonnie had one infection after another and feared she might become a diabetic amputee, but hasn't had a single infection in the two years since she began wearing custom-made shoes. The American Diabetes Association records show that foot problems are the number one reason for hospital admissions, with about 56,000 patients losing a foot or leg each year. Medicare-covered foot care and custom-made shoes are lifesavers for patients and a bargain for taxpayers.

Many services are available to those who make the proper request. For example, once your doctor completes a United States Post Office form verifying you are unable to walk to your mailbox, the mail carrier will deliver to your door instead of leaving your mail in the box. For a temporary disability, a polite request of your mail or paper carrier may be all that's needed.

If your parents have limited income and few assets, they may qualify for programs that help them live independently for a longer time and help you hold on to your assets. Several government agencies have created web sites. The www.govbenefits.gov site and the National Council on Aging site — www.benefitscheckup.org — list benefits and discounts available to older adults.

Ten minutes to complete a questionnaire produced the following possibilities for those that qualify:

- An IRS tax credit to reduce tax liability.
- A Medicare Savings Program that returns the $58 a month currently taken out of Social Security benefits to pay for Medicare Part B and, in some cases, waives the 20 percent co-payment and the $100 annual deductible.
- A Free electronic monitoring system for someone living alone.
- Food stamps

- Grants to meet home heating and cooling costs, insulation, repair or replacement of heating and air-conditioning units.
- Weatherization assistance to insulate attics and around doors, windows, hot water heaters, as well as to pay for possible modifications to furnaces for more efficiency.
- Free library services — talking books by mail — for the vision impaired.

Look at specific prescription drug benefits by selecting BenefitsCheckUpRx. Each state's Medicaid program and 116 company-sponsored programs show savings of 20 to 40 percent on medications. For example, Lilly offers a thirty-day supply of their drugs for $12, and Pfizer offers a thirty-day supply for $15. A pharmaceutical industry patient-assistance program, with forty-eight participating companies offering 1400 different drugs, provided 5.5 million patients with free prescriptions in 2002. Log on to www.helpingpatients.org to see if you qualify.

Although benefits vary by state, eligibility guidelines, program descriptions, local contacts with organizations' names and addresses, and necessary documentation for applying for benefits are provided. Some include toll-free numbers and Web sites. Granted, getting approval is a lengthy process, but the price is right.

British writer Thomas Carlyle said, "The main business is not to see what lies dimly at a distance, but to do what lies clearly at hand." It's clear to me that we can exercise options now to brighten that dimly lit future. Visualize several housing transitions from active to dependent, secure your financial future, downsize the stuff, and you'll have a wealth of options.

Listen and Learn

Listen or thy tongue will keep thee deaf.

— Native American Proverb

"Listen, no #%&@ little PR girl is going to keep me from talking to my manager," George Steinbrener boomed across the long-distance line. The day before, I had left Billy Martin "resting comfortably," as the hospital folks say. I, too, was sleeping comfortably until the predawn phone call jangled me awake.

During the summer of 1985, the New York Yankees' manager and former Ranger's manager was hospitalized with a punctured lung. Martin enthusiastically accepted the hospital's "no information" status, a policy that provides well-known patients with the privacy and quiet surroundings they need to recover.

He could give his room number to family or friends, but information was not available from the hospital switchboard or information desk — no phone calls, no uninvited visitors. All inquiries were referred to the PR office.

Suddenly I found myself in the middle of the long-running and much publicized feud between manager and owner. Martin, whom Steinbrenner fired and rehired three times, used hospital policy (and me) to stonewall his boss.

"Yes, he has a phone in his room, but I can't give . . .," I attempted to explain. Steinbrenner would hear none of it. He huffed and puffed and cussed. I listened, and listened, and listened. Although tempted to hang up, I waited him out.

"Are you there?" he growled. After a moment's silence he was ready to listen. Score one for the PR lady.

"I'll deliver your message and others the hospital operators have collected overnight, but the decision to return calls is Mr. Martin's." As promised, I delivered his message, expletives deleted.

For several days I took calls from ravenous reporters, adoring fans, and admiring females, all with creative stories illustrating why I should let them talk to him. I delivered the messages, he thanked me, and laid them aside. Since I was continually accused of failing to deliver messages, I'm sure few of the calls were returned. I don't know if he returned Steinbrenner's call, but he did finish the season with the Yankees.

One day Martin wasn't in his room, and the nurses couldn't account for his absence. A call from an angry reporter solved the mystery. "Why didn't you tell us Martin was released from the hospital? I just got a tip that he's been seen around town."

Martin, apparently tired of hospital food, sneaked down the back stairs and joined some cronies for a clandestine lunch. When I made my afternoon message delivery, he quickly shut his eyes and feigned sleep.

"How was lunch?" I teased. With more style than most people in a hospital gown can manage, he winked and flashed his charming grin. It was a response I suspect reflects the way he managed baseball and his life — no excuses.

As he prepared to leave the hospital, Martin handed out autographed baseballs to the staff. As he signed the ball for me, a volunteer delivered a huge basket of flowers. He took the card and handed me the bouquet. I'll never know who sent the flowers he graciously passed on to me, but I like to think it was Steinbrenner.

The flowers wilted, Martin died in a car accident a few years later, and I retired, but the basket remains. No doubt Martin appreciates knowing the basket has a place of honor in our bathroom. When I fill it with extra tissue, I imagine him smiling down from that great diamond in the sky.

Another baseball great, Yogi Berra, noted that, "Sometimes you can observe a lot by watching." And sometimes you can learn a lot by listening, although even when we listen, we don't always hear. And what we hear is not always what was said — or meant.

A team leader for the hospital's quality assurance program asked me to prepare some props for a skit on meeting customer needs. I took a list over the phone that included one of those "take one" things. I checked off the items, printed a label with "take one" on it, and stuck it on a plastic brochure holder. Luckily, they had a rehearsal and discovered the miscommunication. They wanted the "take one" clap board used on a movie set. I didn't meet the customer's need, but the incident made a great example for the next training session.

Former Secretary of State Dean Rusk, in the business of persuasion, said, "The best way to persuade others is with your ears — by listening to them." We tend to do exactly the opposite and try and persuade with our mouth. Find the two words in the anagram ENTSLI for a clue to what it takes to use our ears more and mouth less.

One day granddaughter Shelby, three at the time, jumped up on my lap and started pushing my hair back. "Let me see your ears, Grandma." With a sigh of relief, she turned to her older sister and said, "See Chelsea, I told you Aunt Kathy didn't talk her ears off." Indeed not, otherwise we'd be an earless society. If the Almighty gave us two ears and one mouth intending for us to listen twice as much as we talk, we've strayed.

Listening is half the communication equation. In practice, listening-talking splits 80-20 at best. When we should be listening, we're often planning what we'll say as soon as the other person shuts up. No doubt this practice spawned the description of a conversation as a vocal competition in which the one who is catching his breath is called the listener.

I learned this lesson the hard way. My friend Edie called, and before she could say a word, I babbled on about losing my purse with some cash in it and about how I had credit cards to cancel. When I stopped to catch my breath, she told me that her young nephew had been killed in a car accident and his mom, dad, and brother were in critical condition. I felt more foolish than I had that morning when I drove off with my purse on the roof of the car.

Unfortunately, that's not the last time I got caught talking when I should have been listening; but I'm working on it. One of my most embarrassing work incidences involved a brochure for the hospital maternity care unit. Our staff was especially pleased with the clever name — Great Expectations. A few days later, a doctor from one of the obstetric practices stopped by my office and asked why I had used the name after he'd told me they were going to use it. My heart sank. I had no idea what he was talking about.

After several sleepless nights of trying futilely to recall his mentioning it to me, I concluded (for the sake of my sanity) that it was a conspiracy of my inattentiveness and the doctor's dry sense of humor. Apparently, I didn't listen carefully or thought he was joking. Anyway, the obstetrician forgave me, patients probably thought it was a coordinated effort, and the doctor's sense of humor is serving him well in his new role — mayor of the city.

Now hear this

Harry Lorayne, bestselling author of books on improving your memory, trains business executives across the country to strengthen their memory. The *Los Angeles Times* calls him "the Muhammad Ali of the memory business." Here's what he says about learning techniques, ". . . your education doesn't really begin until you start to listen."

Active listening heightens understanding and retention, so untreated hearing loss not only risks social isolation, but it also jeopardizes your learning ability. If you can't distinguish certain words, don't hear the oven buzzer, and often ask people to repeat themselves, it's time to have your hearing checked. You are among the 28 million Americans with diminished hearing.

Don't be discouraged. About 95 percent of hearing loss is correctable with hearing aids — analog, digital, or implanted — available from a few hundred dollars to as much as $15,000 for an implanted device. The adjustment comes easier to those who seek help before significant hearing loss occurs, so although I'm just beginning to miss a few sounds, it's on my ATB list.

Food for thought is fat free

Where the brain is concerned, you can't overdo it. Every other organ in our body suffers from overuse; our brain gets flabby with disuse. A diet of lifelong learning beefs up our brain and keeps us mentally young.

Only in the last thirty years have scientists discovered that brain cells act very much like muscle cells. Repeatedly lifting a weight builds a muscle and improves its function. Repeatedly challenging the brain improves mental function; therefore a well-exercised brain processes more information faster.

A few minutes of mental calisthenics a day improves perception, memory, and judgment — a cognitive trifecta worth pursuing. You're not saddled with expensive equipment, gym memberships, a personal trainer, or specific start times. Everything you need rests between your ears. Which can be a problem — the resting part that is. One savvy tout observed that, "The brain is a mass of cranial nerve tissue, most of it in mint condition!" Mental acuity depends on mental exercise. My thinking? If intellectual conditioning improves the odds that my mind will make it to the finish line at the same time by body does, show me the track.

Dr. Howard Gardner, Professor of Psychology at Harvard University and Professor of Neurology at Boston School of Medicine, is best known for his theory of multiple intelligences. He groups our brain functions into five main categories: language, spatial ability, logic, memory, and creativity.

If you exercised only your right arm, you wouldn't expect your left arm to be as muscular or be able to lift as much. Spinach is good for you, but not if that's all you eat. The brain's eclectic appetite feeds on every type of mental stimulation, creating unlimited opportunities.

It seems our brain thrives on doing several things at once — a stronger area for women than men. We've been multi-tasking for years. Remember balancing a baby on one hip while stirring the spaghetti sauce and calling out spelling words to a first grader?

The best news is that research indicates the mature brain *does* regenerate and add neurons to the thinking center. In *Older & Wiser,* Dr. Richard M. Restak says, "The brain of an older person is not inferior to that of a younger counterpart; instead, the brain of an eighty year old is organized differently than that of a thirty-five year old." He says our brain retains the capacity to function well into our eighties and nineties. So, yes, you *can* teach the ol' gal new tricks.

Great thinkers of science and literature agree that curiosity sparks the engine of lifelong learning. Albert Einstein urges us to "stand like curious children" and Rudyard Kipling tells us that six honest serving-men taught him all he knew — "Their names are What and Why and When; and How and Where and Who."

Senior citizen centers, universities, and colleges begin a long list of places to satisfy your curiosity and answer all of Kipling's questions. Classes on everything from weaving to world religions fill lengthy catalogs. Are you more interested in taking physics or French? Go for it. It's a good bet you'll do as well as the younger students. Remember the wager between the tortoise and hare? Slow and steady won the race. And you can too.

You probably enjoyed playing along with *Who Wants to be a Millionaire* more than *The Weakest Link* — possible influenced by a suave gray-haired male host compared to a younger caustic female. But more likely it was the multiple-choice questions and the slower pace of *Millionaire* that attracted you. It was a friendlier format for mature minds.

The million-dollar question is how to avoid those frustrating senior moments. Eleanor Roosevelt ate three chocolate-covered garlic balls every day because her doctor said it would improve her memory. Now there is "brain gum" that claims to boost memory. I don't think either sound like a tasty alternative.

I'd rather believe the mature brain takes longer to recall things because it has several decades more to remember than does a thirty-five-year-old brain. Or as grandpa would say, "Old timers have more sense in their little finger than those young whippersnappers ever will." The trick is to get the information from our finger to our tongue. Memory experts say those tip-of-the-tongue answers usually rise to the surface in less than an hour. (Mine seem to bubble up around 3 a.m.)

Let's see what rises to the surface with this riddle. Pick a number between one and nine. Got it? You won't need paper and pencil, just follow along. Multiply your number by nine. If the sum is double digit, add the two numbers together. Subtract three. Now give your number a letter: A for one, B for two, C for three, and so on. Name a profession that begins with your letter. What natural resource do the folks in this line of work require?

Urban dwellers likely chose firefighters and rural folks picked farmers on their way to the final answer — water. Experiment with every number between one and nine to see how it works. Now let's carry the fun a little further and relate a farmer's sunup to sundown challenges to our effort to grow a healthy memory. Grab a hoe and come along.

Weed out the negative

Turn over the hardened dirt that says there's nothing you can do about a flagging memory, and break up the clods that say you're too old.

When we get too farsighted to read fine print, we don't anticipate blindness, we have our eyes checked and buy the appropriate glasses. When other physical systems fail, we search for ways to overcome them. Yet, when our memory fails we tend to think there's nothing to be done.

Mind/body researchers say our fear of *certain* mental decline is unfounded. Dementia and Alzheimer's are disease processes. Like cancer and heart disease, not everyone gets them and, as with those diseases, it's possible to reduce your risk.

Unlike Alzheimer's, CRT disease — Can't Remember Stuff — is curable. We spend too much time reflecting on the hereafter — as in walking into a room and saying, "What am I here after?" If we do nothing, those senior moments become hours of frustration. Remember what our mother's told us: "Can't, never could?" Well if you can't remember stuff now, it won't get any better unless you dig out the negative and plant some positive attitudes.

Plow the ground

Set your life into nice neat furrows. Plow under the *hereafter* episodes with *always* and *never* organization. For starters you won't have as much to remember if you get organized. If the scissors, keys, glasses, checkbooks, and your purse all have a place then you won't have to look for them.

Somewhere on the human genome there must be a specific gene that determines if we prefer lists and organization or if we thrive on clutter and spontaneity. If so, my daughters and I got opposite genes. What I call organized — the spices in alphabetical order — they call anal. If you tend to agree with them, at least try one or two of these ideas, then find your own creative solutions.

Have you ever misplaced your toothbrush? I thought not. That's because you *never* walk out of the bathroom with it. How about the coffee? No? That's because you *always* put it in the same place. I lost two pair of prescription sunglasses before deciding I needed to wear them on a cord around my neck. It works.

Apply the always/never theory to everything you frequently misplace. (They're not lost because you know they are in the house; you just can't remember where.) Sometimes getting rid of the clutter helps, and sometimes it's adding something that works better. Hang a key holder next to the door, needlepoint an attractive glasses case and keep it on an end table as a practical decoration. At our house we have scissors in every room — kitchen shears, sewing scissors, ones for clipping articles, and a pair for cutting gift wrap.

Sometimes the worst place to put something is in a "safe place." We've all done it. We can remember that we purposefully put something in a safe place, we just can't remember where that is. The solution? Designate one container — a drawer, a shelf, a basket, a box — as your safe place. For years my place for airline tickets, invitations, receipts for items to be return, and the like went in a carved wooden chest that sat on my dresser. Reflecting changing times, the Mediterranean chest went the way of the shag carpet and harvest gold appliances. Now a Lucite box sitting on a shelf beside computer software boxes serves this purpose. When my other half swears I must have something he can't locate, it's nice to have only one place to look.

Both in their eighties, Bernice and Lou maintain their own home and stay socially active entertaining friends and traveling. On gaming trips to Laughlin or Las Vegas, Bernice doesn't have any problem remembering the rules to the games; but they missed a trip to Italy because she couldn't remember putting the tour tickets safely in a luggage pocket. There was no reason to pack if they didn't have the tickets, so they never looked in the luggage, and the plane took off without them.

Planning a safe place during travel avoids the frustration of constant digging through pockets and purses. What seems logical before the trip often gets lost in the excitement and can't be recalled later. The luggage key in a coat pocket when you leave in freezing temperatures is forgotten when you arrive on a tropical island eight hours later, so develop a plan.

Proximity prods my medication routine. Morning pills sit next to the cups; lunch and evening medications reside in a plastic basket with the salt and pepper; bedtime pills stay in the drawer with floss and night cream. The system only works if I set the pill bottles on the counter while getting the other items and return them to their place *immediately* after taking them. Otherwise I won't remember if I took them or not.

It took a while to find a system for remembering to take medications when eating away from home. Now I carry my brightly colored pillbox along with my lipstick in a small cosmetic bag. Since I usually apply fresh lipstick after a meal, I haven't missed many doses. Only once did I spray the medication for osteopenia in the same nostril two days in a row. A nose full of scabs convinced me to check the calendar and adopt an odd/even day routine. My new medication, taken once a week, creates another challenge.

Lest you think I'm a total dummy, I should explain that about 90 percent of the time I would remember the medications without the proximity cues. But why not go for 100 percent compliance? Since a major reason for nursing home admissions is to administer medications, I'm practicing preventive medicine.

A centrally located collection point saves searching for items at the last minute. The dryer top serves as our staging area. The day before I run errands, I begin stacking things there as I think of them — library books, video rentals, the dry cleaning ticket, coupons. A flat-backed basket hung by the back door serves the same purpose. And don't forget that giant magnetic bulletin board in every home. Everything from grandchildren's art to doctor's appointment cards are in plain view every time you open the refrigerator door.

When you've plowed through the clutter and unearthed some practical ways to organize, you're ready for the next step toward reducing the "hereafter" episodes.

Sow the seed

A nutritious diet and regular physical exercise germinate brain cells. Recommended activities and the approach to maintaining brain health varies, but every author on the subject puts diet and exercise near the top of the list.

Annuals, like our short-term memory, flower then fade and die at the end of the growing season. Perennials, like our long-term memory, bloom year after year, if properly nourished. Brain-wise, with attentive listening and concerted effort, annuals become perennials. Plant a strong seed and it takes root in long-term memory. Without conscious effort to remember someone's name, face, or a sparkling idea, the image flits away like a firefly. You have to be quick to catch a mental firefly and store her in your long-term memory jar where she'll glow forever.

Danielle C. Lapp teaches memory improvement courses and has written several books on the subject. In her book *Don't Forget! Easy Exercises for a Better Memory*, she says, "It isn't enough to know you must be mindful of something you want to remember: You must then do it."

Our brain would become root bound if we remembered everything. What if we remembered every face we ever saw, the taste of every meal, the smell of every perfume, every physical pain, and every emotional slight? We'd go crazy.

A brain chemical, like a once popular song, accentuates the positive and deletes the negative — like childbirth pain. There's no in between. Our mind prevents information overload by tossing out things that are too painful to remember or that we don't value enough to be mindful of. And there lies the clue for how to remember. By employing all our senses we say to our brain, "Hey, this is important, catch it while your can."

The more senses we involve the stronger the message. To root a memory, listen carefully, repeat the information, create a visual picture, and let your brain know that you value the information.

Water and fertilize

We can call on a Greek goddess — Mnemosyne — to feed and water our freshly planted seeds. Ms. Nee-mon-ik, the goddess of memory, is no stranger. She's been feeding anemic memories since grade school; you just didn't know her name. Remember "Columbus sailed the ocean blue in 1492" and 'i' before 'e' except after 'c'? They are mnemonics — formulas and tools to help us remember. So are rhymes, riddles, lists, calendars, and yellow sticky notes.

My neighbor, Ed, offered this rhyme when he saw me struggling with a water hose connection: righty-tighty; lefty-loosy. Now I never have to wonder if I'm turning something in the correct direction.

Using "Thirty days hath September, April, June, and November" is easier than memorizing how many days in each month. HOMES prompts our recall of the Great Lakes. And putting the pal in principal and an 'o' for the dome in the capitol building helps us find correct spellings.

Mneumonics fertilize memory and give a boost to eager young learners as well as to us oldsters. My grandchildren are a great source. Grandson, Andrew, uses "Never eat sour watermelons" to remember the clockwise position of north, east, south, west.

Visual mneumonics teach left from right. Stretch your hands in front of you, palms out, fingers together, thumbs pointing to each other. The left hand forms an 'L' and helps a child remember which is their left hand (although a challenge for my dyslexic granddaughter, when trying to learn which side of the plate to set the fork).

Grandson, Austin, quickly picked up on a multiplication mneumonic. Try it by spreading your fingers apart and putting your left ring finger down. Your left pinky becomes a one, the ring finger a space, followed by eight standing digits to make 18 — 2 x 9. Continue consecutively across the fingers for each answer. The right ring finger indicates 81. Interesting, huh?

Scare away the crows

Farmers constantly monitor their fields to guard against intruders that worm their way into the juiciest tomatoes, rob the cornfield, and infest the grain. They spray insecticide and build straw scarecrows to scare away the birds and maximize the harvest. Fatigue and stress peck at our concentration and wither our memory as surely as drought dries up crops.

Many of us are familiar with the growing evidence of stress that occurs around our waist. Dr. Cynthia R. Green says stress also affects our memory. In *Total Memory Workout: 8 Easy Steps to Maximum Memory Fitness,* she says, "There is growing evidence that stress may directly impair memory function. Research has linked excess stress to shrinkage of the hippocampus, the area of the brain associated with new learning."

Bobby McFerrin's song *Don't Worry, Be Happy!* makes it sound so easy. It's not. Bad times, even happy times, cause stress. I'd like to offer some personal testimony of success in this area, but the truth is I'm a bad example.

In the '70s, Dr. Thomas H. Holmes developed a scale for measuring the stress of adjusting to change and gave a numerical value to forty-three life change units (LCU). Death of a spouse scored 100, a son or daughter leaving home 29, and celebrating Christmas 12. Holmes predicted that anyone who scored over 300 LCU points would develop a major illness in the next two years. Although I took the test several years after the fact, a score of 546 could probably have predicted the lump in my breast eighteen months after Fred's death.

Thirty years later, Tension Tracker 2002, a nationwide survey sponsored by Tylenol, finds Americans more stressed out, with lack of time, financial issues, and terrorism topping the list of concerns.

Most of us know the same-song-second-verse recommendations by heart — exercise, eat a balanced diet, get plenty of rest, organize — yet haven't conquered stress.

My embarrassing encounters with the effects of stress on memory began in high school. Traditionally, sometime during the football game the head twirler leads her squad around the track and introduces the members to the visiting team's twirlers. On one of these occasions, I opened my mouth to introduce the blonde-haired girl on my right and went blank. We had practiced together for two years; and she has such an easy name, you can probably guess it from her initials, C.S. I don't recall if Carole introduced herself or I recovered, but it has given me a lifelong fear of forgetting names.

In researching memory techniques I discovered this bad experience taught me to use many of the expert's suggestions. On the way to an event, Vince and I rehearse the names of people we expect to see, describe them, and try to remember as much about them as we can. This technique proved a real challenge the first winter we spent in a 55-plus RV resort. Fortunately, everyone wears nametags because when gray hair, bald, glasses, hearing aids, and casually dressed are eliminated from descriptions, what's left?

Practicing what I preach (see Chapters 1 and 3) has helped, but controversy and adversity still send me into a tailspin. For example, doctors told me they would have to wait for further tests, but it looked like my mother's spinal problem was cancer (it wasn't). In the following two days, "Ms. Organized" lost her car keys *and* sunglasses, a personal confirmation that stress affects our memory. I don't care to speculate on what tripping over a parking lot speed bump (getting a nasty bruise on the chin) and getting caught picking my nose in public indicates.

Recently I lost a contact lens as I rushed to get ready to meet a granddaughter at the emergency room.

Misplacing things is my cue to back off the throttle and curb the stress. Yoga lessons are on my ATB list. In the meantime, exercise, lunch with a friend, a relaxing bath, a nature walk, or a window-shopping trip ease the tension. It must be working. Psychologists studying the effects of stress on health report that people under stress are four times more likely to catch a cold, and I go for several years without catching one.

If weight gain is your downfall, keep in mind that stressed spelled backwards is desserts and look for a stress reliever other than a trip to the bakery. Pull weeds, do deep breathing, meditate, do yoga, get aromatherapy — whatever works.

Rotate the crops

Successful farmers systematically rotate crops to prevent soil depletion and break up disease cycles. Just as crops with different food requirements build fertile soil, a variety of mental stimulation maintains a vigorous brain and discourages mental decline.

Neurobics, psychologists' word for doing ordinary things in a different way, has the same effect on the brain that aerobics has on the body. For the best results, switch off the automatic pilot and break the routine. Take a different route, brush your teeth with your other hand, learn a foreign language.

With a bushel of ideas for harvesting a fruitful mind (and no doubt overloaded with farmer analogies) you're ready to reap the benefits by turning your mental lapses into memorable moments.

Have you ever missed a memorable family picture because there wasn't any film in the camera? Me too. Likewise, if we neglect to load our brain with a thought, then nothing develops when we want to recall the vision. The brain, like a VCR or tape recorder, is ready and waiting for you to push the "record" button.

Here's an example: You get out of the car, lock the door, and head off to the nearest mall entrance, wondering if the blouse you saw last week is still on sale. After shopping for an hour you walk up and down several isles in the parking lot to find the car and dig through six pockets of your purse to find the keys.

And it could be worse. My neighbor rushed off to the grocery store for some last-minute dinner items; and when he came out, his car was gone. After assuring himself it wasn't there, he called the police. They took a report, including a description of the car, and offered him a ride home. As they turned the corner onto our street, there sat the car he'd described in his driveway. Only then did he remember he had taken his wife's car because he was in a hurry and hers was in back of his.

To avoid such embarrassing moments, try recording your shopping trip. You pull into the parking lot and before locking the car and dropping the keys in the pocket where you *always* put them, say to yourself: "I'm facing east about ten cars from the entrance with the letter 'D' in the store name at the beginning of the aisle."

In a multistory garage, relate the level to something familiar and picture the number with that item. Maybe a seven inside a shoe if that's your shoe size. Or picture your grandchild who is five carrying a big number five. If the floors are color-coded, associate the color with something. The more outrageous, the more likely you are to remember, so have fun. Visualize bright red strawberries spilling out of the elevator or little green men jumping up and down on your car. For the clincher hum an appropriate song like *Blueberry Hill* or *Tie a Yellow Ribbon Around the Old Oak Tree.*

Not only will you never have to look for your car, you'll enter the mall smiling and relaxed. Continue the recording as you enter the store by noticing the merchandise at the entrance — baby clothes, purses, whatever. Tune in to what you're doing. Pay attention.

The Dallas/Fort Worth airport took the color coding and music connection a step further. When they unveiled a new parking system, Elvis impersonators were on hand to keep motorists from getting all shook up. Now with color-coded signage, parking lots, and shuttle buses, you don't need to be a hound dog to sniff your way to the terminal.

Memory experts say inattention is the main reason for forgetfulness. We never recorded the information in the first place so there's nothing to play back. To move information from our sensory memory to short-term memory and finally to long-term memory takes practice.

Whether in a classroom, at the computer, the kitchen table, or around a card table, lifelong learning keeps our mind in shape. A growing body of evidence suggests that mental, physical, and social pursuits may be effective against dementia, even Alzheimer's.

A study at the Rush Alzheimer's Disease Center in Chicago found that "frequent participation in cognitively stimulating activities is associated with a reduced risk of Alzheimer's disease."

A dry sponge sits unused, rough, and brittle until dipped into water. Then, like magic, it becomes soft, subtle, and ready to soothe or scrub. Likewise, our brain soaks up every drop of information offered. Without mental stimulation it dries up. Lifelong learning is the wellspring that nurtures our brain. It's not a new idea. Three hundred years before Christ, Aristotle declared education to be the best provision for old age.

Darline is the poster girl for lifelong learning. She's never let gender, her petite size, or age stop her. At thirteen she lied about her age to get a job at a golf course. When her children were small, she worked from home, tying five-dozen trout flies a day. "I always had a giant vegetable garden, and we raised a couple of beef every year. One to eat, one to sell," she said. "That's really helpful with teenagers."

She and her husband, a retired California highway patrolman, always avid fishermen, built five boats, sanding and varnishing each one to high-gloss perfection. When they retired, she took on a five-pound sledgehammer and twelve-inch nails to help build their log retirement home from a kit.

When we visited them in LaConner, Washington, their home was filled with quilts. Of quilting lessons, she said, "I've learned enough now that I don't need teachers. I can get it from books." The taste of her plums and the flower photograph hanging in my living room attest to how well she's adapted her gardening to the Northwest climate.

At sixty she took up pool, and within seven years she won the Arizona State Senior Olympics Gold Metal in her age group. The next year she won the silver in pool, the gold in archery.

Since I last visited with her, they've sold the log house and bought two smaller places. Never one to miss an opportunity, she's learned you can play year-round by spending summers in Washington and winters in Arizona. A lifelong pursuit of new and varied activities keeps Darline, now past seventy, young in body and mind.

Be a sport

Like Darline, Frances was too busy for sports until she retired. After sixty-five years of freezing Minnesota winters, Arizona sunshine opened new opportunities. Golf provided mental, physical, and social stimulation as she learned the rules, played the game, and made new friends.

When golf and tennis are too strenuous, try pool or shuffleboard. If you're beyond participating, become a fan. Study the rules, calculate your team's progress, and read about the players and coaches.

I keep trying to find something I'm suited for, but it seems anything requiring more coordination than walking and chewing gum is beyond my expertise. In politically correct vernacular, I'm severely athletically challenged, which may explain my admiration for athletes.

My ability scored zero in elementary school and hasn't improved. The best way to describe my position on the fifth-grade softball team is short with not a lot of stop. At golf, I whiffed more than hit; at bowling, I filled more gutters than fall leaves; at tennis, I got tangled in my own feet going for an outside shot and almost broke my jaw (really); my most recent endeavor — pool — is equally embarrassing.

I've not stumbled onto anything my eyes and hands can agree on, but I've always been a fan. My love affair with baseball began with the Houston Buffaloes in the late '40s. A feisty pitcher and future congressman, Vinegar Ben Mizell, and the future Mrs. Bing Crosby highlighted those years. I was in the stadium the night Kathryn Grant was crowned Miss Buff Baseball. A few years later, she married Bing. Poet Walt Whitman declared baseball a blessing. My life has often been blessed with a baseball connection. The incident with George Steinbrenner is just one of many baseball tales. The hospital co-sponsored several health fairs with the Texas Rangers and the Ranger Wives Club. Most old T-shirts got tossed in the downsizing process, but I kept the one signed by all the wives — names like Valentine, Ryan, Buechele, Petralli, Sierra, Lopes and many more.

Fran, one of my new neighbors, belongs to the Texas Rangers Women's Club, a group of volunteers organized in 1974. About 200 women from their twenties to eighties attend games together, provide seats for seniors and disadvantaged youth, and assist the ball club with special promotions. Fran says, "It's a year-round affair. We go to plays together, participate in food drives, have luncheons with speakers who are often coaches and ballplayers. It's fun."

It's never too late to take up a sport or become a sports fan, so join the fun!

Take a different view

There's no one map for lifelong learning. A street map, an atlas, and a globe all represent the earth's surface, yet they provide very different perspectives. Speed around the learning curve by viewing the world from many angles and attitudes. Experience another culture through its games. Mitzi is teaching her neighbors to play mah-jongg — the game the ladies of *The Joy Luck Club* played. Or try, Go, the game played in *A Beautiful Mind.* Read something different, like Michael Pollan's *The Botany of Desire* that looks at the world from plants' point of view or try Diana Gabaldon's historical fantasies. For maximum brain gain, read a mix of fiction and nonfiction, mystery, romance, westerns, and biographies. It makes Jane an interesting woman.

Make up a story

Creating interesting stories helps you focus. Fifty years later I can recall how our study group remembered that Sinclair Lewis wrote *Ring Around the Rosy.* We pictured Sinclair gas pumps dancing around in a circle. Using this device we quickly matched the list of authors to their works and did well on the exam. Stories turn dull facts into easily remembered information. When temptation lurks, long forgotten morality sermons spring to life in Bible parables and Aesop's fables.

While hiking to the Burgess Shale in British Columbia, our guide described the plants, animals, geology, and biology of the area. I recall few of the details of the trek except for Rosemary's description of lichen. It goes like this: Alice Algae and Freddy Fungus took a lichen to each other. Freddy bought a house, Alice moved in to cook, and they lived happily ever after. It's a fun and easy way to remember that the symbiotic relationship of fungus and algae create lichen.

The high-tech folks have also discovered that people remember visual things better than numbers and letters. Pointsec Mobile Technologies has developed a system using pictures to help people remember their password. Users make up a story to go with the pictures they choose, then press the pictured clues in sequence to access their computer systems and electronic devices.

Ninety percent of the brain's sensory input is visual, so add color, motion, depth, and form to your memory bank. Involve as many senses as possible. Recall the scent of a freshly cut pine tree; the feel of your father's rough hand wiping a tear, the taste of your grandmother's apple pie. Make your stories epic productions in living color, with surround sound and irresistible aromas. Preview them a couple of times before putting them on the shelf. When you're ready to replay that special moment, the dusty layers of time will slide right off.

Telephones that retain our frequently called numbers and calculators that respond in seconds contribute to our lazy memory. Mnemonics are great aids, but we don't want to neglect flexing our memory. Make some mental lists and strive to remember some phone numbers. There's no need to remember every telephone number; that's what directories are for, but certain numbers come in handy — Social Security, driver's license, voting precinct, to name a few.

In *Smart for Life, How to Improve Your Brain Power at Any Age*, Dr. Michael Chafetz suggests "chunking numbers." For mental exercise and as a practical way to remember a long series of numbers, slice them into manageable chunks and make up a story associated with numbers you can easily recall. With this method you can remember long numbers by stringing the chunks together into a mental filmstrip. Use clues like 911, 1776, 1492, 33 or 78 (record speeds), 4 quarts in a gallon, 5 points on a star, family birth dates and so on. See if you can find the hidden number in this story. When the stock market crashed, a dozen investments went skidoo in an envelope with no postage due. If you think of 1929, twelve stock certificates going into an envelope addressed twenty-three skidoo and stamped with thirty-seven cents worth of postage, you come up with 1929122337 (unless the postage goes up before this is published).

Douglas Mason, coauthor of *The Memory Workbook*, suggests making up very visual and even funny stories. Test his theory by adding details to a simple scenario like a law officer driving his car down the highway to remember 58866. Having trouble? If so, think of the shape of his badge, a make of car, and a famous route — his 5-point star, Olds 88, and Route 66. Creating a story is fun and great mental exercise. For anyone who thinks grandma's losing it, keep your method a secret and impress the family with your numbers know-how.

Four score and seven years ago

We're well aware that memorized pieces from years past are recalled more easily than what we read in the morning paper; but with practice we can resuscitate the mind that memorized the state capitols, the books of the Bible, the Gettysburg Address, and lengthy verses assigned in high school. Physically you may be beyond collecting seashells or jumping over candlesticks, but reciting poetry, nursery rhymes, and tongue twisters keeps your mind nimble. So does memorization.

Now that you're limbered up, memorize a new poem and write one of your own. For a real workout try Haiku. Here's how: Write three unrhymed lines of five, seven, and five syllables (17 total) preferably about nature.

Haiku I can't do
These seventeen syllables
Show I have no clue

Even a feeble effort like mine, which falls short in two categories, is good exercise. Send your best effort for posting on the *Umbrella* Web site.

The magic of music

To work out another area of the brain, set your poems to music. Sing, hum, whistle. Revive *Name That Tune* and search your memory for the words of once popular songs. Join the church choir, a community chorus, or barber shop quartet. Check out your knowledge of current music with the daily crossword puzzle at www.billboard.com. As with reading, the wider the range of your entertainment — from opera to Grand Old Opry — the greater the benefit.

Stroke patients who have lost the ability to speak often find their first words by singing a familiar song like *Happy Birthday.* Maybe musical skill is like riding a bicycle, something you never forget. At least it's easier the second time around, say the experts, so you remember more notes that you expect.

It's never too late to learn to play an instrument or return to one you played years ago. New Horizons Bands, an organization begun in 1991 by professor Roy Ernst at the Eastman School of Music in Rochester,

New York, has groups in twenty-one states and two Canadian provinces. Sponsors, the International Music Products Association, and the National Association of Band Instruments provide start-up grants to assist volunteer directors in organizing senior-citizen bands nationwide.

In my hometown the senior center supports two bands, a Ukulele Band and a Kitchen Band, which rehearse weekly and entertain in the community. Musicians of any age are welcome to join the Arlington Community Band.

Our winter home in Arizona has weekly jam sessions where young-at-heart musicians pull out old instruments and jam for their own pleasure and that of a toe-tapping audience. Some, like seventy-five-year-old Roland, have taken up an instrument for the first time. Two years later he's a member of a banjo band that entertains community groups.

Patsy only plays the piano for her own entertainment. "I took a few lessons as a kid, but I hated it and Mother got tired of fighting with me about practicing. Now I love it," she says. She resumed lessons until she became embarrassed by the number of times her busy schedule and charity work required her to cancel classes. "I don't play for anyone else, though. It's just for myself. I have a book with easy chords and play all the old popular songs. It's very relaxing."

If your mom once played the piano then gave it up for lack of money or space, consider getting her one of the small, reasonably priced keyboards now available. This advice comes from personal experience with my dear mother-in-law, now in her nineties.

Ruby's brother, sister, and grandchildren disappeared behind a curtain of dementia several years ago. Now the present occasionally peeks out for a brief encore then makes a quick exit. All seems lost until she sits down at the piano. Her eyes sparkle and she sometimes smiles as her crippled fingers slide over the keys, finding enough of the notes to recognize the hymns and dance tunes of her youth. When she plays the piano, she seems to forget the uncontrollable bodily functions and the indignities of dependence. Maybe the melody brings back the mischievous young girl who hid in the tall grass of North Dakota summers, the determined divorcee who moved her family across the country, and the brave woman who overcame her fears to work overseas for the extra money she needed to pay a street assessment and keep her home. I hope so.

Dominos and dice; cards and computers

The nice part of mental exercise is that it's mostly play. "I play dominoes every day," bragged my mother-in-law (I've been blessed with two lovely mothers-in-law). "I'm not like those old women who don't know what day it is," she said at ninety. Maggie dropped out of school during hard times, but she always loved games — cards, bingo, Uno, dominoes. Pictures of children, grandchildren, and great-grandchildren, numbering close to 100, fill her nursing home room, and she can name them all. She left a nightstand full of crossword puzzles in varying degrees of completion when she died at age ninety-five.

Try SET, a card game of visual perception that can be played alone or with a group. It's a game enjoyed equally by MENSA's high-IQ members and children as young as six. Bridge, bingo, canasta, charades, whisk, checkers, chess, scrabble, and a hundred more challenge multiple areas of the brain.

Old standbys like Euchre and Yahoo, newer games like Caverns and Tetris, along with numerous versions of solitaire, can be found online; so test your manual and mental dexterity against yourself, the computer, or an online competitor. Become a video superstar and join your grandchildren's "thumber" world.

Space games, made up games

Jigsaw puzzles, Pictionary (a drawing version of Charades), sculpting, drawing, painting, and video games jog our spatial memory. Flex your spacial muscle by estimating dimensions and mentally rearranging the furniture. Survey a room pretending you'll be asked to describe the details at a trial. Revive the game we played at wedding and baby showers and pass around a bag of hidden objects for participants to finger the shapes and identify the objects.

Liven things up with name games that can be played alone or in a group. Name groupings, like a herd of buffalo, a gaggle of geese, a mob of kangaroos, then try to stump each other with gang, colony, or quiver. Debate whether it's a school or herd of seahorses. My favorite group name? A parliament of owls.

How many names can you come up with for bodies of water? From puddle to sea, the first nine are easy: three begin with a 'c,' a 'b,' and an 's.' Now see how close you can come to twenty and send your list for a surprise reward.

How many male, female, and baby animal names do you know? Buck, doe, and fawn come easy. What about a pen or cob? How many city newspapers can you name? Start with the Boston Globe and work your way west. The ideas are endless. If you're in a retirement home where the lunch conversation often centers on aches and pains and who's in the hospital, give this a try. Soon you'll find tablemates vying to top each other.

While sitting in traffic or waiting in the doctor's office, mentally pack a shopping cart with an alphabet of grocery items, artichokes to ziti; a suitcase full of clothes including socks, T-shirts, and underwear, or a zoo full of animals ending with yaks and zebras. Always repeat the entire list before each addition. With several people playing, players who can't repeat the list or think of a word beginning with the next letter lose. You'll be a winner if you create a mental filmstrip connecting each item to the next.

Create your own versions of the packing game for some interesting results. A generational version has grandma packing a turn-of-the-century valise with undergarments and jewelry like corsets and cameos and her granddaughter stuffing a backpack with thongs and toe rings.

Solve a puzzle

The outside-the-box thinking encouraged by crossword puzzles, as discussed in Chapter 1, is an ideal addition to your mental-fitness routine. Newspapers and inexpensive paperbacks provide several levels of difficulty. Large print, and foreign language versions are available. If you're up to a challenge or want to refresh old skills, get puzzles with clues in one language and answers in another. If you're a beginner, add a crossword dictionary to your library, and you'll soon join a gaggle of gals who jump-start their day with a crossword puzzle.

Add some oomph to your mental workout by making your own puzzles. Begin by writing a word in the middle of a page (graph paper and a long word help) and see how many like things you can attach — sort of a combination of Scrabble and crosswords. Begin with Minneapolis and add cities; or begin with the big-eared exemplar of memory, sit "giraffe" on top of the first letter, hang a "tiger" off the tail, and continue to add animals. Play alone or take turns with an opponent.

Two techniques — visualization and categorizing — spur your memory for this type of puzzle. An imaginary journey across the country or a trip to the zoo spawns a longer list, as does viewing cities and animals in categories. Try naming cities by state and listing all the animals with horns, in the cat family, and so on.

Get the whole family thinking with the invitation to a family reunion. Include puzzle instructions and a challenge. Have them begin with their full name and add as many relatives, first or last names, as they can. At the event award a prize for the best puzzle.

Take a learning trip

In *Our Best Years*, a book based on Helen Hayes' daily radio commentaries, she recounts how young Jewish boys are introduced to the Talmud, "... at the age of four or five — a bit of honey is placed on the book for him to taste the sweetness of knowledge."

You'll find knowledge never tasted better than the confections cooked up by Elderhostel. In collaboration with more than 2,000 colleges, universities, and museums around the world, they offer educational travel programs for older adults. Three-day programs to month-long adventures include lodging, meals, lectures, field trips, and more. An extensive catalog lists these interesting options: "Study Jane Austen in the White Mountains of New Hampshire; explore the spectacular art and architecture of ancient Greece, discover the diverse wildlife of Arizona's Sonoran desert." For a catalog of their adventures in lifelong learning call 877-426-8056 or visit them on the Web at www.Elderhostel.org.

The back pages of *Smithsonian* magazine also list excursions for learning. Actually, all travel is an opportunity to expand your mind. Whether you cruise to Alaska, drive fifty miles from home and stay in a quaint Bed and Breakfast, fly to New York for the best of Broadway, or visit your ancestral home in Europe, travel presents a vast array of sensory stimulation and learning opportunities.

For a threefold benefit, study the place you're going before the trip, soak up the atmosphere while you're there, and relive the experience when you return by making a scrapbook and relating the highlights to your family and friends. If making a scrapbook doesn't appeal to you, dump all the brochures, maps, and pictures in a plastic bag picked up along the way. You'll be surprised at how often you pull out the mementos to enjoy again.

With careful planning, mobility and health concerns don't necessarily preclude travel. Changes brought about by the Americans With Disabilities Act make it possible for wheelchair-bound tourists to wind their way down National Park trails and up special elevators to the top of the Empire State Building. The American Lung Association offers tips for travelers who need supplemental oxygen for an airline trip, and some tour companies specialize in trips for people with limited mobility. The Internet lists several agencies that specialize in travel for older and disabled travelers. A division of Cruise Holidays, At a Snail's Pace, says it best.

If travel at any pace doesn't interest you, then the information superhighway may be just the ticket.

From abacus to amazon.com

The computer age snuck into my life one Christmas as deceptively as earrings wrapped in a shoebox. Ellen brought home discarded materials from her job at Texas Instruments for her craft-loving sisters-in-law. Lou and I folded, stapled, and spray-painted computer punch cards, turning IBM's mainframe waste into wreaths. We made no more connection between these holiday decorations and the beginning of a technology that changed the world than we connected Gutenberg's movable type to the Santas and angels made from *Reader's Digest* magazines.

Historians say this technological journey began in ancient China some 3000 years before Christ with the invention of the abacus — the first numerical calculator. In the 1640s came mechanical adding machines and slide rules. Charles Babbage, considered the father of the first modern computer, introduced his analytical engine in 1830. A century later came ENIAC and UNIVAC the forerunners to the room-size behemoths that used punched cards for engineering and scientific calculations (or for making Christmas decorations).

About thirty years after that came the microprocessor and a decade later, in 1981, the personal computer. Notice we've gone from thousands of years, to hundreds of years, to decades, and as the saying goes, "You ain't seen nothin' yet."

Things really heated up in 1989 when a Swiss fellow, Tim Berners-Lee, a physicist in Geneva, introduced the first Web server. Two years later the server was made available to the public and lit the fuse for the information explosion. The Web went from one to fifty servers in the first year. After that, the timeline is measured in days. In the mid-'90s, Dr. Jakob Nielsen estimated that the number of servers on the Web doubled every fifty-three days. Although saturation has slowed the early proliferation, in April 2001 there were twenty-four million Web servers, and the exponential growth continues.

Why the history lesson? It's good face-saving material. There's no chance we will understand computers the way our grandchildren do. At best we can avoid responding that we're afraid of the water when they asked if we surf—and a little history gives you something to share with them while they're patiently explaining IMing (instant messaging) to you.

If you're a digital diva, burning CDs, surfing the Web for e-commerce bargains, and buying stocks online, you may want to skip the next few pages. Newbies ready to plunge into the computer world, read on.

A computer is no more a luxury than a telephone. You can do without one, but why would you want to? When electric lines dropped into the neighborhood, women plugged in — lights replaced kerosene lamps. Radios, mixers, and toasters followed. Refrigerators replaced iceboxes. Washers replaced rub boards.

Within four years of its introduction fifty million people plugged into personal computers; it took thirty-eight years for radio and thirteen years for television to reach that milestone. And the phenomenal growth continues. The Consumer Electronics Association estimates about 60 percent of American households own computers, with seniors making up the fastest growing segment of the market. Almost half of Americans use e-mail. And in 2001, eighty-one-year-old Pope John Paul II used his laptop computer to send his Thanksgiving message over the Internet.

Computers have the same practical and entertainment potential as electricity. Granted, navigating the electronic world isn't smooth sailing, but you don't want to be left standing on the dock when the ship sails. You can stick your paddle in the water for about $1,000 and learn enough in a few days to e-mail your family and friends. You'll even get thank-you notes from the kids when they can e-mail you! In fact, e-mail pulled ahead of its paper-based rival, commonly called snail mail, several years ago.

And it's not all about fun and games. A survey by Pew Internet and the American Life Project indicates that twenty-eight million Americans, about one-fourth of all adults, have signed on to the Internet to find out more about their faith.

Learning to use the computer and access the Internet assures lifelong learning. Because the computer's logic requirements expand and exercise our mind, researchers credit the overall rise in IQ scores to computers.

Being a what-the-heck-I'll-give-it-a-try kind of gal, Ellen applied to *Bride and Groom* when the wedding she wanted seemed out of reach for two teens in a Dallas public housing project. Her willingness to try paid off. She and Bob were married on TV before he left for Korea

Fast forward fifty years, and Ellen's still giving new things a try. She's tracing the family genealogy, making her own Christmas cards, and e-mailing around the country with no long-distance charges. For Ellen, the computer was a logical step. "It's well worth the $20 a month I spend for Internet access," she says. It was especially worth it when she got to see pictures of her hour-old great-granddaughter transmitted from a hospital in Texas to her home in Oceanside, California.

Ellen took classes at the local community college and bought a computer before her seventieth birthday. Lou, a retired librarian in Houston, told me about her venture into the computer world: "My grandchildren gave it to me for my eighty-fifth birthday, and I love it. They got it all set up, and I've been learning a little at a time. The best part is e-mail. My grandchildren would never write, but I get e-mail from them all the time."

And so can you. Don't let a little mouse with an electric tail freak you out. Anyone who can cook from a recipe or sew from a pattern can learn to use the computer. You got a driver's license by studying the rules of the road and having someone teach you basic driving techniques. In no time you tooled around town without a clue how the internal combustion engine worked.

Using a map and road signs, you can drive from New York to Los

Angeles without once thinking about longitude and latitude. In the same way, you can easily find the entrance ramp to the information superhighway and travel the World Wide Web without mastering the theory behind the technology. Expect a mixture of praise and damnation when you talk to new computer owners; but ask if they plan to give it up, and you'll get an emphatic "never!"

Like buying a car, you need to establish a budget, determine your requirements, and learn something about what's available before purchasing a vehicle for the information superhighway. If you don't have family or friends to guide you through the purchase process, there are classes explaining the basic hardware and software, the difference between Apple products and IBM compatible PCs, how to choose an Internet Service Provider (ISP), and how to protect your investment from power surges and viruses.

You'll have lots to choose from. Computers get smaller, faster, cheaper, and better every year. They've gone from room size to palm size. And iMacs come in five tutti-frutti colors. It's best to check out class availability for each type or choose the type the person you expect to help you has.

A computer ends your search for ways to exercise your brain. A machine with the Shut Down command on the Start menu may be intuitive to a six-year old, not to anyone over sixty. At any age, news that traversing the Internet requires Boolean algebra would have ended my search, but I've been weaving my way around the Web using *and*, *or*, and *not* blissfully ignorant of any algebraic connection.

My point? It doesn't matter if you think microchips are the crumbs at the bottom of the potato chip bag. Just accept the cyberspace jargon and gadgetry like you accept that phonetics isn't spelled like it sounds, and move on. With a few classes, many designed especially for seniors, you'll be on the road to computer literacy.

The Maria-Madeline Project's Experience Senior Power (ESP) brings children to a variety of settings, from senior centers to nursing homes, to teach seniors computer skills. Dell Computer Corporation offers significant discounts on computers to ESP locations, so you may want to encourage an organization in your community to provide a site.

Computer skills broaden your opportunity for fun, games, crafts, and possibly profit. When Roberta's thirty-seven-year marriage dissolved, she headed back to the classroom. "I didn't want to sit around, watch soap operas, and play bridge. I may decide to go back to work. I can use the money; and to get any kind of job today, you have to have computer skills, so I'm taking "Microsoft for Seniors," she says.

Computer peripheries fall in the same category as shoes and jewelry to match a new dress — nice accessories, but not necessary. A scanner is one of these extras. It's a crafters delight that scans printed material, slides, and photographs into the computer for manipulating, printing, or e-mailing. You can convert slides and photos into a digital scrapbook that's easily reproduced to send to every family member or you can make a family calendar. Photographs of past years' celebrations on each month — a July 4th picnic, the family gathered around the Christmas tree — and a small picture of each person on the date of their birth turns a calendar into a keepsake. Additional peripherals let you "burn" digital information onto compact disks and make your own CDs.

Although e-mail's the big online lure, you'll discover that it's the proverbial tip of the iceberg. Any topic you can think of is probably out there on the Web. Entry-level tourists can find their way around; however, with billions of pages on millions of topics, a class in navigating the Net beats floundering around.

Google, just one of many search engines, has three billion pages of information indexed and waiting for your inquiry; and there are approximately five billion more pages at Altavista, Excite, and Hotbot, to name only a few. At Google, a "weight loss" query brings 2,210,000 results. This is when that Internet class to learn how to narrow your search comes in handy.

Is there a doctor in the mouse?

Well almost. Every major health promotion organization — Heart, Cancer, Diabetes, Stroke, and so on — has a Web site. Mayo and Cleveland clinics, Johns Hopkins, and all the other biggies are online. A joint effort of the NIH, the CDC, and the Health Resources and Services Administration at http://chid.nih.gov has a database of more than 100,000 health-related articles.

At the American Institute for Cancer Research, www.aicr.org, site you can look at the latest research, copy recipes using foods and herbs thought to lower health risks, and order a free copy of *Cancer Resources.* The old standbys, the *Physicians Desk Reference* (PDR) and the *Merck Manual of Medical Information* are also online.

Going to the horse's mouth can be heady stuff, so don't get carried away before you check the teeth in online information and services, especially concerning medical information. No doubt, among those two million weight loss sites, there were a few promising dubious herbs and miracle machines to wash the weight away without effort. Dr. Quack and the CDC are both just a click away, so a healthy dose of skepticism is advisable.

The Internet is a wonderful source for answering your medical and wellness questions; however, you need to know who's supplying the answers and how recently they posted the information. Was the article written by a doctor or sponsored by one of the organizations mentioned above? How recently was it updated? If you're unsure go to www.QuackWatch.com. Any site selling products that promise miracle cures should immediately raise suspicion. The usual advice applies — consult your personal health care provider before diving into unknown waters.

Join the click clique

Shopping, gaming, news updates, health information, monitoring the stock market, listening to music, and a thousand other things are at your fingertips. In a one-man crusade to save a failing e-commerce stock he owned, a friend clicked on its site often hoping the added traffic would boost the stock price (sorry, Sid, I thinks it's flown the coop).

You can vote, add your opinion to polls, even click for charity. In exchange for advertising, companies sponsor sites offering charitable contributions. My favorite is www.thebreastcancersite.com. Every day that enough people click on the site, a free mammogram is donated to an underprivileged woman — about seventy a month at current clicking. And at last there is a way to get that rice we didn't eat as a child to people around the world — at least that's what the folks at www.Thehungersite.com say. Pet food is provided for each click at an animal rescue site and each click on the rainforest site preserves 11.4 square feet of rainforest. A good deed is just a click away.

Fantasy becomes fact

It's not surprising that the word cyberspace was coined in a fantasy novel by William Gibson. Just a decade ago, only Toto could have whisked us through this intricately woven Web of information; computers that respond to voice commands; and a Cross pen that zips your handwritten messages into the computer.

We've experienced the dramatic effects of computerized medical equipment on diagnostic and surgical procedures. Now the technological tidal wave is washing up on the home shores. I pooh-poohed predictions of surreal computer applications — refrigerators that make the grocery list knowing when the eggs are gone and when the milk is past its date and televisions that know what I want to watch. Now that TiVo is actually on the market, I'm pampering my old refrigerator hoping for one of those new models that save me from sniffing sour milk. All this, yet Internet pioneers say we stand at the edge of the electronic frontier with more exotic horizons still to explore.

Lifelong learning the key

Scientist say we have as many neurons bustling around in our brain as there are stars in the heavens. It's up to us to generate enough friction among those neurons to keep our mental light shining for years to come.

Here's what Henry Ford had to say about learning and age: "Anyone who stops learning is old, whether at twenty or eighty. Anyone who keeps learning stays young. The greatest thing in life is to keep your mind young." Like our cars, our brain is reliable if we keep it tuned up, so spark your curiosity and oil your imagination with lifelong learning.

Love and Laugh

Age does not protect you from love. But love to some extent protects you from age.

—Jeanne Moreau

To a great extent, the amount of love and laughter in our life determines how we age. The external and internal wrinkles formed by smiles aren't as harsh as those created by frowns. Choosing love and laughter over bitterness boosts our immune system and relieves stress.

In *Anatomy of an Illness,* Norman Cousins credits laughter with relieving pain and helping to cure a debilitating illness. Centenarian studies list a good sense of humor as a major personality trait of those living to 100. Psychotherapists use humor therapy, and cultures around the world are finding that laughter *is* the best medicine.

Long before the Code Talkers created the only code that couldn't be broken in World War II, the Navajos valued the language of laughter. The First Laugh Rite celebrating the first time a baby laughs recognizes the influence of humor in their culture.

The 25,000 members of a laughter movement that started in India have spread their happy talk to North America. Laughter clubs taught by certified instructors are springing up in parks, retirement homes, and senior centers. Laughter class participants in care facilities say it puts everyone in a good mood and that they are more relaxed and energized. Laughing not only lifts the spirits; hearty laughter increases lung capacity and helps you to breathe better.

Notice how often young children laugh; then notice how often you laugh. Are you surprised? I was. I think of myself as a happy person, but my audible reactions wouldn't prove it. It's been a good excuse to get a healthy dose of the comics along with the heavy news. When we're alone, we laugh less than when interacting with others, so that's another reason to stay socially active.

I learned the value of a smile during the stress of adjusting to supporting myself and the children and learning a new job. Each morning, I delivered a one-sheet flyer with the hospital's cafeteria menu and brief news items to each department and nursing station. Along the delivery route, I worried about having enough gas for the car until payday, how to tell a daughter she couldn't try out for cheerleader because I couldn't afford the uniform, and if a creditor would call and embarrass me at work; but I pasted a smile on my face and cheerily greeted everyone I met. The returned smiles lifted some of the burden. Only years later, when Dianna learned of my situation, did she tell me I seemed so happy she didn't think I had a care in the world—a treasured compliment.

If a smile works, think how much better laughter can make you feel. It's a lesson I hope to take into old age. If you want to feel better, act like you feel better. Share a smile, a pun, or a joke instead of a list of aches and pains, and you'll find you've made someone else and yourself feel better.

Once love and marriage went together like a horse and carriage; but after World War II, long-term marriage got left at the hitching post. Rising divorce rates had more to do with options than the virtue of earlier generations, where roles were well defined. He brought home the bacon; she cooked it, served it, and cleaned the platter. If the experience was less than the expectation, couples stuck it out.

Without love and laughter, marriages go stale. A good marriage is like a bread recipe. It takes a little dough, a dab of sugar, a dash of salt, and just the right amount of push and pull. No matter how you slice it, love and laughter are the butter and jam. Those who got the recipe right are celebrating their forty-, fifty-, and sixty-year anniversaries. From dozens of friends celebrating those milestones, I've chosen the stories of two couples who defied the odds and their parent's predictions. I also chose their stories because of their age when they fell in love.

At fifteen, Sally fell for her older brother's best friend. Three years later, her parents still thought Nat was too old for her, so she ran away from home to marry him. Her parent's said it wouldn't last. They were wrong. After the children were grown, for thirteen years Sally cleaned other people's houses in the morning and took care of her own homemaking in the afternoon. "Marrying so young, I never had my own money, so I enjoyed cleaning and felt a sense of accomplishment," she says.

Sally's home mirrors that sense of pride. To get the look she wanted in her kitchen, she spent hours customizing a scalloped wallpaper border with fingernail scissors. (Apparently she was ahead of her time, since now you can buy it like that.) Her home and her children's homes are filled with her handmade treasures, along with rocking horses and child-size chairs from Nat's basement woodshop.

In midlife she and Nat traveled the back roads of North America on a motorcycle, sometimes with her ruffled dress billowing behind the bike as they headed to a square dance. Although the motorcycle days are past, they escape Wisconsin winters in their motor home traveling down life's highway toward their golden anniversary, laughing together about the struggles of the past and challenges of the future.

At sixteen, Pat, the oldest of six children raised in New York City, met the love of her life while working in a restaurant. When she married, her alcoholic father said, "You'll be back." Pat laughs, "Even that young, I knew I loved Dick and wouldn't be back. Besides, I thought I was marrying money. His family had real butter. I never mixed another color-packet of dye into oleo," she says. For her four children, she created all the warm family memories that she never had growing up, and she is loving her grandmother role.

If yours is one of these long-term marriages, cherish it. If not, try and find the humor in your situation. If there's nothing to laugh about, consider a change no matter what your age.

Women of every age find themselves single and considering whether to go it alone or look for someone to share their life. There are many to testify that falling in love at sixty, seventy, or eighty feels no different than it did at sixteen. Some prefer living single, and although it's not their preference, others are making the most of their single status.

Marge, a Seattle sculptor and widow for many years, has decided carving toads is better than marrying one. She travels, sometimes as the artist-in-residence at resort hotels, sometimes teaching, sometimes learning from others, and always making new friends. "I'm one of the happy singles — carving twice a week, taking tai chi, playing mah-jongg, and starting a painting class next month. I'm never bored. I never found anyone who measured up to my wonderful husband, and I enjoy the freedom to come and go as I please," she says.

A few women, desperate to fill the void of a man in their life, reduce themselves to giggly, tongue-tied teen behavior. Since women in this age group greatly outnumber men, the competition is fierce. I've heard stories of women who keep cake ingredients on hand and a casserole in the freezer so they can be the first to impress the new widower with their good cooking.

A friend (who shall remain nameless) swears her husband, who loves food but has never found his way around the kitchen, will succumb to a hot meal before she's cold in her grave. Before making your way to a man's heart through his stomach, be sure you want to spend lots of time in the kitchen.

Look at yourself before looking for someone else

If you prefer a partner, before looking for the man of your dreams, consider your own dreams. Are you a sports fan by default? Is camping your thing or was it his? Did you give up dancing because it wasn't his thing? What did you do as a couple that you will miss most? And least? You don't have to go to the lake every summer just because *we* always did. Think about the things *you* have always wanted to do.

Now look for a man doing those things. Put yourself in those places and patiently wait for the right guy to come along. And if he never appears, you have been doing the things you enjoy.

Take a dance class. If you're looking for someone who's health conscious, join a health club. Interested in civic affairs and politics? Volunteer for a political campaign. Buy season tickets for two and be ready to invite someone who shares an interest in baseball, the symphony, or theater. Don't fret if that someone is a woman. Women are often the link to those first dates. You won't meet anyone staying at home.

Actually, that's no longer true. You may meet your perfect match sitting at your computer. Before you rule out Internet dating, take a look at some of the services. Enter your ZIP code and age into the search box at www.match.com or www.personals.yahoo.com, and you'll see how many people in your age range are looking for a match. The sites offer advice on guarding your privacy and precautions to make it a safe experience. For about $25 a month you can narrow your search by age, interest, and location, then review biographies and pictures. It's not, as you might think, the choice of desperate losers.

I know a successful professional woman in New York City and a professor from San Francisco who found their perfect matches online. Their profiles helped them locate people of similar interests.

Just reading the profiles let's you know there are a lot of folks just like you looking for someone in their life. I can't vouch for the veracity of these personal ads, but if you're looking for someone with a sense of humor, you might take a clue from these examples:

> *Mint condition male, 1932, high mileage, good condition, many new parts including hip, knee, cornea, valves, not in running condition, but walks well.* Or how about *Active grandmother with original teeth seeking a dedicated flosser to share rare steaks and corn on the cob?* Or perhaps *If you're the silent type, let's get together, take out our hearing aids, and enjoy some quiet time.*

In my case, I made a spur of the moment decision that put me on the circuitous route to the man of my dreams. When Paula asked me to complete a foursome for an evening sail, my first thought was of embarrassing myself by getting seasick. But what the heck, I'd been single for a year, and no one had asked me out. Why not? A double dose of Dramamine and a single glass of wine got me through the evening, and to my delight, Bob called the next day.

We dated for several months, but our interests were too different for a long-term relationship. However, our friendship brought several fortuitous events. Introduction to his church singles group gave me the opportunity to meet other single people whose friendship proved invaluable during my struggle with breast cancer. (It saddens me to remember that two of the most supportive women lost their battles with cancer.)

Every Friday after work, the singles group, mostly women, met at Cecil's on the Creek, a neighborhood hangout (okay, actually a bar.). On several evenings I'd spoken to a nice-looking man there with his friends. One evening Bob introduced him as someone he knew from work. After that, Vince began joining our group for late dinners, and eventually he asked me out. Although I had dated several men, I knew immediately that this was different. Here was the man I wanted to spend the rest of my life with. We were married about a year later.

Ours is not a marriage of identical tastes and would have failed long ago without the benefit of laughter. I laugh at him and at myself. He's a Yankee. I'm a native Texan. He prefers a Cadillac; I drive a compact. He appreciates a fine cabernet, while I'm happy with white zinfandel. He likes symphonies and jazz. I like words with my music. I like baseball. He thinks it's boring.

Is our marriage boring? Certainly not. As the politicians like to say, "We've found lots of common ground." We love to play bridge, entertain, and travel together. We have enough separate interests that several months in the confined space of the motor home isn't a problem. The ups and downs over boulders on jeep trips don't make me sick and suffices for the roller coaster rides he misses.

I never expected to meet someone in a bar, just like my friend Linda never expected to meet an old flame at a class reunion. You may find your fellow in the next pew, across a crowded restaurant, down the block — even in the family. Here are the stories of some women who've done just that.

Mary

Mary and Melvin grew up in rural Indiana and had known each other since childhood. They married others, raised families, and occasionally saw each other over the years. After their spouses died, Mary decided to give the "little brother" a chance. At seventy, a five-year age difference didn't seem like the difference it had when she'd married his older brother so many years before. They "put the family back together" and are sharing their love with a menagerie of animals.

Bette

When Ed and his wife pulled their RV into a spot near Bette and her husband, the two couples found they had lots in common and spent several winters enjoying activities together at their winter home. Bette's husband died of cancer, and two years later Ed's wife died of a heart attack. The two kept in touch, so Bette wasn't surprised when Ed asked her for a ride to the airport for his flight to Fargo. "I picked up a box of chocolates as a Christmas gift and then left it on the seat when he got out of the car, so I jumped out, handed him the box, and gave him a quick kiss on the cheek," she says. His family told her later that she was the main topic of the holiday conversation. Now in their eighties, they've been married for seven years, happily sharing their eight children and twenty-five grandchildren. "They all love to come to our summer home on Dead Lake. I enjoy cooking for everyone and watching them play. We have ten boats, so there's something for everyone. We have such fun, I've told Ed that if he decides to get a divorce, that's fine, but I get all the kids — his and mine!"

Linda

He spotted her in a crowded restaurant in Utah and took the initiative. They were both divorced and on business trips. She was from the east; he was a native Texan whose relatives fought at the Alamo. Her business often took her to his hometown, and he managed his schedule to be where business took her. Linda learned the dungarees she scrubbed floors in were called jeans and that in Texas, with a little starch and a crease, you could wear them anywhere — even to your wedding. If fact, after several years of long-distance romance, that is exactly what she did.

After an outdoor wedding in San Antonio, wedding party and guests, all in western attire, boarded riverboats festooned with wildflowers. The Texas theme continued with bluebonnet centerpieces, margarita toasts, mariachi serenades, and food as colorful as the flowers — guacamole, salsa, quesdillas, and enchiladas.

Linda gave up her home and job to move to Texas. She made a long commute to her new job and spent weekends studying for a master's degree. The hat she wore to graduation wasn't the western one from the wedding, but something to cover her bald head, the result of chemo to fight breast cancer. Her grit and gumption paid off with a fast track through the glass ceiling, a promotion, and a job in D.C.

Ed commuted for a while then turned his business over to his son and joined Linda in Washington. Linda's colleagues have had the benefit of Ed's southern hospitality, and she's had the opportunity to support him through a bout with cancer. Although they keep a small place in Texas and return for most of the UT games, no one would have bet Ed would spend his retirement anywhere but on the range. Even cowboys mellow with love — and age.

Rose

"After John died, I never expected to remarry. We had a good marriage, he left me financially secure, and I had lots of supportive friends," seventy-three-year-old Rose explained as we chatted at her maple table with a center Lazy Susan.

When I asked her about dating she said, "It's like being eighteen again. My daughters, sister, and friends called to wish me luck. My first date was with a very nice man, someone I knew from the neighborhood, but I was bored. During dinner I kept sneaking peeks at my watch and thinking, I'd rather be home watching the *Golden Girls*."

During John's illness their social life all but ended and, after his death, Rose avoided the places they had enjoyed together. "People were so nice, it made me cry, so I stayed away." After a couple of years and with the encouragement of friends, Rose went back to "The Son's of Italy" club, where she met Bob.

That ended peeking at her watch. "We had so much in common, we could talk for hours." A widower with five grown children might have scared off some women, but as the mother of six, Rose welcomed big raucous family gatherings. Bob had dated several women, one much younger. Rose said, "He told me he was happy to meet someone near his age who remembered the old tunes and movies —someone who'd lived through World War II." Ironically, John and Bob were both sailors during the war, so Rose could easily relate to Bob's attachment to his buddies on the carrier USS Wasp.

Bob wanted a wife who shared his memories, and Rose had her own ideas about the kind of marriage she wanted. "Rule No. 1," she said, "he has to live in my house; rule No. 2, he has to go to church with me every Sunday; and rule No. 3, he can't yell at me." (She said she'd never been yelled at in her first marriage, but was very disturbed by it in other marriages.)

Bob didn't mind moving into her house and enjoyed having a hand in redecorating. Just as their lives compliment each other, Rose's maple furniture blends perfectly with Bob's choice of a white kitchen with red accents. Attending church together continued a long Catholic tradition for both, and the only yelling that goes on is to be heard over a house full of talkative Italians when their blended family celebrates together.

Rose advises women considering remarriage to realize that at this age neither of you are apt to change, so it's best to discuss things ahead of time. "Does he fit in with your children and friends? Do you like his family and friends? How will you celebrate holidays?"

When it's time to buy the turkey, it's too late to discuss holiday traditions, so Bob and Rose were wise to have this discussion before marriage. For them, it's no problem. They don't mind going their separate ways on occasion — "We have every day together."

"We both wanted a prenuptial agreement, so our children's inheritances are protected. We've even decided to be buried with our first spouses. When we married, Bob told me he didn't want to change my life, he wanted to add to it," she said. And a decade later, their life together adds up to some wonderful memories.

Evelyn

"I took all those hard courses — language, chemistry — and then my Dad said, 'Girls don't need to go to college.' So I did what was expected and got married at eighteen. The next year, my Italian grandmother chimed in: 'What's the matter for you, you're not pregnant yet.'"

Evelyn followed her husband out of state and happily raised a family. Later they moved from Texas to a small town in the Northeast to be near her family. "We were going in different directions. After enduring years of Texas summers, I loved the crisp falls and snowy winters; but he hated it," she says. Remodeling a 100-year-old house together pointed out all their differences and strained the marriage further.

When Bob moved from New York to the same small town to pursue his artistic endeavors, fate intervened. Evelyn did what no one, including herself, ever expected — she got a divorce. "It just wasn't something my family did."

"No one breaks up a marriage that isn't already cracked, but small towns don't see it that way. Our only concern was that our children would be all right with it, and they understood. Today our four children are very close friends. We feel blessed to have such a bonus in our relationship."

Although the book hadn't been written at the time, Evelyn describes her love story as *The Bridges of Madison County* — "except we did it." They married and moved to the Maine coast, where Bob opened a studio.

"We followed our hearts across that bridge into a new life, and I've never regretted it. We've only been apart one night in twenty-seven years — he was in the hospital."

Nearing eighty, and now a well-known artist, Bob was invited to show his work at the library in the town where it all began. "We were overwhelmed at the reception. Half of the townspeople turned out to greet us. Once again we were filled with gratitude for this small New England town —for the wonderful people who live there and for its beautiful covered bridge."

Evelyn's love story and mine could easily have gone in Chapter 4. Neither of us have any regrets about the path we chose. I followed love into muddy waters and discovered that, although it was okay for daughters to live with someone before marriage, it was clearly not okay for their mothers. Love is seldom prudent, so we rationalized the cost savings and convenience of shared quarters and lived together for a few months until we could be legally married.

Since our families lived out of town, we didn't bother to mention our new living arrangement; but before the wrinkles could hang out of Vince's clothes in my closet, we had a surprise visitor. My mother called in the afternoon to say she was coming through town (with a cousin I hadn't seen in twenty years) that evening.

We survived a tense dinner. Unfortunately, Vince didn't survive the mayor's race a few months later, and I damaged my relationship with his daughters. With time, disappointments healed, relationships improved, and family and friends survived any temporary embarrassment.

Like couples without children giving advice to parents of two year olds, it's prudent to reserve judgment until you've been there. Don't judge your single friends. And if you find yourself in conflict with your children over a midlife relationship, remind them that you have the right to live your own life, just as they do. With that said, it's important that we show more responsibility than a teenager might. Your children will soon realize the benefits of a happy mother. Having a life partner takes the pressure off them to provide all your emotional support.

Look before you leap

If he's as honest and wonderful as you think, he won't mind signing a prenuptial agreement. Judy Sheindlin, the "I'm the boss, applesauce" lady doesn't mince words when it comes to prenuptial agreements. Judge Judy says, "A prenuptial agreement doesn't have to be a sour note."

Adult children are less likely to object to a late-life marriage if they know their inheritance isn't going to *his* children and vice-versa. An attorney specializing in estate planning can assist you in updating wills and preparing a prenuptial agreement that protects you both and assures the lifetime care for the surviving spouse. Remaining assets go to the designated heirs.

I'm familiar with at least one case of a woman with a rather large inheritance waiting until family and friends insisted that she get a prenuptial. Presented with the fact that he wouldn't have full access to her money, the groom-to-be made a quick exit the day before the wedding — proving what friends suspected all along.

This is a pay-me-now or pay-me-later issue, so hire your own attorney. Update your will, power of attorney, and medical power of attorney. Work out prenuptial details together, then have separate attorneys review the documents. Read the fine print, ask questions, and make sure there are no discrepancies between the prenuptial agreements and the wills.

Also check with an attorney before setting up household together. At least nine states recognize the validity of common-law or informal marriages and consider assets community property. So, get legal advice before assuming that living in your house with only your name on the deed exempts you from the inheritance laws regarding marriage. Don't believe that it takes a certain number of years for cohabitation to result in marriage status. If after presenting yourselves as husband and wife for a few months, you die unexpectedly, your children could find themselves giving up half the house and furnishings you and their father worked to accumulate. Or your housemate might divorce you and claim half your assets.

So even if you choose "marriage without formalities," seek the advice of an attorney before jeopardizing your financial future. Widows collecting a spouse's pension need to check the rules before formal *or* informal marriage.

It's hard to believe that a woman can follow her military husband around the world for thirty years, care for the family alone while he fights a war, then be ineligible for his pension if she remarries after his death. However, this seems to be the case. I know of a widow relegated to living alone because she can't afford to lose her pension and medical benefits. No doubt there are many more in her situation. To make matters worse, if the new spouse dies or leaves, the benefits can't be restored. Some of our "family friendly" legislators need to address this injustice.

Other federal and state pension plans have specific rules for maintaining benefits after remarriage, some designate a certain age — fifty-five or sixty — when benefits aren't affected, and some allow benefits to be restored when situations change. Don't take a chance. Before saying "I do," get it in writing.

Beauty and the beast

Middle age dating is a beast. The comfort of a long-term marriage leaves you ill prepared for the dating scene. The rules have changed, a sexual revolution has occurred, AIDS has become a health issue for every age group. (The HIV infection rate of those over fifty is increasing at twice the rate of those under fifty.)

And as one wag put it: "Time may be a great healer, but it's a lousy beautician." There's no need to kid ourselves. We're not spring chickens — although the roosters don't have that much to crow about either. The worst thing you can do is try to look and act like the person you were thirty or forty years ago (nor do most of us want to). Wouldn't you rather date an interesting bald man than one with a ridiculous comb-over? Likewise, you won't fool anyone if you can't read the menu without your glasses. Be yourself.

All women, single or married, want to look their best. We just score ourselves a little harsher when we play the dating game. There's no age limit on *being* sexy, but looking sexy after forty is an effort. Foxy at fifty? Maybe, but after sixty, forget perky breasts and concentrate on pristine breath (remember, goals you can control). Our mothers told us "pretty is as pretty does," and with the shape our skin is in, we want to believe that beauty is more than skin deep. Actually beauty involves all the senses, so that's the approach to take, keeping in mind that it takes an attractive wrapping to hold someone's interest long enough for them to find the gift inside.

What we spend on products to enhance that package makes the beauty business *big* business, so it's no surprise that I found some good advice in *The Essential Drucker*, by well-known author of business books, Peter Drucker. To improve career performance, he suggests identifying strengths, remedying bad habits, and "wasting as little effort as possible on improving areas of low competence and concentrating on areas of high competence and high skill." He concludes that some things are a "given" and unlikely to change. This same formula works for identifying our physical and personality strengths. Forget the givens (wrinkles), and concentrate on things you can change.

Let a smile be your umbrella

As the song from the 1948 Hollywood musical, *Give my Regards to Broadway,* suggests, "A smile will always pay." To protect your smile, The American Dental Association suggests brushing twice a day with a soft-bristled brush, using fluoride toothpaste, flossing once a day, and seeing your dentist twice a year for a professional cleaning and routine check up.

Once people believed losing their teeth was a natural part of aging. Not so. Dental professionals believe that anyone who practices good dental health can keep their teeth forever. And those routine checkups could be a lifesaver. Oral cancer has the worst five-year survival rate of the major cancers, so early detection improves your odds. Some studies even indicate that people with diseased gums are at greater risk for heart disease and stroke.

My dentist, Patrick Moore, isn't subtle. A sign on the office wall reads: *You don't have to floss all your teeth, only the ones you want to keep.* That sign and my mother's struggle with dentures prod me to floss. As children we wrapped a piece of string around a tooth to pull it out; now we're wrapping a piece of string around our teeth to keep them in. Who knew?

Dental care professionals recommend replacing toothbrushes every three months. If you use two, so one can dry thoroughly between brushings, replace them every six months. Since few of us brush for the recommended two-three minutes, some people swear by the electric brushes that time your efforts. If you haven't tried water flossing, give it a try. Portable machines and ones that attach to the shower make it easy.

There is one down side to sixty-year-old teeth. After years of smoking and drinking coffee, tea, and red wine, the pearly whites are no longer white. Jeffrey Zygar, a dentist practicing in Kingston, Washington, says, "Research verifies there are no long-term problems with returning teeth to a brighter shade using a bleaching process."

Teeth can be whitened with OTC products or, more effectively, by a dentist. Dr. Zygar says fees vary depending on the material, process, and area of the country. "In our office, for $300 a person can have custom bleach trays fabricated and bleach their teeth at home for thirty minutes to two hours a day for seven to ten days," he says.

If you're willing to pay more, a laser-bleach process can be completed in less than an hour in your dentist's office. Either process lightens the teeth several shades and lasts about three years.

Although an expensive and lengthy procedure, dental implants — artificial teeth secured to an anchor placed in the jawbone — have become a popular alternative to bridges and dentures. The American Dental Association says candidates for implants must have healthy gums, adequate bone, and a commitment to meticulous dental hygiene.

The University of Sydney's magnetic retention system, still under development, may prove a less expensive method for securing artificial teeth. But the best teeth, whether natural, artificial, implanted, or held in place by magnets, are ones behind a confident smile and lively conversation.

First impressions

Dragon breath extinguishes the fire of interest faster than you can say halitosis. The first "Hello" may be your last chance to make a good impression, so put you best foot (that may be a bad analogy) forward with fresh breath.

Bad breath is a serious enough problem to spawn a whole new profession — breath consultants — and in case you missed the celebration, August 6 is National Fresh Breath Day. Don't laugh until you spend a stress-filled evening trying not to get too close to someone for fear that your breath is offensive.

Experts on bad breath have advice to make us all breathe easier. They say the old blow into your cupped hands to check for bad breath doesn't work. The preferred lick-your-wrist-and-sniff technique gives you a clue to where most bad breath odors originate — on the tongue. Certainly, foods like garlic and onion cause temporary halitosis, but most of the problems originate in the mouth.

Clinical studies indicate that 85 percent of bad breath comes from accumulated bacteria on the tongue. The 500 or so species of bacteria swimming around our mouth find the tongue a welcome platform. Personal Breath Consultants say that tongue combing freshens breath three times more than brushing your teeth and should be a part of your daily oral hygiene routine.

Breath experts claim products containing chlorine dioxide or zinc chlorite and solium chorite provide the best results in eliminating volatile sulfur compounds that cause bad breath. These products are just beginning to appear on supermarket and drugstore shelves, but if you have a bad breath problem, it's worth the effort to find them. Dr. Harold Katz, founder of The California Breath Clinic, offers TheraBreath products containing chlorine dioxide online. And Triumph Pharmaceuticals of St. Louis offers TriOral products.

Formulas and claims may differ, but combing the tongue and brushing the entire mouth with these products seems to be the answer. Ingredients in most mouthwashes, mints, and breath sprays merely mask the odor for a short time. Sugars increase bacteria in the mouth, and alcohol, whether in mouthwash or a beverage, slows saliva flow, dries the mouth, and contributes to bad breath. That explains why these new products are not as sweet or smooth as we're accustomed to; however, they aren't unpleasant.

Medications taken by many seniors — diuretics, antidepressants, painkillers, and antihistamines — are among the 400 medications known to slow saliva flow. If you suffer from dry mouth caused by medications, disease, or radiation therapy, ask your doctor about artificial saliva (sounds nasty, but it works). A slightly mint flavored solution, spray or on premoistened swabsticks, containing electrolytes similar to those in normal saliva, moisturize the mouth.

A surprising cause of bad breath: skipping meals. It's the same principle as the P-trap under the sink that holds water and keeps bad-smelling odors from coming up from the sewer. An empty stomach allows digestive odors to escape.

Few of us can claim an empty stomach as the culprit, so if bad breath persists after you've upped your oral hygiene routine, it's time to visit the doctor. Chronic bad breath may be a symptom of underlying medical problems. We know that sinusitis, emphysema, and esophageal reflux are common causes of bad breath. Now, researchers are finding that the microbes in our mouths are possible predictors of serious illnesses, even heart disease and cancer. They are hoping to eventually manipulate the good and bad bacteria as a form of treatment. Let's hope the bad guys are the smelly ones.

Less is more

We refer to bad breath as odor and perfume as fragrance or scent, but even pleasant odors can be overpowering. The same goes for makeup. Soft and subtle should be the motto. Bright red lipstick and glaring purple eye shadow paint the wrong picture.

Cosmetologist Carmen Beyer, who represents a major cosmetic company, says the foundation you choose isn't as important as what you're doing underneath your makeup. Beyer says, "Less is more, where makeup is concerned. For older women I suggest brighter colors on the lips and cheeks, less around the eyes that are often more wrinkled. Although everyone is different, some women wear eye makeup very well. Some find light-defusing face powder softens wrinkles." Dipping your fingers into cosmetic bottles and reusing sponges invites germs. Beyer suggests using one of the new makeup brushes that you wash after each use — "they don't waste makeup like a sponge."

Cosmetologists and dermatologists alike, say cleansing, moisturizing, and wearing sunscreen are the key to healthy skin. SkinCeuticals, a pioneer in the antioxidant field, offers topical antioxidant products for aging skin. Dermatologist Sheldon Pinnell, professor emeritus at Duke University Medical Center and consultant for SkinCeuticals, says the American Academy of Dermatology recommends applying sunscreen twice. "People use only about 20 percent the amount they should use," he says. Since few of us apply enough sunscreen for it to be effective, Dr. Pinnell advises wearing protective clothing and avoiding the sun between 10 a.m. and 2 p.m. in addition to wearing sunscreen.

Dermatologists say most of us keep makeup too long. Although powder and pencils may be safely used for a couple of years and foundation for about a year, mascara, a major cause of eye irritation and infection, should be replaced every three to six months. Write the date on future purchases as a reminder. When the shelf life of several items expires, go for a makeover, usually offered free with a cosmetics purchase.

And while you're trying out a new look, take a peek at your glasses. Like the width of men's ties, glasses change from cat-eye skinny to saucer-size circles. Comfortable glasses that satisfy your vision requirements never go out of style, but glasses that rub makeup off your cheeks leaving white slashes or ones that make red irritated dents on your nose need replacing. Most importantly, prepare for romantic gazes with clean lenses that show off your sparkling eyes.

Donna said, "I always thought older women's eye makeup looked so bad because their hands were shaky." Now I see the problem. You can't do it with your glasses on and you can't see with them off. As she's discovered, we need powerful magnifying mirrors. After the purchase of my first 10X mirror, I felt like apologizing to the people in my office who endured looking at the crunchies at the corners of my eyes and inch-long gray hairs sprouting from my chin, wondering if they should say something or keep quiet. Since I could see the black hairs, I didn't realize young eyes could see the gray ones.

Age lightens our hair, darkens our teeth, dims our vision, and softens scents. The latter frequently causing our perfume to overpower more sensitive noses. It's hard to know how much perfume to use when talc, body lotion, hand lotion, and hair spray are competing for attention. For the best performance from your fragrances, use unscented products, avoid deodorant soap, and layer lotion, talc, and perfume of the same scent.

A signature fragrance, one you always wear, is fun and practical. I can still see the white satin-lined box filled with blue bottles my father gave my mother one Christmas. She smelled of Evening of Paris all year. When the soft smell of L'Air du Temps drifts across my path, I look around to see if it's Marie. That's her fragrance — powder, lotion, and perfume subtly applied. Only when I give her a hug or hang up her coat to I get the full pleasure of the fragrance. If the man in your life compliments your perfume or gives you some, you know what he likes, so add it to your gift list. Long after you're gone, your family may carry a scented memory of you. Lavender always reminds me of my grandmother.

Shifting sands

Just because your hourglass figure has twenty pounds of sand caught in the middle doesn't mean you can't be glamorous. Basic solids jazzed up with bright colors around your face keep attention focused on your dazzling smile and brilliant conversation. Is your fabulous look soft and flowing or tailored?

Author and motivational speaker Parry "EbonySatin" Brown has the right idea. She says for years she thought if she wore certain clothes a certain way, no one could tell she was fat. No more. In *Sexy Doesn't Have a Dress Size*, she writes, "I am not ashamed that I am fat. I am in perfect health. I am a large woman who is physically fit and defy any twenty-five year old to compete with my energy level." Forty-eight at the time, she happily referred to herself as "fat and sassy."

No dress is going to conceal our size and nothing is going to conceal our age. Foregoing sleeveless dresses, shorts, and bright color because "we're too old to wear that" doesn't make us younger, just uncomfortable. After we stayed in a Hollywood, Florida RV park with winter visitors from Quebec, my attitude changed. The women, most a decade older than I, were having a wonderful time. Confident in themselves and not caring what anyone else thought, they wore bikinis to the beach and sundresses to dinner. I've never worn a bikini, but I bought several pair of shorts and sleeveless blouses on that trip and have tried to remember the lesson I learned from those women.

Fill your closet with things you like to wear regardless of your size and age — and don't depend on salespeople to tell you what looks good. Take a friend along for an honest opinion (a brutally honest daughter keeps me on track).

Harder than fitting clothes is fitting a bra. Diana Weiss, a national fitting consultant for JC Penney, says eight out of ten women are wearing the wrong size bra. If the underwire pinches, the straps cut into your shoulders, or your breasts are spilling out, take the time to find a proper-fitting bra.

There are plenty of options from department stores brands to new "suspension-bridge" technology from VMM Enterprises, which claims to "retrain breast tissue." Wacoal offers a free computerized silhouette analysis at major department stores, or you can shop for their bras online. Several companies, like Pennyrich, operate home-based lingerie businesses that offer privacy and personalized service. To get in the mood for bra shopping substitute "boobs" for "ears" in the children's song *When your ears hang low.* (Better to laugh than cry.)

My grandmother modestly concealed her large breasts under heavily starched flour-sack dresses. I never noticed that her figure changed much over the years. My daughter recently told me MamMaw's secret. It seems she would take each flat, waist length breast with nipple facing the floor and roll it up into her bra. Although my daughter was appalled, I'm once again impressed with the wonderful "make-do" genes I've inherited.

If the shoe fits

That's a big if. Finding a proper-fitting shoe is as challenging as finding a proper-fitting bra. Almost all of our foot problems are caused by ill-fitting shoes, but you knew that. How could we not know that high heels and pointed-toe shoes were bad for our feet? Yet we followed the fashions from Mary Janes to saddle shoes to penny loafers before graduating to dyed-to-match pumps, sling-backs, spikes, and platforms.

We pushed, shoved, and pinched the fifty-two bones in our feet into every shape imaginable before athletic shoes hit the market. Now we're paying the price with ingrown toenails, hammertoes, corns, calluses, heel spurs, and bunions.

The Foot Health Foundation of America says bunions tend to be hereditary and can be aggravated by narrow shoes. I can vouch for both. I inherited the tendency and my AAA heel and B-width toes gave me a choice of shoes that slipped or pinched.

After observing older women with misshaped toes, some only able to wear sandals or house slippers that exacerbate the problem, I decided to have my bunion removed. The surgery, a custom orthotic from the podiatrist, and shoes with a large toe box keep me walking comfortably all day.

Wearing properly fitting shoes with arch support, good padding on the sole, plenty of room for your toes to move around, and possibly special-made inserts, prevent or ease most painful foot problems and may prevent falls.

Trading stylish for sensible also helps prevent slips and falls, the second leading cause of accidental death in the U.S. Women tend to fall more often that men because our center of gravity is lower and because our shoes tend to be less stable.

My sister-in-law says some shoes are made for walking and some for lunching (and some are for valet parking). We know the difference. After suffering through receptions and cocktail parties that last even longer than a two-martini lunch, I customized a pair of evening shoes. My ten-year-old cushion-soled, black velvet mules with the bright blue Keds trademark covered with permanent marker are perfect with ankle-length pants and skirts. It's been several years, and the folks in their beautiful evening shoes at the Whitman's holiday party haven't even noticed. So until the "Barefoot Ball" idea comes to Texas, I'll continue to wear my comfy conversions.

With retailers pushing muddy-boot trays and promoting chic slippers to replace surgical booties used by early adopters of the shoe-free phenomenon, plan to add a pedicure to your pre-party routine. Even Emily Post acknowledges the trend by addressing the proper etiquette for asking guests to remove their shoes, a common practice in other cultures.

Pamper your feet and legs with daily moisturizing, proper shoes, comfortable socks, and support hose if you experience swelling and discomfort. They'll carry you several times around the globe during your lifetime.

Hair today, gone tomorrow

It's an old joke, but a major issue as we age. For thirty million of us, our crowning glory is missing a few jewels. Perms and color give extra body to thinning tresses, and teasing may cover the scalp for a while, but over time they make the problem worse.

Since Rogaine, Propecia, and pricey hair transplants aren't on my list, I see three basic options: short, straight hair I can do myself; quarterly perms; or weekly visits to a salon. If your pocketbook supports the latter, go for it. Because my lifestyle dictates shampooing several times a week, I've opted for a scrub-behind-the-ears cut — clean, if not perfectly coifed. When all else fails, I'll buy a wig the same color and style as my hair, be comfortable around home, and don the wig for special occasions. One elderly lady I know keeps hers by the door so she won't forget to put it on when she leaves the house.

For many, the hair on their face is a bigger issue than the hair on their head. According to Bristol-Myers Squibb's research, approximately twenty million American women are affected by unwanted facial hair. We're tweezing, waxing, suffering through depilatories or expensive and painful electrolysis when there's an easy answer — shaving. Why we have such an aversion to this simple solution (me included) puzzles physicians. Dermatologist Mary Adams says, "Shaving doesn't make hair grow back darker or coarser. (If it did we could all shave our heads and wait for thick dark hair to grow!) In fact, shaving may be less harmful to our skin than depilatories.

Dr. Adams recommends using the first FDA approved topical prescription — Vaniqa. In most cases, regular use of Vaniqa Cream slows hair growth enough so you only need to shave once a month. Like any other prescription, it's pricey; and because it's considered cosmetic, it isn't covered by insurance plans.

Although most of us are just experiencing the normal effects of aging skin, those with thick, dark facial hair should ask their doctor about anti-androgen drugs, which block the effect of male hormones.

The magic of moisturizers

The description "a dried up old woman" is unfortunately a fact of aging, so begin with barnacle heels and work your way up — moisturize *everything*!

Luffas and exfoliates take off dry, dead skin; lotions and creams lubricate what's left. It takes both. Body lotions, face creams, cuticle creams, topical hormones, heel balms — buy it all. In addition to the above, sun screen worn year-round, saline nasal spray, lip balm, lubricating eye drops for daytime, and eye ointment at night have become part of my daily routine.

Millie, who began her modeling career at fifty (she won't let me say how many years ago that was), appears regularly in national magazine ads. She describes her skin-care routine in three words: water, exercise, and lubrication. "Everyone knows you have to drink a lot of water," she says. The American Dermatology Association agrees. They say drinking six to eight glasses of water every day keeps your skin moist and your oil glands functioning properly.

"I'm convinced the secret to staying young is keeping fit, but you don't have to spend a lot of money on expensive equipment or department store makeup and moisturizers. I use a vitamin-E stick on my lips and always wear sun block. I also like to break open Squalene capsules and use the shark liver oil extract on my skin. Anything that keeps your skin moist and lubricated works." When a gym isn't available, Millie uses large rice bags as weights. "They're easier to grip than cans."

For those of us who find our eyebrows graying, Millie offers this makeup tip: "Brush on brown or charcoal eye shadow. It's not as harsh looking, and it's cheaper than having your eyebrows dyed."

Because hands and fingernails get the most wear and tear, they need the most care. Gentle care is the key. Nails used as staple removers, screwdrivers, and scraped across the dryer lint filter and hands exposed to hot water and harsh cleaning chemicals show the damage. For hands someone will want to hold:

- Wear gloves for washing dishes and scrubbing chores.
- Moisturize hands, nails, and cuticles daily. For severely dry hands, coat with Vaseline and wear gloves overnight.
- Allow nails to breathe 24 hours between polishing.
- Soak cuticles in warm water then gently push them back with a damp cloth. Pushing back cuticles with a wooden or metal stick invites infection.
- Routinely apply sun screen to your hands.

You can spot the sun damage by comparing the back of your hands. Probably the skin on the left hand, the one exposed to more sun while you drive, shows age more than the right hand. When both hands get equal exposure to the sun, it's not as dramatic as for, say, golfers who wear a golf glove on one hand.

Rings on her fingers and bells on her toes

Dance to your own tune with a confident smile and comfortable shoes. Have two outfits, including shoes and accessories, ready to wear — one casual, one dressy. Have your hair and makeup routine down to half an hour. If someone calls, male or female, or a last minute whim strikes you, you can be ready in less than an hour. Forget what your mother said. Spur-of-the-moment can be fun. In a world of instant messaging and palm pilots, don't expect someone to call a week ahead for a date.

Keep the ingredients for an easy PCC (package, can, and carton) meal on hand, and you're ready to extend a last minute invitation. My friends and I often invite each other over at the last minute. If someone calls and says they're in town for a few hours, I'm delighted to have them come by for a visit.

Make every day a beautiful day in your neighborhood by opening your heart to love. Learn what Fred Rogers taught our children. You don't have to do anything sensational to be loved. It's laughable to think we can look like a Greek goddess as we age (few us ever did), but all of us have the capacity for love and that's the real secret to staying young.

The heart that loves is always young.

— Greek proverb

Accept the Accolades

If you have two loaves of bread, sell one and buy a hyacinth.

— Old Persian saying

At this stage in life, it's time to squeeze the best from every moment, time to accept the accolades — the sweet lemonade you've made from life's bitter moments. Indulge yourself. Take a nap, take a lover, take a trip, thumb your nose at tradition. Buy a hyacinth.

It doesn't matter whether achievements are acknowledged with a quiet smile of approval or accompanied by a brass band — or whether they were earned or the result of good fortune. Bask in the moment!

For me, one of these moments occurred in 1992 at Fort Worth's Worthington Hotel. The spotlight followed each proud step as I made my way to the front of the ballroom to accept an ADDY award for Arlington Memorial Hospital's public relations department. Unlike awards shows on TV, there were no acceptance speeches, no opportunity to thank everyone who contributed to the effort. In my case, the entire PR staff, artists, printers, and a multitude of teachers and mentors shared my two minutes of fame. (I'm hoping the other thirteen minutes come before my wake.)

The Fort Worth Ad Club judged our metamorphosis invitation to the opening of the Women's & Children's Center as excellent. The five-panel piece described the life cycle of a butterfly and the hospital's new obstetrical unit in four simple words — growth, change, transformation, realization.

A bumpy flight to the gold included several mishaps. Butterflies flitted through my stomach at the press check when the printed piece didn't match the art. Finally, six hours later, a touch of yellow ink brought Karen Erickson's watercolor to life.

We smugly dropped our beautiful invitations in the mail only to have them fly back to us with an ugly postage-due stamp bleeding across the verdant leaves. What could be wrong? Suzy had checked everything with the Postal Service, including the odd size, assuming they knew a five-by-five-inch invitation was square! Apparently not. Automated equipment doesn't accept squares — ten cents due for manual handling.

Numerous pleas fell on deaf bureaucratic ears, so we stuck the only ten-cent stamps available on a thousand invitations. Chief Red Cloud camped nobly on the upper right corner.

Lori, Suzy, and I convinced ourselves that an advertising agency would win the ADDY, so we were shocked when our name was called. Like a twist on an old Aggie joke, fifteen years before I'd thought PMS was a monthly problem, not the industry standard for ink colors — Pantone matching system.

Our entry didn't make it beyond the local level, which didn't diminish my delight in the least. When people learn I'm writing a book, the first thing they ask is what is it about? Invariably the next comment is, "Maybe you'll get on *Oprah!*" Certainly that would be nice. So would winning the lottery, but it's not something I expect or that determines success for me.

I prefer to set personal goals high and the accolade altimeter low. My goal, publishing a book that encourages women to roar past the rocking chair, doesn't depend on celebrity interviews. I'm looking for reading awards, not writing awards. I count every book sold as an accolade. The prospect that each woman who reads *Umbrella* might adopt even one small idea that helps her age greatly is heady stuff for me. I consider success enough profit to keep the motorhome tooling around the country so I can share that message.

I want to travel to far north British Columbia to meet Betty Ann's friends in Hudson's Hope; and I want to meet the lady who lives at the end of the tree-lined lane at Exit 154 on Interstate 10 in a house reminiscent of the movie *Giant*. I'm excited about meeting women who share my desire to age greatly, and I'm excited about reconnecting with old friends from elementary school, army days, and Methodist Sunday School classes. Publishing *Umbrella* is the first step in making those things happen.

In one of my favorite books, *The Tipping Point: How Little Things Can Make a Big Difference*, Malcolm Gladwell describes how ideas and products spread like viruses. Just as a worldwide epidemic begins with one contagious person, he shows how little causes can have big effects — from the dramatic fall in the crime rate in New York City to the sudden rise in popularity of comfortable Hush Puppies. A part-time job selling magazine ads exposed me to new possibilities and became the tipping point that lead to the ADDY.

Margaret had written the society column for the local paper for years before launching a woman's magazine. Annelle, my boss at the hospital, helped her with the magazine and mentioned that I could use some extra money. Selling is not my forte; but since it didn't interfere with my day job, I spent a few hours on Saturdays selling ads.

The undertaking paid off when I sold the inside front cover to a jewelry store. More than likely it was Margaret's reputation, not my salesmanship, that sold the ad in our fledgling magazine. Nonetheless, it promised a nice commission.

The Arlington Woman didn't have an art director or ad agency; design was up to the salesperson. The magazine took shape on Margaret's dining room table. Lack of training hadn't stopped me yet, and I wouldn't let a four-color ad be my undoing. As usual, the library saved me. I scanned the ads in the most expensive magazines and searched *Ad Week* for jargon jewels to conceal my amateur status.

Now I was ready for "the shoot." Since the photographer and model were professionals, I thought I could fake it — keep my mouth shut and let the pros handle it. Keeping my mouth shut lasted about thirty seconds.

"I think we better move that palm tree across the aisle; it looks like it's growing out of her head. Why don't we tape the necklace to your back so it falls better in the front? Do you mind if I push your hair back just a little? It's casting a shadow on your eyes." I was too busy to worry about what anyone thought.

As expected, the professionals produced a beautiful picture. I added what I considered the best design elements from *Architectural Digest* and *Cosmo* to complete the ad and collected a nice commission. (Looking back, it's not near as wonderful as I thought at the time.)

A decade later, I attended a writing workshop where best-selling author Sandra Brown was the keynote speaker. After lunch, I approached her and asked if she remembered posing for a jewelry store ad during her modeling career. "Oh yes," she replied, "I like the picture so well, I have it framed and hanging in my home!"

Sandra has her own ashes-to-accolades story. She was a model, television weather-caster, and on-air personality for *PM Magazine* when she was fired. Her husband had a career so she could have taken it easy for a while or wallowed in self-pity. Instead, she chose to do something she had always wanted to try — writing. With two small children in the house, it wasn't easy, so she struck a deal with them. In exchange for some uninterrupted time, she wrote her first romance novels under the pseudonym Rachel Ryan, the first names of her daughter and son.

From the ashes of one career, she blazed a trail to an even better one and is accepting the accolades of a best-selling author.

Accolades from the heart

Trophies tarnish, plaques gather dust, certificates yellow, but accolades from the heart last forever. I don't recall sending Rosemary a teapot and tea with a note saying I was sorry I couldn't be there to share a cup with her, but she has kept the tea pot for more than thirty years and says she thinks of me whenever she uses it.

I'm sure a young Star-Telegram reporter doesn't remember sending me flowers after a particularly harrowing late-night confrontation with dozens of demanding reporters, a few who accused me of lying and withholding information. Scott's note apologized for the behavior of those few and thanked me for my efforts. That kind gesture helped me ignore the rude behavior and remember that most reporters were people like me, just doing their job.

At sixty-five, "Granny Elder" became one of the original volunteers when the hospital opened. She did the usual volunteer jobs, but was known for the hugs and smiles she passed out to patients and employees until she was well into her nineties. I wasn't aware she knew I was getting married until she brought a wedding present to my office. She explained that it was one of her favorite wedding gifts and she wanted to pass it along to me. What an honor. Each time I use the cut-glass bowl the memory of her twinkling eyes sparkle in the deep-cut facets, and the warmth of her hugs returns.

Marilyn's favorite necklace comes from a chance meeting along the Amazon River. When a sudden storm sent her scrambling up a muddy embankment, a woman in a stilted shack offered her shelter and made the red and white beaded necklace while they waited out the storm. Something tangible from that brief encounter keeps the memory alive.

You're younger today than you will ever be again so don't wait for someone else to pass out the trophies. Pass along memory-making accolades. Create your own rewards and include yourself on the gift list. Treat others to your handmade specialties — a thank-you card with a personal message being one of the best. Treat yourself to as much luxury as your budget allows.

Share a gift by taking a friend to the theater, paying for a day of beauty treatment for you and your daughter, or taking a grandchild on a trip. Consumables make nice gifts for those of us living in downsized spaces, as does a donation to our favorite charity.

To honor someone and tackle world hunger at the same time, give renewable resources. Through Heifer International, you can give animals or tree seedlings to help families around the world become self-reliant. Patty says, "After hearing about Heifer International, I donated a goat in the name of each son's family. This year at Christmas I donated a goat for each grandchild. I want to impress upon them that everyone can make a difference, and I like the idea of people helping themselves. Heifer International doesn't just deposit an animal on a doorstep; they teach people how to care for it, and the family signs an agreement to share the offspring with their neighbors. Eventually a whole village benefits," she says. These are gifts that live long after other gifts are outgrown, forgotten, or have outlived their usefulness.

As you know by now, travel is my favorite reward for myself. Boston; Boise; Salt Lake; New York, of course; San Diego; San Francisco; Seattle; Key West; Kamloops; Chicago; Cleveland (yes, even Cleveland); Miles City, Montana; Vancouver; Montreal; Newfoundland's quaint Quidi Vidi; tiny Clair, Saskatchewan, population twelve. I love them all. I've visited every Canadian province and all but three states — Wisconsin, West Virginia, and Alaska. To paraphrase Will Rogers, I've never been to a city I didn't like. All these and thousands of others have educated, excited, and awed. The mountains, forests, rivers, valleys, canyons, deserts, and oceans of our great land defy description. I'm not through yet! More awaits me, both here and across the oceans.

From planning the route and reading the history to the actual visit and the photo reminders when we return — travel excites me. Long after the photos have faded and the souvenirs have outlived their usefulness, I'll have wonderful memories to relive.

Find something you get excited about and pursue it with passion. It won't cure your ailments, but you'll be too busy to worry about aches and pains.

Write your life story; get to your roots

I hope my family stories encourage you to record your family treasures. Things you think are mundane will fascinate later generations. Tell grandchildren about visits to your grandmother's house — the ice wagon, the hole in the wood floor under the icebox. Even ice trays may be a novelty to children who think cubes automatically spit out of refrigerator doors. Write about sticking your arm out the car window to signal a turn and using your foot instead of your hand to dim the lights. A million everyday things bring a new appreciation of the past and present. Writing your life story often heals painful memories and always proves more interesting than you expected. Books and seminars offer formats to trigger your memory.

Genealogy workshops abound. Visit the genealogy section of the library, go to bookstores, and use the Internet to help you get started. To preserve your life story or family tree in book form, check into Publish on Demand (POD) printing. POD technology allows you to print as few copies as you like; so for as little as $200, you can print a small quantity of books with family anecdotes and pictures.

Revive an old art; take up a new one

Keep your mind and hands busy crocheting, cross-stitching, knitting, or quilting. Needlecrafts are making a comeback. Take a class or teach one. With the likes of Julia Roberts, Sandra Bullock, and even Russell Crowe taking up knitting, your grandchildren may show an interest in joining you.

With today's scrapbooking supplies, even the creatively challenged have no excuses. Visit a craft store to jump-start your enthusiasm for turning those shoeboxes full of photos, napkins, and paper scraps into scrapbooks of beautiful memories. A scrapbook of family recipes including pictures and stories of family gatherings makes a memorable gift for every family member.

When I was too broke to buy anything significant, I put everything from his birth announcement to his high school honors in three large scrapbooks for my son's sixteenth birthday. He ranks it the best present ever.

Jan, Mary, and Trish send their greetings and thanks on beautiful handmade creations. If you're creativity leans toward the kitchen, make homemade bread by hand or in a bread machine. Sandra's home outside Vancouver always smells of fresh-baked bread. She shuns store-bought bread for healthy, whole grain loaves baked at home. Lucky friends get to share in the bounty.

Go to camp; go for the gold

Swim, hike, sing, canoe, sail, craft, fish, or relax at camps especially designed for seniors — they're cropping up everywhere. NASA offers a space camp, The New England Culinary Institute offers Whisk Away Weekend cooking camps, Fort Lewis College in Durango, Colorado, offers archaeology camps, Spring Valley, New York, offers a camp especially for the blind. Elderhostel has an extensive catalog of camping opportunities for seniors.

Competition keeps the juices flowing. Enter your bread, jam, scrapbook, needlework projects, poetry, or pies in a competition. Test your athletic skill in the senior Olympics. Sign up for a cooking contest, duck-calling competition, dance contest, or bridge tournament. Whether or not you win, take pride in participating.

Join a group

Join a band, a chorus, a dinner club, a garden club, a bridge club, or become a docent. Grandmas are rodeoing and roller skating, so you won't have a problem locating a group that shares your interest, whether it be growing roses or collecting miniature perfume bottles.

The Heart Association, Cancer Society, or any of a hundred charitable organizations offer an opportunity to mingle with people interested in improving health for themselves and others. If you would like to mentor foster-care teens, who leave the system at age eighteen but still need adult guidance, join the Orphan Foundation of America. Whether a group has a serious goal or is a weekly gabfest dedicated to nothing in particular, it keeps up the social contact.

Strut your stuff

A group of homemakers, teachers, waitresses, and businesswomen from Coeur d' Alene, Idaho, know how to have fun. Spectators applauded, the TV audience howled, and the President blew a kiss as The Red Hot Mamas marched down Pennsylvania Avenue pushing grocery carts in the George W. Bush inaugural parade. They performed their synchronized routine wearing red dresses, aprons, zany hats, and gaudy makeup. Their dedication to the "exploitation of merriment and the enhancement of the ridiculous" makes the old gals a favorite in parades across the country.

I discovered a group of fun ladies in Amarillo. After watching women in red hats and purple dresses pass our table headed for a private dining room at the rear of the restaurant, my curiosity got the best of me, and I asked a lady wearing a large red cowboy hat to tell me about the group. Edna explained that they were members of The Red Hat Society, and that although she was eighty-two, they welcomed anyone over fifty.

Inspired by the words of Jenny Joseph, "When I am an old woman I shall wear purple with a red hat which doesn't go and doesn't suit me," Queen Mother Sue Ellen Cooper of Fullerton, California, founded the group. What began with a few friends meeting for tea in 2000 is now a worldwide organization. Red hats and purple T-shirts are showing up everywhere to meet the demand of middle-aged women dedicated to "verve, humor, and elan." There are no official rules and no requirements for fund raising. They prefer the theme of Mike Harlene's song: "All my life, I've done for you. Now it's my turn to do for me." (I've got my eye out for a red hat so I can join the frivolity.) If you're interested in joining a chapter or starting your own, call 1-800-FUN-AT-50 or visit their Web site.

Organize something

It takes just one person to set a date, place, and time to get things started. Plan a reunion, a slumber party, a picnic, or a progressive dinner. Make it an annual event.

For a large event, begin planning at least a year ahead and enlist lots of help. Use some of the ideas from Chapter 6, along with magazines, books, and computer software to help you organize a reunion. In her seventies, Dolly and some cousins organized a family reunion. Her Norwegian relatives came from both coasts for a three-day gathering at the North Dakota family farm. A decade later she says, "It was a lot of work, but I'm so glad we did it. My brothers are all gone now. Other relatives are unable to travel."

Professional organizers say to consider the off-season if the reunion won't be held at someone's home. Pick a date and stick to it, plan plenty of games and activities for kids and adults, make nametags to avoid embarrassing moments, and prepare or purchase plenty of food. Add flavor to the event with food and activities that reflect your ethnic or cultural background. Hold the costs down by surveying the group before springing for T-shirts, caps, or mugs with the clan name.

Barbara organized a group of neighbors who called themselves WOWs — wonderful old women. For years, they went camping and hiking two weekends a year. Now Barbara arranges speakers for the Oldtimers, a group of men and women from sixty-five to ninety-five, who meet once a month at the Senior Center. As an active member of the Historical Society, she invited a bunch of '50s girls to come to the museum for a slumber party. "They brought boxes of memories and snacks to share. We ordered pizza, laughed at our old photos, and had a great time. The party broke up at 4:30 in the morning, when most of the "girls" decided they were too old to sleep on the floor," she says.

Aleyne helped organize past students to honor a favorite high school band director. After the reunion, the group continued to meet, published a book on his life, and raised money for an annual music scholarship in his name.

A group of "girls" I went to high school with started having a Christmas party our junior year, and fifty years later I can count on getting an invitation to join women like the ones Frances Weaver wrote about — *The girls with grandmother faces* — for a wonderful party.

Does this give you any ideas? Good. Set a date, make a few phone calls, and get something started.

Volunteer

Local schools, libraries, hospitals, senior citizen centers, and women's shelters welcome volunteers. Mentoring or tutoring a few hours a week makes a lifetime of difference for someone struggling with reading or a new language. Organizations like Retired Senior Volunteer Program (RSVP) and Service Corps of Retired Executives (SCORE) help seniors find a program suited to their interest and abilities. At Senior Corps' Web site www.seniorcorps.org you can learn about opportunities in your community.

Women have a long history of volunteerism. While Rosy riveted war material in World War II, housewives did their part for the war effort by growing victory gardens, collecting metal, folding parachutes and bandages, and working for the USO. During the 1920s, among other things, Red Cross volunteers began knitting sweaters, socks, and afghans for soldiers and refugees.

That volunteer spirit continues today. Women around the country, working with the American Friends Service Committee and World Concern, have joined the "afghans for Afghans" effort and knitted and crocheted afghans, mittens, and socks for the people of Afghanistan. No doubt a similar effort will be organized for Iraq.

In my hometown, The Handknitters Guild knits blankets, booties, and caps for premature babies and lap robes for nursing-home patients and people confined to wheelchairs.

At the Family Motor Coach national assembly in Oregon, quilters joined forces with East of the Cascades and Mt. Bachelor quilting groups to contribute quilts for local hospitals to distribute to children.

If your fingers are more comfortable on a calculator than on yarn, consider volunteering to prepare tax returns. AARP offers free IRS-certified tax training for tax-aides who prepare tax returns for seniors in community centers and senior centers. By appointment, the volunteers go to the homes of those unable to come to a center.

Since the advent of automatic garage-door openers and the disappearance of front porches, meeting your neighbors and making friends when you move is difficult. Newcomer organizations are an ideal place to volunteer and quickly find people with similar interests.

My friend Carol went from ex-nun to National Organization for Women officer to the woman whose outstanding sales made her employer scrap their "Man of the Year" award for a more gender appropriate trophy. In retirement, she's using her leadership skills to lead a group of Austin newcomers. "We have thirty-five different interest groups covering everything from hiking to bridge to antiques to a French club to culinary sessions and computing," she says.

For some, volunteering begins close to home. Grandmothers enrich their grandchildren's lives by keeping them a few days a week, taking them to dance classes, or music lessons — things their working parents aren't able to do.

Phyllis and Don, whose grandchildren live far away, tutor third graders in math and reading at Augusta Ranch Elementary near their home. "The kids are so receptive to our being there. It makes our week."

Hospitals depend on volunteers. Some work a few hours a week, others log in enough hours to be considered full-time employees. You see them directing visitors and delivering flowers to patients. Behind the scenes, they're running gift shops and snack bars generating revenue in addition to their service.

Redefine vacation

If you've seen the Eiffel Tower and Big Ben, peered down the Grand Canyon, and taken the road to Hana, what's next? Before retirement some folks take a "working vacation" to stay home and paint the house or build a deck. Now, active seniors are investing their elbow grease in volunteer vacations — building houses for Habitat for Humanity; planting seedlings in Sequoia National Park for Special Assignment Volunteers for the Environment (SAVE); and working as Wilderness Volunteers rebuilding footpaths, cabins, and shelters, and restoring salmon and steelhead habitat on the Oregon Coast. The last group bills itself as vegetarian and nonsmoking, proving there's something for everyone.

Sixty percent of Global Volunteers' participants are women, ranging in age from thirty to eighty. Volunteers for Peace (VFP) offers 2200 programs in over eighty countries, but the accommodations are pretty rustic, a deterrent to many seniors. A wealth of organizations sponsor worthy projects and rewarding experiences for volunteers who want to make a difference in the world.

Volunteer vacations range from a few days to three weeks with fees from $200 to $3,000. You provide transportation and personal gear;

sponsors provide food, shelter (which may be a tent), supplies, and the tools required for the project.

Some people might call how Mike and Vicki operate Duvall Books roughing it — no phone, cash register, or computer. They don't see it that way. "Roughing it is banding hawks," Vicki says. Avid birders, they leave the used bookstore in the hands of longtime employees and go bird watching from South Texas to Iceland. Closer to home, they volunteer two days a week during the six-week hawk migration, banding birds for Hawk Watch International and the Falcon Research Group in Washington's Cascade Mountains. "Monitoring the hawks that are at the top of the food chain tells us how the rest of the bird population is fairing. It's not expensive. We drive up and furnish our own food; but it's hard work in cold, windy conditions," she says.

An Internet search found 4300 sites offering training and volunteer opportunities. The Great Basin Bird Observatory in the northern Mojave Desert needs people with computer skills. At Beaverhill Lake near Edmonton, Alberta, volunteers monitor shorebirds and waterfowl. The Cape Cod Museum trains volunteers to work at the Wing Island Banding Station collecting data to help scientists better understand the migratory habits of various species. And in Big Sur, volunteers are restoring native habitat. Bird watching organizations around the world offer opportunities to enjoy nature and participate in bird conservation for a week or a weekend.

Service and religious organizations often pay all or part of volunteers' travel expenses. When the Red Cross calls, Sandra packs her bag, and she and her husband, Hal, head from their home in Littleton to the Denver airport, where a ticket is waiting to take them to the site of some disaster. Once they spent three weeks serving meals to hurricane victims in Puerto Rico. When Hal's son died while they were in Guam, they became the recipients of Red Cross assistance. "They treated us like VIPs. We were out of Guam in four hours, and a psychologist escorted us all the way back to Denver," Sandra says.

"It costs us nothing but our time, and we get to help people who really need it. Hal and I drove the Red Cross ERV (Emergency Response Vehicle) from Denver down to Louisiana and Mississippi following hurricanes Isadore and Lilly. You don't have to have any special skills. We distributed water and clean-up kits — work gloves, brooms, mops, detergents, and stuff like that. It's a great feeling to help people in distress."

After a forty-five-year nursing career, Katie, whose mother lived to 105, figured she had a lot of years left to serve the Lord. "I knew I wouldn't be happy unless I was contributing . . . being busy and serving others," she says. She's past seventy and planning a trip to Cambodia, her ninth medical missionary trip since she retired. She's been to Belize, Peru, Kenya, Guyana, Dominica, some more than once, and pays her own expenses. "The church pays half or all for some who couldn't go without help. Others donate a little; but, for the most part, I pay my own expenses."

A group of twenty to thirty volunteers from the Church of Christ travel to remote areas and work with the local churches to provide basic medical services and spiritual enrichment. "People, some who've never seen a doctor in their life, walk miles to the field clinic. We clean ears, treat minor injuries, fungus and foot ulcers, and teach mothers how to treat their babies' diarrhea — very basic care," Katie says. She admits working in primitive settings — harsh climates, strange food, Turkish toilets — may not be for everyone. "But working with people who have so little and seeing how happy they are makes you really appreciate your own blessings. I wouldn't take anything in the world for this opportunity to learn about different cultures and be able to serve people in need." Every volunteer I spoke with expressed the same sentiment.

Combine work and fun

If sports or theater are your passion, but you can't afford season tickets, consider taking a part-time job or bartering your time for tickets. Sell programs or take tickets if you get to hang around for the action. Usher theater patrons to their seat if you're allowed to stay for the play.

Earn your travel expenses with a seasonal job at a national park or private resort. Campground hosts assist rangers in national and state parks and U.S. forests in exchange for free space and hookups. Clerking at a local store isn't as exciting as the same job in a beautiful setting. Seniors conduct tours, flip burgers, wait tables, and cashier — then they get to spend their free time exploring the area.

A couple from the Midwest turns the family farm over to their children and spends the summer on Mackinac Island. He cares for the horses and drives a carriage; she clerks in the gift shop. They eat and sleep in dormitories, spend their days off exploring upper Michigan and Ontario, and return to the Midwest in time for the harvest.

Veronica and Shirley, two ladies from Florida, travel the country pulling a tiny twenty-five-year-old trailer. "Angelica's Chariot," painted with pastel flowers and angels, provides living quarters and advertising for the handmade angel products they sell. Lot's of seniors find the craft-fair circuit an ideal way to make their hobby pay for itself.

Shop-until-you-drop types make ideal mystery shoppers. Marketing Systems Unlimited, based in Iowa, hires people in forty-six states to eat at restaurants, stay overnight at hotels, or fill their gas tanks. Mystery shoppers' evaluations and reports help companies improve their service and award bonuses to worthy employees.

Barbara evaluates employees up for a promotion or pay increase — without leaving home. She calls the employee, pretends to be interested in the company's product, scores the employee by company criteria, and e-mails the results. "Working a few hours a month gives me my own money to splurge on the grandchildren," she says.

Finance your splurges by passing out samples at the supermarket, house sitting, plant watering, pet sitting, or poop-scooping. Don't turn up your nose! There's an association of dog-doo entrepreneurs. Start up cost is minimal — latex gloves, baggies, and a bucket. Develop a neighborhood route, get your bending exercise, and collect about $15 for once-a-week pickup from each client. Setting aside one day a week to clean ten yards nets $600 a month to splurge.

Gladly give it up

Some of life's rewards involve giving up something — the sigh of relief when some responsibility or task ends. Naomi Levy, in her book *Begin Again: The Journey Toward Comfort, Strength and Faith in Difficult Times*, describes Judaism's unique perspective on the Sabbath. "Beginning every Friday at sunset, we celebrate it until it ends Saturday night. People tend to think of it as a day of prohibitions — you can't do this; you can't do that. But it's really a day of privileges. It's a day when we leave our week behind and enter into a new plane of being."

Remember when you looked forward to each new milestone as a chance to take another path? With the next raise, I'll buy a new car. When we get the kids through college, we'll buy a cabin on the lake. For our thirtieth anniversary, we'll fly to Paris.

Now it's time to reverse the process and see the pleasure in giving up things you don't like to do and some things it's no longer safe to do. We gave up yard work at sixty — sold the lawn mower and tools, hired a lawn service — when maintaining a yard didn't suit our travel plans. The condo's six-foot flowerbed by the front door satisfies my need to dig in the dirt and anticipate spring blossoms. For other folks, yard work and gardening provide exercise and pleasure they never want to give up.

What's on your phase-out list? Are you tired of having every holiday meal at your house? Put out the word a year ahead that you're turning the hostess hat over to the next generation. If you have the biggest house in the family, suggest everyone else bring the food. When cleaning and shopping are too much effort, hire a weekly cleaning service and give gift certificates.

At seventy, I'm through ironing. It's the age the law requires IRA distributions begin, and some of mine are going to the cleaners. I'll wear silk and 100 percent cotton without concern for special care instructions, starching, and ironing.

When my brother-in-law took his eighty-five-year-old mother to her new home, she showed little interest in the tour of the facility. When they got back to her small room and bath she asked only one question. "No kitchen?" Thinking she was upset, he pointed out the microwave and explained that her rent included three meals a day. She sat down on the edge of the bed and with a great sigh of relief said, "I'll never have to cook again." Since she had never complained, the family had no idea that she was tired of cooking. Long after she turned over the family celebrations to the younger generation, we expected her famous chocolate cream pie and fried apricot pies for these occasions. She graciously accepted the accolades of three generations, and we all thought she loved the attention. What she really needed was for us to say was, "Enough, you can retire, it's time."

Giving up driving is one of the less desirable consequences of aging; but at some point, our diminished sight, hearing, and reflexes require that we sacrifice our independence for the safety of ourselves and others. Now is the time to decide on the criteria for voluntarily handing over the keys before it becomes an emotional issue. Taking AARP's 55 Alive driver safety course, which reviews ways to compensate for age-related changes that affect driving, is a good beginning. Use this information as a dipstick to measure how long you can safely drive.

Before that time comes, keep a record of all the expenses associated with owning a car. You can take a lot of cab rides for what you've been paying to own, maintain, license, insure, and fuel a car. When I give up driving, I plan on treating family and friends to lunch when they chauffeur me to appointments and shopping. If finances are not an issue, keep a car for others to chauffeur you around in. An extra car in the family comes in handy for out-of-town visitors and as a loaner while a vehicle is in the shop.

Shedding the emotional baggage

Shedding responsibilities and belongings comes easier than unloading the emotional baggage collected over a lifetime — kids that went astray, relationships that failed, and missed opportunities. When Fred's name appeared among the fine print listing people with unclaimed assets held by the State of Texas, memories of a humiliating day flooded back across the years.

I was summoned to appear at a downtown Dallas law office for a deposition conducted by attorneys representing a major bank and investors involved in a lawsuit. Greedy bankers hadn't done their homework or they would never have loaned him the money. Now they grilled me for hours about hidden assets, even hinting that Fred might have been murdered. How could they think I would put myself and the children in danger?

Determined not to let these legal eagles reduce me to tears, I visualized the villains of silent-movie days twisting their mustaches while they tied the widow to the railroad tracks. The click-click of the court reporters fingers became the clackety-clack of the approaching train, and I comforted myself knowing the heroine always broke free before the train arrived.

I knew my signature on the loan papers was forged and suspected they knew it too. I had no money, was losing a day's pay to give this deposition, and was worried I couldn't pay the parking fee. I kept my chin up (although it may have quivered a few times) and answered each question honestly — mostly with "I don't know."

Sometime during the interrogation, one of the lawyers let it slip that a private detective had been following me. I smiled all the way home at the thought of private detectives recording my mundane routine. I even laughed out loud at the possibility of them following me as I raced across town at 3 a.m. to a small strip shopping center and up to the barred windows of the all-night pharmacy to fill a prescription for a sick child.

I wondered if they suspected I had money hidden in the furniture and an accomplice in prison. Did they watch us load my sofa and chair into my stepfather's sagging old station wagon and follow him down I-45 to the state prison where he taught auto-body repair to first-time offenders? In another class, inmates learned upholstery work and practiced their skills reupholstering furniture for the price of the fabric. It was cheap, but not quick. Sitting on the floor for two months was a dollar-and-sense decision, a small price to pay for changing the sofa's threadbare avocado-green brocade to plush new velour.

I had a new sofa *and* a new husband when that notice of unclaimed assets appeared in the paper several years after the deposition. Logic told me there was no money in the safe deposit box, but I hoped it held a clue to the life Fred had kept from me in those final months. I filled out the forms and mailed my claim to the state comptroller's office.

One night I dreamed I opened a metal box and wads of crumpled cash spilled out. It wasn't the neatly sorted bills in rubber bands like you see on TV when a suitcase of money is opened. Did my dream mean anything or was it just my recollection of a husband who took a shoebox of unorganized receipts to a patient accountant every year to have our taxes done?

The dream prompted me to check on the progress of my claim. Since I had sent everything the comptroller requested, I was suspicious when told his office needed additional documentation from the bank. Could those attorneys who questioned me fifteen years before still be staking their claim?

Numerous phone calls and two years later, a large envelope arrived. I shakily signed the registered mail receipt, leaned against the closed door and clutched the envelope to my chest. Would the contents shatter the rose-colored glass I'd encased Fred in to protect his memory? Would a large check reveal he was involved in some clandestine scheme giving credence to the rumors he was murdered? Did I have a moral, if not legal, obligation to share it with the unpaid creditors from long ago?

After a few minutes reflection I opened the envelope and stared at worthless stock certificates signed Fred Furgerson, president. The anticlimactic conclusion was actually a relief. There was no opening of old wounds; it provided proof I didn't lie under oath; and it brought no moral dilemmas.

I took the brown accordion file of memorabilia from the top shelf of the closet and added the stock certificates to his birth certificate, army discharge, suicide note, and death certificate. Forty years of Fred's life was neatly packed in a three-inch folder, and it was the end of another chapter in my life.

A new chapter with a new husband and a career didn't change my concerns as a mother. Like most mothers, I just wanted the best for my daughter. Like the fellow looking for love, however, I was looking in all the wrong places. Logic prepared me for rain; I had forgotten the sunshine in my umbrella philosophy.

I understood Kathy's dilemma. The clock was ticking, infertility treatments hadn't worked, and her husband was too old for an agency adoption. After much soul-searching and voicing my reservations, I accepted the idea of open adoption and began to reflect on her joy rather than TV images of toddlers being ripped from their adoptive parents' arms and given to strangers with matching DNA.

One of Kathy's friends tried to be helpful: "Tell your mom you're adopting a black baby. She'll be so relieved you're not, she won't object to anything else."

"But I plan to adopt an African-American child," came the icy reply.

I'd never been a crusader for any cause, but as Martin Luther King suggested, I encouraged my children to judge people by their character not their color. Kathy's choice shouldn't have been a surprise, but it was.

How could I model the role of supportive mom, knowing the heartache she courted? Would a black child raised in our WASP family grow wings of self-esteem or suffer the sting of failure? I learned a lot about open adoption and interracial families. Thousands work; only a negative few make the news. The possibilities kindled a spark of hope, and I began to love this unknown child.

My daughter coached the laboring mom and cut the cord. She

named the baby after her brother. Three days later the birth mother changed her mind. It was back home to a fully furnished nursery and an empty bank account. More ads, more hopeful letters mailed, and finally a request of me.

"You're a writer, Mom. See if you can write a letter that will convince someone we are the right parents for her child."

A dozen times I started the letter, then highlighted the words and pushed the delete key. Staring blankly at the computer screen, I took a sip of tea and thought about the painting hanging in the hall. The watercolor on yellowed paper is dated 1919 and signed by my great-grandmother Sallie Douglas.

I have her genes and inherited at least a bit of her artistic ability, so maybe some of her other talents are floating around my gene pool just waiting for an assignment. I leaned back in my chair, closed my eyes and let my reverie return to the oft-told story. The heartbeat in my temples became footsteps of long ago.

Sallie tiptoed across the kitchen, grabbed her poke bonnet from the hook, and eased the back door shut. She hitched Daisy to the buggy and pulled around the smokehouse as the first rays of sun glinted off the tin roof.

"I'm glad I didn't let TJ talk me out of going to town alone. I'll be halfway there before Tennie comes downstairs. Such a silly name, even if some relative was the first white child born in Tennessee. But how could you argue with a mother-in-law who named a son born on February 22, Thomas Jefferson?

"If Tennie came to town with me, she'd want one of those new brassieres she's been pestering me for. With breasts as flat as the biscuits she bakes, the batiste camisoles are fine. And for the price of store-bought underwear I can buy the watercolors I need to finish the rose picture.

"Real art paper would be nice, but the butter-and-egg money won't stretch that far. Besides, Sara promised me the leftover wallpaper from their upstairs bedroom, and the back of it works pretty well."

The surrey wound past deserted fields where a few straggly cotton bolls waved like white flags surrendering to winter. Sallie ducked to miss the branches of a pecan tree and noticed with delight at least an apron full of nuts strewn among the fallen leaves. She made a mental note to stop and pick up the nuts on the way home. She always made pecan, mincemeat, and sweet potato pies for Thanksgiving. She loved holidays and made every effort to make family gatherings warm and comfortable, unlike her childhood memories of such occasions. "Turkey neck, turkey neck," chanted young cousins, comparing her to the dumb birds they shooed into the barn when it rained. Every year a few drowned looking skyward with their mouths open.

She accepted the ugly duckling image the mirror reflected, but held her head high and patiently awaited the fairy tale's happy ending. Ever the hopeful swan, she spurned the local boys and brought that long delicate neck perilously close to the ax of spinsterhood. TJ rescued her just before her thirtieth birthday.

She shuttered at the memories, clutched the shawl around her against the early-morning chill, and geed the horse as the road veered around the shanties south of town. Daisy and Sallie reacted at the same time. The horse snorted and flicked her ears as Sallie slid from the seat and edged toward the sound coming from beneath the bridge.

Two big brown eyes peered between the wood runners. A small boy huddled under the bridge, his thin black arms clasped around his trembling knees. A tattered shirt covered with mud hung off one shoulder.

"What happened to you?" Sally asked. Soft sobs continued as he shrank against the creek bank without replying.

"Well, come out from under there before you catch your death." Sallie lifted the faded quilt from under the buggy seat and hesitated only a moment before bundling up the boy.

Mama's turning over in her grave seeing me wrap this little urchin in the wedding-ring quilt she made for my hope chest. Oh well, by now it's probably a pretty easy turn for Mama.

A question from the smelly bundle next to her jolted her to the present.

"Where are you taking me?"

She hadn't thought that far. She just knew she couldn't leave him there. That was her problem, Mama always said, leaping before she looked.

She looked toward the railroad station that marked the edge of town as if an answer might appear in the smoke spiraling from the

Sante Fe beginning its trip from Edna to Houston. Then she saw the sheriff at his door and knew where to take her small passenger.

"Did your mama get after you again, George?" the sheriff asked as he carried the boy inside. In the dim light under the bridge, Sallie hadn't seen the wounds. Now, with the quilt puddled around his feet, she winced at the caked blood across one shoulder and down his arm.

George surveyed the plank floor as a single tear edged around his nose and slipped past his quivering chin. Sallie thought of the ruckus one of hers raised after a few licks with a peach-tree switch.

"Surely his mother didn't do this."

"Yes, Mz Douglas, and this ain't the first time. She gets liquored up and takes after him with a chain. I told her if she did it again I'd run her out of town. But the boy's too young to be on his own, and folks out there can't take care of the young'uns they've got.

"I'll have the Doc take a look at him. Maybe he could use a fetch-it. Unless . . . well, no, I guess you couldn't."

On the road home Sallie's mind swirled like the dust devils that danced around the surrey's wheels. Is this one of the Lord's mysterious ways or am I just crazy? Five children, grandchildren, and now I'm bringing home this little guy. He's a little different from the barn cats, runt pigs, and orphaned squirrels I've bottle fed and nursed to health. What will TJ say?

Sallie looked down at little George and remembered the quilt left in the sheriff's office. She put her arm around the boy, pulled him close, and thought again of her mother. Well, this does it. Poor Mama just drilled right through that pine box.

The story ends as abruptly as my reminiscing. My mother only knows how George came to live with her dad's parents. She remembers him pulling her around the yard in a wagon and says he took his meals with the family and knew how to read and write. She last saw him at her Grandmother Sallie's funeral in 1925.

I look at the soft pink roses Grandmother Sallie water colored on the back of wallpaper, then return to the painting of George in hopes of finding some clue to the relationship between him and Sallie. A barefooted little black boy in a yellow gingham shirt, brown knickers, and a jauntily tilted tam smiles back at me. Sallie's love shines through the twinkling eyes and broad smile she painted. Now I can write the letter for Kathy.

I don't know if my prose made the difference, but I'm ready to accept the best accolade I've ever had. My grandson is biracial and beautiful — a rainbow stretching from one generation to another.

This was meant to be the ending for *Umbrella.* Instead it's another beginning. I can vouch for the fact that worrying works because none of the things I worried about regarding biracial adoption happened. I never thought to worry about a son-in-law leaving. I worried about the color of the baby's skin not the state of his mind. Now my daughter is alone raising an autistic child. Our young "Rainman" with Aspergers astounds and amazes, often frustrates and is always loved. Kathy is the fourth generation of women in my family deserted by death or divorce. And like the women of the previous generations, I have no doubt that with her love and nurturing, Andrew will find the perfect niche for his special talents.

Likewise, I'm basking in the knowledge that my children found their places in the world despite any childrearing shortcomings of mine. The strong wills and independent spirits that made them difficult to parent are the same qualities that give them an edge in coping with life's challenges. Like me, they've discovered that past adversities often become future accolades.

There are no rules in the aging game; it's the ultimate game of chance. The past deals us one hand, the cards get reshuffled every few years, and the future lays face down. Ace or deuce? No one knows, but we can increase the odds for success with the *Umbrella* philosophy — forecast sunshine, prepare for rain, and look for the rainbows that follow the rain. Until we meet again, look for me somewhere over the rainbow. I'm the one with an umbrella under my arm.

> *There ain't nothing more to write about and I'm rotten glad of it, because if I'd a knowed what a trouble it was to make a book, I wouldn't a tackled it.*
>
> — Mark Twain's *Huckleberry Finn*

Copyright Acknowledgments

Are Your Parents Driving You Crazy, Joseph A. Ilardo, Ph.D and Carole R. Rothman, Ph.D., Vanderwyk & Burnham, 2001. *At work with Thomas Edison*, Blaine McCormick, Ph.D., Entrepreneur Media Inc., 2001. *A Woman's Guide to Sleep*, Joyce A. Walsleben, Ph.D., Random House, Crown Publishing, 2000. *Breaking the Pattern*, Charles Stuart Platkin, Red Mill Press, 2002. *Don't Forget: Easy Exercises for a Better Memory*, Danielle Lapp, Perseus Books Group, 1995. *Eat More, Weigh Less*, Dean Ornish, M.D., Harper Collins Publishers, Inc., 1993. *Everyone's a Coach*, Don Shula, Zondervan Publishing House, 1995. *Even the Stars Look Lonesome*, Maya Angelou, Bantam Books, Random House, Inc. *The Essential Medication Guidebook to Healthy Aging*, Les Paul, M.D., M.S. and Becky Nagle, PharmD, BCPS, Ballantine Books, 2002. *The Essential Drucker*, Peter F. Drucker, Harper Collins Publishers, 2001. *The Fat Fallacy*, Will Clower, Ph.D., Three Rivers Press, 2001. *How Healthy is Your Family Tree*, Carol Krause, Scribner, Simon & Schuster Adult Publishnig Group Inc., 1995. *The Healthy Kitchen*, Andrew Weil, M.D. and Rosie Daley, Alfred A. Knopf, Random House, Inc., 2002. *Leadership When the Heats On*, Danny Cox, CSP, CPAE, with John Hoover, The Career Press, Inc., 1994. *Living Lean*, Larry North, Simon & Schuster Adult Publishing Group, 1997. *Living to 100*, Thomas Perls M.D., M.H.P., Perseus Books Group, 1999. *Older & Wiser*, Richard M. Restak, M.D., Simon & Schuster Adult Publishing Group, 1998. *The Promise of Sleep*, William C. Dement, M.D., Ph.D., Dell Publishing, Random House, Inc., 1999. *Resilience: The Power to Bounce Back When the Going Gets Tough*, Frederic Flach, M.D., Hatherleigh Press, 1997. *Smart for Life: How to Improve Your Brain Power at Any Age*, Michael Chefetz, Ph.D., Penguin Books, 1992. *Strong Women Stay Young*, Miriam E. Nelson, Ph.D., Bantam Doubleday Dell Publishing, 2000. *Strong Women, Strong Bones*, Miriam E. Neson, Ph.D., Putnam Publishing Group, 2000. *Total Memory Workout*, Cynthia R. Green, Ph.D., Bantam Books, Random House, Inc., 2001. *The Tipping Point*, Malcolm Gladwell, Little Brown, 2000. *The Take Control Diet*, Ian K. Smith, M.D., Random House, Inc., 2001. *To Begin Again: The Journey Toward Comfort, Strength, and Faith in Difficult Times*, Naomi Levy, Ballantine, 1999.

Index